# The Hollow Sun

D.L. Wainright

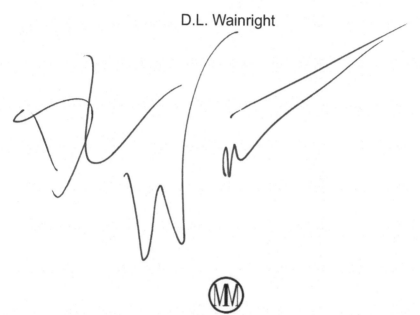

Ⓜ
Minter Media

For Tommy

With eyes the coldest Ice—

Or the hottest Fire—

She watches as the Creature burns

Set upon the Pyre


They never see—those eyes—

The Dangers in the Night—

Surrounding Her with talons bared—

Deluded She's all right


Unheeded warnings—wrapped in Dreams—

Their meanings gone unknown

But such is the young girl's Way—

Not to be told—but shown

# Prologue

The headlights caught on something pale and glistening red among the trees, and Raúl's foot was on the brake as soon as his mind fully registered what he'd seen. Beside him, his sister Julia jerked awake and looked out the windows in confusion. "What happened?" she asked. "You get a flat or something?"

"Someone's out there."

"What?" She turned to him, face scrunched up. "You stopped because you saw someone making a little late night hike?"

At first Raúl didn't answer, too focused on keeping his breathing even, his pulse calm. Then he unbuckled his seat belt with trembling hands and fumbled the door open. "She was hurt," he explained, voice flat with his effort to stay calm. When he looked back towards where he'd seen the woman, all he could make out were the dark, vague shapes of trees. His car's lights were the only source of illumination for miles, the surrounding woods still and silent.

"What do you mean? Hurt how?" Pouring out of the car after him, Julia began looking around with ever-growing alarm. "Where is she?"

"I don't—" He swallowed and jerkily pulled his phone from his pocket to activate its flashlight mode and shine it ineffectually towards the forest. Closer. He'd have to get closer.

"Hello?" he called out, moving cautiously towards the trees. Behind him, he could hear his sister rush to catch up. "Miss? Can you hear me?"

As if in answer, he began to make out the faint sound of sobbing. That spurred him on, concern overriding any fear, and he rushed forward, out of the protective glow of his car's taillights. Soon his world was narrowed down to the small bubble of light from his phone. Trees burst into being for a few clear seconds, only to melt back onto obscurity.

"Where *is* she?" grumbled Julia, her fingers gripping the back of his shirt, twisting, pulling so tight it was uncomfortable. But he didn't chide her, didn't blame her for wanting to stay close. "Hey!" she yelled into the void around them. "We want to help you!"

A trilling came from somewhere, the only animal sound he'd heard so far. The realization of that drew him up short, his sister bumping softly into his back. They'd grown up in woods just like these, only an hour north, and he remembered vividly how loud they were at night in the summer. There were insects, owls, whippoorwills, frogs...the forest was never silent. "Something's wrong," he whispered, gently nudging Julia with his elbow. "We should go back."

"What? No! What about the injured chick?"

"Just. Trust me, okay?"

The trilling started up again, and it reminded him of a screech owl's typical call, but was different somehow. Higher pitched, the notes all running together. Suddenly the crying seemed to be closer, as if just a few paces ahead. There were still no other sounds. "C'mon," he urged faintly, moving his light around and hoping to find only trees.

"She's close," objected Julia, pushing him forward. "I can hear her."

He shuffled a few more steps, and when a figure came into view huddled at the base of a tree, he closed his eyes in dread. "There she is!" Julia cried, suddenly rushing around him. "Hey! Hey there, are you okay?" When he heard Julia gasp, Raúl's eyes flew open and he was hurrying to be at his sister's side in case she needed him. But she was just sitting there staring at the crying girl in shock. "Meghan?" Julia reached out towards the stranger and repeated the name.

And that didn't make sense, unless she'd met some other

2

Meghan since the one she constantly talked about back in high school. That Meghan was blonde with dark, glowing skin and vibrant brown eyes. This woman was pale as milk and had glossy black hair and eyes like spring leaves. She looked like a girl he'd known once, in his freshman year of college. Her name escaped him, but he could still remember how she would smile at him, and how brilliant all her observations in class discussions seemed to be.

Off in the darkness, the trilling began to sound like sharp, manic laughter.

For a moment, the girl before him was a stranger, but then she was looking up at him with those green, green eyes, and he knew her. It had been a few years, but it had to be her. "How did you get way out here?" he asked, trying to smile comfortingly but feeling it twisted too tight in worry. "What happened?"

"Meghan, talk to us."

Slowly the woman blinked and then gave that sweet smile of hers. She reached out and caressed Julia's cheek, and then said in a whisper curling with affection, "Fetch something for me? Just over there." With the hand not caressing his sister's cheek, she motioned off into the darkness.

"Of course," Julia agreed with a determined nod. "Just stay right here."

Fetch what, though? "Fetch what?" he asked, frowning as Julia straightened up and began to walk off without a light or any other guidance.

Instead of answering, the girl turned her attention to him and reached out. "Help me up," she asked with a shy tilt of her head.

Branches rustled. The trilling came again, short and low, before cutting itself off as the night was filled with the sound of large wings beating at the air. "An owl," she said, drawing his attention back away

3

from the sounds. Something fell, out in the darkness, a loud, dull thump.

"What?" he asked, stalled in his motion to help her up.

"Out there," she explained, wrapping her fingers around his wrist. "Just an owl."

"Oh." Of course. He pulled her up and steadied her, his hand instinctively going to her waist. "What is she fetching?"

"Who?"

"My sister. You had her go off to fetch something." Strange noises came from the darkness now. Still no insects or other birds, but something wet and violent. His eyes stung, and his chest hurt, but he didn't know why.

"We're the only ones here," said the girl, moving closer, sliding her hands up and around his shoulders.

"Right," he agreed, because that sounded right.

He dropped his phone so he could wrap both arms around her, and the darkness swallowed them whole.

# Chapter 1
## Day to Day

"Tell me again why I let you bring me here," Lucy shouted above the heavy pulse of the music as it thrummed through the old house.

Kyle tossed back his head and laughed but she could barely hear it. He smelled like cigarettes and beer and heavy cologne. His eyeliner was smudged and the gel in his hair was losing its grip, allowing the dark brown spikes to limp. Of course Lucy knew why she came, but even Kyle's toned chest peeking at her through his skin-tight fishnet shirt could not console her by that point.

Just a few friends, he had told her, nothing more. Some goths from the area, mostly college kids but with a few high schoolers—*like us, Luce!*—allowed to join. Always enjoying the opportunity to spend more time with her friend Kyle, Lucy had agreed to come along. Now she was enduring migraine-inducing death metal and choking on cigarette smoke while squeezing her way through sweaty, vinyl-clad bodies. This wasn't her idea of a fun Friday night.

"I'm going home!" she informed him, yelling the declaration into his ear and knowing he'd probably still have trouble hearing it.

He seemed to have heard it because he frowned a little and gently grabbed her arm. "So soon?"

Giving an apologetic smile, she pulled her arm free. "Early day tomorrow," was her response yell. It wasn't entirely a lie; she had plans to spend the day with her friend Alice, as well as try to make a dent in her English homework. Kyle still looked confused, his big brown eyes taking on a very puppy-dog look. There was a second's hesitation, but then Lucy was ruffling his wilting hair and turning to make her way through the crowd.

Parties weren't really her thing. If it truly had been a smaller gathering she probably would have stayed longer and mingled. The loud music and cramped quarters, however, were not conducive to conversation. Ah, the things she suffered for pretty friends! Friends that she would have enjoyed having as something more, but who most likely would never see her in such a way.

Letting out a sigh that no one would ever hear, Lucy wedged herself past a man in a kilt and a woman overflowing her corset. It was a nice corset, though. Eyeing the design as she continued walking, Lucy considered turning back and asking the woman where she got it. Without looking where she was walking, she was suddenly colliding with someone, and they both stumbled away from each other.

"Sorry!" she yelled with what she hoped was an apologetic tone. The man turned around to face her and the only thing she could think of was that he had surely wandered into the wrong party. He was wearing a beige dress shirt, which had just become as revealing as Kyle's fishnet now that it was soaked through with what must have been the contents of his cup before Lucy had blundered into him. Tendrils of his shaggy black hair were clinging to his face due to the humidity and his dark eyes were regarding her with an unreadable expression.

A man with spiky green hair—for whom, Lucy thought this was certainly the *right* party—slung an arm around his shoulders and grinned. This new man sized her up with lizard-slit eyes that were one of many varieties of contacts Lucy had seen that night. She didn't really understand the trend, but it must have been pretty huge because someone earlier had even asked where she'd gotten hers. Except Lucy didn't wear contacts, her eyes were just weirdly, freakishly pale. When she was little, kids would tauntingly ask if she were part husky. Feeling slightly self-conscious, she crossed her arms in front of her bodice with

6

the pretense of pulling up her arm warmers.

"Ren, you dog! Found yourself quite the catch!" she heard the green-haired man exclaim as he jostled the wet man—Ren, evidently—and laughed.

"Get real," came the response in a rich, almost rumbling tone that Lucy was surprised could carry over the music. "Look at her, man. She's, like, sixteen."

"Seventeen!" Lucy heard herself correct before she could think better of it. She frowned and glared, though it was more at herself than at the men.

Ren's eyebrows shot up and he offered a slight bow, causing his friend to dip as well due to the arm that was still draped around his shoulders. "Well! My mistake, ma'am! Your youthful beauty must have masked your true maturity!"

Biting the inside of her cheek to remind herself to keep a cool head, Lucy brushed past them and continued towards the door. Behind her she could hear the lizard man's pleas for her to come back, and Ren's hearty laughter. She really disliked parties. Truly. Her intrinsic shyness always, *always* resulted in awkwardness. To soothe herself she thought of what it would be like once she got home and could curl up on the sofa with her copy of *Paradise Lost*. Just because she had to read it in order to write a report about it for class didn't mean she couldn't enjoy the experience.

Finally she reached the door and escaped out onto the rickety porch. It was a strange old house that served as the venue, and she absently wondered if it belonged to the host of the party—if there even was a host. The partiers had of course overflowed onto the porch, gathering in clusters at corners and cluttering the steps. Her boots clomped awkward and loud as she tried to navigate through the obstacles of black lace and limbs.

7

The hollow clomping turned to soft crunching as she made her way down the fine gravel path towards the road lined with cars on both sides. Lucy supposed it was a good thing that the party was in the middle of nowhere, where the roads saw little traffic. She trudged her way up the hill to where she had parked, idly swishing her skirt as she walked and doing her best to think of things besides Kyle or mysterious strangers who wore pale colors to a goth party. It was quieter out there on the road, the music and laughter from the house just a faint distraction. Her head still hurt a bit from the noise and the smoke of the party, but the night air was helping to clear it. Even so, the heat and humidity was only slightly more bearable outdoors, which was to be expected of Georgia in the late summertime.

A giggle and the sound of a car door opening drew Lucy's eyes to a car that was parked about five spaces up. The moon was waning and thin and there were no streetlights, but she could see the two figures standing by the car clearly enough. A girl that Lucy thought looked like someone she'd seen at school was smiling up at a man who looked college-aged. They lingered there, the passenger side door opened and waiting while they murmured and kissed. Not wanting to disturb them, Lucy stopped walking and turned away from them in order to lean against the bumper of a sports car.

She leaned her head back and looked at the moon, watching as purple-grey clouds slowly rolled across it. The black trees to both sides of the road hissed and rustled, as the couple got into their car and pulled away. She allowed herself another moment to enjoy the night before pushing off from the bumper and continuing on to her car.

\*\*\*

"So how was your date with Kyle?"

Lucy tripped in her platform boots and shuffled awkwardly for a few steps until she regained her balance. Glaring at her shorter friend, made much shorter with the added boost to Lucy's shoes, she replied with a growl. "It wasn't a date, Alice."

Shimmering pink lips drawn taut in a mischievous smile, Alice gave a little nod. "Riiiight. My bad. So, how was your not-date with Kyle?"

Directing her glare at the sidewalk, Lucy thought about the party and could practically taste the stuffy, pungent air inside that house. She wrinkled her nose at the memory and fiddled with one of her rings. "Bad. I left early."

"Eh? But why?" Alice was the only one of Lucy's friends who knew about her little crush, which had been developing since she was fourteen.

"Wasn't what he made it out to be. Too noisy. Not my scene."

A thoughtful hum came from Alice as they continued to walk, and Lucy tried to distract herself by looking at the clothing on display in the store windows. "You could have suggested that the two of you leave together," Alice offered up at last.

Releasing a startled squawk, Lucy looked back at her friend, not able to believe she just heard those words come out of Alice's mouth. Alice! The girl who had a rule about waiting until the third date before kissing, and who swore up and down that she would save herself until marriage.

Laughing, Alice shoved Lucy's shoulder gently, her gold charm bracelets twinkling softly. "That's not what I meant! I meant you guys could have gone somewhere else. Like go get something to eat or see a movie."

"I think that would be a bit too much like a date for Kyle's liking, Al." A shop window sported a mannequin wearing a black

9

flapper dress and a deep purple wig in the style of a '20s bob. Lucy stopped and looked at the dress, wondering if she should get something like it when prom rolled around. If she was even going to go. Not that she needed to concern herself with that now, since it was still early September. She watched Alice's reflection in the window as it moved to stand beside her own.

They were an odd pair, she mused, one girl in all black and the other in various shades of pink. Despite seeming like such a mismatched pair, Lucy Kincade and Alice Jeong had been friends since they were children. Back then, Lucy wore colorful clothing, and Alice had been a shy bookworm. Time and circumstance had a way of changing tastes and personalities, but not their friendship.

Right then, it looked as if her friend desperately wanted to help her out, even though Lucy would prefer she didn't. She continued to watch Alice's reflection while pretending to be studying the merchandise visible beyond the display. Dark, almond-shaped eyes were staring sadly at Lucy, while perfect white teeth were chewing away at sticky, pink gloss.

Finally, it seemed that Alice had obtained some sort of epiphany, because her reflected face lit up with a smile. "Why don't you ask him out next time?" Alice suggested. At Lucy's continued silence, Alice seemed to feel the need to elaborate. "You know, as, like… friends. Ask him to a place where there will be other people, only not something like last night. Show him what kind of scene you're into, and then maybe he'll know of more places like it that the two of you can… um…go to."

It wasn't a bad idea, really. The only problem would be getting the courage to ask him and in a casual way so that he wouldn't think it was a date. Unless he wanted it to be a date. Was dating always so complicated, or was it just her? Maybe it was just so complicated because he was a friend. Situations like that could be tricky, since one always had to consider any and all repercussions. If she asked him out on a date and he had no interest in her, there was the potential of ruining a very good friendship that had lasted years. On the other hand, perhaps it was exactly because the friendship lasted so long that it could survive any awkwardness that would occur from her bringing such an unrequited love into the light. Then again, there was always that slim chance that he returned her feelings, in which case confessing would prove to be a winning gamble. Too bad Lucy never cared for games of chance.

Alice was starting to look a little apprehensive again, so Lucy summoned a smile and turned back to face her friend. "Yeah. Sounds good." They resumed their walking and Lucy tossed her head back towards the window they were just at. "So, you think I'd look good in a dress like that?"

Glancing back as if she hadn't just gotten a good long look at the thing, Alice gave a shrug and an assuring smile. "'Course. You've definitely got the legs for it, pasty though they are. But where the hell would you wear that?"

Lucy lifted and dropped her right shoulder with feigned indifference. "MnMMmn. The prom, maybe." She couldn't help but grin as her friend burst out laughing, especially when Alice started going on about how at least it would be better than something from Morticia Adams' garage sale.

***

Monday snuck up quicker than expected, and soon Lucy found herself back at school and swept up in the usual routine. Chemistry sucked, as usual, and she made a mental note to ask her friend Krysti for help on homework later.

"And how is my darling Lucille today?" cooed Alice as she locked arms with Lucy in the hall as they walked.

"Perfect now that you're here, doll." Lucy topped the mock flirting off with an over-exaggerated wink that had Alice giggling and shoving against her playfully. "Got your assignment done for English?"

"More or less." Alice wrinkled her nose and released Lucy's arm so they could make their way into the classroom one at a time. "I mean, it's finished, of course. It's just… Poetry is totally not my thing. I do short stories. I like plot and characters and exciting twists."

They made their ways to their seats at the front of the class, side-by-side. Sitting down, they both began to rifle through their backpacks in search of folders and text books. "Well, poems can have those things." Lucy had some trouble finding her pencil, and had to start pulling out random items from that compartment—keys, erasers, crumpled pieces of paper, a compass, a protractor… Ah. There it was.

"Psh. Rarely. And it's not the same. Besides, we were supposed to write a sonnet, not something that spans pages like 'The Raven.'" Alice twirled her long black hair distractedly, staring down at the printed page of poetry on her desk as if it were a plague-ridden blanket.

Pulling out her own assignment, Lucy shook her head at her friend's concern. "I'm sure you did fine. You didn't get into Honors English for no reason, Al. If you can tackle complex plot lines, surely you can compose a few lines of—" The door closing cut her off, and the room fell silent as Mr. Pulchrum walked to the podium in front of the class.

"Good day, class," greeted Pulchrum, a wide smile cutting across his pale face and perpetual stubble. He always had a sort of anemic look about him, and often had purplish bruises lingering around his eyes to denote lack of sleep. Sometimes Lucy worried he wasn't taking care of himself, especially when she'd look up from grading papers for him during her period as his assistant, to find him passed out in his chair, mouth open to release soft snores. Even so, he was always upbeat and would be quite energetic in his lectures on things such as dramatic irony. If Lucy was truly honest with herself, she would admit that she found him more than a little charming.

Purely because of his personality, of course. It had nothing to do with his totally touchable light brown hair and brilliantly shaded hazel-green eyes.

Pulchrum asked if anyone wanted to read their poetry, and Lucy waited until a few others went before she volunteered, so that she wouldn't appear too eager. Afterwards, Pulchrum flashed her a delighted smile and she felt butterfly wings brushing against the walls of her stomach. It always made her elated when people liked her poetry, and she valued a man like Pulchrum's opinion more than that of anyone else she knew. Because he was brilliant, of course, not because of how nicely his shirts clung to his frame.

The happy feeling lingered as she made her way to the cafeteria with Alice after class, which was probably a good thing since it helped keep back any flash of nervousness she would have otherwise felt when Kyle sat down at her table.

"Sorry you didn't like the party, Luce," he said by way of greeting.

"That's okay," she waved it off with a carrot stick and a smile. "Sorry I abandoned you."

"Don't be!" His grin upon saying this made her instantly suspicious. "Seems you were scarin' the girls away. They thought you were my girlfriend or something. Not long after you left, I managed to get, like, three numbers. It was *sweet*. I think one of them was in college. Her name is Gwen or Lynne or something. It was hard to make out."

13

The little butterflies had all gone and Lucy mourned their deaths. Chewing carrots so she would have the excuse of not being able to smile too broadly, she crinkled her eyes in what she hoped was a friendly way. "Good to hear," she said between chews. "Glad I didn't spoil your night." She ignored Alice's soft elbow nudge to her side and ate with the gusto of the starved.

Eva and Jim finally emerged from the lunch line, and were arguing about something, which was nothing new.

"I'm just saying, you complain enough about people mistaking you for a Jamaican, and I seriously doubt the dreads are going to help."

"I can't help it that people here see a black man with an English accent and can't understand that means I'm from *England*." With a full name like James William Lukehurst IV, it was hard to see how much more English he could get.

"At least people don't stare at you for an uncomfortably long amount of time before trying to guess your ethnicity." Rolling her eyes, Eva Kuntz-Tenno slid into her usual spot while Jim took his seat across from her.

"I'm just tired of people asking me if I'm off to a costume party dressed as Jimi bloody Hendrix. It's time for a change."

"Then stop dressing like Hendrix. Like, seriously, do you own anything made after the seventies? But why dreads?"

Jim sniffed, lifting his chin. "They look good."

"Ya, mon."

"Oh, stuff it."

Watching the entertaining exchange, Lucy tried not to look at Kyle, but ended up having to because of the advent of Krysti Van Schuyler at his side. Merrily setting her tray down, the stylish blonde proceeded to inform the group that she was going to join something called a LARP.

"Means live action role-play," she explained with an excited giggle. "I'm going to be a Drow priestess of Lolth!"

"Seriously?" Alice looked scandalized. "You mean…Like those people that run around in the woods wearing funny clothes and swinging padded sticks at each other?"

"Oh, you know what it is!" Neither the look on Alice's face nor her tone must have processed fully in Krysti's mind, since all she seemed to understand were the words. "Looks like fun, doesn't it? I even get to use my D&D character!" Then Krysti suddenly turned her enthusiastic attention to Eva. "You should consider joining, too. I'd think it's right up your alley, since you get to act and all."

A hesitant smile came to Eva's lips and she swirled her cheese into her chili as a distraction. "I dunno… I'm not really into those kinds of things."

"But you can be any kind of character you want. You like wolves, right? You can be a werewolf."

Eva snickered and licked her spoon clean. "A werewolf?"

"Yeah! Well, they're technically called long-tooth shifters, since I think werewolf characters can only be used as monsters, but still! You can howl and pretend you're a shape-shifter or something. It'll be fun. You could be my ally in the battle against the good guys."

The spoon returned to the chili, moving slower this time in its rotations. Eva's green-gold eyes followed it and no longer looked up at Krysti. "Sorry, hon. I'll have to pass." Then a smile came to her lips, but Lucy noticed it did not reach her eyes. "With any luck, I'll get a decent part in the play coming up. If that happens, I won't have much in the way of free time."

Krysti made a noise like a disappointed cat and pouted for a moment before digging into her own meal. When a hand grasped her shoulder, she dropped her spoon and quickly checked to make sure

15

none of the chili got on her expensive blouse. Satisfied that she was clean, Krysti looked up at the girl who was now hovering near her shoulder.

"Sorry to interrupt," the intruder apologized. "Did I hear you talking about a LARP?"

Lucy eyed her, recognizing her as one of the girls from the goth clique which was commonly called the "vamps" due to their penchant for wearing elegant, Victorian-inspired outfits all year long. While Lucy was often called a goth by her peers, she was never a part of any of the varieties of goth cliques found at her school. She got along with most of them, but they were far too concerned with treating it as a lifestyle choice. Lucy liked the clothes and most of the music and certainly most of the literature, but she didn't want to feel restricted from loving other things as well.

When Krysti gave a hesitant nod, the goth girl smiled excitedly. "I had no idea you were into that! Our current role-playing group is thinking about taking things to that level. If you've got the time, you should totally come check our group out. We're always open for new members." The goth's words had Krysti literally bouncing in her seat.

"What's your game about?" she asked, a squeal of delight to her voice.

"It's a sort of creatures of the night thing, called *Chains of the Damned*. A fairly new game that's not really got a lot of attention yet. Don't see why, though; it has such a fascinating system and world. Also, you'd love our GM. He's a brilliant storyteller, and he keeps things running smoothly. Probably helps that he's the creator of the game." Lucy was amused to see that Krysti's eyes were gleaming by this point and that she was hanging on every word.

With a soft chuckle, Lucy turned back to her food. Her gaze brushed past Kyle and caught for a moment. He was laughing at

16

something Jim just said. In that moment—that little insignificant speck of time—Lucy realized that she had a thing for smiles. Truly, she was a sucker for a man with a handsome smile. Kyle's smile made his cheeks and chin poke outwards until they formed a heart together. This always caused his eyes to crinkle up into sparkling slits. He had a smile that warmed her when she looked at it.

"Hey, you were at the party Friday, right?" a new voice asked, snapping Lucy's attention away from Kyle and making her look towards the source of the question. It seemed that another of the vamps had wandered over to join her friend in discussing games with Krysti, and she was studying Lucy with an uncertain smile. It was the girl whom Lucy had seen leaving with the older man, and for an instant Lucy felt a little nervous that she'd be recognized from that moment as well. Maybe she thought Lucy was peeping at them or something. Trying to shake off her nerves, Lucy brought her hand up to tuck some hair back behind her ear and fiddle with the black loop of her cartilage piercing.

"Ah. Yeah, I was there. So was Kyle," she added, nodding towards the boy in question.

The vamp's smile brightened and she nodded. Her posture relaxed to suggest friendship and familiarity, as if having gone to the same party meant they shared something special. "Great party, right? I ended up running into our GM, actually."

At this, the first goth girl broke from her conversation with Krysti to turn to her friend. "Really?" When she got a nod of confirmation, the first girl's smile turned almost shy as she asked "Did he say anything about me?"

The second vamp's lips twitched at one corner before gliding smoothly into a smile. "We didn't really get a chance to talk that much," she offered in apology.

"The music was too loud for conversation," Lucy tossed in, for

17

some inexplicable reason feeling as though she should help her out. Evidently their game master was quite the contested piece of meat. Hopefully Krysti wouldn't go to their games, or else Lucy worried she'd fall for him, too. As much as she adored the girl, Lucy found it ridiculous how quickly Krysti fell in and out of love. Granted, Lucy's head could be turned by a hot guy, but she didn't insist it was her true love each time.

"Looked like you were conversating just fine, Luce." The teasing implication in Kyle's voice had her whipping her attention back to him with a start.

"What are you talking about? I hung out with you in mostly silence, then went home." Then, as an afterthought, she mumbled, "And 'conversating' is not a word."

He smiled one of his big, warming smiles at her, curving the edges up slightly in a devilish way. "Ah, but not before stopping to flirt with some college boys. Nice job soakin' his shirt, by the way. Man, this is why I say sexism goes both ways. Had I done something like that in order to get a similar view of a girl's chest, I'd have been slapped and called a pervert." Kyle was laughing by now, and everyone else was looking at Lucy with interest.

"It was an accident!" she squawked, but evidently that was not excuse enough.

"You didn't tell me about playing wet T-shirt contest with some hot college guy! You told me you had no fun at all!" Alice was looking torn between amusement and anger.

"I'm coming to the next party!" declared Jim, raising his hand as if volunteering for something in class. "If she's going to go about making clothing transparent on hot young men, I want to be there to witness."

Eva snorted after swallowing a spoonful of chili. "Purely for artistic reasons, right, Jim? Studying the human form so you can better capture it through sculpture?"

"Oh, you know it! And since it's to improve my sculpting, of course I'll need some hands-on experience. So that I can better memorize curves and texture, of course."

"Of course." Smirking, Eva exchanged a devilish leer with Jim.

"Wait," Krysti interrupted with the urgent tones of someone who just caught up with the conversation. "Lucy was rubbing all over some wet guy at the party on Friday?"

For a moment, all Lucy could do was gape like a fish trying to breathe on land, while Eva and Jim snickered and Kyle grinned. Alice seemed to accept this new statement as truth, and she was starting to go off on Lucy with a voice made high-pitched from shock. "Lucille Kitt Kincade! What on earth has gotten into you, going around molesting wet men! But most importantly, *why did you not tell me?*"

The vamp from the party offered a conspiratorial smile and leaned down over the table beside Krysti. "Was he cute?"

"Well, he was, actually," she said without thinking. Then, after a beat: "I did not rub all over him!"

"So you only rubbed part of him?" Eva asked by way of elaboration, eyebrows raised and mocking smirk tugging up a corner of her mouth.

"Ooo, did you get his number?" inquired the vamp, who Lucy felt was taking far too much interest in her love life.

"I—there was no rubbing! And no, I did not get his number. I'm not even interested in him!"

"Aw, too bad." The vamp straightened back up with a pout playing on her deep burgundy lips. "I was going to suggest you come to a party that my friend's throwing this Friday, since there's a chance he might show up at that one, too. But, if you aren't interested…"

19

"I'd be game," Kyle piped in, one of his wide grins aimed full-force at the vamp. "I had fun this past Friday, and I met some people I'd like to hang out with again."

Lucy changed her mind; Kyle's smiles were goofy and stupid and he gave them out too freely. "What time is the party?" she asked the vamp.

"Eight," was the response, and it appeared that she was pleased to have obtained two more guests for the event. "I'll give you directions tomorrow at lunch."

"Sounds great," said Kyle, still smiling at her as she left with her friend to rejoin the rest of their clique. Lucy viciously stabbed her applesauce with her spoon.

# Chapter 2
## Shadows

"Halloween come early this year?" Friday evening found Lucy standing in her doorway staring at Eva and Jim as if they'd gone insane. The two of them were on her welcome mat and dressed to the nines in gothic wear.

Eva was wearing black slacks tucked into red combat boots, a black dress shirt with red pinstripes with a vest over it of reverse colors, and a solid black fedora that had a small red feather tucked into its strap. Lucy only ever saw Eva wearing make-up when she was on stage, so she was even more shocked to notice the smoky eyeliner and shadow, as well as the deep red lips lined with black. Eva's long black hair was in its customary braid and trailing down her back, which exposed her dangling earrings that were comprised of little black heart fragments suspended by fine red chains.

Taking a different approach, Jim's ensemble looked more casual. His black denim pants were flared towards the end and hid most of his Converse sneakers, and the legs of the pants were loaded down with pockets, rings, and straps. Practically painted onto his chest, his shirt was black with a giant grinning skull stretched across the front, which went with his Jolly Roger hair kerchief very well. He wasn't wearing any special jewelry, his usual silver loop glinting from his right earlobe.

She had no idea where they got all that stuff, since neither of them were the kind to wear such things, but she was a little afraid to ask. "Sorry, kids, but I don't have any candy."

"Guess we'll just have to egg the house," Eva replied with a shrug.

"We came to join you for a fun-filled evening of wet clothing!"

21

Jim flashed a grin before cringing as Eva elbowed him in the ribs.

"I'm closing the door now." Which Lucy promptly began to do, except she found it difficult to complete the task while Eva had a large combat boot in the way.

"Don't be like that. We're not going to get in your way of wooing Kyle." Letting her usual sardonic mask slip away, Eva gave Lucy a sincere look.

The alien expression on her friend's face almost distracted Lucy from her words. "Who said anything about wooing Kyle!"

Just like that, the mocking smirk was back on Eva's lips. "Oh come on, Lucy. It's obvious."

"No it isn't!" Oh, God, how she hoped it wasn't.

"Yeah. It is." This time it was Jim who tossed in his two cents, and Lucy looked at him in alarm. He offered her a little smile which she was sure was probably intended to comfort. "Don't worry, though. I don't think he's noticed."

"Probably the only person who hasn't," snorted Eva.

"In any case," said Jim, "we wanted to come. Eva's offered to drive us. We know how your mum is reluctant to let you borrow the car, so we figured this would be a good incentive to bring us along."

Lucy stared blankly at Jim for a moment. "Why do you want to come, though? Despite what your current costumes would suggest, I know you two aren't into this kind of crowd."

Eva shrugged. "I'm bored and this provides a chance to play dress-up."

Jim grinned. "I'm shopping for models!"

Lucy sighed. "I'll grab my shoes."

\*\*\*

A few hours later, Lucy found herself alone in a crowd. Evidently Kyle had found one of the girls he'd met at the last party, or perhaps simply hooked himself a new one. Either way, he was chatting up a girl with cough drop red hair and brown roots. Lucy couldn't hear what they were saying over the music from such a distance, but she could guess. The girl's body language was suggesting they go somewhere to get better acquainted, and Kyle's smile was suggesting a dark corner away from prying eyes. Feeling her stomach liquefy and drain down to her toes, Lucy looked around for her other friends so she could find support. Jim was talking with some boys, employing his usual wide, emphatic hand gestures to illustrate his points. Eva was nowhere to be seen. Perhaps she'd gone outside. Intent on finding her, Lucy made her way to the door.

Eva wasn't anywhere on the wrap-around veranda, nor could Lucy see her in the yard amongst the other kids. Right when she was going to give up, she noticed someone with dark hair and a light-colored shirt lounging alone in the tall grass. She climbed down the porch steps at the back of the house and wandered out onto the expansive and horribly overgrown lawn. When she drew close enough, the figure turned and Ren was staring at her with impossibly dark eyes. At first his expression was blank, and then the spark of recognition flickered across his features and he smirked.

"Come to pour more expensive beer on me?" he asked, and his teeth flashed brilliantly in the dim moonlight.

"I was looking for a friend of mine, actually," Lucy responded, with perhaps more defensiveness to her tone than was warranted. She *had* been looking for Eva, though—at least at first.

"I don't think your boyfriend and I look very much alike, so I can't imagine you saw me out here and mistook me for him."

Lucy's cheeks burned and she hoped the night washed the color out. "Kyle's not my boyfriend." Then, a breath later, she added: "Besides, it was my friend Eva I was looking for."

The confused and insulted expression on Ren's face made Lucy feel much better. "You mistook me for a *girl?*" Shrugging, Lucy didn't vocally respond, but she did allow herself a satisfied smirk which practically mirrored the one he'd worn earlier. Ren shook his head and turned away from her in order to lie back in the grass, pillowing his head on his folded arms.

Uninvited, Lucy sat down beside him. "Where's the lizard guy?" she asked, her attention directed upwards towards the stars.

"The wha—? Oh. You mean Nick. He's around. Somewhere. Bastard abandoned me as soon as his ex showed up. He's been trying to get her back, and evidently he's succeeding."

"Well, why aren't you in there mingling, making new friends?"

"Why aren't *you?*"

She raised and lowered one shoulder in a falsely careless shrug, visions of red hair and sharp smiles flitting before her eyes. "Not really my scene," she said softly.

"Why come, then?"

No response came to mind that didn't make her sound pathetic and foolish. Eventually she sighed and pulled her knees up to her chest. "Because I'm an idiot."

"So he's not your boyfriend, but not for lack of wanting on your part." It wasn't a question, so she didn't feel compelled to answer. Instead, she continued hugging her knees and gazing up at the stars. A whippoorwill was calling in the distance, and the trees surrounding the house whispered like waves on a shore. A soft breeze carried the scent of pine and Ren's scent—some kind of cologne or aftershave that was spicy and earthy.

Before the silence stretching between them could grow too

awkward, she broke it with a question. "What about you? Why do you come to these things? Judging by the way you dress, this isn't your kind of scene, either."

"Maybe you shouldn't judge people by how they dress." His cliché admonition caused her to turn and look at him. The moonlight made him seem to glow ever so softly, with his pale shirt—was it baby blue tonight?—and fair skin. Instead of finding him beautiful like that, she was struck by how ill it made him appear to be. He looked washed out like an old photograph. The sallow tone of his skin suggested it was not his natural shade, and that he was meant to be tan and olive-toned. Dark brown, seemingly black eyes looked up at her from shadowed sockets, the skin around them bruised from chronic insomnia. His shaggy hair was the same color as his eyes, and it brushed his shoulders and spilled over his folded arms. He was grinning cheekily at her, and she noticed his teeth weren't as perfect or as white as she had thought a moment ago. They seemed to crowd each other in places, and they showed signs of him either being addicted to coffee or cigarettes.

She must have been staring for a while, because the grin shifted ever so subtly. "I don't do replacement work."

"What?" She blinked at him and searched his dark eyes for a clue as to what he was talking about.

"I'm not interested in replacing your crush."

Refusing to turn away, she glared down at him. "Good, because I'm not interested in you. Period."

"Now, I know that's a lie." Oh, how she wanted to wipe that smug look right off his face. "If there was no interest, you wouldn't have made yourself at home next to me like this. I'm also willing to bet I don't really bare such a striking resemblance to your girlfriend."

Gritting her teeth, Lucy thought up and vetoed several responses before finally just grunting in frustrated defeat. "Fine, let me

25

amend that. I'm not interested in you *romantically*."

His eyebrows shot up, and it looked like he was trying to fight off a laugh. "No strings attached sort of deal, huh?"

"For someone who claims no interest, your words seem to suggest otherwise."

The laugh finally escaped him, and it made any thoughts of illness vanish from her mind. In that moment he reminded her of wild tricksters of old—satyrs, imps, foxes. "I said I had no interest in being a love replacement. Never said I had no interest in other things."

"There you are!" The voice behind her provided a second's warning before hands fell on her shoulders with a momentum that nearly knocked her over. She tilted her head back and saw Kyle's upside-down face beaming back at her, warm brown eyes crinkled in amusement.

"How unfortunate," Ren bemoaned as he sat up and finger-combed his messy hair. "You totally ruined the moment."

"There was no moment," Lucy gritted out with a glare towards Ren.

Kyle didn't seem to pay any attention. "Luce, sorry to interrupt or whatever—"

"You're not interrupting."

"—but I just thought I'd let you know I'm heading out," he finished. Lucy shifted in preparation to stand, but Kyle's hands on her shoulders gently held her down. "With Nova." Her stomach gave a sickening twist. He leaned in close and smiled wide. She could smell that overpowering cologne of his, and the sweet tang of spiked soda. "So don't worry about me," he assured with a wink. "Seems you're having your own fun." Then just as suddenly as he had arrived, he was gone. In a daze, she watched as he ran across the yard towards the redhead. She wanted to throw up. Or cry. No, not cry. Especially not in

26

front of Ren.

"What an ass. And *that's* the guy you're interested in?"

Without responding, Lucy rose to her feet and started walking off towards the woods. She wanted to be alone, away from that stupid party with its stupid people, and especially away from that *stupid* Ren. He was calling out to her, but she didn't care; she just kept walking.

There was a small footpath which seemed to be slowly getting eaten up by the untamed forest. She followed along the barely-existent trail, letting the trees blot out the faint moonlight as well as the sounds of youthful revelry. It was here in the concealing solitude of the forest that she allowed herself to let go and cry.

She was nearly silent, even as her sobs shook her body. The art of silent crying was something she had mastered years ago, after her father's death, when she'd lie awake in the early hours of the morning and cry until the sun crept into her room. She felt ashamed now as she stood there crying over some boy. There had been many times in the past when she'd been disgusted by girls who were doing the very same thing. "*You think something like that hurts?*" she'd ask, fresh wounds and frustration making her eyes burn. "*Boyfriends, at least, can be replaced.*"

Why did it matter now? Why had she become the very thing which annoyed her? *I'm pathetic*, she thought to herself as her chest heaved with another painful, gasping sob. *He's not worth this. Why am I letting him get to me so much?*

"Lucy?"

Frantically Lucy wiped her eyes and forced her breathing back to normal before Eva could get close enough to see that she'd been crying. Thank God for waterproof mascara.

"Hey, Eva," she greeted jovially, turning to face her friend with the best smile she could muster. "I'd been looking for you earlier.

27

Where ya been?"

"I could ask you the same thing." Eva was close now, and even in the grey darkness Lucy could see worry etched clearly upon her face. "I got caught up in a discussion about Tennessee Williams, and when I turned around, you were gone. Then I see Kyle macking on some hair stylist's nightmare, and I figured you'd need some company. Trouble was, I couldn't find you. Asked around and was directed to some shaggy-haired guy, who said you'd bolted into the woods as soon as Kyle left with Kool-aid head."

"I wanted to be alone for a moment." She turned away, feeling the tingle of newly developing tears. "I'm fine, though. I'll head back to the party in a few minutes."

Eva was silent, but Lucy heard her boots crunching on the carpet of dry leaves as she stepped closer. Then, with a hushed voice that both confused and alarmed Lucy, Eva whispered near her ear. "Come back now. With me. Quietly."

Lucy opened her mouth to ask Eva what the deal was, but her friend's hand suddenly grasping her upper arm stopped her short. Her mouth snapped closed and in the ensuing silence, she heard something from beyond the bushes to her left. Turning her head towards the sound, she made out the mingling figures of two people pressed against a tree. The couple was producing wet, sometimes sucking-like sounds, occasionally accompanied by a growl or groan. *Kissing*, was Lucy's first thought, *They're just two kids from the party making-out in the woods*. Something in the way Eva was gripping her arm and radiating tension made her question her initial assessment. Listening more closely, she noticed with a cold tremor that the sounds weren't right for kissing. A memory popped into her mind of her older brother Mick doing his best to annoy her as he chewed an excessive serving of steak with his mouth open, smacking the meat with his teeth.

28

Shifting slightly, she strained to get a better look at the couple, even as Eva started tugging at her arm. The wind assisted her by blowing enough on the bushes that she caught long, clear glimpses of them. They were a few yards away, and the shadows were as thick as the vegetation, but moonlight has a way of highlighting certain things. There was a woman—and Lucy could tell it was a woman by the curves—pressing against a man, the tree at his back. It was the man who was facing towards Lucy, and she saw skin glowing pale blue in the moonlight as he tilted his head back with a moan. The woman's dark head moved down along his cheek, his chin, working towards his neck. As soon as his entire face was in clear view, Lucy had to use every scrap of willpower not to scream. Eva was pulling more urgently at her arm, and this time Lucy allowed herself to be pulled away. Her eyes never left the scene, staring even as the increasing distance and shifting branches made them seem to be nothing more than obscure shadows.

The next few minutes passed by in a confusing rush. Eva pulled her back to the house, where the yelled conversations and the pounding music seemed as distant as they'd been while she was in the woods. On the other hand, that distinctive, wet smacking sound seemed to linger in her ears. Jim was there, objecting to Eva's insistence that they leave. Then he must have seen Lucy's face, because his objections came to an abrupt end and he was asking about what had happened, and was Lucy alright? Bodies bumped against her, and Eva's grip on her hand hurt, but Lucy said nothing as she was pulled through the crowd.

"What happened?" Ren's face was in front of her suddenly, his look of concern confusing her. Why would he be so worried about a stranger? It didn't seem right or real. Nothing looked or felt real, and instantly it made sense to Lucy to think the entire evening had been a dream.

Eva must have offered a satisfactory excuse, because Ren was

29

backing off and Lucy was being pulled along again. They climbed into Eva's car, Lucy in the back, and the thought of being there alone made her grab Jim's shirt in sudden panic. Without question, he got in next to her and shut the door. She didn't let go, even after Eva had started the engine and left the party behind in a cloud of dust. The trees whirling past her window looked more threatening to her now than they ever had before, and she drew away from them, clinging to Jim for dear life.

The image would not leave her head, the sounds still ringing in her ears. She felt sick again, like after Kyle left but worse. Much worse. She was sick and dizzy and cold, and her body was trembling.

"Eva," she said, the first words she'd spoken since the woods. Her voice was barely audible over the whisper-quiet engine, and each sound was cracked and crumbling like dried clay. "Eva, we need to call the police."

"Not right now," Eva said distractedly as she concentrated on navigating the dark roads without breaking too many traffic laws.

"We have to," Lucy insisted, letting go of Jim's shirt in order to grasp the front seats and pull herself forward. "He was still alive! We have to call for help!"

Eva shifted gears, her tan knuckles turning white as she gripped the clutch. "By the time help arrives, he'll be dead and she'll be long gone."

The small part of Lucy's brain which was still capable of rational thought despite her panic understood Eva's reasoning. She knew it was true, but she didn't want to believe it. She didn't want to believe any of it.

"Who'll be dead?" Jim's eyes were wide, and he sounded confused as well as more than a little frightened. "What the hell happened?"

"Lucy and I saw someone being attacked in the woods," Eva

offered as explanation, her eyes on the road ahead of them.

"Attacked?" Lucy and Jim chorused in unison, but Lucy continued with: "He looked like he was enjoying it! Oh, God, how could anyone…" She felt bile rise in her throat, and she swallowed down as she sank back into the cushions of the seat.

"Enjoying what? Being attacked? Will someone *please* tell me what happened!"

Lucy squeezed her eyes shut and hugged her stomach. The image was there behind her eyelids, just as clear and surreal as it had been as she'd witnessed it. Moon pale skin and dark, irregular shadows that gleamed, sticky and wet. "A girl was…eating…some guy's face." The words sounded so odd to her once they came out of her mouth, and she was torn between laughing and vomiting.

The car rumbled on in silence for a few moments, and though she kept her eyes closed, Lucy was certain Jim's face was twisted up in disgusted disbelief. "Seriously?" he finally asked.

"Seriously," Eva deadpanned back.

Jim cursed under his breath and leaned back to join Lucy. She felt his arm come around her and she leaned into his warmth. The rest of the commute passed in silence as Lucy watched the scene play on loop in her mind.

\*\*\*

Eva took them to her house, which Lucy had visited many times since childhood, though it was a first for Jim. As soon as Eva had the front door unlocked, she was rushing in and calling out, "Papa! Mama!"

Her father came into the living room looking anxious and concerned. Eva's father was Dr. Hartmut Kuntz, a dark-haired German immigrant with vivid green eyes and a strong physique. Even though he must have been middle-aged, he still looked quite young and fit, only a few streaks of grey in his hair betraying his true age. He was wearing his usual ensemble of slacks, a dress shirt, and a sweater vest, his hair perfectly arranged without a strand out of place.

"What is it, Eva?" he asked with an accent coloring his words. "You are home early."

Grabbing both of her father's hands, Eva erupted into rapid German rambling that was assumed to be entirely lost on Lucy and Jim. Well, at least it was entirely lost on Lucy, if her blank expression was anything to go by. Jim's face, however, was a mask of concentration as he watched the two of them talk. "Do you understand any of what she's saying?" Lucy whispered to him.

He flicked her a quick glance before fixing his eyes on the conversation again. "Some. Not much, but some. Like something about walking in the woods and seeing a man and a woman..."

Turning her attention back to Eva, Lucy listened more closely, as if trying to see if she could identify any of the words from the severely limited German vocabulary she had picked up from Eva over the years. Looking back to Jim, she saw he was squinting now, his face squished in perplexed contemplation. "What? What's wrong?" she asked, maintaining her hushed tone.

Turning his head slightly towards her but keeping his eyes on Eva, Jim whispered back. "*Scheusal.*"

"Huh?"

"*Scheusal.* Eva said something about the woman and her being a '*scheusal*,' but I have no idea what that is. They're using it a lot now, though." Jim then tried to relay what he could decipher to Lucy, speaking as softly as possible so that Eva and her father wouldn't hear. Dr. Kuntz asked if Eva was certain about whatever it was she had said, that part Jim said was easy to translate. When Eva nodded and prattled

32

out her anxious response, Jim said it felt like he was listening to a radio station that kept fuzzing out in static. Only bits and pieces were clear to him, but the gaps between the familiar made the entire thing incomprehensible. All he was certain of was that this *scheusal*, whatever it was, had Eva upset. He also was able to translate what he was confident had to do with the man's face getting eaten.

"Why are they talking in German?" Lucy asked, suspicion seeping through her shock and fear.

Having no explanation, Jim simply clenched his jaw and shook his head.

They continued watching the animated conversation, until Eva's father suddenly turned on them with a somber expression. "You will stay here tonight. Both of you. You will be safe."

"Um. Okay." Jim looked surprised by the sudden command, most likely because he'd never been ordered to stay the night at a girl's house before, let alone by the girl's father. "I'll take the couch then, yeah?"

"You can take Günter's room," Dr. Kuntz offered as he attempted to manage a smile despite his eyes now looking haunted and preoccupied.

"Where's Günter going to sleep, then?"

Eva looked at Jim as if he were an idiot. "His apartment."

"What, I'm supposed to know! There are many people who still live at home while in college."

Rolling her eyes, Eva motioned for Jim to follow her down the hall. "I'll show you where you'll be stayin'."

Just as Lucy took a step to join them, Dr. Kuntz stepped into her path. "Will you please join me on the couch for a moment?" His smile was still screwed on firmly, but Lucy felt none of the warmth which he tried to convey. He sat on the plush leather couch and patted the seat next to him, which she sank down onto without comment. There was an awkward moment as Dr. Kuntz stared blankly at the Persian rug and Lucy tried not to fidget. Then his strong shoulders rose and fell in a heavy sigh and he straightened his posture as he turned his head to face her. "You had quite a scare tonight, didn't you?"

"We need to call the police." Lucy didn't want comforting, she wanted to help the man she saw, or at the very least bring his assailant to justice.

Dr. Kuntz studied her for a moment, his fake smile wiped away. She felt odd under his scrutiny, as if he was looking into her, beyond her, and seeing things she'd never comprehend. "Yes. I will go take care of things now. I just wanted you to know that you are safe here. No one will get you here."

Her eyebrows drew together and she tried to read his eyes like they were reading her, but they were as indecipherable to her as his native tongue. "Thanks," she heard herself say, and the sound was small and meek to her own ears. He patted her shoulder, a wan smile passing across his lips, then stood and walked into another room. Seconds later she heard the beeping of a cell phone's buttons followed by his rich voice talking in low murmurs.

As she sat there puzzling over what just happened, a low whistle from the hall drew her attention and she rose to investigate. Jim was standing in front of a frame containing various family photos, his eyes fixed on one image in particular.

Moving to stand beside him, Lucy followed his gaze and found herself looking at a photo of Günter laughing in the sun as he stood on a beach in only damp swim trunks, the sea at his back. His shoulder-length black hair was blowing in the ocean breeze, and his dark tan skin was a stark contrast against the white sands and pale sky. Even though Eva had some of her Japanese mother's features, she looked more

34

European than Günter, who must have taken more strongly after their mother. Lucy felt herself smile a little as she looked at the image. She'd had a little crush on the guy since she and Eva were children, but she always knew nothing would ever come of it. Günter saw her as another kid sister, and that perception would likely never change.

"What?" Eva was standing to the other side of Jim, crossing her arms and looking between him and the photo. "What is it?"

"Nothing," Jim replied with a nonchalant shrug and a smile, "just surprised that he's related to you. I mean look at him—he's gorgeous!" Growling, Eva bopped Jim upside the back of his head. He laughed and rubbed at the offended area, tossing his other arm around Eva's shoulders. "Hey now, my Artemis, you know you're lovely."

Relief flooded through all of them in that moment, heralded by the banter and laughter. The world hadn't ended. They'd all be okay.

A staged cough alerted them to Dr. Kuntz's presence, and the three of them turned to see him standing there with a cell phone in his hand and his brows knitted together. He was giving Jim an assessing look, probably reconsidering the wisdom of having a teenaged boy stay the night in his house with two teenaged girls—especially his daughter.

Sensing his thoughts, Eva nodded her head a little towards Jim as a smirk tugged at one corner of her lips. "It's okay, Papa; girls aren't his type."

Jim shoved at her playfully and averted his gaze away from Dr. Kuntz while Eva grinned wolfishly. The physician's eyebrows rose, and then his considering look returned, but it seemed more calculating than concerned.

"Günter will be coming over for dinner this Wednesday. You two are welcome to come and join us. I'm sure he would love seeing you again, Lucy. He also would like to meet more of Eva's friends, I'm sure."

35

Jim looked a little startled, but he quickly recovered and a smile bloomed. "Sounds lovely, sir. I'd be honored."

Smiling in return, Dr. Kuntz nodded at Jim, then looked questioningly at Lucy. When she offered a little nod of her own, his smile grew. "Excellent. Now, before you all settle in, might I suggest our guests call their parents? Being one myself, I know how much they worry."

*

Lucy slunk away to Dr. Kuntz's den in order to make her call. Closing her eyes, she took a few steadying breaths before pressing the buttons to activate her speed dial.

"Kincade residence." her younger brother Donnie's voice caught her off guard, having braced herself to talk to her mother.

"Hi, Donnie. It's me."

"Lucy? Are you okay?" The worry in his tone had her working harder at masking the lingering shock and fear.

"I'm fine. Just tired." She sat down heavily in Dr. Kuntz's insanely comfortable desk chair, its gleaming leather creaking loudly in protest.

Evidently her attempts at masking her emotions were failing, because Donnie wasn't buying it. "What happened? Did someone hurt you at the party?"

She laughed, the action eased by the absurd thought of a twelve-year-old boy charging in to save her from the bad guys. "I'm fine, really. Can I talk to Mom?"

"Fine." Despite his acquiescence, it was obvious that the subject would be revisited in the near future.

During the brief pause, Lucy again tried to rein in her emotions

36

and hide them beneath layers of believable calm.

"Hello?"

Hearing her mother's voice made it very hard for Lucy's resolve, a lump trying to inch its way up her throat. "Hey, Mom. Um. Dr. Kuntz offered to have me stay the night, so I was just calling to see if I may?"

"Oh, of course, dear! How are Hartmut and Jomei?"

"Well, I haven't seen Dr. Tenno yet tonight. She might be out at the moment. But, um, Dr. Kuntz seems well."

"Good to hear. Is Günter still down in Atlanta?"

"Uh. Yeah. Yeah, he is."

"I hope he's enjoying college. Mick says they still talk all the time. We should invite him over when Mick's back during the winter break, don't you think? Well, I mean, we should invite all of them, actually. It would be wonderful having them all over for dinner some evening."

"Yeah, Mom. Sounds great." The desk's surface was so dark and polished that it reflected Lucy's hand with almost mirror perfection. She watched as her fingers danced along the wood, the tips kissing their shadowy twins. It helped to distract her, to calm her.

"Well, you go have fun. Don't stay up too late, so that you don't disturb Jomei and Hartmut."

"Yes, ma'am."

Her mother's voice came warm and sweet across the line, and that lump finally wedged itself forcefully in Lucy's esophagus. "Thank you for calling, dear. Good-night. I love you."

Tears pricked sharp and hot at Lucy's eyes and she strained to keep them from her voice when she answered. "Love you, too."

She quickly ended the call before she was tempted to spill everything, overcome with the impulse to cling to her mother for comfort and protection. There was no way she would do that, though.

None of the Kincade children had allowed themselves such a luxury in years. No, quite the contrary: they resolved to be there for their mother, should she ever need *their* support.

God, she missed her daddy.

Barely keeping the sobs back, she quickly punched at the phone's screen again and stared at the glowing picture that lit up the screen as it rang. Mick's pixilated smile looked back up at her, his glasses slipping down his nose as his eyes looked cheekily over the rims. He was growing to look so much like their father. Like Mick, Lucy also had their father's jet black hair, cadaver pale skin, and frost-colored eyes. Mick was the one with the bone structure and a similar nose, though.

"Hello?" And the same voice.

"Mick." She let the pain show in her voice this time, knowing it was safe to do so with him. He was the support for his younger siblings, and he'd always performed his job well.

"Lucy? Lucy, what's wrong?" She heard him shifting around, and could imagine him sprawled out on his dorm bed, books surrounding him that sported formulas and theories that she'd never understand.

After crying for a solid ten minutes as he husked gentle words of comfort in her ear, she told him. She told him everything.

"You're safe now, though, yes? Christ. You called the cops?"

Breath still hitching, Lucy nodded even though Mick couldn't see it. "I think Eva's dad did."

"You *think*?"

"I'm sorry! I'm sorry!" she choked.

"No. No, no, no…shhhhshshshhh. Calm down, it's alright. You didn't do anything wrong. I'm sure you're right, and that he called. Everything's fine."

"Mick. Mick, I'm scared. I wish you were here."

"I know, Lucy, me too." His voice was so gentle, so sweet, and so very much like their father's that it broke her heart even more. "If you want, I can take a few days off and head down."

"No." She tried to muster up the strength she feigned with her mother. "No, don't cut. Your scholarship…"

"Lucy, it won't be a problem. I'll submit my assignments electronically, and—"

"No." Taking a shuddering breath, she again tried to fight back the tears. "If you come, Mom will suspect something."

"I'll just tell her we had the days scheduled off as school holidays or something."

"Mick, please." She had to whisper to prevent a whine.

"Lucy, you need to have someone there for you. You can't carry this on your own."

"I have Eva and Jim with me right now. I'll be fine."

Mick sighed and gently knocked the phone against his forehead in frustration. "Dammit, why couldn't I have just gone to Tech?"

Despite everything, Lucy found herself smiling at the very thought. If he had gone to Georgia Tech instead of M.I.T., then he'd always be nearby. "That would be nice. I miss you so much."

"God. I miss you, too, Lucy. When winter break comes, you realize I'm not letting you out of my sight, yeah?"

Her smile grew, and the dried tear tracks made her cheeks feel tight. "Sounds like fun."

\*\*\*

That night, as Lucy lay on a roll-out futon on Eva's floor, she watched the play of light on the ceiling from the outdoor lamps shining through the trees and curtains. Outside, the surrounding forest was alive with insects. Lucy lived in a more suburban area, where the insects were quieter and the cars provided a soothing hum for a lullaby, so the more rural sounds around Eva's home were strange to her. They always had been, whenever she'd stayed the night, but at least she could get over them eventually and manage some sleep. Not tonight, she suspected, gripping the soft covers so tightly that her nails jabbed her palms through the thick layers.

Dr. Kuntz had said she'd be safe there. For some reason, that scared her more than if he had never said anything at all. Saying such a thing would imply that she would have something to fear outside the house. It was a silly notion, and she knew it, but it would not leave her mind. Why would she think that the woman from earlier would be able to track her down? The woman probably didn't even know that Eva and Lucy had been there!

There was a howl from somewhere deep in the woods, and Lucy sat up with a reflexive start. "It's just a coyote," Eva said softly. Turning her head, Lucy saw Eva staring at her from where she lay in her bed, the light and shadows of the room casting her calm face in sharp relief and making her eyes seem to gleam. "There are a few that hang out around here. Nothing to worry about."

"Coyotes?"

"'Course." Eva yawned, even though neither her face nor her voice gave Lucy the impression that she was sleepy. "What did you think it was?" she asked. "A werewolf?"

A hollow laugh came from Lucy's throat, and she slowly lowered herself back onto her thin bed. "No. I'm just a bit jumpy, I guess."

There was a thoughtful hum from the bed, then the soft sound of fabric sliding against fabric and creak of springs. "Lucky we're not further north, in the mountains. There are mountain lions up there, as well as screech owls. Both of them sound like someone screaming bloody murder. Sends chills down your spine to wake up to that in the middle of the night."

"I'll bet." Just thinking about it sent a chill down Lucy's spine, so she could only imagine what she'd feel upon hearing such a thing. The room fell into silence again, save for the creatures of the night chattering amongst themselves outside. Time passed, and Lucy wasn't sure if Eva had fallen asleep or not, but she felt she had to ask something, or she'd surely never get to sleep. "Your father called the cops, right?"

At first she was certain Eva had been sleeping, because she received no answer. Just as she closed her eyes to try to force herself to sleep, however, Eva's steady, quiet voice carried over the chirping and howls. "He handled it. Don't worry."

It was hours before Lucy could find sleep, and when she did, she was plagued with strange, macabre dreams. In the last one, which was the clearest and most vivid, Mr. Pulchrum was there, and he had gathered her and several other students together for a special test outside. The landscape was made of white linen, which she had at first mistaken for snow. Dark, rusted fences marred the white as they wound through the oversized folds, boxing off lopsided rectangles. Pulchrum led them to where an old-fashioned lamppost stood near one of the fences. They gathered in its glow, and the rest of that cloth world suddenly seemed so dark and veiled. "Stay in the light," he said with a grin. "Stay in the light, or they'll get you. But what you have to do is get *them* before they can get *you*."

"How?" a boy asked—a dream person whom Lucy had never met in real life. She could see his face, but was unable to focus on any one feature at a time.

Pulchrum was suddenly massive, peering down at them as if they were toys on a table. Somehow, Lucy knew that comparison was accurate, since that's exactly what they were. The street lamp was a table lamp, and the linen landscape was a sheet stretched carelessly across a table. "That's the test," the giant Pulchrum replied with a grin. He held a cage up and shook it somewhere in the shadows. "Stay in the light," he repeated. "Stay in the light and never leave it."

The shadows—nearly every shadow anywhere—was suddenly swarming with things. Whatever the creatures were, they were as dark as the sky during a new moon, but their bodies sometimes glistened with a slimy slickness. There were wet clicking sounds when they moved, but they did not growl or snarl. All around her, the students were erupting into a panic, screaming that they needed more light, needed weapons, needed to get away.

She looked up at Pulchrum and asked calmly, "Can they get into any shadow?"

"Any."

"Even the shadows on my face?"

"Especially the shadows on your face."

Her heart raced, but she did not let her fear show. "I need to get rid of the shadows, but I don't know how."

"Stay in the light."

"Light causes shadows."

Eyes twinkling, he nodded. "Then you'll just have to fight them off, won't you?"

"Before they can get into the shadows on my face?"

"Yes."

Lowering her attention back to her table-top world, she saw that everyone else was gone. "They've run off," Pulchrum's voice explained. "They went to find better light."

42

"There are shadows between the light posts," she observed, looking around and being unable to see anyone else beneath any of the other lights—lights which she had never noticed until that moment.

"There are always shadows, Lucy." Above her head, the lamp flickered. "Time to run."

Around her the shadows clicked and writhed with creatures and Lucy raised her head to Pulchrum again. "I can't."

"Run or don't, it doesn't matter. There are shadows on your skin."

"It hurts." And it did, though it was the first time she realized it. There was clawing and biting from anywhere on her body that existed in shadow.

"Run."

So she did. She ran through the darkness, the clicks loud near her ears and the sharp claws scraping at her flesh, but she never really saw the creatures. Beneath her feet, the sheet shifted and the world was suddenly whirling around her as the fabric rose and she lost her footing. She was falling, her hands grasping futilely at the cloth.

Twitching and gasping, she opened her eyes to find herself on the floor in Eva's room. Sunlight was cutting sharply through the gaps in the curtains, streaking the hardwood floors with gold and blazing a trail across Lucy's face. Squishing her eyes closed against the light, she made no effort to move away, her mind still lingering halfway in her dreams.

*It'll keep the shadows off my face*, a voice in her head reasoned.

# Chapter 3
## The Grin Reaper

Perhaps she should have accepted her mother's offer to stay home on Monday, even if her mother mistakenly interpreted Lucy's state as being ill. But Lucy had spent the entire weekend in a funk, and so forced herself to get it together and go to school. There was something positively unreal about the world moving around her in the same way it always had. Most of all, it was strange knowing that everyone expected her to act no differently. No one else had been there that night except her and Eva. To Lucy, it felt like something had shifted, the foundations beneath her quaking. She was reminded of the first time she had gone back to school after her father's death. Everything was just the same as when she had attended before he died, it was just her that was different. Things took on a different perspective.

At the age of ten, Lucy's entire outlook on the world had changed. Over the years, this outlook slowly faded, blending with that of the average teenager. Things started to matter again, things which she had once considered to be insignificant and foolish. People had told her back then that time heals all wounds, and she'd wanted to believe them. In truth, time could only make the wounds more bearable, but they would never heal.

Now it was as if someone had stripped away years of scabbing, exposing the wounds to the harsh elements once again. How was she supposed to focus on things like chemical reactions, when there was a murderer on the loose? What did trigonometry matter if you were just going to get your face eaten off in the woods by some maniac!

"Luce, you alright?"

Looking up from her seat on the floor in one of the hallways, Lucy watched numbly as Kyle slid down the wall to join her. Oh, that's right; she'd have to explain the events of that night. Repeatedly. Just like back when she was ten and over the years since then. *"Your father died? Oh, you poor dear. How did it happen?"*

Luckily, Eva came to her rescue. "There was some trouble at the party after you left," she explained, taking a seat on the other side of Lucy and setting her backpack in her lap.

"Trouble? Like what? Did someone try to hurt Lucy?" Kyle moved closer, as if he could protect her from something that happened days ago.

"No." Eva unzipped her bag and started looking around for something, her eyes focused on her task. "She and I were taking a walk in the nearby woods, and we saw a man get attacked."

At this, Kyle was leaning closer more out of curiosity than protectiveness. "What was it that attacked him? A bear or something?"

Not really wanting to face Kyle, Lucy was watching Eva, so she saw the ironic smirk that visited her friend's lips for only an instant. "A woman, from what we could tell," Eva replied with an almost clinical calmness that Lucy envied. She wished she could be as calm, brushing the incident aside as if it were no worse than stubbing her toe on the school steps.

"So, you witnessed an assault? Did you call the cops?"

"My dad did. After Lucy, Jim, and I went back to my place. Truth be told, I just wanted to get us all out of there. It was...creepy." For the first time during her explanation, Eva's voice shook, even if for just a second. Abandoning her search—or the pretense of—Eva turned away from her bag and looked at Kyle.

Like Jim, Kyle cursed at the news, but he was unlike Jim in that he wasn't caught up in the moment of fresh terror and adrenaline. His cursing was more subdued, more like the response to watching a random character get shot in a movie. Even so, he wrapped an arm around Lucy and pulled her up against his side in an effort to comfort her. "That must have been terrifying; no wonder you look so spooked. You gonna be okay, Luce?"

Life was unfair, she thought. Here she was pressed against her crush, her head resting against his shoulder, and she couldn't even enjoy it. Actually, she wanted to pull away. "Fine. Just haven't gotten much sleep."

"I'd imagine." He started stroking her arm, pulling her even closer and planting a kiss at the top of her head. "I'm here if you need me, Luce."

She didn't want this. If there ever came a time when Kyle wanted to hold her to him, she wanted it to be out of affection, not sympathy. "Thanks," she whispered halfheartedly, as she carefully pulled out of his arms and tacked on a smile. "I'll be alright, though. See you later." Without another word, she gathered her things and stood, slinging her backpack over one shoulder. When she glanced back down at Kyle, he was looking up at her as if he didn't recognize her at all. That was fitting, she supposed, since normal Lucy would have loved to linger in his arms until the bell rung. Perhaps she'd be kicking herself later, but in that moment, she couldn't stand him holding her for another second.

Eva rose to stand next to her, seemingly intent to walk with Lucy to class despite the fact that they had two different subjects next. Leaving Kyle behind, they made their way down the halls together, shoulders occasionally brushing. "What was that?" Eva asked after they were out of earshot of Kyle.

"What was what?"

"That. You brushing Kyle off like that when he was all over you."

Lucy shrugged her free shoulder, the backpack weighing the

other down. "Don't like pity hugs."

Eva snickered at that. "Pity hug. Cute." Then the right side of her mouth was tugging up in her usual smirk and she was leering askance at Lucy. "No, but really. You changin' your mind about Kyle? Maybe switched your sights to a certain shaggy-haired guy from the party?"

"What are you talking about?" Brows coming together, Lucy paused in her walking to glare dumbfounded at Eva.

"He seemed awfully concerned about you."

"Who?"

Groaning, Eva rolled her eyes. "Are you *trying* to be impossible? You damn well know who."

"Eva, I really don't want to talk about this right now." Which was true, because she was in no mood to be teased or to discuss guys.

Sensing that Lucy was serious, Eva actually backed off. "Sorry." They resumed their walking, this time an awkward silence weighing down around them. Finally Eva gave out a sigh like a deflating tire. "Don't dwell on it." When a glance towards Lucy provided her with a blank stare for a response, Eva shook her head. "There's nothing you can do to change what happened."

"I know. It's just hard to get out of my head. And I keep having...strange dreams."

"It's only natural. But just," Eva paused as she tried to find the right words. "Look, if you find yourself thinking about it, try to think about something else instead. Think of a book you're reading or a movie you saw. Hell, think of shaggy-haired guy or Kyle or Johnny Depp. Just something, *anything*, that isn't that night."

"Yeah..."

"I'm serious, Lucy."

"I know."

"It's not healthy to dwell on it. You've got to get over it. The world isn't going to stop spinning just because you witnessed something seriously messed up."

"This is my room." They stopped in front of the door, and Lucy made herself face Eva with a smile. Her friend was looking apprehensive, even though she was trying to cover it up with her usual indifferent mask. Something inside her heart twisted, and Lucy reached out to pull her friend into a one-armed hug. "Thanks," she breathed into Eva's hair. "For everything you've done. Thanks so much."

When they pulled apart, Eva's smirk looked more like a lopsided smile, and her eyes seemed to twinkle. "Take care."

***

Red pen poised over the paper, Lucy stared at the words without seeing them. Eva's advice, wise as it was, was easier said than done. As she sat there grading papers for Mr. Pulchrum, Lucy's mind kept wandering, though not necessarily to the incident itself. She also thought about that strange dream—or, at least, what she could recall of it—and of Dr. Kuntz's assurances. Something was poking at her in the back of her mind, trying to fit pieces together in order to show her something. The trouble was that the pieces never clicked and appeared mismatched as though taken from multiple puzzles. Still, she knew there was *something* about that night, something important yet evanescent.

"Are you alright, Lucy?" Pulchrum was standing beside her desk, but to her chagrin, she had no idea how long he'd been there.

"Just tired," she said, eyes falling back to their blank study of the paper. It wasn't entirely a lie; she had gotten very little sleep since that night.

A warm, dry hand brushed aside her long, side-parted bangs in order to press against her skin. "You're freezing," he hissed with dismay, moving the hand from her forehead to her cheek in order to assess whether the temperature was uniform. "I'm no stranger to insomnia myself, but this is bad. Maybe you should see the nurse."

"No, I'm fine. Really." His hand's warmth felt soothing, and she had the dangerous impulse to lean into it. Instead, however, she forced herself to be still as stone, and closed her eyes to stop from turning them up to study his close face.

"You sure? Your skin's as cold as ice." His hand left her skin, and she mourned its loss and the heat it had provided.

Will power giving in, she opened her eyes, instantly being caught by the interwoven greens and dark ambers of his eyes. Much like Dr. Kuntz's gaze, Pulchrum's seemed to stare into her, then beyond her, easily seeing through her lies. For one foolish moment, she feared that he could read her thoughts, that gaze piercing straight into her innermost secrets. "I'm sure," she said, trying and failing to summon a smile.

He moved away, scratching at the back of his neck in thought, and Lucy felt a breath release that she hadn't even been aware of holding. Those eyes she'd just admired and feared now flicked around the room as if searching for a solution to the current predicament. His lips squished together up towards his left cheek, giving him the comical appearance of having a puckered mouth on the side of his face. Finally, he sighed and let his shoulders slump before directing his attention back to his pupil. "Maybe you should take a nap," was the brilliant plan he had managed to formulate. "You can use my chair, since it's cushioned. I'll finish up the grading."

It was the first time a teacher had ever told her to neglect her work and take a nap. "You sure that's alright?" she asked, eyes wide.

49

His comforting smile slid easily across his lips. "More than alright. There've been plenty of times when I've fallen asleep on you. I'd say your turn is long past due."

Perhaps a nap would help, she reasoned to herself as she rose from her desk and made her way towards his. As soon as she sat in his chair, he was at her side again, blanketing her with his tweedy grey trench coat.

"There now," he murmured, his voice turning the words into endearments that warmed her more than the coat. As Pulchrum walked away to take her place at her desk, Lucy shifted around in the chair. It creaked and made dull clicks, and then fell silent once she had found a comfortable position. Pulling the coat tighter about her, Lucy settled in for a nap. The coat smelled like walks on crisp winter nights through ancient forests. That was her final, barely coherent thought as she drifted off to the sounds of a pen scratching against paper and Pulchrum's tuneless humming. For the first time in days, no nightmares visited her in her sleep.

\*

When Pulchrum gently nudged her awake some time later, Lucy felt herself smiling without having to force it. His return smile made his eyes twinkle—or perhaps that was just the late afternoon sun shining in through the blinds on the windows.

"Sorry to wake you," he apologized softly. "It's time to go. Do you feel any better?" His hand returned to her cheek for a moment. "You feel a little warmer, at least."

Black hair tickled at her neck and shoulders as she yawned and stretched, bones popping pleasantly. "Oddly enough, I feel even more tired." Even so, she was surprised to find that she felt in better spirits.

His chuckle was rich and pleasant, and Lucy's smile grew as the sound traveled through her. "That'll happen," he said with laughter lingering in his voice. "Your body liked that little nap and is greedy for more. You should take another nap when you get home. Or, at the very least, get to bed early tonight."

"I might do both." After so many days without smiling, her lips and cheeks were actually feeling a little sore from all the exercise they were getting in his presence.

With how often and easy Pulchrum's smiles came, Lucy was sure he never felt any similar aches. "Sounds like a plan." He reached out towards her again, and she thought he might return his palm to her cheek or perhaps—just perhaps—run his fingers through her sleep-mussed hair. Instead, he wrapped his fingers around the coat and gently pulled it off of her. A pang of disappointment spiked up deep inside of her, and she instantly chided herself for it.

Something must have shown on her face, because Mr. Pulchrum paused and studied her, smile wilting. He sighed and pulled up a student's desk to sit beside her, facing her, his expression suddenly serious. "Something is obviously bothering you, Lucy."

She opened her mouth to lie, but felt that every time she told him a falsehood it was like adding weights to her shoulders. "I saw something this past weekend. An attack."

His fist clenched on the desk and his eyes seemed to flash with intensity and alarm. "An attack. Lucy, why didn't you tell me sooner? Have you told anyone?"

"Yes. Yes, the police were notified." Although she didn't tell him who made the call.

For some reason, that didn't seem to satisfy him, his muscles still tense with a strange sort of energy that bled into her and made her start to tense up as well. "Where did this happen? What did you see,

51

exactly?"

Looking into his face, she wondered if she should tell him the whole truth. It wasn't that she didn't trust him. Mostly she worried that he wouldn't believe her. That he'd think she was just making up some wild yarn for attention, and that would instantly make her lose credibility in his eyes. She couldn't endure that. Yet, if details of the attack ever made it into the news, he'd know she lied by way of omission. So, with a ragged breath and determined gaze, she told him. She told him everything.

At the end of it, he was glaring at his fist, looking for all the world as if he were fighting back the angry impulse to rise and chase after the cause of her grief. "That is a difficult thing to witness. No wonder you're so shaken." With great effort of will, he slowly relaxed his fist and gave her a gentle smile. "Of course, it probably doesn't help that I brought it up, because you really shouldn't be dwelling on it. What you need to do is get your mind off of it, focus on something else."

The laugh that tried to surface from her throat died before reaching air. "That's easier said than done."

His eyes turned distant again, slipping away from her and staring blankly at the windows as he fell into deeper thoughts. "I'm sure the proper authorities will handle everything," he assured her, glancing at Lucy with a flicker of his usual self before drifting off again. "You shouldn't worry about it."

She nodded just as the bell chimed electronically over the intercom.

"I need to get going," she said with what she hoped was a steady voice.

He stood and stepped aside, that wide smile returned to his lips and shining in his eyes as if he hadn't just been off in solemn thought.

"I'll see you tomorrow, Lucy. Take care."

"You, too."

For the rest of the day, she would look back at those moments with Pulchrum, analyzing them and wondering if she had behaved oddly. Or, if he had perceived any of her words or actions as odd, and that was why he'd behaved strangely towards the end. She worried that he would think she had a crush on him, which was a silly notion. Lucy certainly wasn't the kind of girl who would want to get involved with a teacher. Of course not. Even if he was young and handsome and an excellent conversationalist that always made time for her. Besides, even if she were interested—which she most certainly was not!—it wasn't like he'd ever be interested in a kid like her.

She couldn't wait until she was finished with high school and all of its unnecessarily complicated romance.

\*\*\*

"*…of a brutal attack this weekend involving the mutilation of a young man's face. More after th—*"

Blinking heavily, Lucy pulled herself up from the realm of sleep and into waking, the living room's overhead light temporarily blinding her. She turned her head and squinted towards the television, watching as Donnie flipped through channels with only brief pauses between clicks of the remote. Quickly rolling to the side, she pushed herself up into a sitting position, propping her still tired body up on her right arm. "Turn it back," she demanded, voice pitched with urgency.

"To what?" Donnie looked at her over his shoulder from where he sat on the floor, his brown, wavy hair obscuring most of his face from her view. Donnie was only twelve years old, and yet he already tended to act like a petulant teenager. He sat there in his well-worn jeans and faded King Crimson shirt—another abnormality for his age was his love of prog rock—staring at her as if she were an idiot. "I've covered nearly all the channels we have."

Lucy scrambled off the couch to sit next to Donnie on the carpet, and reached for the remote. "The news. Turn it back to the news."

Donnie looked like he was about to protest, his face scrunched up as his grey eyes flicked between her and the remote in his hands. Finally he sighed, shrugged, and handed the device over. "Nothing on right now, anyway."

"Thanks," she muttered distractedly once her fingers were wrapped possessively around the smooth plastic remote. Thumb working quickly, she flicked back through the channels until she found the evening news.

"—ce received an anonymous phone call late Friday evening, reporting a supposed attack that involved the gruesome mutilation of the victim's face. The assault was said to have taken place in the woods near an old abandoned house in north Fulton County. The house is evidently frequently used as the site of teen gatherings, as was the case this Friday during the time of the attack. After hours of searching the area, police had discovered no evidence of foul play, and are considering the possibility that the call was a prank."

Lucy watched the lovely blonde anchorwoman with rapt attention, horror slowly dawning on her face at the suggestion that it might be considered a joke. "No," she seethed, gripping the remote so hard it hurt. She *knew* they should have called sooner. Perhaps the police would have been able to make it in time to catch the culprit red-handed.

A pink-faced man with sagging cheeks and deep wrinkles suddenly appeared on the screen, replacing the anchorwoman. His uniform was perfectly pressed, and his balding head reflected the glare of flashbulbs as he addressed a small audience of reporters clustered around him. A graphic with the station's logo and the words "Deputy Dwight Tucker" faded into existence at the bottom of the screen.

"While it is likely that this could merely be a hoax," he was saying with a mild southern accent and a voice graveled with age and cigarettes, "we have not ruled out the possibility that this report was genuine. There are three missing persons reports of young men fitting the victim's description which have been filed since Friday night. One of them, as it turns out, was last seen by his friends at that very party. This is startling information, and it leads us to believe that there may be some truth behind the reported attack. Now, whether or not the mutilation elements are real, I can't say. All that I can say is that we have swept that house and surrounding area multiple times and have found no traces of blood or other indications of an attack. Right now we would like to ask that anyone with information concerning the event or the possible whereabouts of Ronald Kent to please contact the Fulton County Sheriff's Office. Thank you."

The beautiful anchorwoman reappeared, a photo of Ronald Kent digitally added to the area left of her head. She reiterated the deputy's request as the Sheriff Office's phone number flashed momentarily across the bottom of the screen. Then, with barely a beat, the attention shifted to her male counterpart, and he launched into the details of an unrelated story. Lucy continued staring at the screen even while the anchorman prattled on about "new medical studies" and what they revealed concerning the toilets in public restrooms. She wished futilely that they would return to the other story, or at least show Kent's photo again.

"Were you there Friday?"

Snapping out of her daze, Lucy turned away from the TV and

found him studying her with an intensity she found disturbing. Shifting uncomfortably under Donnie's scrutiny, she looked away and back towards the screen. "No," she lied. "I just heard something about it at school."

Donnie didn't respond, and she didn't dare glance at him to see whether or not he seemed to believe her. Instead, she watched the last of the toilet seat report with feigned interest. The next report, minor details of which were offered up as a teaser before switching to commercial break, sparked very real interest. "The serial killer that has been eluding authorities for a year is on the move once again. Could Atlanta be his next target? Stay tuned; more after this."

"Serial killer?" she asked, as if addressing the can of chunky soup that just appeared on the screen.

"Yeah," Donnie answered from beside her, assuming the question was up for grabs or maybe even directed his way. "She's probably talking about the Grin Reaper."

Brows knitting together, Lucy turned to look at her brother as if he'd grown a second head. "The what?"

"Grin Reaper. That's what everyone's callin' him," he explained with a bored tone as if this was old news. "He's called that because when they find the victims, their lips are cut off so it looks like they're laughing or grinning. Hence, *Grin* Reaper."

"That's sick." Lucy didn't specify whether or not she was referring to the state of the victims, or the ridiculous nickname the killer had acquired because of the disfigurement. She felt the description could be applied to both.

"That's not the half of it." Donnie smirked a little, a gleam in his eyes to show that he was actually more interested in the conversation than his earlier tone had suggested. "All that's left of the victims are their heads…on sticks."

"Sticks?"

"Yeah, like poles. Stuck into the ground. The heads are stuck onto the top, usually positioned next to a window so that it looks like it's just people standing around laughing inside."

"Inside? How does he stick the poles through the floor?"

A shrug. "Dunno. He just does. Guy must be real strong, though. Evidently he tears the bodies up like paper."

Skeptical, Lucy glanced back at the TV to see if the news had returned, but continued her confused study of Donnie when she found only an advertisement for facial tissues on the screen. "How do they know he tears the bodies up, if the heads are all that's left?"

"Well. They're all that's left that's whole. There's also usually tons of blood and little bits and pieces everywhere. Still, with all that mess, they haven't found even the guy's footprint."

"Seriously?"

"Yeah."

"You're making this up."

Donnie glared up at her as he crossed his arms defensively. "Am not."

She opened her mouth to respond, but aborted the action when the speakers emitted the musical theme to denote the return of the news. The camera suddenly zoomed in on the blond anchorwoman as the words "Grin Reaper" slammed dramatically onto the screen beside her head. "Many Americans are familiar with the Grin Reaper, the serial…"

"See?"

"Shut up."

"…terrorizing ten states, and claiming over thirty known victims. His pattern has been seemingly erratic, with no indication as to which state he'll relocate to next. So, what's caused the FBI to believe that Atlanta is the next target? Missing persons reports. According to the

FBI, they keep a close watch on missing persons trends, a sudden leap in submissions being a red flag for the potential location of the killer. The Grin Reaper has fallen dormant in the past month, which has led investigators to believe he is on the move, and possibly has already begun again somewhere new. His last known location was in Nevada, where he claimed seven known victims in the Las Vegas area. Four of these victims appeared in missing persons reports prior to the first discovery of victims' remains.

"This rise in reports also occurred in the other states visited by the Reaper, which is why investigators have been drawn to Atlanta. Within the past month, the number of people reported missing in Atlanta and the surrounding area has shot up at an alarming rate. As was the case in the other states, most of the missing persons are young people, on average between the ages of sixteen and twenty-five. Many who are familiar with the Reaper will know that all of his victims have also fallen within this age range, as he seems to target young adults specifically."

"One of the good things about still being a kid, I suppose." mumbled Donnie from beside her. A glance his way revealed a rare glimpse of naked fear in his eyes.

"I should go finish my homework," Lucy heard herself say, forcing her body to release the remote and stand up.

Donnie looked at her, a curtain of steely concern shuttering the earlier fear. "Next time you're out, be careful. Don't talk to strangers."

"Yes, *Mom*. And I'll hold a grown-up's hand when crossing the street." Her voice was softened by his concern, coming out more affectionate than snotty.

Without another word passing between them, she headed upstairs to the computer room, which was more of a store-all space combined with a small, family-shared office. She pushed the power button on the tower and plunked into the wobbly chair while the fans inside the box hummed to life.

Instead of doing homework, however, she spent nearly an hour rummaging through websites on missing persons and the Grin Reaper. What she found was confusing, to say the least. Near as she could tell, there did indeed seem to be a trend with missing persons reports suddenly spiking in an area just before any confirmed Reaper victims. The odd thing was, however, that the sudden increases in missing persons would almost always start while the Reaper was still conspicuously active in another state—sometimes across the country.

"The hell is going on?" she whispered to the screen, as if its words would suddenly rearrange themselves to provide the perfect answer. With a frustrated growl, she slumped back in her chair and glared at the ceiling. Also plaguing her were the amateur pages about the Grin Reaper, and how they talked about theories that he was cannibalizing his victims.

What did it mean, and why was she even obsessing over all of it so much? Did she really think the Grin Reaper had anything to do with what happened at the party?

Maybe. Maybe he did. Maybe it wasn't one man acting alone. The only way to really explain the trends in disappearances would be to assume that he was working in conjunction with someone.

Dr. Kuntz's expression that night flashed suddenly through her mind, his words echoing in her ears. Eva had been upset, yet at the same time she seemed level-headed about the whole ordeal. It was as if she knew something—something her father also knew about, because they could talk about it with familiarity. Not only that, but they also talked in German as if they were shielding the information from their guests. Eva's father had lived in America for well over twenty years, and was probably more fluent in English than Lucy was. There was no reason for Eva to switch their conversation to German, unless she didn't want Lucy and Jim to understand.

Jim *had* understood, however, even if just a little bit.

Leaning back in her chair, Lucy fished her cell phone out of her front pocket. She unlocked the screen and called Jim. He answered after three rings with a "Hey, Lucy" that sounded friendly yet distracted.

"Hi, Jim. Um… Is this a bad time?"

"Naw, just sketching out concept ideas for my next piece. What's up?" That's when she noticed the cavernous echo quality to his voice, which let her know he was in his studio. She could picture him hunched over his drawing desk, pencil working in a dance of jerks and fluid strokes.

"I was just wondering if you could tell me how to spell that word from Friday night?"

There was a slight pause, followed by a confused "I'm sorry, what?"

"That word. That Eva and her dad were using Friday night. Remember? Schnitzel or whatever."

"*Scheusal?*"

"Yeah, that's the one. How do you spell that?" She switched the phone over to her left ear, freeing up her right hand to type awkwardly at the keyboard. Using one of the windows already open for Grin Reaper research, she searched for online German to English dictionaries and clicked the first link.

"Why?"

"Just humor me. Please."

Jim released a long sigh that sounded as if he was stretching. "Alright then. Ah, let's see. It's probably s-c-h-e-u-s-a-l. Got that?"

Lucy typed it in with one hand then paused to examine the word. "You sure that's right? Looks like it should be pronounced 'shoosal' instead of 'shoisal.'"

"The 'e-u' makes a sort of 'oi' sound in German. That's the correct spelling, or I'll buy you lunch for a week."

She clicked the search button and scrolled down a little to read the results that appeared in less than a second. The twisting in her gut got worse and she licked suddenly dry lips. "Are you really sure that's how it's spelled?"

"Why? No results?"

"No, there are results... It's just... Are you sure that's how it's spelled?"

"What does it say it means? What are you looking it up in?"

"I'm using an online dictionary. It says that it means 'monster,' 'zombie,' or 'fiend.'" She clicked the back button a couple of times to return to the search results for dictionaries, and opened pages for several more on the list, checking the word in those and finding the same results. "All of them say it. Was Eva using it to describe how the woman attacked, do you know?"

Jim had fallen silent, and Lucy hoped he was actually thinking about the conversation in question and not just going back to his art. Finally he broke the silence from his end, mumbling that maybe that was it, with a tone which suggested he knew full well it wasn't.

Holding back her frustration at his lie, she pressed again about whether he was sure. It seemed to her a strange thing to use the word so frequently in conversation if it was just to describe one element of the event.

"Maybe it was just a nickname Eva gave the woman," Jim reasoned, voice uncertain like he was trying to convince himself just as much as Lucy. "You know, since she does that a lot. Identifies someone by a certain feature and proceeds to address that person by that feature from then on."

This was true of Eva, but Lucy remained skeptical. Finally it looked as if the puzzle pieces were making a little more sense, their colors and curves matching up and falling into place. There were still a few elements missing, however.

A little notice popped up next to the instant messenger program's icon on her task bar, letting her know that mercutioswidow had logged on. Grinning with determination, Lucy brought the program's window out of hiding and clicked on Eva's screen name. "I'll call you back later, Jim. Thanks for your help."

"Ah. Yeah, sure." His voice sounded a little lost and confused, but then he terminated the connection.

Lucy set her phone aside so she could have both hands free to type. She popped her fingers and took a few calming breaths as she thought about how she was going to phrase her questioning.

**notSteelsAffair**: Hey, Eva. :)
*mercutioswidow*: oh hey lucy! you feelin better?
**notSteelsAffair**: A little. How are you?
*mercutioswidow*: me? psh i'm fine.
*mercutioswidow*: so what's up?
**notSteelsAffair**: Actually, I had a question for you. Well...a few questions, really.
*mercutioswidow*: shoot

Lucy hesitated, fingers hovering over the keys. There was really no other way to ask it other than simply spitting it out, she supposed.

**notSteelsAffair**: Well, you see... Friday night, while you were speaking to your father in German, Jim could understand some of what you were saying...

She waited a few seconds to see if Eva had any response to that, but nothing came and the bottom of the window didn't say anything about how her contact was typing a message. Chewing her lip, she pressed onward.

**notSteelsAffair**: And there was this one word you guys kept using that he didn't know the meaning of, and it was driving him a little crazy at the time.
*mercutioswidow*: I didnt know jim knew german
**notSteelsAffair**: He doesn't. Well, not fluently. Evidently he knows some, though.
*mercutioswidow*: ah
*mercutioswidow*: ok
*mercutioswidow*: so what was the word? you want me to translate for you?
**notSteelsAffair**: Well, I just did a translation of it, actually. Using his help for spelling and searching several places online. They all said the same thing for it, so I guess it's accurate enough...
*mercutioswidow*: alright then. so what's your question?
**notSteelsAffair**: My question is... Why were you calling the woman a monster?

There was no response from Eva. Lucy waited, tapping anxiously at the desk and watching that little bar in the bottom of the window to see if it would say Eva was starting to type a reply. Nothing happened.

**notSteelsAffair**: Eva?

Perhaps she should call Eva, instead. Then again, Eva might just ignore the call.

**notSteelsAffair**: Hello?
*mercutioswidow*: yeah. i'm here. sorry
**notSteelsAffair**: I was starting to think you left or something.
*mercutioswidow*: no. still here.
**notSteelsAffair**: You just don't want to answer the question?
*mercutioswidow*: blunt arent you?

Lucy smiled at that.

**notSteelsAffair**: Must have gotten it from you.
*mercutioswidow*: oh ha-ha
**notSteelsAffair**: Well, you always did prize honesty. Isn't that what you always say? That it's not that you're mean, you're just frank.
*mercutioswidow*: this is true
*mercutioswidow*: and frankly, I dont want to talk about this right now
**notSteelsAffair**: Is there a time when you will want to talk about it?
*mercutioswidow*: most likely not. no
*mercutioswidow*: but I will.
*mercutioswidow*: just not now
**notSteelsAffair**: When?
*mercutioswidow*: i dunno
*mercutioswidow*: you coming to dinner weds?

In all honesty, Lucy had forgotten about the invitation extended to her and Jim by Dr. Kuntz. She considered it for a moment, then

64

decided she would probably be able to get her mother's permission.

**notSteelsAffair**: I should be able to go, yes.
*mercutioswidow*: alright. we'll talk then.
**notSteelsAffair**: You'll talk about this at dinner?
*mercutioswidow*: I was thinking more afterwards. its not exactly good dinner conversation.
**notSteelsAffair**: Good point.
*mercutioswidow*: i'm full of those.
*mercutioswidow*: it's why I'm usually so prickly. ;)
**notSteelsAffair**: lol
**notSteelsAffair**: I'll see you in school tomorrow.
*mercutioswidow*: k but I still wont talk about it then. dinner weds.
**notSteelsAffair**: I know. I won't even bring it up tomorrow. Scout's honor.
*mercutioswidow*: you were a girl scout?
**notSteelsAffair**: ...er...well, no.
*mercutioswidow*: =/ didn't think so. that sort of thing just clashes with my image of you
**notSteelsAffair**: Hah! Well, I had wanted to be one. Never joined, though.
*mercutioswidow*: why not?
**notSteelsAffair**: That's something I quite frankly don't want to talk about right now. Sorry.
*mercutioswidow*: touchy subject? girl scouts?
**notSteelsAffair**: Not so much the Girl Scouts as the memories that time brings up.
*mercutioswidow*: ...oh. alright, yeah I understand. sorry.
**notSteelsAffair**: No problem.

**notSteelsAffair**: See you later.
*mercutioswidow*: yeah. later. get some sleep tonight, ok?
**notSteelsAffair**: I'll try. ;)

After shutting down all the running programs, Lucy logged off the computer and rose from her chair with a bone-popping stretch. Her questions had been left unanswered, but at least she felt she was on the right track. Now she just had to be patient and wait for Wednesday night.

# Chapter 4
## Through the Looking Glass

There were times Lucy was reminded that Jim's upbringing was vastly different than her own. As they all sat around the Kuntz-Tenno dinner table, Jim shed his usual casual demeanor and donned the air of a true gentleman. Unlike Lucy, Jim did not fidget in his chair at all during dinner with the Kuntz-Tennos. No, he'd been raised better than that. Proper gentlemen did not fidget, nor did they rest their elbows on the table or talk with their mouths full.

Though Lucy was fairly certain gentlemen weren't supposed to ogle their best friends' siblings, no matter how discreet the attempts. Fighting back a smirk, she gently elbowed Jim and leaned in to whisper as much.

"I know," he hissed back, "but have you *seen* him? Damn if that boy isn't bloody *fit*."

"Eva tells us that you plan to go to Emory next year, Jim." Dr. Kuntz's jovial voice boomed from the other end of the table. He smiled at Jim's nod, and gestured towards a blushing Günter with his fork. "Günter's there for pre-med, you know. He could probably show you around and such, I'm sure."

The glowing smile Günter offered Jim at this was brighter than the overhead light. Günter's dimples were in full force as well, and Lucy was entertained to watch Jim's eyes glaze over at the sight.

"Hartmut and I went to university together," Dr. Tenno said as she showed off where exactly Günter had inherited those lovely dimples. Her voice was sweet and gentle, every line spoken with a song-like cadence. "What will your focus be?"

"Business," was Jim's initial short reply, and he smirked a bit at the blank faces all around. "Minor in visual arts. I plan to run my own

67

gallery someday, so it's best I learn exactly how." Both of the doctors made pleased little sounds, and Günter seemed to study Jim with a gleam of respect in his stunning amber eyes.

"That's very practical and well thought out," praised Dr. Tenno. "Your parents must be so proud of the quality man you are."

Inclining his head, he offered up a simple, respectable: "Thank you, ma'am. You are too kind."

Glancing around at everyone, Lucy wondered not for the first time exactly what the big secret was that Eva would reveal. Everyone seemed perfectly normal, pleasantly enjoying the delicious roast Dr. Kuntz had prepared. Well, all except Eva. Eva just seemed withdrawn, as if she was trying to prepare herself for something.

Lucy must not have been the only one to notice, because a moment later Dr. Tenno was whispering Japanese to her daughter and trying to coax a smile. Eva pretended to give in, but the expression was melting away as soon as Dr. Tenno turned her head.

Dr. Kuntz, Lucy saw, had also noticed how his daughter was behaving. He watched Eva for a long moment, allowing his wife to lead the discussion as it turned to Jim and Günter's hobbies and whether or not they shared any between them. All the while Lucy watched askance the now duo of somber faces.

Eventually Dr. Kuntz set down his fork and smiled his big, friendly smile at them all. Eva's eyes would crescent in just that same way, on the rare times she allowed herself a full-on grin. "I think perhaps we are full, yes? We should carry on our talking in the living room."

Lucy perked up at his suggestion, and eagerly rose from her seat. Everyone else looked at her with flat mouths and apprehensive eyes, except Jim, who was just confused.

"Alright. Well." Günter cleared his throat and also stood,

extending a hand towards Jim. "Eva and I will clean everything up. It was great to meet you, Jim. I'm sure we'll see each other again."

"I'm not going anywhere," replied Jim, who rose to his feet and shook Günter's hand just the same. A look of mild surprise passed across Jim's face once their hands touched, and he glanced from Günter's hand to his face in something like confusion.

"You're not?" A strange sort of panicked worry flickered in Günter's eyes, and his hand clenched reflexively before sliding away. "But, I thought…" He glanced quickly between his family and Lucy, as if wanting one of them to clarify.

"Lucy was my ride here. She stays, I stay."

"But," Günter repeated, his dark tan skin blanching to an ashy grey.

"C'mon," muttered Eva, grabbing her brother's arm and dragging him into the duty of clearing the table.

The doctors were standing near the doorway to the living room, smiling gentle encouragement. "Lucy had some questions," Dr. Kuntz said, his voice so calm and fatherly and foreboding. "We think it's only right we answer them. Only right you know."

So Jim and Lucy followed them into the living room, taking seats beside each other on the couch while the spouses took chairs facing them. Jim glanced between them all, then back towards the dining room. Maybe it hadn't been a good idea to carpool, Lucy realized. Eva had promised to explain things to Lucy, not to Jim. Perhaps the family didn't want anyone else to know. Though, the doctors seemed unconcerned with the addition of Jim's presence at the reveal, so perhaps it wasn't that big of a deal.

"What questions?" Jim wondered aloud, but seemed to realize a heartbeat later—"*Scheusal.*"

Lucy felt a strange split in her feelings as she sat there facing

69

the doctors. Part of her was excited to finally be on the cusp of learning the full story, while part of her was simultaneously terrified of what the truth may mean. It was as if something deep inside her already knew the answer, but had been keeping it from her out of protection. It raged at her to run, to cover her ears, to tell them she'd changed her mind.

Dr. Kuntz's gentle eyes regarded her and Jim with a guarded expression that did not suit his face. "'*Scheusal'* was not the correct term to use," he said, voice steady and gentle. "Eva should have said *angreiferin*. Her German, while practically fluent, is not perfect. She merely tripped up on the right word to use."

Jim tensed beside Lucy, then leaned forward a bit as he tilted his head in confusion. "Setting aside the fact that *angreifer*-slash-*angreiferin* is a far more common word than *scheusal*, why was she speaking German to begin with?"

At that, Dr. Kuntz merely blinked at Jim before again breaking out his wide smile. "Why, because I'm German."

It reeked of a lie, and a blatant one at that. Lucy glanced between Kuntz and Tenno, trying to figure out why they said they would explain everything, only to lie like that. As if hearing Lucy's thoughts, Eva slammed open the door from the kitchen and glared fiercely at her parents. "She deserves to know," Eva insisted, voice tight and lips tighter. "You said you'd tell her."

While Tenno seemed unsure, Kuntz's shoulders stiffened in firm resolve. "It isn't our place to say. There are *rules*, Eva. They are there for a *reason*."

"Mother's family aren't part of the Treaties," Eva shot back. Behind her, Günter stood in the doorway with sad, almost fearful eyes on an otherwise calm and closed-off face.

"Maybe we should do as Father says," Günter whispered, barely loud enough for the guests to hear.

Glancing around the room, Lucy tried to make sense of everything. It was Jim who interrupted the family dispute, though, with a simple: "What, was the attacker an *actual* ghoul?" His words dripped sarcasm and he was falling back against the couch cushions with a snort, but the Kuntz-Tenno family were suddenly, tellingly, very still.

Kuntz cleared his throat and turned it into a scoff. "Well, surely anyone who could do such a terrible thing is ghoulish."

This was pointless.

Suddenly sitting up in alarm, Lucy fished out her phone and pretended to check the time. "Crap, I forgot I'm supposed to get the car back for Mom to use. I'm really sorry, but we gotta head out." She stood, offering apologetic smiles to the family, lying through her teeth. Eva caught her eye and gave a little nod, before following her lead and pretending like it was just the end of a normal dinner together. Jim seemed eager enough to end the weirdly tense turn the evening had taken, and gladly accepted Lucy's excuse.

"It was lovely," he said to their hosts. "Thank you again for inviting me. Günter, it was wonderful to meet you."

"Great meeting you, too," Günter replied, stepping more fully into the room in order to shake Jim's hand again and give Lucy a brotherly hug. "Have a safe trip home, both of you."

"See ya in school tomorrow," Eva added with a shadow of a smirk.

\*\*\*

"Lucy," whispered a shadow in the corner of her room, startling her awake. "Shhh, don't scream," it hastened to say. "It's me." Günter was then stepping into the light from her window, his amber eyes seeming to flash gold in the streetlamp glow.

71

"How did you get in here?" she asked, sitting up more fully in bed, wondering if she was still asleep and this was nothing but a weird dream. It certainly wouldn't be the first time she'd dreamed of Günter in her room.

He nodded towards the window in answer. It was then that Lucy noticed that her window was open, the screen for it set propped against the wall. "But, this is the second floor," she said slowly, still trying to figure out exactly what was going on.

"I'll get to that," he assured, licking his lips nervously and glancing towards the window again then around at the rest for the room. He avoided looking directly at her, she noticed.

"What?"

"Our parents were supposed to tell you the truth tonight," he said instead of answering her question. "Eva insisted they should, because you deserved to know the truth." Günter seemed rigid as if bracing himself for something. "What you saw at the party. It wasn't...human."

Lucy snorted and shifted to sit on her knees, scooting down towards the foot of the bed and closer to him. "What, was it really a ghoul?"

"Eva had intentionally used the wrong word that night. She was doing everything she could to hide the truth from you two, because that's how we were raised. After some consideration, though, she realized you had the right to know the truth. And, well, I agree." His voice was stilted and hesitant on the last words.

"What's the right word, then?" she asked, studying his eyes. For a moment, they again gleamed a bright gold instead of their usual dark amber. It was just a trick of the light, Lucy reminded herself.

"*Vampir*," Günter answered quietly, the word recognizable even through the smooth German accent he curled around it.

72

"A vampire?" Lucy hissed incredulously, leaning away from him and wondering if maybe this was all just a prank. Or a dream. She was more than willing to revisit that theory. "I thought vampires drink blood, not eat your face."

Günter bit his lip and glanced out the open window, as if contemplating just jumping right out. "Father told us stories about different types of vampires," he explained in hushed tones. "Most feed on blood, but some will consume more of the body than just that."

Lucy felt dizzy, and she rubbed a hand over her face. "There are multiple types of vampires?" she asked, wondering if she should just humor him until the joke was played out and done.

"Multiple types of most things," Günter returned with a shrug. "Just like with any type of creature. Fish, birds, mammals...every region of the world has different variants. Supernatural creatures are no different in that regard. My father's clan for instance," there he cut himself off with a snap of his jaw.

Sensing that maybe there was something more going on than just some stupid prank, Lucy raised back up on her knees and focused fully on him. "What about your father?"

"I think I should show you how I got in." Clenching his jaw with a determined look, Günter started pulling off his shirt. Now Lucy was certain this had to just be another inappropriate dream about her friend's older brother. She barely had time to fully admire the way his muscle tone looked in the shadowy light, when her attention was caught by a strange crackling sound followed by a loud swish. Günter shifted a bit where he stood, and large wings unfolded out from the shadows behind him to display themselves to her. It was too dim to really see what color they were, aside from dark and glossy and amazing.

"Please don't scream," he beseeched, looking so worried that it verged on terrified.

"I'm not going to scream," Lucy assured, stunned by how calm her own voice sounded. She could feel her heart slamming frantically against her ribs. "Just... What's happening?"

"As I said, Eva wants you and Jim to know the truth. She's at his place, now, revealing what we are to him. So, I'm showing you."

Hesitantly, Lucy slid from her bed and padded over to Günter. "And you're what? An angel?" Seriously, this *had* to be some weird dream.

He laughed a little, deep in his throat, and shook his head. "Eva and I are hybrids, actually. Crossbreeds. The wings are from Mother. And this," he said, holding out his hand to show her as it shifted from human in appearance to being covered in dark fur and—*holy God*—tipped with black claws, "is from Father."

"I still don't-"

"Mother is a tengu," he explained gently. "It's a type of bird-like monster from Japan." His voice tripped a bit on "monster." "Father is a certain type of werewolf." Günter stood rigid, as if bracing himself for her fear or condemnation. It was the banked dread in his eyes that really convinced Lucy, made her realize that this wasn't some sort of joke or prank.

Lucy tried to force her mouth to say something, but she couldn't. All she could do was stare and try to get herself to understand that these people she grew up with were not people at all. It was hard, bordering on impossible, to accept. Memories were flickering through her mind like a strobe light. Dr. Tenno's graceful hands as she demonstrated tea ceremony, the subtle curve of her spine as she bent over the clay bowl. Dr. Kuntz's hearty laughter as he would pick Lucy and Eva up in the lake, tossing them into the water as they laughed and squealed. Günter carrying her into the house after she'd twisted her ankle while they all played in the backyard. His warm fingers as he inspected the swelling joint, his gentleness making her fall head over heels. Then, of course, there was Eva. Eva under the sweltering stage lights, her usual snarky persona stripped away to make room for some other character's emotions, her clear voice resonating throughout the auditorium. Eva smiling one of her rare, pure smiles as they sat together beside Lake Lanier, watching the rest of the family splash and laugh. Eva as a quiet little girl, shutting herself off from the rest of the world, just as Lucy had, the both of them standing away from the other children and away from each other, before being drawn into the light together by Krysti and her smiles.

Lucy had read *Alice in Wonderland and Through the Looking Glass* when she was in middle school; and as she stood there in her room staring at a man she'd thought she'd known since childhood, she couldn't help but wonder if she'd stepped through a looking glass of her own. Any minute now she'd awaken to find that it was all a dream, and she'd dozed off while her older brother Mick read to her. Perhaps she'd be able to believe that theory better if Mick wasn't off attending college in Massachusetts.

"This was what Eva wanted your parents to reveal tonight, after dinner?" She hesitantly reached out to touch a wing, waiting for his consenting nod before making contact. The feathers were unbelievably soft, and taut muscle could be felt shifting just beneath the silky covering.

"This," said Günter, "and everything else. But Father insisted that we shouldn't. His clan are part of the Treaties that forbid revealing such things to humans. Mother's clan isn't, though, which is why Eva and I think it should still be allowed for us to tell you." Günter's shoulders seemed to lose some of their tension, the more time that passed without her freaking out on him.

His words caught Lucy's attention from his wings back to his face, and for a moment she was distracted by how his eyes again seemed to burn a bright gold. "Clans? Treaties?"

He shook his head and folded his wings back into himself now that Lucy was finished inspecting them. It was just as amazing to watch them get drawn back into his back as it was to watch them unfurl, like a flower blooming in reverse. When it was done, his skin was perfectly smooth and unmarred. "Well, like I said, there are many different types of supernatural beings. Over time, they've formed different groups and organizations, usually familial in nature but sometimes based on what type of supernatural they are or even just regional alliances. There are some groups that are protectors of humans. Father's clan was like that once, but in the Middle Ages his kind and others were hunted and subjected to trials and gruesome executions. So, the Treaties came about, which withdrew the clans' protection of humans and also put into place certain rules about secrecy."

"But you're telling me all of this, despite those rules, because your mother's clan isn't part of the Treaties?" she asked, uncertain. When he nodded, she nodded slowly back. "Okay, and your mother is something bird-like. And your father is a type of werewolf."

His bright golden eyes studying Lucy closely, Günter nodded again. "I'd fully shift into an actual wolf to demonstrate what Father is," he said, dropping eye contact with her and looking askance with a blush, "but it would require I strip down. Otherwise, I'd tear my pants." He cleared his throat and made himself look at her again. "Father can only shift between human and wolf, he can't do a partial shift, like I showed you with my hand. I get that ability from the tengu genes, we think. Eva can do it, too."

"Are-" Lucy worked her mouth soundlessly, then swallowed and tried again. "Are you immortal?"

Günter blinked and then shrugged as he bent down to retrieve

76

his shirt. "We aren't sure about me and Eva. And, I suppose it depends on what you mean by that. Father's kind pretty much stops aging after reaching adulthood, due to their healing abilities fully kicking in by then. He's been dying his hair grey and using makeup to make himself look older for years, now. Mother's kind age, but very, very slowly. She's really fifty-three, like she says, but if she drops her glamours, she looks my age. Father looks about my age, too, without all the makeup and such. He's actually over five hundred, though."

"Five *hundred*?"

"Give or take a few years, probably. He claims he's lost count." A small, fond smile flitted across Günter's lips and he slipped his shirt back on as he continued. "Anyway, aside from the aging stuff... Father's kind are incredibly difficult to harm. The only physical item that can do lasting damage is mistletoe. Wounds created by anything else heal literally as soon as they're made, so it's practically impossible to kill them. Well, except with fire. Complete bodily combustion was a common method of execution of his kind during the Middle Ages."

Shaking her head, Lucy rubbed a trembling hand across her mouth. "This is insane," she murmured to herself. As she took a steadying breath, she looked back up at Günter. "What about tengu?"

Günter scratched at the back of his neck, mussing his long, black hair. "Slower healing factor than Father's kind, but still faster than humans. It leaves them more vulnerable, however, especially since they are susceptible to all things instead of just mistletoe. So, either way, Eva and I heal faster than humans. We just don't know *how much faster.* Or how invulnerable we are. It's not exactly something we want to experiment with."

"Right, no, yeah. That makes sense." Lucy offered him a weak smile, then shook her head again. "I can't believe I've known you and your family most of my life, and I never knew or even suspected."

77

"You weren't meant to. Humans aren't supposed to know, for safety reasons." His face was somber, and Lucy's mind flashed back to his words about executions in the Middle Ages.

"Hey," he said softly, taking a cautious step towards her. "You okay? I know this can be a lot to take in all at once."

She looked up at him, his hair messy from just pulling back on his shirt, his face caught between concern and apprehension. Her mind tried to reconcile all the new knowledge with everything she thought she'd known about Günter and his family. Part of her wanted to feel betrayed, wanted to scream she was looking into the face of a stranger. Still, another part of her wanted to do nothing more than wrap him in a tight hug and promise him nothing had changed between them. It was the second voice she heeded, flinging her arms around him. Günter wrapped her up in just as tight of an embrace, and she could feel him trembling against her. This boy had been like a brother to her in so many ways, and she couldn't imagine turning her back on him or anyone else in their family. Besides, Mick would never forgive her for hurting his best friend, no matter the reason.

Wait. Mick.

"Does Mick know?" she asked, pulling away from where her face had been pressed against his chest, but not loosening her hug by much.

Günter frowned and shook his head with averted eyes. "Remember, we aren't really supposed to be going around telling humans."

She wondered how much that must have killed Günter and Eva, to always have to lie to their friends. Jesus, Lucy just couldn't imagine it. "Can we tell him now? Since Jim and I will know?"

It felt like Günter was about to pull away from the hug, so she gripped his shirt tightly with her fingers and moved her head until she

78

forced him to make eye contact. "We can't," he said, and it looked like the words were cutting him open to force their way out. "Please, Lucy. No one else can know. Promise me."

Lucy didn't like it. This would be worse than Günter and Eva lying to their friends, because Lucy would have to lie to her *family* as well. The very thought made her queasy. Still, she understood why secrecy would be so important to them. How it could be the difference between life or death.

"I promise."

# Chapter 5
## Insomnia

Needless to say, that night was another sleepless one, Lucy spending most of her time sitting curled-up in a chair beside her window and watching the occasional car happen by. Her street was lined with arching lampposts, and they kept most of the sidewalk awash in sepia-toned light. Everyone's yards stretched out like small black pools with muted green ripples. Some houses had their porch lights on, and they stood as beacons, looking alluring and safe compared to the homes with dark doorways.

It was strange, she thought, how a single evening could throw one's entire world out of whack. In one night, you could realize just how little you knew about your friends, no matter how many years those friends had been like family. This was different from when her dad died, and different from how she felt after witnessing the attack. No, this kind of perspective change was more all-encompassing, turning the world into an alien landscape before her very eyes. There was no one else to blame for it but herself, though, and she knew it. She had hunted the White Rabbit down and wouldn't let it go. Now she had to deal with the consequences of her unrelenting curiosity.

Across the street, an animal that looked like it might have been an opossum scurried from one bush to another, and Lucy watched it, wondering if it was something else. Dogs barked from somewhere, a quick burst of frenzied conversation before the neighborhood again fell silent. A lone figure made its way down the sidewalk, baseball cap and flannel shirt looking dull and washed-out in the artificial light. Lucy watched him walk down the street, until her angle prevented her from seeing him anymore. At her back, the house creaked with its familiar night sounds. The floorboards settling, her mother had explained, when

Lucy was little and frightened of her lonely, dark room.

There had been more than sounds which had frightened her back then. Closing her eyes, she remembered being four or five and staring at the shadows of the room, convinced they moved. She recalled thoughts coming to mind, images of creatures melting from the shadows and shifting—ever shifting—into countless grotesque forms. One tried to look like a bunny, a sweet, harmless bunny. However, its body was melting darkness and its eyes were hollow holes, and it frightened her more than any of the others. She had screamed and then her parents were there, turning on the lights to a phantomless room and wrapping her in their protective arms.

Night terrors, she'd been told was the cause. Something she would grow out of in time. No one was really sure what caused them, but it was just a strange kind of nightmare that usually only small children experience. Eventually, just as they'd said, she outgrew it.

The world, just like five-year-old Lucy, had trained itself to no longer see sinister creatures in the shadows.

Opening her eyes, she stared out at the light, refusing to turn around and return to bed. For the first time since she was a child, she felt scared of the shadows, convinced that they would start to shift if she looked at them. Would her mother come, though, if she screamed? Would the light be turned on, banishing all the demons? Would it be the same with only one pair of comforting arms?... Better to not risk it. It was better to stay there, in the soft glow of the street lamps. Once the sun started to rise, she would go to bed, but not before then.

Looking out at the deserted street, she pondered on how many creatures, their numbers having gone unchecked for centuries, lurked in the shadows. Her mind entertained images of them crouched there, amongst the perfectly pruned shrubbery and tasteful shade trees, staring back at her in hunger. A more terrifying thought then came to mind—

how many lived among the humans, no one the wiser? She wondered if this was what being a paranoid schizophrenic felt like, watching shadows and waiting for something menacing to emerge from them. Watching faces and wondering how many of them were really human.

A chill trickled its way down her spine like a thick drop of water, and she stiffened. The puzzle pieces inside her mind finally all snapped together, the image staring her in the face as clearly as her reflection on the windowpane. The Grin Reaper. A cannibal with incredible strength and an uncanny ability to elude authorities, managing to leave not even a footprint. He didn't sound human, but more like some sort of boogeyman from an old story. Considering everything she now knew to be true, Lucy was willing to bet he was exactly that.

And his next stop was Atlanta, just forty-five minutes away from where she lived.

She trembled and turned her attention to the sky, remaining in that position long past dawn. When her alarm clock sounded, she made no move to shut it off, her body too tense from the tremors and curled-up position. Eventually her mother came in to investigate, and the woman stopped short at what she saw.

"Lucy?" Diana Kincade asked cautiously, venturing closer to her daughter. "What's wrong, dear?"

"Don't feel good," Lucy whispered in reply, turning her head to her mother and trying to control the trembling.

Diana moved to tap the alarm off before approaching Lucy. "You look like you haven't slept a wink all night."

Lucy thought her mother was a beautiful woman, and not even the fine wrinkles developing on her face or the streaks of grey slowly peppering her brown hair could mar that beauty. She wasn't like Tenno or Kuntz, who both looked far younger than their ages despite their attempts to mask the truth. Diana looked, at best, a few years younger than the forty-five that she actually was; but her dark grey eyes were often twinkling with youthful vibrancy. Diana's parents had been big into the hippie scene and never really left it, so she was like a walking remnant of that era. She'd even opened a store, back before her husband Walter had died, which sold organic soaps and oils. As a result of spending so much time at the store, she often smelled like what Lucy could only describe as dusty flowers, which was a combination of the incense and floral aromas that permeated the entire shop. Since Walter's death, she had struggled to keep the store running and bringing in enough income to support herself and three children. Mick, Lucy, and Donnie understood the kind of stress their mother was under, and so always tried their best not to make things worse.

Despite her lips still trembling as if she were freezing, Lucy attempted a smile for her mother. "Couldn't sleep," she said lamely.

Diana considered her for a long moment, forehead wrinkled with worry as she tried to determine how to remedy this situation. "I want you to stay home today," she eventually announced, her warm hand reaching out to pet Lucy's messy hair. "You've been having trouble sleeping since Saturday, and I'm concerned. Do you need to see a doctor?"

Trying her best to stop the trembling, Lucy shook her head. "I'm not sick. It's just…there are some things I need to deal with. Some issues I need to work out, I guess."

That seemed to distress Diana even more, and she bit her lip for a second. "Do you need to see a counselor?" she asked, fingers still combing her daughter's hair. "Or would you like to just sit and talk with me for a little bit? Keeping it inside will just make it worse."

It was tempting, so very tempting. Her mother was generally excellent at counseling Lucy whenever something upset her. This was a special case, however, and she had promised Günter that she would keep their secret.

Shaking her head, Lucy looked pleadingly up into her mother's eyes, silently imploring her to understand. "No. I just can't right now. But if it gets worse, I promise I'll come to you."

The hand in her hair shifted to caress her face, and Lucy surrendered to the impulse she had fought with Pulchrum, leaning into the touch and letting her eyelids droop. "Alright," Diana whispered, comforting smile lighting up her face and making Lucy feel warmed from the inside out. "I'll go call your school. You try to get some sleep. I don't want to come home tonight to find that you've been up all day. Would you like me to make some lavender tea before I leave for work?"

Lucy shook her head, then sighed softly when the hand left her face. With a kiss to Lucy's forehead, Diana was walking away, leaving behind only the lingering scent of dusty flowers. For a while, Lucy stared at her doorway and listened to the sounds of her mother and Donnie getting ready for the day.

Eventually she turned and looked back out the window, watching as the world came alive. People got in their cars and drove away, joggers took advantage of the milder temperature before the Georgia sun rose too high, and children darted off to bus stops. She spotted Donnie as he walked with some neighbor kids, his shoulders slumped while the others talked animatedly.

The house shook a little as the front door opened and closed, the clicking of the key in the lock resonating through the lifeless rooms. After Lucy watched her mother leave in their beat-up sedan, she made a move to head to bed.

Having been kept in one position for so many hours, her muscles and joints protested the sudden shift, and she cringed as she stood from the chair. Leaving the curtains open, she hobbled to her bed and crawled under the navy blue covers. She lay there on her back, staring blankly up at her ceiling fan's rotating blades. The familiar sounds of the daytime worked to soothe her. A combination of birds, cars, lawn mowers, and people's voices provided a comforting white noise that lulled her to sleep at last.

\*

Later she awoke to the sounds of Donnie returning home. Rolling onto her side, she faced the window and stared out at the blue sky, uncaring about the sunlight burning her eyes. Her brain, foggy with sleep though it was, told her that she was being ridiculous. What was she going to do—spend the rest of her life afraid of the dark? Would she never sleep normally again, too worried about monsters and ghouls that might not even be there? She'd survived seventeen years without being gobbled-up in her sleep, hadn't she?

She tossed back the covers and headed to the bathroom to belatedly prepare for the day. A plan had started to form in her mind, nurtured by new-found determination. She wasn't going to let the fear defeat her; instead she would defeat what she feared.

A memory came to mind of when she was very small, and she'd encountered a snake in their yard. Her father had told her to remain calm, saying that the snake won't bother her if she doesn't bother it. *"They're just as much afraid of you as you are of them,"* he'd said. As far as she could tell, the supernatural creatures were like the snake.

Humans had hunted monsters before such creatures were believed to be confined to fiction. Now the creatures hid beneath those new beliefs, cowering in fear of discovery. Creatures like vampires were just as afraid of humans as humans had always been of them. It was possible that the years without hunts may have made the vampires start to act in hubris, however, which would explain the boldness of the

85

one Lucy had seen at the party and perhaps even the Grin Reaper.
Perhaps it was time for them to be reminded of that old fear.

# Chapter 6
## Best Laid Plans

On Friday morning, while everyone was hanging out in the hall before classes started, Eva barely acknowledged Lucy's approach. Deep inside, Lucy's gut twisted at the realization of how her friend likely viewed her absence the previous day. The Eva that sat there before her was so much like the child that Lucy had once known, who sat away from everyone else and kept the world outside carefully constructed walls. Now those walls threatened to come between them again, and Lucy could smell the fresh plaster with distinct unease.

Without saying a word, she sat beside Eva and leaned against her shoulder in her usual familiar way. Eva tensed for only a second, and then her muscles melted and she leaned against Lucy in return, a rarely genuine smile ghosting across her lips. "What happened to you yesterday?" Eva asked, looking askance at Lucy. The walls were still weak, still vulnerable from being freshly laid, and Lucy could see them slowly crumbling. Eva didn't want them there any more than Lucy did.

"Stayed home sick," was the only response Lucy could think of to explain her absence.

Eyebrows rising, Eva tilted her head to better be able to see Lucy's face. "Did dinner Wednesday not agree with you?"

Letting out a little hum, Lucy rested her head on Eva's shoulder. How was she to tell Eva about her little breakdown without making it sound as though she was afraid of or repulsed by Eva?

Krysti, sitting on the other side of Eva, leaned forward so she could see Lucy. "Did you guys have sushi? Dr. Tenno makes excellent sushi, but I got sick last time I had it, because it turns out I'm allergic to —what was it that I was allergic to, Eva?" Krysti's dark blue eyes switched from Lucy to Eva, blinking questioningly up at her.

"Uni," was Eva's amused response.

"Yeah, uni. Did you have uni, too?"

"Ah... No, her dad cooked. We had roast beef." Lucy smiled at Krysti until the blonde sat back and was no longer within view. Smile fading, Lucy whispered to Eva, making sure her voice was pitched low enough that no one else would hear. "There's something I need to talk about. Meet me in the library at the start of lunch, and bring Jim." Hopefully the knowledge that Jim was involved in the discussion would ease any worry Eva had about the topic potentially pertaining to her friendship with Lucy.

The two girls looked across the narrow stretch of hallway to where Jim sat, and he looked up from his history book to dart a glance between Lucy and Eva quizzically. Lucy was happy to notice that he seemed to have recovered from his shock on Wednesday fairly well, barely a hint of nervous tension about him. She wondered if he'd had a private little breakdown when alone, too. Before Jim could ask them what was up, Kyle plopped down beside him.

"Good morning, peoples." Kyle sported one of his charmingly impish smiles that had Lucy feeling in suddenly better spirits. "Now, that's hardly fair. How come Eva gets all the girls?"

Rubbing her cheek playfully on Eva's shoulder as Krysti leaned in to do the same on the other side, Lucy gave Kyle a devilish grin. "Because Eva's a sexy beast," explained Lucy with a purr to her voice, which brought about a choked laugh from Eva.

Krysti gave a throaty moan of agreement. "Everyone knows that snark is dead sexy."

Trying to control his laughter, Jim began to make sounds in the form of bad porn music. Beside him, Kyle was staring with wide eyes and a loose jaw. "Damn," Kyle murmured. "And me without a camera."

"Is this 'Girls Gone Wild: Jailbait Edition,' or something?" Eva asked with a laugh, shrugging her friends off of her.

"Aw, baby, don't make them stop," moaned Kyle beseechingly.

"Sorry, sweet cheeks, but class is about to start. Maybe if you're a good boy we'll host a wet T-shirt contest for you after school." Rolling her eyes, Eva gathered her things and stood to leave.

"I'll hold you to that," Kyle warned with a cheeky grin, which Eva returned with a mild glare and sarcastic smile.

The warning bell rang to let the students know it was time to head to class, and the rest of the group also gathered their things and stood. Krysti and Kyle headed one way, while the other three headed the opposite direction. Once Kyle was out of earshot, Jim shoulder-bumped Lucy and leaned in to whisper to her. "Honestly, what do you see in him?" he asked.

"I think shaggy-haired guy is better." Eva gave this input with a solemn, sagely nod.

Lucy raised a brow at her, then shook her head. "You don't even *know* him. And his name's Ren, not 'shaggy-haired guy.'"

"Point is," continued Jim, "you could do better. Not to be cruel, but you've got the Devil's luck when it comes to guys."

"That's a good thing," interrupted Lucy, not really in the mood for a lecture about love, but resigned to its inevitability.

"It's what? No, it isn't. The Devil's bad, right?" Jim reasoned. "So wouldn't his luck be bad?"

"No, it's an expression for someone who has uncannily good luck, when all the odds are stacked against him. Like as if he'd made a deal with the Devil, I guess."

Jim stared at her, trying to process this, but he just looked doubtful and confused. "That's stupid," he concluded, face twisting up like he'd tasted something foul. "Then what's a phrase meaning really rotten luck?"

That caused Lucy's face to scrunch up like his as she considered the question. "Um...not sure."

"Well," he said "whatever it is, it can be applied to your luck with guys."

Yes, she could see that was where he was taking things, but she glared at him all the same. "Thanks," she deadpanned.

He raised a hand up in placation, his other hand still gripping his bookbag's strap over his shoulder. "Hey, I'm only stating facts. Your history with guys sucks. You constantly fall for guys who never return the favor. Then, in the rare cases when they do, they end up being jerks or losers. Like the appropriately named Dick, and how he cheated on you with three other girls—that we know of."

"Or Ron," added Eva, "who thought carving your name into his arm was the epitome of romance."

Jim waved his hands towards Eva as if she had just brought out a chart that further illustrated his point.

"But this is different," insisted Lucy. "I've liked him the entire time I dated some of those guys. I mean, seriously, this crush has been going on for years. You just... You don't know him like I do."

"Oh, please." Eva actually stopped walking and shot Lucy a look that seemed to yell *You must be kidding me.* Okay, so maybe it was a rather cliché thing to say, but it was accurate.

"What?" Lucy asked, defensively—though more for herself than for Kyle's honor.

"He's a fisher," said Eva, as if that simple phrase could close the argument.

"A what?" The snag was that it couldn't end the argument if Lucy had no idea what it meant.

"Fisher. He likes to hook girls, reel 'em in, cut 'em lots of slack, then reel, then slack, and so on. And, if he does decide to reel the fish in

90

all the way, he'll turn around and toss her aside. He's in it for the sport, not the prize."

Lucy opened her mouth to object, but the second bell rang. They quickly parted ways and ducked into their respective classrooms before the tardy bell could sound.

***

At lunchtime the library was nearly deserted, save for the librarian and two students who served as assistants. Lucy, Eva and Jim procured one of the small study rooms for their discussion. Its walls were mostly glass, baring its contents to the rest of the library, but it was practically soundproof. Considering the topic of their conversation, there was more concern for people overhearing than for them watching.

"Won't take too long, will it?" questioned Jim, who looked antsy. "Barely have time to eat after getting through the line as it is; don't imagine it'll be better if we're late."

As if not hearing a word he said, Lucy dropped her backpack on the table and turned to face them. Her ice blue eyes were set with determination, and the expression stilled Jim's fidgeting. "We need to do something." At her friends' blank stares, Lucy elaborated. "About the vampire. We need to do something to stop her."

"Stop her?" echoed Jim, with the hesitant tones of one who just realized he's entered a conversation with a lunatic.

"Yes. Somehow, we've got to put an end to the killing. There has to be *something* we can do."

Eva regarded Lucy with a stoic expression, her eyes reminiscent of Dr. Kuntz and his inescapable scrutiny. "The only way to really stop a vampire is probably to kill it," she said, her voice giving no more away than her expression.

The room fell silent after that, Jim and Lucy both turning that concept over in their minds. As Lucy's face hardened in steely determination, Jim's eyes widened in dawning, horrified realization.

"Oh *hell* no," he exclaimed, shaking his head. "I'm not playing Buffy the goddamn Vampire Slayer with you."

"Why?" Lucy asked, her eyes starting to gleam with excitement as ideas were planted and taking root in her mind. "Humans have a long history of killing vampires. If a backwoods farmer can do it, why can't we?"

"Because the farmer was older, stronger, and most likely wasn't alone!"

"If we fight together, we won't be alone. It'll be three against one."

"Four," corrected Eva, a smirk threatening to shatter her iron mask for the briefest of seconds. "Günter will want to fight, too."

Jim looked at Eva as if she'd betrayed him. "Why are you encouraging this? You're mad. You both are. Or suicidal. Though, I'd consider suicidal a type of mental, so you'd just be doubly mad."

Lips drawn taut in a firm line, Eva stared back with conviction that matched Lucy's own. "It hasn't sat right with me, knowing she's out there somewhere, her atrocities going unpunished." Her eyes then locked on Lucy's, boring into them with a weight and intensity that Lucy could physically feel. "But are you sure about this, Lucy? Are you absolutely certain this is what you want to do?"

Lucy's initial impulse was to reply with an emphatic affirmative, but the seriousness of Eva's expression and tone made her hesitate. She gave herself a moment to think about everything—all the recent trauma and realizations and reawakened fear. Her mind replayed the scene from that night, which reminded her of all the nightmares she'd had since. No more sleepless nights, she'd promised herself.

Something had to be done. Somehow she had to find the strength needed to overcome all the fear.

"I'm tired," she finally replied, her voice a whisper that was practically inaudible in that quiet little room. "I'm just so tired of the nightmares."

Eyes still penetrating Lucy's psyche, Eva asked in a soft, steady voice, "You really think taking her out will make them stop?"

Lucy tore her attention away and stared off into middle space, reevaluating everything again for what felt to be the hundredth time. Honestly, she thought it might make the nightmares worse. It would make all of this irrefutably real, and prevent her from any attempts at delusion. Still, it felt like something she had to do, or else she'd never feel right. It was as if the vampire was a loose end, and Lucy simply felt compelled to tie it off, even if it resulted in a noose. Bracing herself, Lucy let her gaze reconnect with Eva's. She said nothing, but let her determination show in her expression.

Eva's countenance softened an inch, and she nodded. "Then, as long as you're certain, my brother and I are with you."

The gleam in Lucy's eyes returned, and a manic smile was starting to bloom on her lips. "See, Jim! We'll be better off than the backwoods farmers of old, because we'll have the added bonus of fighting alongside two—um..." The smile flagged into a thoughtful frown. "What exactly do I call you? Since you're a hybrid?"

Eva's eyes widened and a grin broke out on her face, effectively banishing her previously grim expression. "You know, I never really thought about that, but you're right! We should really come up with a name for what Günter and I are, since we're totally new creatures and the only ones of our kind." She laughed and Jim raised his eyebrows. "It's like discovering a new species and getting to name it whatever you want—except *I'm* the new species."

"You've…seriously never considered that?" Lucy asked, bemused.

Shaking her head distractedly, Eva wandered to the table and sat on it, her feet in a chair. "Should it be a German term, or Japanese?" she muttered to herself.

Lucy watched Eva for a few seconds, then shook her head as if snapping out of a daze. "Anyway," she continued, turning back to again face Jim, "if we all work together on it, we'll be fine."

Jim still looked skeptical, his eyes flicking between the girls. Finally his shoulders slumped and he tilted his head back to glance at the ceiling in a quick, silent prayer. "Fine," he sighed, already sounding as though he was ruing the decision.

Lucy beamed at him and gave him a hug as if he'd just agreed to go to Six Flags with her and pay for everything. He patted her indulgently on the head before gently dislodging her. "Yeah, yeah," he grumbled, though a corner of his mouth was tugging up suspiciously. "I'm going to lunch."

When he opened the door, Eva called out to him, stalling him as he gave her a questioning look. An impish grin came to the shape-shifter's lips and she tilted her head. "If you die during this, can I have all the artwork you've made?" she asked. "I'm sure they'd be worth a fortune after your death." He flicked her off and she winked. Lucy smiled as the tension that had been looming turned to smoke and dissipated into nothingness.

"One more thing," Lucy announced, drawing the others' attention to her once more. "I was thinking we could get together tonight to do some planning and research. Mom's going to be working the closing shift, so won't be home until late, and Donnie's staying with a friend. So I thought we could meet up at my place. Four-thirty an okay time?"

Thinking for only a second, Jim shrugged and nodded. Eva seemed to take a little longer to mentally check her schedule, however. "It's no problem for me," she eventually said with a shrug. "Günter probably won't arrive until later, though. He has to drive up from Emory, and I don't know when his last class of the day is."

Lucy nodded. "That's fine. Whenever he can come will be alright." She was about to make a motion that they actually go grab food now, but another thought occurred to her. "Oh! And if you guys could bring some vampire movies or something, that'd be great."

"Vampire movies?" questioned Jim as he closed the door to return their privacy. "Why? Want to get yourself in the slaying mood, Miss Summers?"

Ignoring his jibe, Lucy grinned back at him, her eyes alight with anticipatory excitement. "Research."

\*\*\*

"So that's another one that confirms decapitation is an effective form of termination." Lucy made some notes on the pad of paper set in her lap. Sitting beside her on the couch, Jim was staring at the screen as the credits rolled, a look of horrified uncertainty twisting his features.

"You really sure about this?" he asked her, eyes still glued to the screen. "I mean, that guy had to become one of them in order to defeat them."

From her seat on the floor, Eva gave an amused snort and swallowed her mouthful of popcorn. "There was also an entire village of vampires that he was up against. We'll only be facing one. The odds are in our favor."

"Exactly," agreed Lucy, reaching for the remote and stopping

95

the DVD. "So, what's next?"

Günter appeared in the doorway from the kitchen, carrying four bottles of soda. "I picked up a couple on my way over. Put in one of those." He proceeded to hand Lucy and Jim their bottles while Eva rummaged through the plastic bag Günter had left on the floor when he first arrived.

"The hell—this is a comedy, *genius*." Eva shot her brother a mocking glare. "You really an Emory student?"

He bonked her on the head gently with a bottle before letting her take it from him. "It's about Dracula, isn't it? So it's a vampire movie."

"It's a *satire*. Could you not tell this by the goofy cover image and the fact that it's Mel Brooks?" Eva uncapped her bottle and took a swig as she tossed the DVD at her brother's head, which he easily caught before it made contact.

"I like Mel Brooks," said Jim as he fiddled with his bottle. "Maybe we could watch that one next, anyway. I mean, to lighten things up after the more gruesome ones we've been watching.

Günter sat down next to Jim with a smile. "See? Jim thinks I made a good choice."

Eva rolled her eyes and returned her attention back to the bag, mumbling "Jim's suckin' up so you'll be his model, is all."

Smirking in amusement, Lucy tried to focus on her notes. Under the header of "Fatal Weaknesses" she had a list of "sunlight, garlic, dead man's blood, silver, (were)wolves, UV lamps, stake through the heart, crosses, holy water, decapitation." Under "Restrictions" she had "cannot cross running water, cannot enter a home uninvited, cannot tread on hallowed ground, must return to their home soil to rest, cannot appear in mirrors." She tapped the pen against the notepad as she reviewed everything, wondering if there really was anything they could possibly be forgetting.

"I don't get why you two don't know all about this stuff already," griped Jim before taking a swig of his soda.

Günter shifted on the cushion and cleared his throat. "Just because we're supernaturals doesn't mean we know everything about all other supernaturals. Father and Mother have taught us things, sure, but mostly about how to identify different supernaturals and what they typically do. Like, 'That's a vampire. They drink blood and sometimes gobble people up, so try to avoid them.' That sort of thing. Nothing explicit about anyone else but our own kind, really." He was frowning as if disappointed in his own lacking knowledge.

"Do you think we could ask your parents about some of this?" Lucy asked, tilting her head and chewing her pen.

Jim also turned to the older man, hope shining in his eyes. The wince that passed over Günter's face, however, stomped out any spark of hope Jim or Lucy may have had. "If we ask, they'll figure out what we're up to."

"If they figure out what we're up to," Eva continued as she tossed DVDs aside in successive veto, "then they'll do everything possible to stop us."

"Why?" The notepad on Lucy's lap slipped down and her eyes darted between the siblings in confusion.

"The Treaties." Eva glanced up, then looked at the back of a video case with rapt attention.

Günter released a sigh echoing the soft hiss of his bottle's initial uncapping. "Father insists that we must abide by the Treaties that his clan have signed, despite our arguments."

Lucy stared blankly down at her notes, her guts slowly sliding together to form a knot. "So are you guys comfortable doing this, then? If it breaks the Treaties?"

97

A snort came from the floor, and Lucy looked over to see Eva grinning like the wolf she was. Well, half was. "The Treaties don't fully apply to us, since we aren't *really* part of Papa's clan." The grin on Eva's face morphed into a secretive smirk. "I think Yemon-jiisan would take issue with us being considered part of any clan but his own."

Günter bent down to steal the bowl of popcorn from Eva and offer some to Jim. "Yemon-jiisan—Grandfather Yemon—insists that we be part of the Tenno clan," he explained. "As far as he's concerned, we have no werewolf blood in us, but are only tengu. It's one reason we visit every summer, to seek guidance and training from him in the ways of the Tenno clan."

"But it's kind of hard to ignore that your grandchildren are half-breeds when they run around as wolves with their father." Eva laughed, Günter chuckled, and Lucy and Jim smiled twitchy, unsure smiles.

"What about your mother's side, then?" It was Jim who was asking this time, and he leaned back into the couch with a masterfully feigned nonchalance. "Would she be okay with what you're doing?"

Leaning back to be level with Jim, Günter raised and lowered one broad shoulder. "The Tenno do not tolerate injustice. But, unlike Father's clan, they traditionally deal with issues of humans against humans, not so much supernaturals against humans. So, Mother would not approve of our involvement in this, since it's not our place to protect humans from the other creatures of the world. Technically, though, neither her clan nor any of the ones found in Japan are part of any of the Treaties, so at least it wouldn't be breaking a Treaty law." But he didn't look fully convinced of his own words, adding a mumbled, "At least, I don't think it does."

"Forget what our parents' clans say, though." Jaw tight and eyes glaring at something—or someone—not there, Eva crawled towards the DVD player with a new movie in hand. "We don't care if they'd approve or not. We're doing this because we feel it's right."

Günter nodded as he took a sip from his bottle. In the ensuing silence, Eva moved back to the couch to grab the remote.

Lucy looked down at her notebook, scribbling random squiggles in pretense of writing, unsure of what to say. She agreed, of course, and in a sense she was doing the exact same thing by going around behind her mother's back. It wasn't the same, though. Not really. The only family Lucy had was her mother, maternal grandparents, and brothers. That was far different than defying sacred Treaties and entire ancient clans of immortal beings. God, that was a weird thought— immortal beings. Glancing surreptitiously through her long bangs, Lucy watched the siblings. Günter, followed soon by Jim, tossed popcorn at Eva while she clicked for the DVD to start. She laughed despite her outrage and threw the fluffy ammo back at them. Who knew that immortal beings could be so…normal?

The movie started, showing an animated sequence of a chariot riding through a village as all the crosses bent and the fountain's running water froze. "We're watching a cartoon?" Lucy turned to Eva with a questioning look. "You veto Günter's choice because it's satire, but you put in a cartoon, instead?"

Looking highly offended, Eva abandoned the popcorn battle to settle in her place amongst the pillows on the floor. "It's anime, not a cartoon. And it's actually incredibly well-done. Better than the other crap we've been watching."

Lucy gave a little grunt of still-skeptical acquiescence and turned her attention back to her planning. Her notes seemed woefully inadequate all of a sudden, and she felt a slick, roiling knot of fear form in the pit of her stomach. Still, she tried to tell herself that they'd be fine, that this was the right thing to do. It wouldn't just be her going up against a monster alone, after all. Her fear didn't matter, anyway. The vampire had to be taken out so that it couldn't harm anyone else.

Biting her lip, she scribbled "Friday" down in the margin of her notes, circling the word repeatedly as if the loops could reinforce her conviction. It gave them only a week to prepare, but they had all decided that they needed to act fast to prevent more victims. So, next Friday night it was.

Their best idea was to go to another party thrown by the same crowd and hope to find either the vampire herself or a strong lead as to where to track her down. It wasn't much of a plan, about as solid as their concepts of how to fight it, but it would have to do. Ready or not, they were going to do what they could to track and kill the monster.

Hopefully, it would go off without a hitch.

# Chapter 7
## Dancing with the Devil

"You're going to wear a bathrobe?" Jim asked Günter when the older boy had stepped from his SUV in order to help load the gear.

Günter paused in his steps, his wooden thong sandals making one final clack against the paved driveway. He ran his hand down along his navy blue robe and frowned a little. "Yukata," he corrected.

Lucy looked up from where she was bent checking the contents of a duffel bag, and grinned. She always thought Günter looked quite fetching when he got all decked-out in Japanese attire. It was really quite a treat to watch him practice archery, when he'd slide his robe off one shoulder.

"I what-a?" Jim gave him a perplexed look as he tossed his duffel bag into the back of the vehicle.

"That's what he's wearing," Eva clarified, elbowing Jim out of the way in order to carefully store her bundle of weapons. "A yukata is a cotton kimono. It's the casual wear of old Japan."

"Ah." With this new information in mind, Jim took another look at Günter's attire and glanced at the swords amongst the weapons. "Is it what one usually wears while sword fighting, too?"

Günter's cheeks reddened, and he scratched at his neck while glancing away. "Not...exactly. But, it's easier to slip on and off in case I need to transform."

Jim's eyebrows rose at that, and Eva gave a confirming nod. "If either of us is going to transform, it's going to be Günter," she explained. "A lady's gotta keep her modesty, after all." With a pat to her bag of weapons, Eva gave a wink. "Besides, I'll be armed enough without the need for claws and fangs."

Somehow Jim's eyebrows managed to slide a little higher, until they were practically hidden beneath his headband scarf. "So Günter's going to run around in the buff while we do this?"

"Ah...heh..." Cheeks burning hotter, Günter used arranging the luggage in the back as an excuse to look away. "Not all the time, no. And I'll be in animal form whenever I'm out of the yukata. It's necessary, though. Otherwise my clothing would be ruined, and I'd have nothing to wear if I changed back into human form."

Eva clucked her tongue against the roof of her mouth and glared askance at nothing. "If we had more of our mother's abilities, we'd be able to manipulate things around us like our clothing. So far, it seems our transformations carry with them our father's limitations of only being able to manipulate our own bodies."

"We're still training, though," Günter offered, seemingly more as comfort to his sister than as explanation for Jim and Lucy.

Frowning, Eva gave a slight shrug and moved towards the front passenger door. "Let's just get going."

***

The party was already in progress when they arrived, people still slowly trickling into the area where the bonfire was lit. There would be no house this time, just a large clearing surrounded by dark trees and neglected dirt roads. Some large logs were scattered around the fire to provide seating, and a pickup truck was parked in the clearing to provide a tailgate and music. By the looks of things, this gathering promised to stay relatively small in attendance, causing the trio to doubt that the vampire would even show.

They claimed a log that was far enough away from the fire to avoid the overbearing heat, but still within its flickering glow. Eva's eyes were darting every which way, her nose sniffing so often she seemed to have a cold. Having not actually seen the vampire clearly and not being in possession of a superior sense of smell, there was nothing Lucy could really do but sit stiffly on the damp log and try to act natural. Beside her, Jim's leg bounced and he seemed fidgety and restless. No doubt he was still asking himself why he agreed to everything.

As each new group of revelers arrived, Eva looked them over, and Lucy did her best to compare the females to the shadowed form from that night. Obviously needing something with which to distract and calm himself, Jim started up a running commentary on the new arrivals.

"Never understood why guys wear skinny jeans that are so loose they fall off the arse. It's like they want the combined look of an ostrich and a prison bitch. Oh dear God…talk about muffin tops! Well, that group obviously *wants* to be vampires; though my money's on them just being overly-dramatic twits who feel their lives are dark pits of black despair."

Jim's comments got Lucy chuckling, and even Eva smirked while releasing some snickers. "You're awful!" Lucy's attempted reprimand was somewhat spoiled by her smile.

"I'm honest," was his response, false smug indignation plastered on like a cheap paper mask.

Suddenly Eva stood up, and the other two went rigidly silent. "Relax," she said, waving off their tension like a bad odor. "I'm just going to do some asking around. Be back in a bit."

She walked off, leaving the others feeling on edge. Lucy's eyes wandered to the trees, and she stared into their dense blackness, watching the play of light on the foliage closest to the clearing. She tried to keep calm by reminding herself that Günter was out there somewhere watching over them.

"Feels eerie," murmured Jim, his attention also on the trees. "Why would anyone want to have a party in the woods like this, after what happened week before last?"

"Honestly I'm surprised people are still having parties when that Grin Reaper guy is rumored to be heading this way," Lucy added. The shadows shifted deep within the forest, and Lucy told herself it was just the wind in the trees—or better yet, Günter. "But, I don't know. Maybe the idea is that it's easier to keep an eye on everyone in a place with no walls. You'd be able to better tell where your friends are and notice if anyone's missing."

Grunting in acknowledgment, Jim continued to stare uneasily out at the wilderness. "Still creepy."

"Back!" announced Eva, plopping herself proudly down between Jim and Lucy on the log. "Got a way of identifying her now."

"How'd you manage that?" asked Lucy, eyes flicking from Eva's face to the ever-growing crowd.

"Your boyfriend, actually," Eva replied with a smirk. At Lucy's perplexed look, Eva's lips pulled wider into a devilish smile. "I found that Ren guy and had a little chat with him. Asked him if he'd noticed anyone heading into the woods before you, or anyone leaving after us. Seems he's a witness the cops really should have questioned."

"He saw her?" Lucy brushed aside the boyfriend comment, and clung hopefully to the rest of the news.

"Yep," confirmed Eva, eyes flickering orange and gold in the firelight. "He's going to let me know if and when she shows up tonight."

With a short bark of laughter, Jim clapped Eva on the shoulder. "Way to go, Eva! Also, I'm liking this Ren bloke more and more. Maybe you really should consider him seriously, Lucy."

"Consider who?" Kyle's smile was warm yet questioning as he

strolled up to the trio, eyes focused primarily on Lucy.

Devious leer in place, Eva leaned back a little on the log and regarded Kyle through lowered lashes. "Ren. The guy Lucy's been talking to at each of these parties."

Lucy discreetly kicked Eva's foot, her face turned down slightly to hide her flush. This, naturally, caused Eva to chuckle sadistically.

"I'm going to grab some drinks," Jim informed everyone as he stood from the log and brushed his vintage bell bottoms clean. "Eva, come help me carry them." Without giving her time to refuse, he was pulling her up to follow him.

Once they were alone, Kyle sat beside Lucy, taking his turn to look out at the surrounding trees. "Are you still shook-up over it?" he asked, his voice soft and concerned.

Raising her head, Lucy watched the shadows once more. "A little."

Out of the corner of her eye, she saw him look away from the trees for a moment to study her face. "I'll stay by you tonight. If you get scared, or anyone makes you feel even slightly uneasy, let me know."

A smile came unbidden to her lips, and she looked at him with sad amusement gleaming in her eyes. "And what will you do, then?"

His smile sent a heat through her that surpassed the bonfire at their backs. "Whatever the situation demands—get in a fight, give you a ride home, give you a hug, whatever's needed."

"Thanks," she whispered, and wondered if it would be alright to hug him right then, without the presence of a threat. He beat her to it, wrapping an arm about her shoulders and pulling her into a one-armed embrace. Resting her head on his shoulder, she allowed herself the indulgence she had shirked the previous week.

As she sat there absorbing his warmth and tasting his scent with every breath, she realized that part of her motivations for hunting the vampire were to protect him. If someone was going to these parties and targeting young men, Kyle was just as much at risk as anyone, if not more. What if he hadn't left with the redhead, but with the vampire instead? Shuddering, she pressed closer and even dared to cling to his shirt.

"What's wrong?" he asked, hushed voice little more than warm breaths in her hair and vibrations beneath her cheek.

Her eyes watched an ant crawl along the dirt, but she wasn't really seeing it. Swallowing around a dry throat, she tried to organize her concern into words. "I don't think I'm the one that needs to be so careful," she said, and he leaned in closer to better hear her. "She probably only goes after guys."

Fingers combed through her hair, brushing soothingly at her scalp. "I'll be careful," he assured. "No more going off with strangers."

What did he mean? What was happening here? Was this normal —just a comforting hug from a concerned friend? Heart racing, Lucy silently waited for Kyle to make the next move and give her some indication as to the nature of his actions.

"You really like that guy?" he asked, fingers playing idly with her hair now.

The question was unexpected, and its tone ambiguous. Had he asked out of jealousy or genuine curiosity? If she said yes, would he proceed to devise a plan to help her snag him? If she said no, would he sigh in relief, pull her closer, and brush a confession against her lips between kisses?

"I don't really know him," she replied, too much of a coward to try a definite answer.

The fingers in her hair stopped moving and he seemed about to say something, but then Ren was there in front of them, pulling a cigarette lazily from his lips in order to speak. "Sorry to interrupt, darling, but your friend sent me to fetch you." His dark eyes glanced between them, his trickster grin made of viscous honey as it spread across his face. "Aw, did I spoil the moment? What a shame."

As soon as Ren had appeared, Kyle had felt tense against her. Looking up at his profile, Lucy saw that he was staring intently at Ren with a tight smile. Reluctantly, she pulled free from his embrace and stood from the log. She smiled down at Kyle, trying to project assurance. "I'll be back in a few minutes," she said, implying he should stay and wait for her. He did, but not before employing his puppy expression on her as she walked away with Ren. As endearing as the expression was, it caused her to be even more confused. He rarely ever used that to express his honest emotions, using it more as an exaggerated jest.

As she walked away, her smile faded and her mind became a tangle of thoughts. Ren walked alongside her, blowing smoke out in the other direction as a courtesy. Even so, she could still smell it, even amongst the wood smoke of the bonfire and the sharp scent of spilled beers. It didn't smell like a normal cigarette, but it wasn't cloves or pot or anything else she could readily identify. For some reason, its rich sweetness made her think of old men.

She knew he was studying her out of the corner of his eye, but she had no desire to look at him or strike up a conversation. The tension she felt between them was strange and awkward, and she wished he would just go away.

"You seem to be doing a bit better," he said casually. When Lucy gave in and glanced his way, he was looking ahead with apathetic eyes. "Never saw someone get so upset over a guy before."

Confusion jumbled her thoughts for a moment, until Lucy realized he was referencing *that* night, and the state she was in after Eva brought her out of the woods. "It wasn't a guy that had made me so upset," she felt the need to explain.

He looked at her then, his steps slowing as he took a drag from his cigarette. "Yeah? Then what was it?"

There didn't seem to be a filter on the end of the cigarette he wrapped his lips around, and Lucy noticed it wasn't quite a perfect cylinder. Suddenly the scent made sense, as she realized it was hand-rolled, straight tobacco. Who the hell rolled their own tobacco cigarettes anymore, she wondered. "Nothing." She looked away from him and picked back up the pace as a not-so-subtle hint.

Keeping stride with her, Ren let out a disbelieving hum, but let the subject drop.

When they finally reached Eva, Lucy noticed that her friend was alone and avidly watching the crowd. Following Eva's gaze, Lucy spotted Jim chatting up a scantily clad woman with long, chestnut hair. Ah, so the vampire had indeed made an appearance. By the looks of things, the plan was going smoothly so far. Jim was doing an excellent job of charming her and holding all of her attention.

After a little bit more talking, Jim motioned towards where people were gathering to dance. Smiling with delight, the vampire nodded and let him lead the way. Lucy gaped as she watched them move together to the pounding beat of the music. It was obscene, and certainly not how she'd ever imagine Jim dancing with a girl. Not that she ever really thought about how Jim would dance, or ever really thought it would be with a girl. Though, she supposed that she had harbored the impression that should she ever find Jim dancing, it would be perfectly executed swing or ballroom dancing—something that suggested a level of class. Considering his retro attire, perhaps she could see him doing disco, too. Of course, she had no idea that she'd be chastised for such a thought, since his brand of retro predated disco. In any case, what he was engaged in now was little more than dry humping in time to goth electronica.

"Your friend has horrible taste in partners." Looking away from Jim, Lucy found Ren watching the dancing pair, his infinitely dark eyes as unreadable as ever. He took a quick drag from his cigarette, lips curling around it in a smirk. There was a stream of smoke, once again pouring away from Lucy, and then the smirk was nothing more than a ghost of a shadow on his thin lips. "Then again," he said as he flicked ash to the dirt below, "didn't think she'd be his type, when I met him."

"First impressions are rarely as accurate as people claim they are," Eva said to explain away the contradiction that was Jim. Lucy stopped studying Ren and turned her attention onto Eva. Her friend had not once glanced away from the pair, watching them with a calculating intensity that was reminiscent of a predator stalking its prey. Lucy wondered if Günter was watching from the shadowed trees with the same expression in his usually gentle eyes.

Ren also took to studying Eva's face, a secretive smile on his lips that he failed at hiding with his cigarette.

"What are we watching?" Kyle had evidently grown bored of waiting, and had snuck up behind them to wrap his arms around Lucy's shoulders. Eva and Ren glanced at them for the briefest of seconds, mirrored expressions of fractionally raised eyebrows flitting across their faces. Then Eva returned to her tunnel vision, and Ren casually disposed of his cigarette butt in a small silver box that was some sort of pocket ashtray. Ignoring them both, Kyle pulled Lucy back against his chest and rested his chin on her shoulder. "What's so fascinating that's got you all standing here staring?"

"Jim's hooking up with someone." Trying to control her racing heart and relax against Kyle, Lucy watched her friend dancing with the vampire.

Eventually Kyle spotted them in the crowd, and he let out a

confused "huh" before whispering into Lucy's ear. "That's not quite what I expected. Man's full of surprises."

Lucy was about to respond with a comment about how she agreed, but the words evaporated into a gasp when she saw Jim kiss the vampire. It wasn't just a chaste little peck, either; it was hot and heavy and made Lucy's jaw drop.

"You all have very odd pastimes," commented Ren with a glance towards the three of them. "I don't think it's normal to stand around watching friends make-out."

"You're here, doing the same thing," Lucy pointed out, feeling slightly indignant that he could be so condemning while being baldly hypocritical.

Ren shrugged, smiling at her as one would a particularly stupid child that was endearingly pitiful. "He's not *my* friend."

"Ren!" The guy Lucy had seen at the first party, who had spiky green hair and lizard contacts, strolled up to them flanked by two girls.

He had his arm around the waist of the girl to his right— perhaps the ex who may no longer be an ex, Lucy assumed. She was a petite black girl wearing a blood red vinyl sundress that successfully accentuated her figure. Her hair fell to her shoulders in tight spiral curls, and the bonfire's glow revealed red highlights throughout. Much like the green-haired boy, she wore strange contacts, hers designed to look like circular flames.

The other girl was staring at Ren with interested shyness as they approached. She was so pale that Lucy wondered if she were wearing clown greasepaint. Not that Lucy really had room to criticize, since she had the complexion of something born and raised in the deepest recesses of a cave. This second girl's outfit was comprised of black skinny jeans and a long, purple and black striped baby doll tee adorned with neon-colored hearts and skulls. Her hair fell mostly in her face

110

over one eye and was choppy and disheveled in back. It was bleached platinum blonde, but there was discoloration towards the tips to suggest that she'd previously dyed it black.

"Now, *he's* my friend," said Ren with a grin as the trio approached. "How goes it, Nick?" he asked, clasping Nick's hand with a smack and giving it a quick shake.

"Someone I want you to meet," Nick announced with a self-satisfied grin. He then motioned towards the blonde as if he were Vanna White and she was a completed word puzzle. "This is Bridgette. She's a junior at UGA, and very cool. Bridge, this is my friend Ren I told you about. His real name's René, but he gets all grumbly if you call him that. It's cute, actually, so I suggest you do it often."

Ren shot Nick a playful glare before taking Bridgette's hand for a polite shake. "Pleasure to meet you," he told her with a charming smile that shocked Lucy almost as much as Jim kissing the vampire. Plus, he'd delivered the salutation in a rumbling purr, which Lucy marveled could be heard above the din of the party.

When Bridgette offered her own greeting, Lucy was thrown by how *adult* she sounded, despite looking like a punk teenager. That was when Lucy took a better look at her, and noticed a maturity in the way she carried herself. Absently Lucy wondered if Bridgette was younger or older than Ren. Nick had said she was a junior in college, but had not volunteered equal information concerning Ren.

Evidently having maintained a constant focus on Jim, Kyle whispered a shocked curse against Lucy's ear, prompting her to scan the crowd for her friend. When she spotted him, she let out an expletive of her own. Jim and the vampire had relocated to a log, where they sat practically atop each other, locking lips between intimate murmurs in each other's ears. She fervently hoped that Jim was just a surprisingly good actor, and that the vampire hadn't put some kind of charm on him.

111

"Childhood education? Sounds interesting. Mine is psych. Do you plan to teach once you graduate?" Ren's voice started to distract her again, but then Jim and the vampire were getting to their feet.

Jim paused and looked around, smiling and waving once he spotted them watching. He and the vampire then started walking off towards the direction planned.

"Now that's something I'd never thought I'd see Jim do—go off with some girl. Or...well...*any* girl, really." Kyle shook his head, chin still on Lucy's shoulder so that his cheek brushed against her hair with the movement.

"Speaking of leaving, Lucy and I need to head home." Tearing her gaze away from her prey, Eva turned to start towards the road.

Kyle's arms around Lucy's shoulders squeezed tighter, keeping her firmly pressed against his chest. "So soon? But it's still early, and I'd wanted to dance with Luce."

Eva paused and looked back at them, her eyes glancing apologetically at Lucy before sternly regarding Kyle. "My brother is picking us up now, so we have to leave."

"I could take Lucy home," Kyle offered, nonplussed by Eva's sharp tone.

Holding back a groan of frustration, Lucy reluctantly pulled free of Kyle's arms. "Sorry," she said with a wistful smile when she turned to face him. "Another time. I really gotta go now."

Much like he had that Monday morning when she'd pulled away, Kyle stared at her as if she were some pod person. She ruffled his gelled hair affectionately and told him she'd see him Monday.

As she started to turn to follow Eva, Lucy glanced over at Ren and tossed a casual good-bye, successfully pulling his attention away from the blonde. His dark eyes landed on her and he grinned with sarcastic sweetness. "Fare thee well, odd voyeuristic girl with mild stalker tendencies! Do take care."

Unsure how to take that, Lucy gave a wan smile and proceeded to follow Eva. As she turned away, she thought she saw Kyle glaring at Ren, but she was moving too quickly to be certain. She and Eva walked briskly towards the road where everyone parked, and turned down the way that would curve back towards where Jim had gone.

Soon they were moving beyond the last car, the music and the laughter from the party starting to fade. Pulling out small, key chain flashlights, the girls continued on until they found a poplar tree with a subtle cross scratched into its white bark. They glanced around and then stepped into the woods behind the tree.

There were diverging paths that the group had made earlier in the week, and they exchanged a glance before parting ways. Enough branches and underbrush remained on the small paths to snag at Lucy's clothing and trip her feet. Little pieces of reflective tape had been placed at intervals in order to keep her on the right trail, and even with her tiny flashlight pointed downward, she could see them glowing in the darkness ahead of her, like little fallen stars. She moved as swiftly as she could, dodging the obstacles she saw and jerking impatiently free of the ones that caught her by surprise in the insufficient light.

Eventually she came upon a tree that had a longer strip of tape on its trunk, and she eagerly squatted down to rummage amongst the tall ferns at its base. Hoping that Günter hadn't chosen a patch of poison sumac for a hiding place, Lucy continued to feel around until her fingers felt cloth. With a triumphant grin, she hefted the duffel bag onto her shoulder and started running down the path.

It was happening—really happening! She was rushing towards a battle against an undead, cannibalistic monster, and she was armed with a bag of wooden stakes, garlic, and crosses! A laugh burst from her throat like a ragged exhalation, and she wondered at how her fear and apprehension only served to make her run faster.

The woods around her suddenly dropped away, and she found herself in the chosen clearing. On the battlefield. For a dazed moment she stood there panting from her sprint and trying to process what her eyes were seeing.

Jim was crouched in the grass, body tensed and poised ready to spring. It was his beige tunic standing out against the darkness that made him so easy to spot. Beige was such an impractical color to wear to a battle where you could get covered in blood, but it had seemed that Jim didn't want to do the goth thing this time around. Perhaps it was simply a case of his usual vintage clothing providing a sense of comfort for him at a time when he was nervous and afraid.

A couple yards away from him, his back towards Lucy, stood Günter, though his dark yukata and long black hair made it easy to miss him in the shadowy night. When he shifted slightly, it looked like moonlight was trickling from his right hand. As he turned to face Jim, Lucy could better see that it was his katana, and she chided her foolish mind for the earlier fanciful thought.

It was only then that she noticed the crumpled body at Günter's feet, and the dark, spherical lump not far away. Realization hit her along with a surprising amount of disappointment.

"Well, that's rather anticlimactic." Eva's words echoed Lucy's feelings, as the shape-shifter emerged from her path. Her quiver and bow were on her back, her own katana hanging at her hip. All of it was unnecessary weaponry, like the stakes in the bag on Lucy's shoulder.

A stench started to rise up from the corpse, as if it had been dead and decaying for months. Rising from his crouch, Jim staggered over to the bushes, where he doubled over as he puked. Lucy knew she should have been happy that it all went so smoothly, and that the vampire had been killed without a fight. Instead, however, she felt

114

hollow. Could it really have been that ridiculously easy? How could such a creature be the cause of so much fear, when it was so easy to exterminate?

It was difficult to believe that the boogeyman was just as vulnerable as a mortal man.

# Chapter 8
### Grilled Vampire and Fried Eggs

Lucy and Eva stepped out further into the clearing while Günter rushed to Jim's side. He rubbed his free hand soothingly along Jim's back and murmured comforting nonsense in his rich timbre. Eva wrinkled her nose, face scrunching up in disgust. "Don't blame him," she said with a choke. "That thing smells *foul*."

Not wanting to really look at it, Lucy cast a brief glance at the corpse, then took a step closer to her friends. "What should we do with it?" she asked, realizing belatedly that all their planning had revolved around killing it, with no consideration for method of disposal.

The siblings adopted twin calculating expressions, and Jim just tried to catch his breath between heaves. For a long moment, the only sounds came from Jim and the trickling creek. Without any wind, the surrounding trees were merely lifeless masses, barricading them off from the outside world and painting them in shadow. Perhaps not entirely lifeless, however, as Lucy heard a soft whisper like the rustling of branches. No, that wasn't right. It was more like a dragging sound than a rustle. As soon as that assessment of the noise fully sank into her brain, a cold tension cascaded down along her nervous system. Judging by their stiffening postures, the siblings had caught onto it as well. Without really wanting to, Lucy forced her head to turn and look at the corpse again. What she saw made her want to immediately follow Jim's example, but her mouth settled with expelling a scream.

The corpse was dragging itself through the grass towards its severed head. Günter cursed and Jim started yelling denials, but Eva kept a focused, steady composure.

"I think we can safely scratch 'decapitation' off the list," Eva said evenly as her eyes followed the sluggish movements of the headless body. "Lucy, why don't you try the traditional method of a stake through the heart?"

Lucy nearly yelled, "Why don't *you*?" but she bit back the words. Frantically looking around the little clearing, she felt the strong urge to drop the bag and run. Perhaps she should just toss it to Günter and have him do it, instead, she reasoned. With a shaky breath, she shoved such selfish thoughts from her mind. All of this had basically been her idea, so she couldn't very well back out by this juncture. This was what she had wanted, right? A chance to fight the thing—a chance to kill it.

Fingers trembling, Lucy struggled with the duffel bag's zipper and was fairly certain she managed to break it. Regardless, it had opened, and she grabbed a stake before dropping the whole thing to the ground. At the same instant, the vampire had grabbed its discarded head. For a petrified moment, all Lucy could do was stare in morbid fascination as the vampire reattached her head to the bloody stump of a neck. Carefully the vampire pulled herself back to her feet, testing the healed neck by stretching it and tilting her head every which way.

While the vampire was still absorbed in such motions, Lucy started charging her with the stake. Before she could allow herself to think about it, Lucy plunged the wooden stake into the vampire's chest. It didn't feel as if it went very far, and Lucy wasn't strong enough to break it through the bone. This had looked so much easier in the movies, and reality was knocking her off balance. All she could do was stand there as the vampire sneered disdainfully at her. *This is it*, she thought with an odd mixture of fear and acceptance. *There's nothing we can do, and she's going to kill us all.*

"Lucy, move!" She spun around at Jim's voice, and managed to jump aside in time to avoid his shoe hitting her square in the chest. Instead it made contact with the vampire, forcing the stake deeper with

117

a sickening crack.

The vampire screamed and stumbled back, hands clawing at the small bit of wood still protruding from her chest. While the vampire was distracted, Jim grabbed Lucy by the shoulders and pulled her with him to get behind Eva and Günter. At some point, the vampire had found purchase on the stake nub, and was pulling the wood out as she made pained sounds like a wounded animal. Once it was removed, blood gushed from the hole, and the vampire swayed as she gripped at the wound.

"That hurts, you know. Idiots..." Her voice was just a raspy whisper, and her shoulders heaved slowly with her heavy breaths. Then she was removing her hands from her chest, revealing the absence of a wound or even a hole in her black leather halter top. If not for the blood on her hands and staining the grass at her feet, no one would be able to tell that she'd ever been injured. She looked at the four of them in a way reminiscent of how Eva had studied her at the party. Never mind that the four of them had come to hunt her, she saw *them* as the prey. "This is pointless," she chastised in sweetly teasing tones. "We can go like this for hours, but you know I'm just going to end up eating you." A mouthful of knives smiled pleasantly at them.

Terrified gaze locked on the vampire, Lucy noticed Günter only out of the corner of her eye. She registered that he'd dropped his yukata only a split second before she saw a wolf leap at the vampire, his maw snapping at her neck. Just as hope started to work its way into Lucy's mind, the vampire was twisting away, falling onto all fours and snarling with a lupine face.

Günter was beautiful, like no other wolf Lucy had ever seen— not that she'd ever seen an actual wolf in anything other than pictures. In the moonlight, Lucy could see that most of his back was dark grey, his sides and legs being primarily light with dark grey streaks. As he

118

moved, the coat caught the moonlight and reflected it back with an iridescent sheen that reminded Lucy of bird feathers. The vampire looked nothing like Günter, even though she also appeared to be a grey wolf. She seemed rabid and mange-ridden, with teeth far too long to fit into her snarling mouth.

They circled off and then lunged at each other, forcing them both to rise onto their hind legs. Günter's forepaws shifted into large talons, and he clawed viciously at her sides. She yelped in pain, and tried to pull away, but his talons held fast. Taking advantage of her distracted struggling, Günter bit down on her neck and jerked his head violently. Snarling, she ignored how every motion caused more tearing, and managed to smack him in the face with her paw. He was startled off of her, crying out with a high-pitched sound that tugged at Lucy's heart. The vampire was then able to break free, and the two circled each other once more. Their hackles were raised, and Günter's had become reddish and more feather-like in appearance than just their sheen. With that and his still-transformed forearms, he looked like some confused rendering of a griffin.

Without turning her face away from the wolves, Eva sidestepped over to where Lucy had dropped the bag. "Let's see if this, at least, was true," she mumbled to herself as she knelt and rummaged impatiently through the bag's contents. Finding what she wanted, Eva drew bulbs of garlic out with her left hand while simultaneously pulling a handful of arrows out with her right. She then started stabbing the bulbs with the arrows, smearing their sticky, pungent juice over the heads and shafts. Satisfied, she took one arrow and rose to her feet as she nocked it. Taking aim, she yelled out something to her brother in Japanese. Günter dashed to the side, the vampire lunging to follow. The vampire never made it more than a few steps, the force of the arrow hitting her in the shoulder knocking her to the ground.

119

When she hit the ground her fur was fading and her body was melting back into that of a woman. Eva bent down and retrieved another laced arrow, quickly preparing for the next shot. As the vampire started to pull herself up, Eva loosed the arrow, this time striking the creature's side. The vampire opened her mouth as if to scream, but the sound was garbled and choked. Tenaciously, the vampire again struggled to get up, though she only managed to pull herself up onto her hands and knees before her body convulsed. She coughed and gasped, breath sounding strained and asthmatic. Blood started oozing from her mouth, a mix of bright, fluid red and black, congealing gunk.

Despite the vampire's condition, Eva picked up another arrow, nocked, and aimed. When the vampire suddenly jerked up to stand on her knees facing Eva, it was the combined force of two strikes that knocked her flat onto her back. Eva's third arrow had hit the vampire square in the chest, but a large metal bolt had effectively nailed the creature's head to the ground.

"Great shot, Montenegro!"

The group turned around at the sound of the unfamiliar voice, and watched in stunned silence as people started entering the clearing. Günter, still in hybrid wolf form, grabbed up his yukata in his mouth and dashed behind a tree. There were three strangers at first, but after a rustle and thump, a fourth followed. Their faces were shrouded by cadet caps and the night, leaving only impressions of features in Lucy's mind. A white grin here, pale eyes there, but nothing discernible. All that Lucy could really make out was that they all wore hunting camouflage without the regulation neon orange, and that there were three men and one woman. They moved quickly, three of them heading to a spot between the vampire and the bubbling creek. The fourth went to kneel beside the vampire, which was starting to regain its wits.

"Did good usin' tha garlic," said the kneeling man, his voice old and gritty, and his accent obviously local. He then pulled something from his pocket and stuffed it into the vampire's mouth. "They can't stand tha shit."

One of the other men had a large metal disk on his back like a silver turtle shell, and he had been working to unfasten it. As soon as it was freed, he positioned it on a bald patch of dirt, cradling it on a spidery wire stand. From that point on he left it to the other two, and proceeded to join his companion over at the vampire. During all of this, Lucy had caught snippets of conversation exchanged between the strangers.

"It's a good spot. Running water." That had been the woman's voice, her accent also local but not as thick.

"Handy. Makes our job just that much easier." The turtle man that time, but his accent was some type of European variety that was unfamiliar to Lucy.

"Phil, hold 'er down."

"Coming, coming. You got it from here, yeah?"

"Yeah, I'm good."

Not once did the third man speak. He stood near the creek, crossbow in his hands, and watched the trees.

The four friends unconsciously drew closer, Günter having wandered back out tying his obi. Jim had a protective arm around Lucy's shoulders, and Günter stood with his shoulder between Jim and the strangers. Eva stood to Lucy's left, also situated between her friends and the newcomers, with her bow still clutched in her hand. Eyes barely glancing at the two by the creek, Eva kept her gaze solidly on the ones with the vampire.

"What are they?" Lucy asked in a whisper, reaching out to touch Eva's sleeve.

"Humans." Eva didn't look Lucy's way, but shifted subtly

121

closer. "One of them, though…" She never finished her sentence, distracted by watching what they were doing to the vampire. Günter glanced at his sister, then bent to retrieve his discarded sword.

While the foreigner held the vampire's arms down, the local man drew a large hunting knife. Lucy smelled charcoal and liquor seconds before the clearing was illuminated by a large blaze from within the metal bowl. The fire allowed for everyone's features to be more discernible, but they flickered like old film.

Standing beside the fire, the woman's dark skin glistened with stuttering gold. She was young, Lucy noticed, possibly in her twenties. More than the fire was reflected in her eyes, however. There were ghosts and pain and burdens, far more than anyone her age should have.

Screams muffled by a mouthful of what must be garlic, the vampire tried to struggle free. The man pressing her down maintained a firm hold, and the local man began slicing into her chest. Stilling the knife, he glanced at Eva. He was old and scarred, but he had stood taller than them all when they had walked into the clearing.

"Montenegro," he called, slowly working the blade through flesh and bone as if it were no more an obstacle than Jell-o. "These arrows are in my way."

At the call, the silent man abandoned his post by the water and went over to kneel on the other side of the vampire, setting his crossbow beside him on the grass. The arrow in the vampire's shoulder had been ruined, but he salvaged the ones in her side and chest, leaving his own in her skull. Eyes nearly as black as Ren's regarded Eva for a moment, and then the archer was taking the arrows back to the creek, where he squatted with his back to everyone.

The local man then proceeded to fully tear open the vampire's chest with the large knife. Lucy had to turn away, burying her face in Jim's shoulder and wishing she could plug her ears up against the sounds. Like a train wreck, however, she could not help but to be drawn to take another look. She peeked in time to see the local man stand, a slimy dark blob in his hand. The vampire's heart, Lucy realized, watching him carry it towards the fire. What was most disturbing was that it still seemed to be pulsing, but she knew that was ridiculous—it had to be just a trick of the firelight.

"Hot enough, yet?"

"Have to be in Hell to be hotter."

The local man smiled, and it was a perfectly normal smile, as if this were a perfectly normal exchange on a perfectly normal evening. "What a coincidence," he said with a chuckle in his gruff voice, "that's just where our friend 'ere is goin'." His weathered cheeks dimpled—or was that just scarring and wrinkles?—as his smile grew.

More muffled screams erupted from the vampire, and Lucy looked back at the thing in shock. Hadn't the heart been removed? How could it still be alive? How could it still be thrashing so wildly, as if in pain and terrified? The foreigner maintained his hold, which also marveled Lucy, because he seemed so lean. She'd think the vampire could easily toss him.

With a glance at the vampire, the old man started carving away at the heart with his knife. That close to the light, Lucy could see his dark camouflage outfit was soaked with blood, splatters cutting across his face like sticky shadow. More blood squirted onto his clothing and dripped from his red hands as he cut the organ into pieces. Each piece was dropped unceremoniously into the flames as soon as it was cut, and each time the vampire released a muffled cry. Except the final time, when her body fell limp, and she made no more sounds. No longer needing to restrain her, the foreigner released his hold and rocked back onto his heels. The clearing now smelled like they were having a cookout, and Lucy scrunched her face up at the thought.

Montenegro was suddenly stepping in front of Eva, holding her arrows out to her. He was a broad-shouldered, stocky man with a deep tan and black hair in a crew cut. There was no expression on his face, and he stood there holding the arrows, radiating a sense of limitless patience. When Eva reached for them, her nostrils flared in a deep sniff.

"What did you do to them?" she asked.

Behind Montenegro, the woman and foreigner were drawing small axes.

Montenegro's voice was low and flavored with a faded Spanish accent. "Rinsed them with red wine. It purifies them. Gets rid of the creature's taint."

Eva accepted the arrows with a nod of thanks. He returned it, respect showing clearly in his eyes. With a glance spared to Eva's bow, but none for her friends, he turned to join the local man by the fire.

The other two were now chopping at the corpse, breaking it apart like a butcher would a pig. Again Lucy had to look away or risk becoming sick. Instead, she watched the local man, who watched her back while washing his hands with wine poured by Montenegro. Eventually he motioned for the archer to stop, and he rubbed his hands dry on the parts of his pants that were free of blood.

"There's a diner an exit down from 'ere," he said to Lucy and the others. When all he received was silence in response, he walked up to them, a friendly smile softening his rugged features. "You kids go get cleaned-up if'n y'all need it, then meet us there. We can all have breakfast together."

The woman and foreigner were dropping pieces of the vampire into the fire, causing heavy black smoke to billow up. A combination of smells followed that smoke—burning hair, roasting rancid meat, and garlic. Lucy's stomach turned over, and her throat convulsed in a heaving gag.

"I know, I know; it's a bit early fer breakfast." The old man shrugged, and Lucy found her eyes drawn to the streaks of black blood still marring his face. Over his shoulder, Lucy could see Montenegro doing something with the fire. Suddenly the repugnant smells gave way to the scent of burning cedar wood. "Still, I think we all should sit an' chat, an' it's always nice to do so over coffee."

"We'll see you there." Günter's voice and response both came unexpectedly, and everyone, even Eva, turned their eyes to him. Jim reached out to tightly grip his shoulder, but Günter continued to lock gazes with the old man.

Pleased, the old stranger nodded and returned to his younger associates. The matter was closed now, the course set, and Lucy felt like demanding a recount. She, for one, had no desire to spend more time with those people. By the way Jim was still clutching Günter's shoulder, she was not alone in such sentiments.

"Come on," said Eva, grabbing up the stake bag and remainder of her arrows. Feeling mildly betrayed, Lucy followed her friends out of the little clearing and onto the path that would take them to Günter's SUV.

*** 

They had made a quick stop at their campsite—what better excuse to give their parents than a friendly camp out?—to drop off their weapons and allow Günter to change. Jim also took the opportunity to gargle mouthwash in his attempt to rid himself of the taste of "vomit and shame," as he put it. Cringing, Günter ran his tongue over his teeth, then decided to follow Jim's example. While Jim may have had the misfortune of kissing the vampire, Günter had been the one sinking his teeth into its rancid flesh.

Words were rare, awkward things tripping between them, even after they found themselves in a booth at the designated diner.

"Who do you think they are?" Lucy asked the table in general as she watched the condensation trickle lazily down the glass tumbler of her apple juice.

"Gehealdan, most likely," replied Eva, Günter nodding in agreement across from her.

"What?" Jim looked up from his idle coffee stirring to leer accusingly at Eva. "The hell is that?"

Unfazed by Jim's glare or tone, Eva took a long sip of orange juice before replying. "Enforcers of the Treaties. Keepers of the secrets. They were established to serve as a non-biased third party, and now are kind of like supernatural police. Well, and judges and executioners. Like Judge Dredd." She snickered at her own joke.

"How is that funny?" Jim hissed, his coffee spoon cutting into his palm due to his grip. "And don't you think you should have told us about them *before* we did all of this? Seems like our part was not only unnecessary, but also likely more illegal than you led us to believe."

"Technically, killing someone is going to be illegal no matter —"

"*You know what I mean.* You said that we wouldn't be breaking any Treaties!"

"I said my *mother's* family—"

"You also never mentioned that there were already people who would take care of this mess for us. You led us to believe that we were the only ones who could take the vampire out. Like humanity's only hope, some bloody Obi-Wan Kenobi. So you put me through—you put your *brother* through—"

Günter, sitting next to Jim, gently placed one of his hands over the one of Jim's clutching the spoon. Instantly Jim's eyes snapped from

Eva to her brother, but their new focus drained the fiery anger from them. "It was nothing I can't handle," assured Günter in calm, soothing murmurs. He gave Jim's hand a small squeeze, and then slowly retreated. "And neither Eva nor I meant to mislead you. We were uncertain that the Gehealdan would even act on this case. We'd rather be sure the threat was taken out than sit idly by and hope the proper authorities might eventually get around to handling it."

Jim's jaw clenched behind his closed lips, but he swallowed down anything else he might want to say. With a deflating exhale, he turned his attention back to his coffee and gazed moodily into its murky depths.

There was a clattering of dishes and utensils from behind the counter as the cook went about preparing their food. The waitress was laughing about something, the cook nodding and smiling as he flipped bacon. Some pot-bellied trucker was sitting at the counter, poking at his omelet.

Picking little holes in her napkin, Lucy waited to make certain Jim had settled before she continued with the conversation. "Do you think the Gehealdan will hurt us?"

Eva dripped orange juice onto her crumpled straw wrapper so that it grew like a soggy snake, all the while darting surreptitious glances at Jim through her bangs. "No. That's not how they work. Usually humans who find out about the truth are given two choices— join, or forget."

"Forget?" Lucy asked, glancing anxiously at the door. "What do you mean?"

"Magic," was Günter's matter-of-fact response, even if the word itself sounded absurd. "While Gehealdan are usually made up of humans, there's always a mix of supernaturals among them. Each chapter has at least one member with the ability to alter memories."

127

"It's the usual method of dealing with humans who learn too much," added Eva. She then shook her head, frowning at her drink. "Evidently, it's what most humans prefer."

There was a jingle of bells above the door as four people flowed into the diner with familiar ease. In normal clothes and under the bright, spherical lights, the Gehealdan seemed like completely different people. They took the booth across the narrow aisle from Lucy's group. The old man and the young woman took the outside seats, while the implacable foreigner and Montenegro took the respective inside seats. The waitress arrived with the food for Lucy's table, and the old man told her they'd be taking their usual. Once everyone was settled, he turned to acknowledge Lucy's group for the first time since arriving.

His eyes were a faded, dusty grey, but one of them looked clearer and more focused than the other. The clear eye was surrounded by jagged scars, however, which led Lucy to theorize that it was a false eye. Scars peppered his entire face, which was the color and texture of cracked leather. He smiled at them from beneath the brim of a threadbare denim baseball cap with "#1 Dad" embroidered on the front in fraying thread. "Hey there," he greeted in his gravelly voice. "Now we can get better acquainted. I'm Caesar Hayes, but jus' call me Czar, like the Russian leaders. Not Russian m'self, but an' ol' friend use ta call me that, an' it stuck."

Lucy's table remained silent, the four of them only nodding in understanding.

"This is mah right-hand man, ri'chere," he continued, patting the shoulder of the foreigner beside him. "He's Philandros, but jus' call 'im Phil."

Phil leaned forward a bit and offered the group a dimpled grin that crinkled the corners of his greenish-blue eyes. In the light, Lucy noticed that he had incredibly long hair, but it was hidden, woven into a braid that slithered down his back. His skin glowed with a rich, healthy tan, and his brown hair had sun-bleached highlights throughout. If Lucy didn't know that he was a Gehealdan, she'd think he was just a surfer or beach bum. As he shifted in his seat, however, it became obvious that there was nothing but lean muscle beneath that tan skin. A few scars also caught the light, some striping his arms and two faint ones cutting across his left cheek.

Everyone nodded again, and Lucy privately pondered on the national origins of a name like Philandros. Maybe Greek?

"Then we got the lovely Carmen, 'ere." Czar motioned to the young woman across from him. Her hair was styled into cornrows as tight and severe as her expression. Carmen smiled thinly and gave them a nod, but Lucy though that her brown eyes still seemed so weary. When they had walked in, Lucy had noticed that Carmen was the second-tallest next to Czar, and her cargo pants and T-shirt had done little to hide her incredible figure. In another life, perhaps Carmen would have been a runway model instead of someone who chopped up monsters. Such a thing would likely be difficult for her now, with her smooth, midnight dark skin marred by pink and ivory scars.

"Last, but most certainly not least, we got Montenegro." The stoic Latino man also gave a nod. His was curter than Carmen's, and no smile accompanied the gesture.

Once the introductions of the Gehealdans were complete, Lucy's table glanced at each other, wondering who should start on their side, or if they should have a single representative like Czar. Before anyone could move to speak, however, Czar was talking again. "Some of y'all I know. Well, know *of*, should say. You two," he said, pointing at Eva and Günter, "are Hartmut and Jomei's kids. Either that, or hybrid wolf-birds are more common than I thought."

Günter rubbed at his left wrist and hand, shifting a little on the

129

bench. He then lifted his head and met Czar's gaze. "You're right, we're Günter and Eva Kuntz-Tenno. The other two aren't like us, however; they're humans."

"I'm Lucy." Czar's eyes switched to her, but his face remained pleasantly unreadable. "It was my idea, what we did tonight," she continued. Eva looked at her, but said nothing.

"And I'm Jim." At the new introduction, Czar's eyes again shifted without any other muscle even twitching. "I was against the idea for what we did tonight," assured Jim. That got a reaction, the corners of Czar's mouth twitching upwards before he seemed to give in to the inevitable grin.

"More 'n one thing wrong with what y'all did tonight, not the least of which bein' yer research. Lemme guess—y'all used movies?"

Guilty glances were exchanged around the Lucy's table.

"Thought so." Czar sighed affectionately while Phil snickered and Carmen rolled her eyes. Montenegro merely continued his silent study of everyone and the diner.

Suddenly Montenegro glanced at Czar's face, then over the older man's shoulder. Czar relaxed casually in his seat, letting the conversation rest while the waitress arrived with his table's drinks. He flirted playfully with her while she served them. Phil teased him as he did so, calling him a dirty old man, then tried to charm the lady himself. She inoffensively brushed them off, but gave Montenegro an extra-bright smile. Carmen hid a smirk behind her coffee mug.

Once the waitress had moved away to chat with the fry cook and check on the trucker, Czar slurped his coffee and turned back to Lucy's group. "Movies are tha last place y'all should be goin' to fer accurate info on vamps." Another slurp. "Mosta tha crap in movies is written by vamps or us or others jus' trying ta maintain tha secr'ts of what's real."

130

"Or just people who never do *actual* research, and merely build off earlier films," Phil added while pouring obscene amounts of sugar into his iced tea. Czar nodded in agreement.

"So, they're intentionally wrong?" asked Lucy, confused and more than a little surprised at discovering such a conspiracy.

"Some are," corrected Czar. "Like Phil said, some are just accidental results of laziness. Think it started a while ago, with books. Don't think the actual authors were vamps, mind, but I reckon the vamps were feedin' 'em a load of bull on purpose. Tha Gehealdan jus' kept on tha tradition, is all."

"Works, too," added Carmen. "You guys failed at killin' it, which is part of the goal. Plenty of vamps signed the Treaties, and the Gehealdan serve all who have, so long as they keep to the codes." A small, cruel smile flitted across her full lips. "Unlike our friend tonight, who was a Treaty breaker."

"Where do we find accurate information?" Lucy asked, earning a glare from Jim.

Czar shook his head. "Never you mind that," he rumbled. "Ain't none o' y'all's concern. We don't need ta save yer asses because y'all up and went after another Rome." He then frowned and scratched at his grey stubble, muttering mostly under his breath, "There've been an awful lotta 'em 'round, lately, fer some reason."

"Rome?" Eva and Lucy asked simultaneously, in matching tones of perplexity.

"Romanian," supplied Phil with a dimply smirk. "Also known as strigoi."

Montenegro cleared his throat, and everyone fell silent as the waitress again approached the table. This time she carried two trays laden with food. Setting one down on a neighboring table, she started passing out dishes for Czar's booth. While Lucy's table had opted for small orders—toast and eggs, mostly—Czar's crew had plates piled high with artery-clogging goodness.

"If y'all need anythin' else, just holler," the waitress offered with a wink at Montenegro that the young man seemed not to catch. She wandered reluctantly away, returning to her gossip with the cook.

"Anyway," continued Phil as he mixed his eggs and hash browns together, "Romanian is what you'll typically run into, when it comes to vamps. It's a type now, more than a nationality. There are strigoi of probably every nationality nowadays."

"Spread like tha plague, they do." Czar growled a little as he stabbed his omelet. "In fact, folks use ta think it were jus' plague, when many times it were Romes."

Lucy chewed at her toast while her mind chewed on the information. Ever since that Wednesday night when Günter visited her in her room, a block had been steadily chipping away, allowing her a more complete view of the world. It was like switching everything from grainy analog to digital HD, all the tiny details now becoming crystal clear. She was fascinated. Putting her toast down, she focused her attention squarely on Czar. "Could you teach us?" He squinted at her and her question, but remained silent. "About vampires," she elaborated, assuming that's what his silence was requesting.

Scratching at his scarred, stubbled chin, Czar cast a cursory glance around Lucy's table before exchanging looks with his own. "You an' Jimmy-boy do have a choice," he conceded, "'bout how we go from 'ere. One option is that y'all forget—as in we've a way to take all these mem'ries away. Tha other option is ta join up with us, an' trainin's jus' part of tha package. So, a course I'd be teachin' ya 'bout vamps and all sorts a others. Bein' Gehealdan ain't easy, though. You up fer it?" He smirked sardonically at her before taking another bite.

Eva set down her fork, her fried egg mostly untouched. "Can I join, as well?"

Still chewing his heaping forkful, Czar raised his grey eyebrows. A chuckle followed his swallow, and he shook his head, not even bothering to turn enough to face her. "Why tha Hell for?"

"You know my lineage," said Eva. "You know neither side likes to stand by and watch innocent people get hurt."

"Not all your momma's folk are like that," Carmen said, her eyes on her hash browns as she shook hot sauce on them. "Some like to be the cause of such hurt."

Both of the siblings bristled at that. "Mother's family isn't like that," Günter insisted in a low, dark tone.

Czar stabbed a fresh piece as he finished chewing and swallowing the last. Before bringing it to his chapped lips, he attempted to diffuse the situation. "Pardon mah ward's error. She meant no slight, I'm sure." He then ate the waiting forkful, not once glancing their way.

"I'm sure your momma's family is just chock full of human compassion," added Carmen, barely glancing up.

"Considering our grandfather is a Buddhist monk," snapped Eva, "I'd say yes."

"If we choose to forget," Jim interrupted, drawing all eyes back to him, "how *much* would we forget?"

On the table, Günter's hand twitched as if he was going to reach out to Jim in comfort again, then curled tight into a fist and slid away. Czar eyed Jim silently, but Phil leaned forward a bit and cocked his head. "How much do you *want* to forget?" Phil asked, brows crinkling in obvious concern.

Jim's cheeks jerked a bit as he clenched and unclenched his jaw. "I'm not certain that's what I want," he evaded. "I'm just weighing my options."

"Weigh 'em quick," grumbled Czar around another bite of food.

133

"Need ta know by tha time we're done 'ere."

"If we join up," Jim said slowly, sharp gaze sliding along each of the Gehealdan members, "do we have to fight? Are there other jobs? Different positions in the organization?"

That brought something almost like a smile to Czar's lips. "Why? What skill ya got that's useful in an alternate capacity? Ya know how ta craft weapons? Maybe know computers? Got some sorta political connections could do us some good?" He stared Jim down, then pressed on when there was no immediate response. "What I see when I look atcha is a young man with strong arms. Got some good muscle on ya there. Saw how ya kicked tha stake inta tha vamp. So, ya obvi'usly had some sorta trainin' in fightin'. Don't see why that can't be put ta good use."

Shifting in his seat, Jim took to studying his hands wrapped around his empty coffee mug. "Can I at least never be used as bait again?"

Czar snorted. "No promises," he gruffed, smirking and winking as if to imply he was only kidding. Lucy didn't believe the gesture, and for some reason felt the hair on the back of her neck stand up a little.

"Just remember to eat a lot of bananas," Phil chirped with another cheeky grin. "Goes for all of you. Just in case, bait or not."

Lucy's table exchanged looks, before Jim finally asked, "Bananas?"

"Vitamin K," Carmen explained. "Helps blood clotting."

Before any of them could ask why they'd need that, Czar was gracing them with a small lesson about some sort of enzyme or something in vamp saliva. "Prevents clotting, so's ya bleed out better. Easier fer 'em ta feed." He licked his fork and swiped his lips with his napkin, before turning to better face Günter. "Which reminds me. You bit?"

Günter blinked, but quickly shook his head. "No, she scratched me a bit, but those are already healed."

Czar's lips were a thin line as he regarded them all. "Any of y'all look into its eyes?"

Slowly, hesitantly, Jim lifted a finger. Without warning, Phil was tossing him a small bottle of what looked like dirty water. "Drink that," Czar commanded, scrutinizing Jim as if searching his features for something.

Jim held the bottle up to get a better look, shaking it around. Even from across the table, Lucy could see the blackish debris floating about in it like some sort of grungy snow globe.

"It's the vampire's ashes," said Phil, his grin gone. "Any who may have been cursed by a vampire must drink its ashes mixed with water. It's the only way to break its curse. Otherwise, you get sick and wither away and die."

After a steadying breath, Jim uncapped the water and downed it. Afterwards, his dark skin looked a bit ashen, and his face was screwed up in obvious disgust. "Well, at least it's an improvement in taste from when it was alive." He held the bottle up in silent question to Phil, but the man shook his head.

"Keep it." Suddenly the grin was back, accompanied by a wink. "Like a souvenir."

"I'll cherish it always." Jim's sarcasm made all the Gehealdans smirk a bit, even Montenegro.

It felt as if some of the tension was easing up a little, and everyone started to go back to working on their food. Of course, such a reprieve was to be disappointingly ephemeral.

"One more thing." Phil's voice had Czar's chewing slow to a stop. The young man's eyes were a thin veneer of calm sea over a tempest. "Not all vamps are hostiles," he said, the thumb of his right

135

hand idly playing with a gold band on that hand's ring finger. "I'm sure present company can appreciate that not all of a creature type are exactly alike. Some vamps used to protect humans, once upon a time, same as werewolves. As mentioned, many are even part of the Treaties. Just because someone is a vamp, it doesn't mean he's an enemy."

Lucy glanced at Eva and Günter, who were both studying Phil. A message of understanding passed between the three, it seemed. Perhaps Phil wasn't entirely human, Lucy wondered. Hadn't Eva been about to say something about one of them, before? Then there was the bit about how the Gehealdan had a mix of humans and supernaturals.

"Besides," continued Phil, but he paused and looked at Czar as if silently asking a question. Though Lucy didn't see the old man's expression change, Phil must have found his answer, because he was soon staring across the way at Lucy's group again. "Generally, vamps don't even make kills. Because of the Treaties, they're usually cautious about their feeding habits, so as not to draw too much unwanted attention. It seems that something's changed their minds about that, though. Used to be we didn't need to hunt down Treaty breakers but once every few months. Now it's weekly. Sometimes more than once a week, at that. Also seems like their numbers in the area are increasing, both in terms of freshies and in oldies. So just be careful, yeah?"

Montenegro asked Czar for the salt, and the waitress arrived with the bills. Czar reached out and intercepted her before she could lay one down on Lucy's table. "I'll be treatin' mah friends, 'ere," he told her with a smile.

Returning the smile, the waitress handed him both slips. "You're such a sweetie, Hayes."

"Taste sweet, too. Care for a sample?" he asked with a wink of his glass eye. She laughed and batted him playfully on the shoulder before strolling away. Once the waitress was out of earshot again, Czar looked back at Lucy's table. "Go on, get outta 'ere. Get some sleep, fer shit's sake."

They tried to thank him, Günter insisting on handling the bill himself, but Czar waved them quiet. "'Fore ya go," Czar said, shifting to reach his back pocket and retrieve his wallet, "take this." He pulled a business card from the folded leather and tossed it onto the other table. "I expect y'all there Wednesday after yer all done with school. I'd have ya over sooner, but we're plum booked solid till then."

Günter pulled out his own wallet and slipped the card into one of the pockets. "Thank you," he said to Czar, nodding low. "We owe you a great deal."

Czar smiled at him, but his dusty eyes looked troubled—even his false one. "Don't owe me a damn thing."

Before taking a step to go, Lucy bit her lip and steeled herself to ask Czar one last question. "Do you think the Grin Reaper is a vampire?"

All of the Gehealdans stared at her, and Lucy could feel her friends giving her confused looks as well. Eventually Czar gave a slow nod. "He is. How'd ya know?"

"I didn't. I just. Well, I suspected."

Czar's eyes reminded her a bit of Donnie, both in coloration and in their disturbing intensity. "Suspected?" When she merely nodded, unsure how else to respond, Czar's mouth stretched into a secret smile. "Int'restin'. Now, don't ya mind that none right now. He's not ta be any concern of yers, child. He's mah business, ya hear?"

Lucy gave a hesitant nod, and let herself be led away by Jim.

As they reached the door, Lucy was sure she heard Carmen murmur "Shoulda taken the blue pill."

# Chapter 9
## The Cost

"Boo!"

The cry coupled with the pair of hands suddenly falling on her shoulders had Lucy nearly toppling over where she knelt. All of the books she'd carefully been stacking and sorting slid and scattered into a miserable heap. A girl's delighted giggle helped Lucy's heart calm down and start pumping anger instead of fear.

"Krysti, how did you—when—what?" Spinning into a tense crouch, Lucy glared at her amused friend.

"What? I knocked. Donnie let me in. So, whatcha dooooin'?"

Damn it all, but it was impossible to remain angry with the cute blonde. "Cleaning."

"Cool. I'll supervise."

Lucy tried to sigh in annoyance, but it came out more as a laugh. "No, that's fine. I'll just deal with it later." Tossing a dark look at the spilled pile, Lucy stood and moved to her bed. She fell back onto it in exhaustion and loudly smacked at the empty space beside her.

Krysti bounded onto the bed at the invitation, platinum hair spilling around her in gentle waves. "How is my Lucy?"

"Your Lucy has had a very trying few weeks." She turned her head towards Krysti, but focused on their hair and how it mingled. Strands of black and icy blonde.

Krysti stared at the ceiling, for once looking serious instead of playful or pouty. "Eva told me about the attack."

Of course she did. Eva told Krysti anything and everything. *Except what she really is*, Lucy thought, though even her mental voice was flavored with doubt. *Had* Eva told Krysti the truth about her family?

138

"And I hear from Kyle that you guys went to another party on Friday." When Krysti rolled her head to look at Lucy, her dark blue eyes were shot through with brighter, luminescent ripples from the glare of the overhead light. It made Lucy think of the ghostly effect produced from light on water, the swirling projections dancing languidly along walls and skin.

"Nothing happened Friday," Lucy lied with surprising ease. She had never lied to Krysti. Maybe she could have offered little white lies to anyone else, even her own mother, but never Krysti.

Something flickered across her friend's expression, and Lucy knew that Krysti had detected the fib. It was almost enough to make Lucy start babbling apologies. Krysti deserved better. After everything she'd done for Lucy over the years, Krysti deserved more than pathetic lies.

"It's dangerous, Lucy." Krysti rarely used that soft, serious voice, and its tone chilled Lucy. "Haven't you heard what they're saying on the news? That Grin Reaper guy is supposed to be coming here."

Lucy almost felt contrite, but then a realization made her squint speculatively. "What about you and your LARP?"

Krysti just rolled her eyes. "We aren't even to the stage of LARPing, and even if we were—"

"I thought you said you were joining a LARP. How can a LARP not be ready for LARPing?"

"Ah. I didn't join that one. Instead I joined that gothy RPG, *Chains of the Damned*. Darin—the GM and creator—is still tweaking the LARP mechanics. But, *anyway*. We'll be in a more controlled environment, where only the group will be present. No strangers coming in to try to chat anyone up and spirit them away. Plus we'll have radios, and several players have medical training. It's all very safe. Unlike random parties."

139

Without thinking about it, Lucy reached over to play with some of Krysti's long, silky hair. "Eva and Jim were with me. It was safe enough."

"They were with you when you witnessed an attack, too. Look, I know Eva's badass and all, but she's not invulnerable. And believe me, I gave *her* a lecture, too."

Lucy bit her lip to keep from snickering about the invulnerable comment.

After an awkward silence, Krysti slid her hand over to hook her pinky with Lucy's. "You tell your mom?" she whispered, because Krysti knew better than any of her friends how Lucy sheltered her mother.

"No. Only Mick."

Krysti's pinky tightened for a second. "What'd he say?"

Thinking of her brother, Lucy couldn't help but give a tiny smile. "He was ready to drop everything and come down. The idiot."

The blonde snorted. "That is probably the most inappropriate word for him. Ever."

"Psh. What, so you sayin' 'psychopath' or 'hideous' are more appropriate?"

"Ugh, no, totally not what I meant!" For a wonderful, brilliant moment, Krysti looked like her usual cheery self. Then the shadows returned to her face and voice. "You miss him?"

"Of course I do." Saying the words made Lucy's chest hurt and her throat clamp closed. She shut her eyes to fight back their sudden sting. "That doesn't mean I'm going to let him skip school just to come down and give me a hug."

"Why not? He probably needs one, too."

Behind her eyelids, Lucy saw Mick as he was at fifteen—standing strong and determined in a black suit while their mother wept on his shoulder. Already he had started to look like their father, and

Lucy remembered how she both loved and hated to look at him for a very long time.

"Winter break isn't too far away," she said, forcing her eyes open.

Krysti offered a gentle smile, warm and calm as the first rays of a sunrise over the ocean. "True. Also means fall semester will be done by then. Maybe he can transfer down to Tech for his doctorate?"

"He mentioned the possibility. I think he misses the family."

"No doubt. I'd miss you guys, too."

They smiled at each other, and then Krysti tried to shift the conversation to lighter things. "So, Kyle tells me you've got a crush on some college guy."

Brows wrinkling together, Lucy turned her head and frowned at the ceiling. "College guy?"

"Yeah, some guy with dark hair, who evidently smokes. A smoker, Lucy? Really?"

As soon as she realized whom Kyle had been talking about, she laughed and rubbed a hand over her face. "No. No, that's Ren. The guy from the first party that I spilled beer on. I don't have a crush on him. Trust me."

"Oh." Krysti seemed a little disappointed, and that made Lucy glare askance in betrayal. "Well, I suppose that's good. Wouldn't want you getting lung cancer from secondhand smoke and all. But, you know, Kyle sounded a little jealous when he was telling me about that guy."

"Pfft. Kyle? Jealous? Not likely."

"He was! And he was all concerned for you, because that guy was evidently *all over* some blond chick as soon as you left."

Despite her doubts, Lucy couldn't help but smile at the thought that Kyle might be jealous of Ren. "Well, Kyle *was* a bit…friendly."

"Oooh?" Squirming where she lay, Krysti grinned at Lucy in anticipation of some juicy news. "He finally make a move?"

"No. Hah, no. Nothing like that. He just…held me for a bit. Tried to act all brave and noble, talking about how he'd protect me if anything bad happened again."

"Ohmygod, that is *so sweet.*"

Lucy blushed and looked away. "Shut up. He was just being a friend."

"Uh-huh, riiiight. So, what else did he do?"

Remembering everything that had happened, Lucy felt her blush burn hotter. "He may have wanted to dance with me, and kept his arms around me constantly, and didn't want me to leave."

The squeal that came out of Krysti was so high-pitched that Lucy was willing to bet all of the dogs in the area were going nuts. "He totally loves you!"

"He totally doesn't!"

"Mrs. Lucille Raposo. It has a ring to it. Oh, wait, you won't have to, like, adopt all of his other names, will you? He's got like a million of them."

"Please stop planning my wedding. And no, I'm pretty sure you only take the family name."

Rolling her head to look directly up at the ceiling, Krysti bunched her brows together in deep contemplation. "Why do Portuguese have so many names?"

"I'm sure they wonder why you only have three. And he's half."

"Didn't cut his amount of names in half, though, did it?"

"You are so weird."

"What?" Krysti adopted an offended mien and rolled back to face Lucy. "Just because I take interest in learning about the ways of different cultures? Really, Lucy, you are so closed-minded and ethnocentric. It's sad."

Lucy responded by grabbing a pillow and whomping Krysti in the face.

*** 

"Knowledge is power."

The night was the darkest of blacks, but the bloated moon literally cut a path, weaving its light into solid road. A lone tree stood at the side of the path, and a man stood beneath the tree. Somewhere in the distance, a horn was blowing. It wasn't like a car horn, but something caught between music and alarm.

Slowly turning, the man beneath the tree looked at her, one eye as clear and bright as the moon, the other nothing more than a marred hole. "Power comes at a cost," he said in a voice as old as the world.

Lucy walked towards him along the path, recognition giving rise to a feeling of security. Czar wouldn't let anything attack her from the shadows. "What can I pay?" she asked once she was closer to him and the tree. "I've already lost so much."

He smiled, and there was a pain in that smile that Lucy would never understand. "Removing the veil means not that you have lost." One weathered hand rose to touch the equally weathered bark. "To gain something great, there must be sacrifice."

"But I've nothing to sacrifice."

His hair and beard were white as snow, both long and flowing, decorated with elaborate braids. Lucy realized belatedly that he wasn't Czar at all. The horn no longer sounded. Overhead the wind pressed at the tree's branches so that the air was filled with wooden moans.

"You are not the one," the stranger explained, "who is to name the price."

A low growl erupted from the darkness on the other side of the path. Deep within Lucy bloomed a primal fear, instinctive and biting. When she turned towards the sound, the only features the moon allowed her to see were the mouths. They were of various sizes, all sharp-toothed and snarling. Gnashing at the night, they growled in limitless, ageless hunger.

*

Lucy's eyes flew open and she stared sightlessly at her bedroom ceiling. A car drove by, causing light to dance through the gaps in the curtains. Closing her eyes again in relief, Lucy started to roll over— only to discover that she couldn't move. Something heavy was pressing at her chest, holding her down where she lay. Her heartbeat quickened and her breath came ragged with panic.

Another car drove by, and in the whisper of tires on asphalt she thought she heard her name. She kept her eyes squeezed closed, praying silently that it was just in her head, knowing it wasn't. The weight finally shifted, feeling as though something crawled off of her chest and onto the bed then thumped onto the floor. Only when she heard the creak did she open her eyes, which went immediately to her door. Never did she go to bed without closing the door tight, not since becoming a teen and desiring a heightened level of privacy. The door was ajar, however, and slowly opening further. From the hall, the crescent moon plug-in nightlight was leaking its pale blue glow into Lucy's room.

*What should I do?* she asked herself, eyes darting a frantic glance around her room before returning to the door. The duffel bag was beneath her bed, still packed with stakes and crosses, though the garlic had been removed. She supposed she could arm herself with that,

144

but then remembered that such things were actually quite useless against a vampire. Then again, this might not have been a vampire. There were other creatures, she reminded herself, other things that lurked in shadows and lured people to their deaths.

There were also good things, however.

Still uncertain, she slid out of bed and straightened her skull-print pajamas. The door had stopped moving, and so she looked away from it in order to search for something to use as a weapon. On her desk was the antique letter opener that had been her father's. With nothing better coming to mind, she quietly crossed the room to fetch it. Once armed, she slowly eased the door open enough to pass into the hall.

From that point on, she had no idea where to go. Should she check on Donnie and her mom? Well, it was the best plan she could come up with, so why not? Turning, she took a few soft steps towards her mother's door.

From downstairs came the distinctive—though very faint—sound of a door opening and closing. Lucy froze, straining her ears to hear anything else, but the house was still and silent. With a steadying breath, she altered her direction and moved to the top of the stairs.

The little glass moon only cast its faint artificial beams halfway down the stairs, darkness smothering the rest until it melted into a formless void. Biting her lip to keep from whimpering, Lucy started slowly down into the nothingness. No boogeyman had jumped out at her by the time she reached the bottom, so she figured she was safe—for the moment, anyway. The floorboards had barely even made a sound beneath her feet, thanks to years of experience from sneaking down to watch television past her bedtime. Peering unseeingly into the darkness, she fumbled with her free hand along the wall for the light switch. If she was about to face some spooky entity, she'd be damned if she was going to give it an advantage over her.

Her fingers found the switch, and light came like a breath of relief, casting all the fear away. There was nothing there, just her house with all its familiar clutter. Not about to let her guard down quite so easily, Lucy clutched her letter opener tightly as she went from room to room, switching on all of the lights.

Nothing.

Not even the front or back doors showed signs of having been opened, both securely locked tight. Lucy leaned her back against the island in the kitchen, feeling quite silly and ridiculous.

"Is anyone there?"

Silence answered, and she laughed softly, setting the opener down in order to rub at her face with both hands. "Maybe the price is my sanity." She laughed again, but it sounded suspiciously like a sob. "This is stupid. It was a dream."

Lowering her hands, she glanced around once more with her puffy, red eyes. It had all just been her groggy mind playing tricks on her. Surely she'd be better after getting more sleep. Sighing, she grabbed the opener and left the kitchen, flicking off its light on the way. Once she had gotten halfway across the living room, her brain finally processed something her eyes were seeing. Her feet whispered softly against the carpet as they dragged to a halt.

Ahead of her was the archway which led to the foyer, providing access to the front door and stairs. Beyond this archway, however, was darkness.

She took a step back, mind whirling. Hadn't she turned all the lights on? Hadn't the foyer's light been the first? Were there any lights she'd extinguished aside from the kitchen's? No, she was fairly certain that had been the only one. There was a possibility she could be wrong, though. It was, after all, habit for her to turn off lights when exiting a room.

Steeling her nerves, she clutched the opener and stepped forward towards the darkened archway. When she peeked up towards the top of the stairs, however, what she saw had her immediately retreat. The nightlight upstairs was out, too, its pale glow no longer trickling down the steps.

After moving back into the center of the living room, she found herself trapped by the darkened archways on both sides. With a whimper she couldn't suppress, she walked to the couch and sank down into its cushions, which could provide none of the comfort she needed. The clock on the cable box read a quarter to one. It would be at least five hours before dawn. She could be brave and walk through the darkness to her room, or she could try to stick it out there in the living room until sunrise.

Grabbing the remote from the end table, Lucy turned on the TV and quickly clicked the volume down to whisper level. She pulled the quilted throw from the back of the couch and wrapped it around herself as she settled in for a long night of movie watching. Lucy had underestimated her exhaustion, however, and fell asleep before reaching the conclusion of some golf movie. Luckily there were no strange dreams this time, and she managed to get several hours of uninterrupted sleep.

*

Morning birds woke her, the amber light of dawn peeking through the curtains. She stretched lazily on the couch before pulling herself up into a sitting position. So, she'd survived the night, it seemed. With a self-deprecating laugh, she picked up the letter opener from the coffee table and twirled it idly in her hands. There had probably been no reason for her fear, anyway, she knew. Most likely her mother had roused at some point, and seeing the foyer light was on, switched it off before heading back to bed. Yes, that was probably it.

When she reached for the remote, she noticed that the TV was turned off already. In that moment, she also noticed that the infant sunlight was the only source of illumination. Above her, the overhead lamp stared down at her with grey indifference. Her mother again, she reasoned with herself. That was the most logical, rational explanation, so that had to be it.

Floorboards creaked wearily as someone came down the stairs, and Lucy looked towards the foyer with an apprehension she tried to kill. Diana entered, her long hair in a messy braid, and her fluffy bathrobe draped over her raw silk pajamas. She blinked blearily at Lucy, a smile etching crow's feet at the corners of her eyes.

"You're up early, Lucy."

# Chapter 10
## Chasing Shadows

"Oh my God, Beowulf is such a prick!" Alice moved her hands emphatically as she talked, nearly smacking a passing freshman in the face. Half-lidded eyes staring ahead into middle space, Lucy nodded dumbly. "The way he brags! It's, like, if he were real and I were listening to him, I'd be totally calling bull, you know!" When Lucy didn't even nod, Alice ceased her ranting and grabbed her arm. They came to a stop just outside of the door to Mr. Pulchrum's classroom.

"Lucy, are you alright?"

"Hm?" Blinking away her thoughts, Lucy made her eyes focus on her friend's face. "I'm fine. Just zoned out for a moment, sorry."

"Was I that boring?" Alice pulled a hurt face, pouting her lips cutely.

Lucy smiled and shook her head. "No, I was interested. And, I agree—Beowulf was a jerk. Only fought monsters for glory and fame, not to help his fellow man."

"I know, right!" Instantly Alice's face brightened, sufficiently assured that her friend was well.

Pulchrum was at his desk already when they entered the room, which was rare for him. When he spotted them, he smiled in a strange way that didn't reach his eyes. Pulchrum always smiled with his entire face, so it was jarring to see him do anything less. He motioned for Lucy to approach, which she did after giving Alice a quick, questioning glance.

"I thought you might have use of these," he said, pulling a large stack of old books from his deep bottom drawer. A cursory glance at their spines revealed that they were all pertaining to folklore, especially chronicles of oral traditions. When he saw Lucy give him a startled look, his strange not-smile flitted back across his face. "I'm told you got a new part-time job that requires some extra study."

Lucy's pulse raced and her stomach twisted. "You—"

"You and the others need to get these read by Wednesday." Pulchrum glanced back down at them with a wry chuckle. "Or, at least as much of them as you can. I realize they're not exactly light reads."

When Lucy only stood there gaping at him, Pulchrum held them up at her pointedly, urging her to take them. They were heavier than expected and Lucy staggered a moment under their weight, before clinging them firmly against her torso. "I don't understand," she tried to say, mind whirling at the implications. Was Pulchrum a member of Gehealdan? If not, then he had to be something that wasn't human. The only humans that could know of the Gehealdan were members of the Gehealdan, after all.

"Wednesday," he simply said, making no indication if he meant that's when he'd explain or if he was just reiterating her reading deadline.

She nodded weakly and started to turn away, but Pulchrum reached out and stopped her with a hand against the stack of books. "Never let your guard down," he whispered, and his hazel eyes seemed to become almost as golden as Günter's for a moment.

***

"That's not reading."

"Astute observation, Eva. Surely you'd make a great detective." Jim's voice came to them with a slight echo quality as it bounced off the bare walls and picture windows of his studio.

An eighteen-year-old with a fully-stocked art studio was such a strange thing for Lucy to wrap her head around at first. Then she had seen what he could do, and it was easier for her to understand why his parents had built him a professional-quality studio. It probably didn't hurt much that his parents were also obscenely wealthy, so could afford to indulge his artistic passions. There were two studios on their property, actually, since Jim's mother was a world-renowned artist in her own right. It was thanks to her that he was so easily able to break into the art world and feature his works at galleries, even though he was still in high school.

"Stop drawing and come help!"

"I *am* helping. I'm letting you use my studio for this horror fest of a study group." Jim didn't even look up from his easel as he spoke, charcoal working across the large paper with soft scratching sounds that were amplified in the cavernous room.

"All of us are supposed to read these," Lucy reminded him. "You said you were going to join the Gehealdan, so you have to study these, too."

"You lot can give me the Cliff's Notes version, I'm sure. Keep me apprised of all the important bits."

"Your dedication is truly inspiring," snarked Eva.

The banter died down as the three at the table started their reading. It was then that they realized how old the texts were, most published in the eighteen hundreds, and another published around 1915. From that moment on, they handled the books with the utmost reverence and care, knowing that they'd likely never be able to replace them if they were damaged.

"These are from your English teacher?" asked Günter, his amber eyes scanning the front pages for publishing information.

"Like I said, I think they're actually from Czar."

Those eyes turned to her, wide with amazement. "And he's letting us borrow them?"

Eva gave a hum of interest as she flipped slowly through the pages in search of strigoi. "I think we're glossing over the real issue here."

"Pulchrum is either Gehealdan or a supernatural," Lucy said softly, staring blankly down at a random page.

"Or both," shrugged Eva. "It's common enough. Though, I've never noticed him smelling particularly special." She suddenly sat up stiffly as if just realizing something. "In fact, I've never really noticed him having a smell. Like, at all."

"He smells like the woods," Lucy corrected, remembering his coat draped across her as she napped. "Reminds me of nighttime in the winter."

Eva and Günter both eyed her speculatively, either wondering why she knew that or what type of creature had that smell. "Maybe he's something special," Jim called over, still scritching away at his paper. "Something that can mask its scent."

The siblings frowned and exchanged a glance. "Maybe," conceded Günter. "It's certainly not like Eva or I are experts on everything out there. We pretty much only know a few scents in particular, and have only met a few different types of supernaturals that are friends of the family." He tapped his fingers on the book open in front of him. "I'm actually really excited we have these, so I can learn more." Smiling, Günter bowed his head to return to his reading.

"Which reminds me..." Lucy opened one of the books and ran an idle finger along its table of contents. "I want to figure something out. Or, well, identify it." None of the topics mentioned creatures that snuffed out lights.

Günter looked up from his book, tension seeping into his posture. "What?"

Meeting his eyes for only a moment, Lucy continued to scan the

152

contents. One chapter was about the causes of eclipses, which wasn't quite what she needed but perhaps close enough. She flipped through the book to find the correct page as she replied. "There was something in my house last night and this morning." She paused, considering the ways it all could very well have been a dream, and added softly: "I think."

Everyone remained silent, watching her expectantly, so she recounted all that had happened. After she finished, Jim walked over to the table and sat down heavily in the empty chair beside her. He was muttering to himself in a language comprised primarily of swear words, his eyes staring blankly at the table as he thought about what she'd said.

"Nice of you to join us," said Eva.

Snapping out of his daze, Jim looked at her as if she were nuts. "This is serious, Eva."

When he looked into her eyes, his mouth clicked shut, and the intensity he found there had him diverting his stare. "I *am* serious," said Eva with a low, even tone.

In a far gentler voice, with calm, calculating eyes, Günter asked Jim if he had experienced anything like that since Friday night. Wincing, Jim shook his head. "I don't usually remember any dreams, let alone have nightmares. I'm also a heavy sleeper, so I wouldn't have noticed any noises, if there were any."

Releasing a grunt-like hum, Günter glanced around the studio as if he could spot an anomaly in a room which was new to him. "If I may, I'd like to spend the night, just to make certain."

Jim's gaze didn't quite touch Günter, wandering over the cluttered table and flitting from one old book cover to another. "That would be kind of weird, though, yeah? I mean, I haven't had a sleep-over since I was a kid. Might be a bit odd for some college guy to just drop by and stay the night."

153

"Why not just use the excuse of Günter serving as your model?" When Lucy suggested it, Eva stared at her with shock, obviously dismayed that she hadn't said such a thing herself.

With a nervous laugh, Günter shifted in his chair and played with his mechanical pencil. "I don't really think I'm model material."

"You're kidding, right?" Eva looked like she was about to bop her brother upside the head. "Jim's wanted to use you as a model since before he even met you. Besides, of course you're model material; we're from very good stock, you know."

Still looking quite unsure of it all, Günter glanced around at the studio again. This time, however, he was searching for some indicator of what he'd be getting himself into, as opposed to trying to find some malicious creature lurking in the sparse shadows. "What exactly would this modeling entail? And what's it for, exactly?"

Head still lowered towards the table, Jim raised his eyes, finally looking directly at Günter. "You'd just have to sit or stand for a long time. That's really it. It's for a marble sculpture I'll be crafting for my next exhibit."

Eyebrows practically disappearing into his hairline, Günter regarded Jim with a new level of respect. "You're a professional artist? I mean, I know you said you like to sculpt, but…"

Eva leaned back in her chair until it stood on only two legs, the wood and metal releasing dull creaks as she balanced her weight perfectly. "Ya see that statue there in the corner?" Her head jerked subtly towards the corner of the studio, where a marble statue of what appeared to be a Greek goddess stood. "That's me. As Artemis. I was his test subject, to make sure he could pull off the Classical Greek style."

"I want my next exhibit to be a sort of homage to Classical and Hellenistic Greek art," explained Jim with a smile sneaking onto his lips. "But with a bit of a modern twist, of course. A sort of marriage of the old and the new."

"Like a neo-Renaissance kind of thing?" asked Günter, standing to go inspect the statue.

Jim watched him, eyes alight. "Yes, exactly!"

Lucy was tempted to join him at the statue, even though she'd already seen it many times. There was just something enchanting about the way the figure's hair and tunic flowed along her body as if they'd actually be soft to the touch. It was also incredible how he was so perfectly able to capture Eva's likeness in the mysterious eyes and slightly smirking mouth. Even if it was just a test piece, Lucy thought it was one of the most beautiful statues she'd ever had the privilege of seeing in person. By the awed exclamations emanating from Günter, it seemed he felt the same, which made the smile blossom more fully on Jim's lips.

"Yes, I'm quite beautiful," agreed Eva, letting the chair drop loudly onto all fours. "Time to get back to business, though. We need to read these books *and* try to figure out what the hell was in Lucy's house. Not to mention I've got real homework to do. So, let's get crackin'!"

"Maybe the thing in Lucy's house was a vampire," suggested Jim, who actually seemed to be ready and willing to join the group, at last. He even pulled a book closer, as well as a sheet of paper and a pencil. Perhaps all he needed was to be bribed with a willing model. "I mean, it was gone by daybreak, yeah?"

"Well," Lucy hesitated, but then gave a reluctant nod, "I think so, but…I couldn't really tell." She just didn't think that was what it was, though. For reasons she could not explain, she had the sense that it was something else entirely.

Undeterred by her uncertainty, Jim continued reasoning out that

155

angle. "In any case, it didn't seem to like light." Suddenly he sat bolt upright and leaned closer to her while examining her neck. "Do you have any bite marks? Feel drained or ill?"

With an exasperated sigh, Lucy fell back in her chair and stared at the stark ceiling. "No. Just tired from sleep loss."

"Eva, stay at Lucy's house tonight," Günter commanded as he eventually returned to the table.

His sister looked at him as if he'd just told her to go skinny dipping during a blizzard. "But it's a school night."

"So? I'll talk to Mother and Father, should they take any issue with you staying over there on a school night."

Eva chewed her lip, then gave a determined nod. "Fine. Let's actually get some of this researching done, then call it a day."

***

"Well, I wasn't able to smell or sense anything in the house." Eva pulled the covers back and crawled into the bed beside Lucy. "If it was a vampire, it would have left a lingering stench that I'd be able to detect."

Lucy rolled her head on her pillow towards Eva, watching as her friend got situated. They had done their homework together and had dinner with Lucy's family, and nothing strange had transpired. There had been no flickering lights or moving furniture. By the time they were preparing for bed, Lucy was ready to accept that it had all been in her head. Perhaps she'd just been sleepwalking. Yes, that sounded plausible, even if she'd never done such a thing before in her life.

"In any case," Eva continued, all snug under the covers and smiling with well-feigned bravery, "I'll be here if it shows up again."

Not being an actress like Eva, Lucy didn't even try to hide the fear in her smile. Gratitude shone in it, as well, making Lucy's eyes glisten with the conflicting emotions. "Thank you for doing this."

All the sharp lines of Eva's smiling face were rounded off, and her mask removed. A genuine smile pressed at her lips and shone in her eyes, but behind that smile peeked a resigned despair. "That's what friends are for, right? I'll always be there when you need me."

Needles pricked at Lucy's chest, making her turn away from Eva to study the steady rotation of the ceiling fan. She could not present the same offer to Eva, she knew. Eva would be around long after Lucy was dead and gone. What was that like, Lucy wondered, to know that you'd outlive all your friends? What had it been like for Eva's father, watching nations rise and fall through ageless eyes? Lucy thought she might hate it and all the pain that would accompany it. Even though vampire stories had been inaccurate about most things, she felt perhaps they'd gotten the parts about envying mortals right. Immortality seemed so lonely and sad.

*

"Everything changes."

A man sat at a scarred wooden table, an oil lamp his only light. The rest of the room—of the world—was a grainy, sepia-toned rendering of a rock-walled hovel. Lucy walked up to him, watching as he scratched leisurely at the parchment in front of him with his quill. His lanky black hair was pulled back messily, wisps of it falling around his face like a tattered veil.

"Death is change."

As soon as she reached the table, he looked up at her. Ever-shifting, his face was an indistinguishable blur. The quill kept moving, kept writing out messy lines of foreign text, but he no longer seemed to be paying attention to the actions of his own hand. Standing this close, Lucy saw that some of the scars on the table were actually crude carvings scratched into the wood by a knife. They looked like stretched-out animals, tying themselves together into elaborate knots.

"It only hurts if you forget."

She looked at him in confusion, tried to focus on his shifting eyes. Perhaps she knew him, she thought, but she'd only know if she could make out his features. "Forget?"

"Forget that nothing lasts forever."

"Some things do," she objected.

He laughed, and it echoed in the darkness until it became someone else's voice. "Nothing does. Not even gods."

The oil lamp snuffed out, plunging them into nothingness. She called out for him, but he did not answer. Spinning around in a panic, Lucy scanned the void for something—anything. There! A small speck of light, a star, winked at her. She walked towards it, and the speck grew into a flame.

It was just a small flame, eating away at a match head as it was moved by some unseen hand. A wick was lit and the match shaken until the fire died. The candle cast more of a glow, illuminating the figure of a man as he lowered something towards the flame. Suddenly the light was manipulated into casting the image of a grinning face against the darkness.

Lucy stared at the jack-o-lantern with a foreboding she didn't understand. The carved face stared back at her with its fiery eyes and flickering grin.

"Do you like it?" asked a whispery male voice. "I made it myself."

"It's not Halloween yet. It'll rot by then."

"Not for Hallow's Eve. For the people. For my brothers and sisters, and all my friends." The voice was calm, almost gentle, and snake-hiss faint.

"A pumpkin?"

"No. It's not a pumpkin."

"Yes, it is. I can see it."

"You don't know what you see."

She did, though. It was a carved pumpkin. Anyone would be able to tell that. Never mind, that wasn't important. What *was* important was... "Who are you?"

"It was common once, you know. It wasn't so strange. Well," a chuckle, "at least it wasn't so shocking."

Lucy stepped back, away from the light. Something wasn't right. She shouldn't be there. She had to find some way out of there, but there was only empty space. No, not empty; there were things out there, lurking. Waiting. Waiting for her to move blindly towards them. "Who are you?" she asked again.

"The Magician's Hand."

"The—"

"But I'm not the one you want."

Off to the side a grin appeared, floating in the darkness like the Cheshire Cat's. Obviously able to see her take notice, the grin stretched wider—impossibly wider. Beside it, another smile cut through the darkness, followed soon by another, then another. Countless unseen figures were grinning at her, surrounding her on every side. That's when the laughter started.

As many voices as there were hovering mouths began to laugh and guffaw and giggle. They melted together, bounced off each other, and tried to outdo one another. It was too much for Lucy, and she pressed her hands to her ears in a futile attempt to block them out.

Even though she was surrounded, she tried to run. The ground beneath her was slick, however, so she only made it a few steps before she slipped and lurched forward. As she fell, her stomach clenched, and she feared that she was falling into some infinite abyss. The hard floor met her quicker than she had anticipated, her hands and knees striking it with loud smacks. Her hands started to slide on the wet floor, and she hurried into a sitting position before she fell on her face.

The lights flicked on, illuminating a large room that made Lucy feel as though she were inside a chamber of the heart. Red glistened wet and sticky from the walls, ceiling, and floor. All of the grins remained, their owners revealed as nothing more than heads on sticks. The dead, vacant eyes gazed ahead blindly, though she was certain some were turned to lock onto her.

*

"Lucy!" someone hissed.

She opened her eyes and saw Eva's concerned face looking down at her. Seeing that Lucy was awake, Eva turned her eyes away, staring towards the door.

Keeping her voice low, Eva tried to explain the situation. "I woke up, feeling that something was wrong. There was…a thing…on your chest."

"A thing?" Lucy sat up with a start, pulling her legs protectively towards her chest. "What kind of thing? Is it gone?"

Eva shook her head, still looking at the door, which Lucy just noticed as being ajar. "I growled at it, and it fled. I don't know if it's totally left, though."

"What was it?" Lucy repeated. "What did it look like?"

Perhaps it was just a trick of the nightlight in the hall, but Eva's eyes looked golden, their pupils reflecting an iridescent copper. "I don't know. It was...I don't know. For a second, I thought it was a person."

"What?"

Again Eva shook her head, closing those glowing eyes as she tried to remember. "Wasn't. It was bent...oddly. Hunched over and gnarled. But its face...looked almost human."

Lucy whimpered and hugged her knees. "Why is it here? What was it doing?" she wondered aloud, knowing that Eva had no more of the answers than she did.

Opening her eyes, Eva looked at Lucy. Gold slowly dulled into the usual mixture of light brown and green. "It was just sitting there. I honestly have no idea, Lucy." Eva seemed scared, which heightened Lucy's own fear.

Eva slid out of bed, the soft creak of springs sounding too loud in the silent house. "I'm going to look around." Eyes once again an unnatural gold, Eva looked at Lucy in question. "Do you want to come, or stay here?"

What a choice! Stay and be without help should the *thing* return, or snoop around in search of the thing while in the company of someone who *might* be able to fight it. Feeling her throat clench, Lucy forced herself to get out of the bed. "I'll go with you."

Nodding, Eva padded softly to the door and peeked through the gap. Without looking away from the hall, Eva motioned for Lucy to follow. They both slunk out into the hall, looking everywhere and seeing not even a shadow out of place. "Downstairs," Eva mouthed, and Lucy nodded in understanding.

The stairs made a few groans beneath their feet, and Lucy clung to the sleeve of Eva's T-shirt. They were able to make it to the foyer without incident, but Eva held out her arm to still any move Lucy might attempt. After scanning the darkness with her predator eyes, Eva slowly stepped towards the door. She kept her back pressed close to the wall, so Lucy followed suit.

"Should I turn on the light?" Lucy whispered near Eva's ear. The shape-shifter shook her head in reply, and nodded towards the door. "It's out *there*?" More whispering, and Lucy prayed that Eva was the only one to hear.

Again Eva shook her head, then angled it back towards Lucy while keeping her eyes on the door's decorative window. "Something else."

"What!" That whisper had perhaps been a touch too loud, and Lucy cringed at her own folly. In a quieter voice she asked, "What about the first thing?"

Eva shrugged and cautiously advanced closer to the door. "Can't sense it. Don't hear, smell, or see it. It's as if it just…vanished."

"And this other thing?"

Shifting so that it would be easier for her to see out of the window, Eva tried to stay out of sight of whatever was out there. "Heard it. Then saw it moving."

"How do you know it's not human? Could just be someone out for a walk."

The streetlight filtering through the window was reflected back by Eva's eyes. "Because. It's coming this way. With purpose. And…"

Lucy drew closer, stretching the fabric in Eva's sleeve with her grip, and tried to peek out the window. "And?"

"And it's making the hairs on my arms and back of my neck stand on end."

In the faint light, Lucy was able to see that Eva was right, which resulted in her own body reacting similarly. "You don't know what it is?"

"No." Eva's body suddenly became impossibly more tense.

162

"But it's spotted me watching it."

Again Lucy tried to peek through the window to see what Eva was seeing. The streetlight outside her house flickered, and she thought she saw a dark figure that was about the height of a man. It stood in the center of the street, looking like a shadow cast upon an invisible wall.

Suddenly the upstairs lights came on, making the glass slightly reflective. The shadow form had to compete with the ghostly images of Lucy and Eva to be seen.

"What are you girls doing?" Diana rarely got mad. Even in that moment, she sounded more confused and concerned than she did angry.

On reflex, Lucy turned away from the vigil in order to face her mother. Eva, on the other hand, pressed closer to the glass to get a better view. Diana walked down the stairs, looking between them as she awaited an explanation.

"Someone was outside," said Eva, finally turning away from the window. "I think he was trying to break in or something."

Lucy and Diana both looked at her in shock. "Should I call the police?" Diana asked.

Eva seemed to consider it for a moment before shaking her head. "I think it scared him off to see that someone was up and moving about."

"You sure?" Diana walked over to the door and peered out through its window, cupping her hands between the glass and her face to block out the interior light.

"Yeah. Besides, it's not like he was in the process of breaking in. We can't call the cops on someone without just cause. I could have been wrong; he could have just been going for a walk."

Diana looked at her, grey eyes studying hazel as best they could in the poor light. "You woke up and decided to walk downstairs, and then just happened to see someone pass the window?" It was obvious in her tone that Diana was starting to grow skeptical of their story.

Eva didn't even twitch. "No. I heard a noise. I thought I'd check it out, and ended up waking Lucy when I got out of bed. So, we both headed downstairs to make sure it was nothing. That's when I heard someone outside, so went to the window to check. It looked like there was someone casing your house—walking around, checking to make sure everyone was sleeping, checking to see if you have a security system, that kind of thing."

It seemed that Eva had woven a believable enough story, and Diana once again looked outside with worried eyes. "God, I wish Walt were here," Lucy heard her mother whisper, and knew she wasn't meant to catch it.

"Leave a light or two on to help make it look like someone's still up, and it should be fine," Eva assured.

Diana nodded distractedly and shooed them back to bed. As they ascended the stairs, Lucy glanced over her shoulder to find Diana still gazing out into the night.

"You sure it's gone?" she asked Eva once they were back in her room.

"It ran away, but that might mean anything." Eva moved to the window and scanned the deserted street below.

A dog howled from not far off, which Lucy thought nothing of until she saw Eva's reaction. Cupping her hands over her lips, Eva made a strange, choked-off sound and jerked away from the window. Slowly, she lowered her hands, her jaw clenched tight.

Lucy rushed to her side, but stopped just short of touching Eva, unsure as to whether or not it would be safe or welcome to do so. "You okay?" she asked, hand hovering helplessly beside Eva's shoulder.

A nod answered her inquiry, and Eva tried relaxing her jaw enough to speak. "Sorry," she eventually gritted out, again moving to the window. Her eyes had a wild urgency about them as they searched the neighborhood. "That's never happened to me before." Sharp teeth gleamed in the moonlight as she spoke, and her eyes looked distinctly lupine, not just tinted yellow. Lucy even thought she heard a slight growl to Eva's voice.

"What happened?"

Those feral eyes glanced Lucy's way before continuing their fruitless search. "That howl...I started to... It made me involuntarily start to reply. I couldn't control it."

"Was it another werewolf?" Had that been what was in her house last night? How could a werewolf have gotten in and moved about so quietly, however? More importantly: *why*?

"No." Eva shook her head in emphasis, firmly rejecting Lucy's budding theory. "Werewolves have never made me react that way. This thing's different."

"How can you tell?" Lucy wrapped her arms around herself, suddenly feeling very cold.

Finally giving up her search, Eva turned away from the window. "I just can." Her tongue ran along her teeth, and she seemed to just realize that she had partially transformed. A faint furrow came to Eva's brow, and her eyes and teeth slowly reverted back to normal.

"You see," she continued, meeting Lucy's eyes without shame, "werewolves can really only transform, and that's it. This—whatever it is—can obviously do more. It's something else, something powerful."

She was only trembling because of the chilly night, Lucy told herself. "Am I— Is my family in danger?"

Eva dropped her gaze as she thought about it, and every second which ticked by with her continued silence wound the coil of fear tighter in Lucy. "I can't say for sure about that, but that howl didn't sound angry or hostile," was the eventual response. The corners of

Eva's eyes tensed as she continued to stare down into middle space. "It was…sad. Really, really sad."

# Chapter 11
## Cats and Black Dogs

World Street antique book store was hardly much to look at from the outside. It was tucked into the left corner of a dead strip mall, all of the other businesses long having closed shop. Well, to be fair, there seemed to be a café three doors down, but it didn't even sport a name. Speaking of names, the final "T" in the book store's sign was hanging precariously to its side, as if a strong wind would be enough to send it to its doom.

Günter frowned at the shop's façade and checked the business card in his hand again, as if it would magically change its address. "This is the place," he announced flatly, tucking the card into his pocket.

"Czar owns a bookshop?" Lucy asked, both confused and intrigued by such a discovery.

"Would appear so, yes."

Eva darted off to make a quick check of the area, but there wasn't much else to be seen. A rundown Mexican restaurant was across the street, advertising one dollar taco specials for lunch. To the right of the strip mall stood a dirty gas station, plastic bags over all of the pump handles except one. That was pretty much it, aside from some unmarked buildings that may be offices or warehouses. It was a strange, quiet little pocket just off of Buford Highway, somewhere between Duluth and Sugar Hill. Eva returned from her perimeter check with a silent nod to suggest the all clear.

"Well, the place looks sufficiently creepy. Sure they have lots of fun hunting ghosts around here," said Jim with a sarcastic grin.

"Looks to me like the only ghosts around here are people's dead dreams."

"How poetic, Lucy!" Jim's jesting praise drew a laugh from Lucy's throat as they all advanced on the decrepit shop.

Nothing prepared them for what they would find inside.

Sharply contrasting its exterior, the inside of the shop was clean and well-maintained. The hunter green carpet and dark wood shelves spoke understated elegance, and gave the impression of having stepped into a rich lord's private library. Rows upon rows of shelves trailed off to the right, no doubt occupying what had previously been other shops. There seemed to be a break in the rows, where a large open area housed wingback chairs, couches, and tables. The very corner of a counter was also visible, and Lucy assumed that was the café.

"Welcome!" The voice was Carmen's, but her cheery tone shocked them all as they swung around to find her among the looming shelves. She had been smiling pleasantly, but it instantly drained away when she saw who they were. "Oh. You." Dismissing them with her eyes, she turned to a book cart beside her and began stocking the shelves. "Czar is dealing with cataloging the newest arrivals, and Phil is busy in the back with non-book-related business. Montenegro's working as barista, so you guys can go get coffee or something while you wait."

The four of them exchanged a look, but then shrugged and moved towards the area with the café.

Montenegro's black eyes drifted over them, settling on Eva and anchoring. Whether he was recognizing her as their leader, or merely showing her elevated respect for being a good archer, Lucy couldn't tell.

"Reporting for duty," Eva announced, giving a little salute. She leaned on the counter, sparing a second's glance at the menu. "Also, we have a bit of a problem."

"What's wrong?" he asked, not one to waste words on small talk.

"There're two creatures we cannot identify, both of which have infiltrated Lucy's house."

The muscles around his eyes tensed, and he moved closer. "Describe them."

So, she did, giving him as much detail as she could for the bent little thing on Lucy's chest and the phantom man with the mournful howl. When she was finished, Montenegro was frowning.

He glanced towards the door just as a couple of cars pulled into the lot. "It's nearly time for the regulars to start arriving," he said, eyes following the cars through the windows. "We shouldn't talk about this here."

He pulled a phone from its wall mount and punched a few keys. After a short pause, he was talking with Czar on the other end of the line. "The greenies are here," Montenegro informed him, "and you will be quite interested in what they have to say, I think." There was another brief pause while Czar responded.

Little chimes announced that people had entered the café, and Lucy turned her head to watch them. Six people of about college age or older were filing in, four of them women. They were chattering with animated hand gestures and happy laughter.

"Czar wants you to meet him in the back. Phil will be out in a moment to show you the way." The phone was replaced on its cradle, and Montenegro went about making lattes with a silence that killed any thoughts of continuing the discussion. As he finished each drink, he set it on the counter, and the college kids collected them with such an air of familiarity that no words needed to be exchanged.

"Make one for me, while you're at it." Phil's voice preceded him as he made his way out of the labyrinth of shelves. "Hey, kids!"

Lucy had opened her mouth to respond, before she realized the greeting had been directed towards the customers. A pony-tailed brunette with red-rimmed glasses squealed excitedly and abandoned her drink for the sake of embracing Phil. Laughing, he hugged her back and rocked them side-to-side. "Margot, my dear! Back from Crete so soon?"

Margot pulled back from the hug but kept an arm around his waist. "Next time, I'm taking you with me."

With another laugh, Phil slid out of her reach and moved towards Lucy's group. "It's not time for me to go back, just yet." Smile not quite reaching his eyes, Phil leaned on the counter beside Eva and accepted his coffee from Montenegro. Since it was the first time seeing him so close, and with them all standing, Lucy realized Phil was actually rather short. He didn't seem to be much more than an inch or two taller than Lucy, who stood just shy of five foot five in her flat-soled tennis shoes.

After taking a loud slurp of his coffee, Phil turned to again face everyone. "Would love to stay and chat, but I've got to take these guys to Czar." He motioned towards Lucy and the others with his coffee cup while talking to Margot. "Perhaps later you can fill me in on all the details of your time abroad."

"I haven't seen you guys around, before," said Margot, tuning her voice to be higher and sweetly questioning. There was a smile on Margot's lips as she studied the strangers, but Lucy sensed a subtle air of hostility.

Phil pushed off from the counter with his hip and started towards the shelves. "Lucy's Czar's granddaughter," he explained with a nod towards Lucy and a covert wink. "As such, Czar's granting her and her friends a favor by giving them some part-time work." Without pausing in his step, he effectively forestalled any further comments from Margot or any of her friends. Lucy and the others hurried after him, casting silent glances at the college kids.

"American girls can be so clingy," Phil commented as a casual observance once they had moved out of earshot of the café. "No offense," he added with a cheeky grin and pointed glances towards Lucy and Eva.

"Perhaps we are just helplessly drawn to exotic foreign men with interesting accents," quipped Lucy with a cheeky grin of her own.

Phil preened a little as he walked, grin growing. "Ah, yes, I suppose you're right. Americans are suckers for sexy foreign accents. Jim empathizes, I'm sure. Beating them off with a stick, I'll bet." A wink was tossed at Jim, accompanied by a friendly smile that made Phil's tanned face glow warmly in the cold shadows of the bookcases.

"More like stakes," corrected Eva with a snicker, earning her a vengeful shove by Jim. Phil laughed a rich, hearty laugh that worked to soothe all the tensions from the group. Lucy liked Phil; there was something about him that projected a sense of kindness and comfort. Without a doubt, he was probably just as haunted as Carmen and Montenegro, but he seemed to deal with it on a far more advanced level. Just being in his presence made Lucy feel safe.

They went through a heavy door of weathered wood, a small plaque in bronze beside it warning that only employees were allowed beyond that point. It led to a short hallway with burgundy, tight-weave carpet that had been worn nearly bald in certain spots. Four dark wooden doors broke the drab monotony of the faded olive green walls, two on each side of the hallway. At the very end, an exit sign's red light flickered above a reinforced steel door. Phil led them to the second door on the left, which turned out to be Czar's private office.

The old man was sitting at his desk, reading glasses perched on his nose as he examined a very old leather-bound book. He glanced over the silver frames when he heard the visitors arrive, but then went right back to work. Phil motioned for everyone to enter, then followed them in and shut the door. Despite the office being decently large, it was so packed with books and boxes that it felt suffocating and oppressive with so many people. In order to allow the kids more space, Phil moved over to sit on the side of Czar's solid oak desk. Aside from the one Czar sat in, there were no chairs, and the visitors shifted anxiously where they stood.

"Sorry I didn't meetcha at tha door, kids, but we jus' got a new shipment in. Don't you worry none, though; yer trainin' will still be startin' soon. Likely won't get into too much tonight, though." Even as he talked, Czar's eyes remained on the book, examining its spine as he made notes. "Now, Montenegro tells me y'all have some sort of problem needs solvin'?"

"There was something in my house," said Lucy, taking a small step closer to the desk and trying to overcome the irrational nervousness which had come upon her. "Well," she paused and her face contorted into a pained smile, "two somethings."

That worked to get Czar's attention, and he took off his glasses as he turned his eyes to her. "What were they?"

Lucy shrugged, eyes wandering to the antique lamp on his desk, with its stained glass shade in the pattern of leafy branches, and blown glass base that twisted like an old tree. Returning her gaze to his face, haloed by messy hair like frosted fire, she shook her head. "We don't know. Can't even figure where to start, even though we've been tearing through the books you—ah—passed along to us." Which Lucy was itching to ask him about just as much as the creatures in her house. Because, seriously, what the hell did Pulchrum have to do with all of this?

"Have ya tried the Internet?" His question threw them all off, and everyone but Phil stared at him in confusion. Chuckling at their reaction, Czar leaned back in his chair and picked up his #1 Dad hat from the cluttered desk. "Sure it's mostly crap, but there's still enough truth in there sometimes ta at least help ya know what ta look fer." He ran his hand back through his mane and slipped on the cap. "In any case, might as well jus' tell me 'bout the critters."

Again Eva described what she'd seen. Czar and Phil listened with shuttered expressions, absorbing every detail and processing it in the databases of their minds.

Once Eva had finished, Czar heaved a sigh through his nose and shared a look with Phil. "The first thing ain't no big deal," he said. "Sounds ta me like it's jus' a nightmare." As both Eva and Lucy started voicing objections, Czar raised a single hand to call for silence. "By that I mean a *mara*, which means 'mare,' an' is where we even get the term 'nightmare.'" The girls' mouths snapped shut, and Czar smiled a little as he scratched his rough chin and neck. "They're annoyin' little buggers that sit on yer chest an' cause yer dreams ta rot an' turn dark. Also cause sleep paralysis until they get off ya. Other than that, they ain't much harm. Sometimes they go 'way on their own once they get bored with ya."

Lucy thought about having to feel that thing on her chest again, and shuddered. She'd been hoping that Czar would tell them how to get rid of it, or even offer to come and terminate the thing. Certainly she hadn't expected him to brush it off as if it were nothing, and even suggest she simply put up with it for the foreseeable future.

"Tha other thing is a different matter," he said, smile draining away as he leaned forward and rested his elbows on the desk. "I'va a few theories, but..." Czar's eyes stared blankly at his hands on the desk while he thought. "Think you could stakeout the place, Phil?" he asked, expression still introspective.

"I could," agreed Phil with a hesitant nod as he fiddled with the ring on his right hand. "But, if it's not a vamp, the ring won't be of any use."

"Your ring detects vampires?" Jim asked, stepping up beside

173

Lucy to get a better look. "How does one go about obtaining such a thing?"

Phil laughed softly at his phrasing and extended his hand so Jim could get a better look. Lucy leaned in to see, as well, and felt Eva press close on her left while Günter hovered between her and Jim at her right. At first it looked to her to be just a woven gold band, but then he shifted his finger slightly and she saw a face. A screaming Medusa head stared sightlessly up amid an intricate tangle of golden snakes, the serpents slithering around the entire finger in order to form the band.

"Why Medusa?" Lucy asked, mesmerized by the detail of the terrifying face.

"It's a Greek thing, something frequently used to ward away evil and intimidate the enemy." Phil pulled his hand back to look at the face himself. "My—ah—stepfather has a tendency to be a traditionalist." There was a slight laugh to his voice on the word "stepfather," as if he was amused by his own word choice. A private joke played out in his mind, stretching his wide grin.

Holding it so they could again see it, he pointed to the different features on the tiny face. "The eyes will glow when a vamp is nearby, and a Greek letter will appear in her mouth to tell me which kind. As to how to go about obtaining one of your own…" He laughed at another private joke, his eyes never leaving the ring. "I suppose you'll have to go get yourself adopted by a very old and very protective strigoi."

There was a loud, collective inhalation as all four youths readied themselves to speak at once. Czar cut through the stunned pause with his rough voice like a serrated edge. "Take 'em to Branislava. I don't suspect it's a vamp, so yer ring, as ya said, won't do no good. Branka'll be able ta scry or whatever tha hell it is she does. Might still wantcha ta stake out tha place tonight, though, dependin' on what she says."

174

As Czar talked, Phil's face went from laughing eyes to serious professionalism. He nodded at his orders and stood from the desk. When he moved towards the door, everyone started to follow, except for Lucy, who dallied near Czar's desk. The old man stared up at her expectantly, the pupil of his real eye constricting as he studied her. She split her attention between his eyes and the streaks of amber and green light splashed across his leathery face by the close proximity of the lamp.

"Thank you," she eventually said, voice soft and respectful.

A smile softened his weathered face, but it made her feel suddenly and intensely sad. There was a coldness with the sadness. Not an indifference or an emotional coldness, no. There was just a sudden sensation of ice and the prick of frostbite winds. Something must have shown in her face, because Czar's smile had twisted into a confused frown, and his shoulders had become tense. Lucy tried to smile reassuringly, tried to shake her head to convince him—convince her—that it was nothing. Without saying another word, for really she could think of nothing to say, she hurried out to rejoin the others.

They all walked silently through the shop, the forest of books insulating them from the laughter in the café. It wasn't until she was outside that she realized she'd forgotten to ask about Pulchrum.

\*

By the time they were pulling into a driveway behind Phil's Jeep, it was dark. They had gone north, eventually exiting off the interstate in order to take highways and backroads until they were somewhere between Gainesville and Cleveland. The house was the last one on its road, after two lanes had been reduced to one, and pavement became dirt and gravel. It was a rather unimpressive house, looking like so many other rural homes in the area, with its chipping whitewashed boards and screened-in porch. An electric blue hybrid coup was parked outside, with a large black-and-white cat sprawled lazily across the hood.

The screen door wasn't locked, and Phil entered the porch to knock on the front door. Everyone else wandered after him, eyeing the area and wondering what was so special about this Branislava. They didn't have to wait long after knocking before the door was opening to reveal an attractive woman with long, curly brown hair. She wore a wrap-around skirt and a halter top that seemed to be fashioned out of a long scarf.

"The old man called and said you were coming," she said with a tired smile, Caribbean green eyes giving Phil a once-over before darting assessing glances at his company. She had a voice like threadbare velvet, with an accent that sounded almost Russian. "Might as well come in and get this over with." Branislava stepped aside to let them pass, then closed the door before a calico cat could follow. "Which one of you is Lucy?"

"I am." Looking away from her study of the living room and its battered, eclectic furniture, Lucy approached the woman.

"Of course you are. I'm Branislava, but all of you may call me Branka." Her gaze ran over them all again, and Lucy noticed that there were islands of brown flecks in the woman's tropical sea eyes. A faint, seemingly sarcastic smile thinned otherwise full lips, and long, slender fingers brushed back defiant curls. "Not sure if Hayes told you, but I'm a striga."

"You're a vampire?" Jim asked, looking from her to Phil in questioning alarm.

Branka laughed without humor and walked to the coffee table, where a pot of tea and six cups had been set. "No. Strig*a*, not strig*oi*. I'm what you may call a witch, but I implore you not to confuse me

176

with anything like a neo-pagan or Wiccan or the like. Those are humans who like to sometimes try their hands at magic. I am a different creature entirely."

She started pouring tea, then motioned for everyone to have a seat. Jim, Günter, and Eva took the couch; Phil leaned against the wall by a window; and Lucy took one of the arm chairs. "So, you have a mara and something unidentifiable plaguing your home, yes?"

"Yes." Lucy accepted her tea with a nod of thanks. The taste of it reminded her of wet-hot spring days in the woods, with the fresh, sharp scent of broken saplings and the sweet aroma of honeysuckle in full bloom.

"It howls," Eva added, accepting her own tea. "It made me nearly return the howl. And it was the saddest sound I'd ever heard."

Finished passing out tea, Branka was silent as she took a seat in the other arm chair. As she slurped from her own cup, she studied Lucy intently. The weight of the scrutiny was too much for Lucy, and she squirmed awkwardly in her seat. A lump in the cushion beneath her caused her to shift some more until she'd finally found a decently comfortable spot.

Finally Branka looked away, setting her cup down on the ring-stained coffee table. Surprisingly, she switched her attention to Günter, and held out a hand to stop him from taking a sip of his tea. "You won't like it. Just a moment." Her fingers did a little dance, twirling about in the air. As they moved, Günter's tea began to swirl, and then little wisps of golden honey pulled themselves from the liquid. They danced over to Branka's fingers, and she pulled all her digits back except for her index finger, using it to spool the honey. "There," she said with a smirk before sucking the honey from her finger. "Should be fine for you, now."

Günter gaped for a moment, but then seemed to remember his manners, and gave a low nod of thanks. To his right, Eva sipped her tea with laughing eyes. At his left, Jim was setting his untouched cup back down upon the table.

Leaning back in her chair, Branka returned her attention to the matter at hand. "Tell me about yourself, Lucy."

"What do you want to know?" She didn't see why Branka would be interested in her personal life, instead of trying to get more details from Eva about the mystery creature. Perhaps there was a purpose to it, however. Lucy really had no idea how striga magic—or any magic, for that matter—worked. Sliding her tongue along the roof of her mouth, Lucy sought out the taste of honey in her tea.

Branka poured herself more tea, watching amber fluid fill the floral print cup. "Let's start with your family. Whom do you take after most? I've noticed you have quite beautiful eyes—from your mother?"

"Father. Mom's eyes are more of a grey than a blue, and are darker."

There was a kindly smile on Branka's lips before they were obscured by the tea cup. "She must be wise, then. Many with grey eyes are known to be wise."

Pride swelled in Lucy's chest, and she smiled. "She is, yes."

"Your hair," Branka continued, returning to the original line of questioning, "is it also from your father?"

"Yes. Mom's hair is lighter."

"What about your siblings? Are there any, and after whom do they take?"

Again Lucy wondered what this had to do with the creature in her house. She looked around at her friends on the couch, who also seemed confused. Then she looked at Phil, who offered her a reassuring smile and encouraging nod. Hoping all of this really did have a point, Lucy answered the new questions. "Two brothers, one younger and one older. The younger one, Donnie—"

178

"Donnie?"

"Donovan," said Lucy, assuming Branka had been asking for his proper name. "He resembles Mom, but he reminds me more of Dad than any of us."

"How so?"

"His personality, sometimes, which is odd considering Dad died when Donnie was too young to really know him that well."

"I'm sorry for your loss. My father died, and despite it having been many years since his passing, the pain of loss still lingers."

Lucy looked at Branka's face with more of a considering eye. The woman looked to maybe be in her thirties, but Lucy thought it possible she was like Hartmut Kuntz, forever youthful and centuries old.

Lowering her eyes to her own tea, Lucy murmured a thanks in reply to the words of sympathy, even though she never cared for such sentiments. Some may find comfort in learning that others share in their pain, but Lucy just felt like it made things worse. She had no desire to find camaraderie in grief. She also just disliked pity in general. Never once did she ever try to use her father's death as an excuse or as a reason for people to feel sorry for her.

Branka's voice disrupted her thoughts with an expectant "So." Once Lucy had looked back up at her, Branka continued. "How is your Donovan like your father?"

"Oh." Using the tea as a means of stalling, Lucy took a long sip to gather her thoughts. "Well, Dad always had a sense of... melancholy?...about him. Not like he was depressed or anything. It was more like he was distracted or preoccupied by some ever-present concern. Could have just been the stress of opening the store with Mom, and trying to get it to all run smoothly. Don't really know. But, Donnie's like that a lot. I don't know what kinds of concerns a kid his

179

age can really have, but...he'll get the same look in his eyes."

For some reason, this seemed to pique Branka's interest more than anything, and she set her teacup down in order to give Lucy her full attention. "Is he the only one who gets like that? Would you say that he's depressed, perhaps? How about you or the others? Would you say depression was common in your family?"

The hinges in Lucy's jaw slipped loose, and it was difficult to get the thing working again. "Excuse me? What does that have to do with—"

"Could be a Black Dog."

"No." Lucy shook her head. The hinges in her jaw were now suddenly far too tight, and the tension was starting to hurt. "I don't think a dog would have affected Eva the way it did."

Branka's smile suddenly looked strained and slightly annoyed. "Not a dog that is black, child, but a Black Dog. Often can show up right before something horrible happens, but also tends to linger around areas of sadness. Some say they are attracted to the melancholy, some say they cause it." She shrugged, retrieving her cup. "In any case, that could be what we're dealing with."

"What, like that thing in *Harry Potter*? The Grim or whatever?" When all eyes turned questioningly to Günter, he crossed his arms defensively and tried to glare defiantly back. "What? I like that book series, and happen to think some of the movies are pretty good."

"Something like that, yes." Branka's eyes twinkled with amusement, and she took another sip of tea.

Lucy leaned forward, setting her cup down on the table with a dull clink. "How do I get rid of it?"

"Oh. You don't."

Surely Branka had to be joking. So, what, they had all wasted their time asking Czar and Branka about this, since she was just supposed to live with the existence of both mystery creatures? "I don't?"

"No. It will leave on its own."

Groaning, Lucy fell back in her seat and closed her eyes. "That's exactly what Czar said about the mara. I *really* don't want to have to live with these things creeping me out every night."

"He wants you to leave the mara alone?" Now it was Branka's turn to look shocked and confused. Also a little repulsed. "The man is disgusting. No, I will give you incense to keep it away." Curls bobbed and swayed as Branka rose and moved about the room in search of the promised incense. Eventually she returned carrying a long, thin box.

Lucy accepted the box, and opened it to take a whiff of the sticks, smiling at the familiar scents which reminded her of her mother. "Smells good. Like lavender."

"Lavender's used, yes, among other things." Branka must have read the worry in Lucy's eyes, because she waved it away with a tsk. "They're perfectly harmless, I assure you. It's just a combination of things which repulse creatures such as mara, while simultaneously helping you get a good night's sleep."

Lucy chuckled with relief and took in another deep sniff. "You should work with my mom. She makes stuff like this, too, and sells it at her shop."

For the first time, Branka seemed to have a genuine, warm smile. Yes, Lucy could totally see her mother and Branka hanging out together. They seemed cut from the same cloth, even if they were different species. Just as suddenly as it came, however, the smile faded, leaving a twisted half smirk in its wake. Branka moved towards the door, and Phil pushed away from the wall to follow. "It's time to go, now. My favorite show starts soon, and I don't want to miss this episode."

Confused, the kids started to trickle out onto the porch. Günter and Eva softly thanked Branka for her hospitality as they passed, neither one meeting her eyes. Jim gave a nod and flinch of a smile before slipping out to linger near the screen door and speak in low tones with Phil. Before Lucy could cross the threshold, however, Branka stopped her with a touch to her shoulder. There was no way to read the striga's face; no way to decipher the subtle tensions or entrancing eyes. Staring at that face, Lucy wondered if this entire form was nothing but a disguise, masking a more animalistic creature with the face of a beautiful woman.

"Sometime," said Branka quietly, "I want you to come back and tell me what you dreamed."

Lucy nodded, unsure if she'd want to return alone, even if she could find the place again. Thinking Branka was finished, Lucy took a step backwards through the doorway. She was mistaken, however, as the witch continued, her voice pitched softly for only Lucy's ears. "It's possible they meant to warn you of something, or deliver an important message. You must remember everything they showed you, child."

A chill sprinting up her spine, Lucy nodded and quickly stepped fully onto the porch. The others had been waiting, watching the exchange along with several cats that perched on the rotting deck furniture. Phil looked at her, his smile seeming so suddenly fake that it filled Lucy with disgust. It was like seeing his smiles for the first time as they truly were, though she sincerely hoped she was wrong.

Branka's voice drew her attention away from Phil's false smile, and she politely faced the witch as she spoke. Again Branka's voice was quiet and private. "The information you need will be found in the book written by Yaxley. Chapters five, thirteen, and twenty should be most beneficial."

Lucy's lips parted, but Eva's voice was the first to be heard on

182

that rickety little porch. "About vamps?" No one seemed to feel the need to question how Branka even knew of their research books, let alone any of the authors.

The striga looked straight at Eva, her lips caught between a smirk and a frown. "About useful things. There are other chapters which will be good for you, as well, but I'm seeing those numbers as brightest."

"Good to knooooow," Jim said cautiously, edging surreptitiously towards the door.

Phil merely grinned wider, and slapped Jim on the shoulder with a laugh. "Thanks for your help, Branka. These kids are still learning the ropes, you see."

Her eyes gleamed with amusement as she studied Jim, even while addressing Phil. "I know. They barely have any blood on their hands, yet. That will change very soon, however."

"Great!" Seemingly delighted, Phil cast everyone an approving look. "Anyway, that's it for tonight. Come by the shop Friday, and we'll get you started in actual training. You guys alright with finding your way home?" he asked, turning away from Jim and opening the screen door. That conversation, evidently, was officially finished. Never mind that Lucy was still trying to make sense of everything.

Günter assured him that they'd be fine, thanks to his GPS, so Phil waved and trotted down to his Jeep. The others walked to the SUV with the trudging slowness of dazed minds. Some of the cats—and there seemed to be more of them each passing minute—meandered about their feet, meowing loudly for attention. One of the cats jumped into the SUV when Eva opened the door, and she had to shoo it out. The others were then more careful getting in, keeping the cats at bay with their feet.

"I'll read up on strigas tonight," Eva announced, once they were on paved road again.

"Good idea," agreed Lucy, even as she clutched her box. "I mean, I know Czar seems to trust her and all, but…she's kind of…"

"Creepy," Jim supplied. "She's creepy."

"Honestly, we'll probably have to be cautious about whom we trust, from now on," Günter pointed out, his voice trying to sound hard-edged, but coming off as depressingly bleak. "We've chosen dangerous roles in a dangerous world."

# Chapter 12
## Each a Role to Fill

Phil was waiting for them beside the door when they next visited World Street, and he greeted them with his friendly smile. Few words were exchanged as he led them to the back rooms, and they caught a glimpse of Montenegro stocking books as they passed by the dark alleyways of shelves.

Instead of taking them to Czar's office, Phil led them through one of the doors across the short hall. It opened to another hall, far starker than the previous one. Bald of carpet, the floor was a glossy river of grey that reflected the bluish glare of the naked fluorescent lights. Bare, white walls stretched on for what was likely the entire length of the strip mall, interrupted only occasionally by dark doors on first the left and then eventually also the right, further down towards the end. As they passed each door, Lucy noticed that they were all grey-painted steel with keypads on the handles. She also noticed that each door had a different creature sketched out on its surface in black and white inks. Most looked like people with random animal features—part fish, bird, or dog, for example. One looked like a normal human upon first glance, but its feet were on backwards.

The door they stopped at had the image of an old, twisted man with hands like claws and a murderous grimace. His hat looked heavy and wet, little trails of moisture sketched out across his wrinkled forehead in black ink. In his left hand he held some type of jagged spear. Lucy had to stiffen her spine to prevent a shudder, and was grateful when Phil stepped between her and the image in order to key open the door.

Inside was a large box of a room, housing a round table at its center that could seat eight. Along the bottom of every wall stretched fully-stocked book shelves and filing cabinets of various colors. Above those, taking up nearly every spare inch of wall, were maps. They ranged from world maps to local street maps. Some dotted with pins, others checkered with sticky notes.

When Czar spotted them, he rose from his seat at the table that was blanketed with clusters of papers. "Welcome to the War Room, ladies and gentlemen." There was a grim smile on his scarred face, and his baseball cap cast sharp shadows over his eyes.

The time for their training was at hand.

He started them off in the same manner they'd already begun: research. It was imperative, he stressed, that they know the creatures they were going to face, that they understood their weaknesses and strengths. No amount of combat training would prepare them if they simply ran into a situation blindly, as they had before. Plus, more often than not, they would have to deal with supernaturals in a civil capacity, and so should learn about them in an effort not to offend. Czar provided them with more books and even some pamphlets, but Lucy kept privately going back to the book Branka had specifically mentioned.

Since they were just starting out in the Gehealdan, they were given the lowest-ranking job: executioners. They were to quietly terminate and dispose of Treaty breakers, much like Czar's team had done to the vampire in their initial meeting. Czar explained that at first he'd give them easy cases, where they already knew the location and identity of the guilty. Even so, he expected them to know everything possible about the type of supernatural they were and how they could effectively kill it. Because strigoi were the most common type to be breaking the Treaties in that area, their research would start with learning everything available about that particular supernatural.

The Yaxley book told them (in chapter five, pages 48 through 53) to ignore the ones who were pale; that was something else the

186

movies lied about. Instead, look for the ones with a rosy complexion, as if they had just run a mile or were suffering from sunburn. Those who wore lots of perfume or cologne were also potential vampires in disguise, trying to mask the scent of decay. The book said that strigoi have hoofed feet, so it was safe to rule out anyone who was barefoot or in sandals. Not that detection was really a necessity for them, because Czar insisted they were only going to be sent to deal with confirmed strigoi at the location of their graves. Still, it was good to know for future reference, if they were ever upgraded in their duties.

Lucy was only able to get a brief look at chapter thirteen, but it seemed to be about some type of creature that caused eclipses by eating the sun and moon. It wasn't relevant to what they needed, so she decided not to worry about it for the moment. Focusing purely on the strigoi chapter, Lucy didn't even bother to look at chapter twenty.

Once they got the technicalities of how to identify one down pat, they had to focus on methods of killing the thing. Czar explained that the best recourse was to locate where it slept, its grave, and to return on a Saturday evening in order to kill it. For some reason, strigoi could not rise on Saturdays (Yaxley 52). Since it couldn't rise, they also didn't have to worry about fighting it, which was something Czar thought they were far from ready to do. They were to strike in the evening only because they needed to rely upon the shroud of night to hide their actions. After all, it wasn't exactly acceptable behavior to dig up graves and cut away at corpses.

"You only execute the ones we tell ya to," Czar said firmly. "There're plenty Romes ain't done a thing wrong, an' we need ta leave 'em be. Eventually, you'll be learnin' 'bout how the Gehealdan system works. Such as nons registerin', and all tha laws laid down by the Treaties. Ultimately, it's up ta us to maintain tha secrecy of the nons and the sanctity of their Treaties. We ain't jus' some blood-thirsty killers

187

huntin' down nons for sport, ya see."

"Nons?" asked Jim.

"Non-humans," Czar explained, with a nod to Eva and Günter.

Lucy wasn't sure she liked that term. It seemed...pejorative. At the very least, it certainly lacked the hint of respect that came with calling them "supernaturals." It seemed to be one of the slang terms used by the Gehealdan members, though, like *Rome* and *freshy*.

When it seemed the new recruits had had their fill of books, Czar took them down the hall to a room with a dancing, armored bird creature on its door. There, he showed them the tools they'd need to "execute the guilty."

*\*\*\**

On the first Saturday evening of October, Czar sent them on their first execution. They'd been given a file with a photo of a man with wavy blond hair and a smile that could turn heads. Sawyer Jackson, his file said, human from 1949-1995, strigoi from 1995-present. Evidently he had died at the age of forty-six, and yet he had seemed no older than twenty-one in the supernatural registration photo.

"What was his crime?" Eva had asked.

Czar had stared her down and simply said, "He broke one of the Treaties. That's all ya need to know."

"What rule do you suppose he broke?," Lucy asked later, perched at the edge of the pit which was formerly Jackson's grave plot.

Jim nearly hit her with a large helping of dirt as he shoveled it out of the hole. "Shouldn't you be tending the fire?"

Scooting over a few inches, away from the freshly-tossed mound of dirt, Lucy brushed at her pants and shoes to make sure they hadn't been hit. "It's ready. I'm just waiting for you guys."

Suddenly there was a loud thunk, and Günter let out a victorious laugh. "Won't have to wait too much longer!"

"Finally!" exclaimed Jim. "Christ! I did *not* sign up to perform hard labor. Pity they use some sort of weird vampire hoo-doo to get out of their graves without disturbing the soil, because it would certainly come in handy if the ground was already softened up for us."

The shoveling went faster, accompanied by banging and scratching sounds as they unearthed the coffin.

"Would you rather be fighting the thing, instead? Lucy, pass me the axe."

Lucy scrambled to oblige while Jim pulled himself from the pit. "No," said Jim, crouching beside the discarded shovels. "This does seem to be the slightly more preferable choice, thus far. Let's hope ol' Mr. Jackson here doesn't wake-up. Otherwise, we'll still have to fight a vampire, on top of having dug a six foot plot."

Günter swung the axe repeatedly, a loud bang resounding through the graveyard with each moment of contact. Sitting further from the edge than she'd been, Lucy turned her attention skywards. She could just make out the shape of a large bird circling overhead in the inky sky. Leaning back on one arm, she waved at the figure. A piercing hawk cry responded, and she smiled.

"Bingo!"

At Günter's yell, Lucy and Jim leaned over the edges enough to see into the grave. A man lay in the coffin, turned on his side as if sleeping. For having been dead for so long, he looked in astonishingly good health.

Günter set the axe on the ground beside Lucy and called for his bag of medical tools. She quickly fetched it, pulling the disposable scrubs from it and passing them over. Once Günter had donned them, thus protecting his clothes from any of the creature's blood, Lucy began

189

passing him instruments as if she were an OR nurse. At first she tried not to look at what he was doing, but morbid curiosity took over, and she tilted her head to see over his shoulder.

The scene reminded her of operations she'd seen on hospital shows, except the conditions here were far from sterile. Splinters of wood and clumps of soil surrounded the body and tangled in matted blond hair. Günter had opened its chest, and blood was flowing thick and black over the dirty cloth interior of the coffin. As he cut out the heart, bright red blood sprayed like a small fountain from the still-pulsing organ, causing Lucy and Jim to jerk back in alarm. Günter cursed and scrambled out of the pit with one hand, the other clutching the bleeding heart.

"He must have eaten somewhat recently," Günter said as he hurried to the burn disk and carved up pieces of the heart to drop into the awaiting flames. "There was fresh blood."

A thumping sound arose from the pit, and Lucy and Jim looked back in to find the vampire convulsing. Blood was gurgling up through its mouth and trickling uselessly from severed veins into the cavity of its chest. Lucy made herself watch, made herself fully witness the death throes of what would be the first of many. *You chose to do this*, a voice in her head said, something similar to her own but with a harder edge. *You've no right to look away.*

Jim watched until he could take no more. Turning his face away, he looked towards Günter and the fire. "Do you think destroying the heart will be enough?" he asked.

Günter turned towards him, his mind calculating and considering. "Most of the sources said it would be enough."

"But Czar said the strigoi is able to regenerate if even a tiny piece of it was not destroyed," Lucy reminded, still watching the vampire, which had gone still.

190

"Might have just been a particular variation which did that." Jim didn't seem to care for the idea of burning the entire body, and Lucy couldn't say she blamed him.

"Yeah," said Lucy, "strigoi." Would she be able to hack a human body to pieces, she wondered. *Don't think of it as a human*, that voice explained gently. *Remember when you carved that roast chicken? This is no different. It's an animal, and it's already dead.*

Before she could change her mind, Lucy pulled another set of disposable scrubs from Günter's bag and quickly tugged them on over her black T-shirt and black denim pants. Jim called out to her, asking what she was doing, but she barely heard him over the sudden roaring in her ears. Adrenaline, she knew was the cause—adrenaline and fear.

Climbing down into the pit, she ignored Jim's questioning voice and the slight tremble of her hands as they reached up to grab the axe's handle. It was heavier than she'd anticipated, and her shoulders flinched painfully when she raised the axe too quickly. She ignored that, too, and swung the tool down with all her might. Somehow she had managed to accurately hit the shoulder joint on the vampire's right side, cleanly cleaving it off from the torso. The blade stuck a bit in the bottom of the coffin, and Lucy grunted as she jerked it free.

Above her, Jim was cursing, and had pulled himself farther away from the pit. She figured he was afraid of getting blood splattered on him, so she continued ignoring him in order to focus on her task.

Lift the axe, aim, swing, repeat. At certain points, she had to shift the body by nudging it with the axe head in order to get a better angle. *It isn't human.* Her arms ached with the vibrations from striking bone and wood. *It's already dead.* She missed a joint and the long bones splintered and cracked, her clumsy attempts crushing the area to a messy pulp. *It isn't human!* The head rolled to the side once freed, getting tangled in sticky wet hair.

191

Eventually, the litany in her mind faded away like the receding tide, and her pale eyes surveyed her handiwork with clinical detachment. Yes, she supposed it was in small enough pieces. After putting the axe back up onto the grass, she proceeded to toss the vampire up, piece by piece, out of the pit. Even through the gloves, the flesh felt slippery and softly yielding. Sometimes it was difficult keeping hold of the pieces, and they tried to slither back down to the coffin before she could toss them. When she could find no more bits, not even a tiny chunk of flesh, she carefully pulled herself up. It certainly wasn't easy as the ground crumbled away and she slipped a little on all the blood despite the tread of her boots.

Across the pit, Jim was staring at her with wide eyes, the whites of them nearly glowing in the flickering light of the fire. That's when she realized that it wasn't the blood which had frightened him. There was no time to worry about that, however.

Looking away from him—but not in shame! She had no reason to be ashamed!—Lucy started picking up body parts to take to the fire. Tanned arms moved alongside her pale ones, and she looked up to find Günter crouching beside her, his face shuttered and his eyes on the pile of flesh. Together they moved all of the pieces, taking several trips before the pile was gone. The burn disk Czar had given them was large, and they managed to get all of the pieces into its flames. Vampire flesh burned like dry kindling, Czar had said, and he was right. Lucy had worried that the wet flesh would smother the flames, but it only drove them hotter and higher.

No one talked while the two of them worked. At some point, Jim had risen to his feet and began refilling the pit. The rhythmic sound of his shoveling helped to soothe Lucy's erratic pulse. By the time all of the pieces had been put into the fire, she was no longer trembling.

She and Günter removed their scrubs, tossing them and their

gloves into the fire. Her nerves returning to normal, Lucy was able to feel the sticky wetness on her face, but Günter grabbed her wrist before she could touch it. He let her go in order to fetch the bottle of cheap red wine they'd brought, uncorking it as he returned. He also brought the roll of paper towels, tucked under an arm to free his hands. Once the bottle was open, he pulled some of the paper towels off and wet them.

"Here," he murmured, rich voice comforting, just as he'd been with Jim that first, failed hunt. Lucy let his warmth and voice wrap around her like a blanket as he ran the wet paper towels gently along her face. "Hold out your hands." She did, letting him wash them with wine. When he was done, he handed her some more wine-dyed towels. "For your shoes."

She took them and looked down at her boots. The firelight caught the blood on them, lending the impression that the boots themselves were nothing more than masses of congealing gore. Carefully pulling up at her pant legs, she bent down to cleanse the worn leather.

Günter cleaned himself off as best he could, tossing the paper into the fire when he was done. He then joined Jim, and the soft hissing chinks of two shovels echoed in the graveyard. A shadow-black and moon-grey church watched them work from across the small expanse of headstones, its many eyes gleaming predatorily with reflected moonlight.

Finished with her shoes, Lucy tossed her paper towels into the flames. Bones were cracking open inside the blinding radiance, and their sounds reminded her of popping logs in a campfire. It stank, like it did when they'd witnessed Czar's team take out the other vampire. She walked over to her duffel bag and retrieved the bag of cedar chips they'd brought.

Those managed to improve the smell, so she remained by the

193

fire while the boys worked. There was another crack, and the mass within the flames shifted, revealing a blackened skull. It stared up at her, grinning cruelly. For an animal, its skeleton looked so very human.

Was that what her father's bones had looked like, when the accident happened? So little was left of him, the car hardly more than scraps of twisted metal and burnt rubber.

Her throat clenching was the only warning before the hot tears began to roll down her wine-scented cheeks. There was no need to cry; it was all over. She'd done well, hadn't she? There had been nothing wrong with her actions. They were necessary.

Closing her eyes against the sight of the burning skull, she saw the terrified face of Jim projected on the inside of her eyelids. There was no reason for such an expression! It wasn't like she had murdered the thing! All she had done was carve it, like a giant chicken. Besides, the thing wasn't even human!

So caught up in her thoughts as she was, Lucy didn't even notice when the shoveling stopped. A hand touching her shoulder startled her, and she opened her eyes to see Jim's profile as he watched the fire. "You okay?" he asked in a half whisper.

"Yeah." She was disappointed to hear a hitch in her voice. Her disappointment grew when she felt the floodgates release and the breath convulse in her lungs.

When Jim looked at her, there was no sign of fear, only pity, which for some reason made her cry harder. Without saying a word, he pulled her into his arms and let her cry into his shirt. Hands stained with blood and wine clutched at him, chipped black-lacquered nails biting at his skin through his shirt fabric. No protest or cry of pain issued from his throat; he merely tightened his embrace and gave her the stability she so desperately needed. He didn't let go until she'd finished crying, and she didn't stop crying until the fire ran out of fuel and choked itself to death.

When they parted, the area was dark and still, except for the crickets and the whispering trees. Günter released an avian screech, head tossed back. A similar cry replied from somewhere in the darkness above, followed immediately by the loud flapping of large wings. Eva swooped down, landing across the burn disk from Lucy and Jim. In the faint orange glow of the embers, Lucy could just make out the shape of a large bird standing Eva's height, her hawk beak sleek and sharp, and the moonlight bouncing off her golden eyes. Rough, taloned hands reached out and gripped the side handles of the disk, lifting it effortlessly from its stand. The tengu's massive wings slapped at the air, and she was airborne once more.

Once the ashes were dumped into a nearby stream, she'd return to take her human form and get dressed. Eva had less concern about modesty when she was confident it would only be the four of them. Plus, she and Günter had argued over who would dig and who would serve as sentinel, and Eva had come to the conclusion that she'd rather fly around naked than shovel dirt.

The other three went about loading everything into the SUV. No one felt much like conversing, the situation pressing down on them with a practically tangible weight. When they had everything loaded, Lucy took a flashlight and made a final sweep to be certain. On her way back, she shone the light on Jackson's gravestone and wondered with a new, piercing ache if he was someone's father.

\*\*\*

Czar had been pleasantly surprised by Lucy's actions, and for the next execution, Lucy was given a machete and a smaller axe, like the ones Phil and Carmen used. He had also given her the choice to pass them off to Günter. She didn't. She spent her free time that week learning to slice with efficiency, and maintained the blades to keep them perfectly sharp. These weren't people, they were monsters who broke the rules, and she resolved to stop feeling sick and guilty.

Their second execution had gone off without a hitch, and Lucy had only felt slightly shaken once it was over. It had been a woman that time, and she'd bled so much that Günter and Lucy each spent over an hour in the shower afterwards. They had taken to staying at Günter's apartment on kill nights; abandoning the whole tedious camping process in favor of showers and climate control.

She also wondered if the machete could have caused the increase in gore, since it required more whacks in some places in order to get through all of the layers of muscle and meat. Next time, she decided to try switching off between the axe and the machete more, since some parts required the subtle, thin blade of the machete, while others needed the brute force of the heavy axe head.

Their third execution had been an odd one. For the first time, they saw a creature more accurately matching the descriptions from lore. Isaiah Cartwright had hooves instead of feet, a tail, and a face as red as blood. His nose was nearly rotted off, but the overall decay was minimal, despite the tombstone claiming he died in 1816. This was a fully matured vampire, they'd realized, while all of the others had been metaphorical children. Much like Jackson, Cartwright had looked vastly different in his file. He'd looked like a charismatic man with perfect skin and stylishly wind-tossed brown hair.

His flesh and bones burned particularly well.

*The Hollow Sun*

# Chapter 13
## Strangers

The smell of gunpowder still tainted every inhalation, and her hand ached. Walking down the long, stark hallway, she absently massaged her hands together, her eyes flicking to each door she passed. *Ghul, näcken, kappa,* she mentally recited. *Nu...er...* Her mind stumbled over the pronunciation of the Japanese vampire creature with a detachable head. *Nukeku-something...* Her shoulder gave a little twinge, and she rolled it to loosen the tense muscles. Next time she was going to do double the stretching before allowing Eva to throw her around on the practice mats. Even a hot shower hadn't been enough to relieve all the strain from yesterday's training.

Eventually, she stopped in front of the door with the twisted old man. "Redcap," she whispered aloud, studying the streaks of ink and paint so that she wouldn't have to look at his hateful eyes. "Dunter. Powrie."

Achy fingers punched in the key code—one of the few she'd been told, despite even the broom closet there having a keypad.

"-loween, then?" Günter was asking Czar, papers and books spread out in front of them on the table. Across the circle from them sat Eva, who was absorbed in her own notes.

Czar shook his head. "Some nons are affected by different parts of tha year, it's true, an' some even like certain dates fer whatever reason. But, far as I know, Romes don't give a damn 'bout that date. Most don't. I think they just like takin' advantage of all tha ruckus at that time, if anythin'."

The men noticed she was standing there, and turned away from their discussion to greet her with small smiles and smaller nods.

"How'd ya do?" asked Czar, and he actually appeared to be

interested in the results.

Grinning, Lucy rolled her shoulder again. "Hit mostly next to the bullseye, both in the chest and the head. A couple actually hit almost perfectly."

Czar returned her grin, and his voice was warm with approval. "Atta girl."

"Where's Jim?" Günter leaned sideways in his chair, as if trying to see if Jim was somehow hiding behind Lucy. Never mind the fact that she was probably a good head and shoulders shorter than Jim was.

"His aim was still pretty off, so Phil kept him to run through the exercises again."

Günter frowned at this news and rose to his feet. "I should probably go and…ah…see if I can help out or anything."

There was a snort from the other side of the table, but a glance at Eva only found her deeply engrossed in her reading. Ignoring his sister and the annoyed expression on Czar's face, Günter pushed past Lucy and headed down towards the shooting range at the end of the hall.

"Boy needs ta focus," she heard the old man grumble. "Anyway, Lucy, you go over there with Eva an' start reviewin' tha organizations an' such." A smirk drew his features out from their dour shadows. "Y'all will, o' course, be tested on it."

Lucy groaned, even as she made her way over to sit next to Eva. "I'm still memorizing the list of nons you gave me."

They'd been working with Czar's team for nearly a month. In that time, Lucy had learned many skills, such as how to escape an attacker's grasp, how to shoot, and how to prepare a triple mocha latte. When she wasn't being trained or reading about various nons, Czar put her to work at his shop. It provided her with a good excuse to give her mother for the near daily visits, and even came with a paycheck. The antique book trade must do better than Lucy thought.

"Váli." Eva's voice snatched Lucy's attention away from her article about marine monster factions and families. Across the table, Czar was setting down a book with Chinese characters comprising the title.

He smiled grimly and removed his reading glasses. "I was wonderin' when he'd come up."

Feeling as though she missed something, Lucy scooted closer to Eva in order to read over her shoulder. "Who's Váli?" The name seemed vaguely familiar, and any attempts to dredge up a memory of it resulted in echoes of her father's voice.

"He's the one who created my papa's kind," explained Eva, not even looking up from the page she was reading. There was an emblem of a wolf chasing the sun printed across the top of the page, in a sort of simplistically stylistic fashion. "SKÖLL" was in large font beneath the image. "There are several types of werewolves in Europe," Eva continued, voice low, "but our kind was made with magic that used his and Baldr's blood."

Czar made a small sound of agreement, but otherwise remained expressionless.

Baldr. Another familiar name. The sound of it sparked sweet, sadly fading memories of her father telling her stories about gods and giants as she settled in to sleep. His big, warm hand stroked her hair as his gentle voice guided her consciousness towards the realm of dreams.

"The Norse gods?" Lucy asked. She remembered now that Váli was the son of the trickster Loki, and that Baldr had been a son of Odin. There'd been a murder, and severe punishment. *"Too severe,"* her father had whispered, a wrinkle between his brows as he petted her head.

Eva finally turned her attention to Lucy, smiling slightly at the revelation that her friend knew some of the story already. "Yeah. Váli never forgave Odin for cursing him by turning him into a ravenous wolf and setting him upon his own brother, so he set out to create soldiers to stand against him. Using his blood and that of Odin's late son, Baldr, Váli got a woman skilled in magic to create a method for him to spread his curse. Baldr had been given protection from all things in the world except mistletoe, so those with the new strand of curse would have this protection as well. It's why Váli used Baldr's blood, to ensure his soldiers would be nearly invulnerable. So that's why my papa's kind are so hard to kill, and only weak against fire or mistletoe."

"But why fire?" Of all the many questions to ask, Lucy had no idea why that one was the one to spring from her mouth.

Shrugging, Eva looked back down at the paper. "Maybe because it isn't a *thing*, really. Or maybe because of Váli's blood, considering he's the son of Loki, who had a strong connection with fire." She traced her fingers along the emblem at the top of the page, then raised her gaze to Czar. "So are Hati and Sköll not real wolves, then? Not like Geri and Freki?"

The old man cracked a smile, his faded eyes twinkling. "Naw, they're just groups. One for nocts and one for sunnies, respectively."

"Because Hati eats the moon and Sköll eats the sun," Eva murmured to herself in realization.

"Same for Fenris." Czar barely paused in his words, despite Eva's mutterings. "But, far as we know, Váli only serves as head fer Sköll."

"Fenris?" Eva repeated, brow crinkling. "Fenrir? The giant wolf?"

"One an' the same, just a different spellin', is all. But, said organization is considered by many ta be merely a rumor."

"I remember Fenrir, but who are Geri and Freki?" To Lucy, this conversation felt like a pathway winding through dark woods with only partial illumination. Just when she thought she was following along, she'd be plunged back into the shadows and lost.

Luckily, she had a friend who could see in the dark.

"They were Odin's wolves, and the reason Papa's clan no longer follows Váli. Over time, they convinced several of Váli's creations to stray, then pulled them all together into one solid clan. Instead of working towards the destruction of Odin, the new clan did what they could to protect humans from other supernaturals. So long as they did not directly interfere with Váli or his followers, Váli didn't really mind their loss." Eva paused, frowning. "Will we ever interact with Váli, Czar?"

He also frowned, considering. "Possibly."

"You know the power he has over my father's kind, right?"

Somehow his frown tugged down further. "Yeah. I know."

Before Lucy could ask about the exchange, there was a faint beeping from the door to herald the arrival of Günter, Jim, and Phil. The latter sprawled out into a chair beside Czar and cocked an eyebrow. "Agent Belobog is arriving any moment," Phil reported. He then glanced pointedly at Lucy and the others, then looked back to Czar.

"It's time they meet him," Czar simply said, going back to his book as if the matter was settled.

"Agent?" Günter asked while he and Jim took their seats around the table. "Agent of what?"

"The Gehealdan," said Phil.

Lucy glanced at her friends in confusion. They'd been reviewed on titles and positions within the Gehealdan, but they'd not been told about the position of "agent." Czar was a High Commander, and Phil was a Commander. Carmen and Montenegro were considered Keepers, while Lucy and her group were still trainees yet to be full Keepers.

Seeing that this was a new opportunity for educating the

trainees, Phil leaned forward on the table and smiled at them. "An Agent is a special member of our illustrious organization, in that they are not registered as serving under any one particular chapter. They transfer from region to region, reporting to the local Commanders, and ultimately receive orders from the few High Commanders. They serve different functions, but generally they are in charge of smoke screen. They do what they can to divert suspicion away from any sort of supernatural explanations of strange events. Sometimes, they have other jobs, however. Such as Agent Belobog's recent assignment, which was as a monitor. When there are a number of children who are nons in an area, it's imperative to have a monitor."

Suddenly Lucy knew who Agent Belobog was. No sooner had the realization came to her, than the heavy metal door beeped and opened, revealing Mr. Pulchrum. "Sirs," he said with a respectful nod at Czar at Phil. "Kids," he added, casting Lucy and the others a wary glance and weak smile.

Across the table, Czar was watching Lucy closely. It was unnerving, and she tried to block it out of her peripheral awareness while she stared at Pulchrum. "Why didn't you just tell me, when you gave me the books?"

Pulchrum entered the room and closed the door, glancing around at everyone as if wondering if he really needed to answer that question or could just ignore it and move on to other matters. "It's not really something that should be discussed in public," he explained gently. "I thought you might have come to the proper conclusion on your own, because why else would I be passing along books from Czar."

Her face was burning at that, because of *course*, it was so obvious. In a way, she had assumed as much, but without confirmation it was all just speculation.

203

"So, you were monitoring us?" Eva asked, narrowed eyes studying him.

When Pulchrum looked back at Eva, he seemed to project an air of power and calm that Lucy had never before seen him possess. "I was serving as a monitor at your school," he said, which sounded neither like a confirmation or denial.

"What are you?" asked Günter, who wasn't being entirely subtle as he scented the air. "Why can't I smell you?"

That seemed to amuse Czar, who smirked a bit as he looked between Günter and Pulchrum before waving a single hand out as if to say *"Well, tell the boy."*

"A special type of werewolf," divulged Pulchrum, matching Czar's smirk. "Slavic. Not like the Scandinavian sort you're born from."

"It's weird," Günter insisted, with Eva offering a shallow nod in agreement. "Lucy's right, you smell like the woods and wintertime."

Pulchrum glanced at Lucy, then cleared his throat. "It's just how my kind is. It helps us be particularly good hunters."

"We should go ta mah office," prompted Czar, rising from his seat. "Ya gotta give me yer report, and I gotta go over yer next orders." He barely allowed Pulchrum enough time to nod good-bye to everyone before he was pulling him out the door and they were both gone.

"Finish up your readings," ordered Phil, as he got up to follow them out of the room.

Everyone was silent for a moment, and then Eva leaned closer to Lucy and whispered, "Keep an eye on him."

\*\*\*

"What's been up with you lately?" Alice didn't even look at Lucy as they walked to English, and her tiny shoulders were stiff beneath the straps of her pink backpack.

Lucy bit her lip, then cleared her throat and turned her attention ahead of her at the busy hall. "What do you mean?"

"Don't," Alice practically snapped. Then she took a deep breath and stopped walking to finally turn and face Lucy. "You're always busy, never talk to me or Krysti or Kyle anymore. But for some reason, Jim and Eva get to be in the loop, get to spend time with you. Every weekend, you're off with them. And I only know *that* because Jim let it slip."

For a moment, Lucy felt herself flounder, but then she sighed and shook her head. "We all have part-time jobs at the same place," she explained. "Right now, we're kind of in the training process, so it's been kind of intense."

The stiffness in Alice's shoulders seemed to let up a fraction, but she still looked skeptical. "So, what, you'll have more free time once the training's done?"

"Maybe?" Lucy bit her lip, helpless to come up with something to say that would placate her friend. "It depends on how many hours we get scheduled for, I guess."

Alice wrinkled her nose, and they both turned to continue on to class, aware that the bell would ring at any moment. "What kind of job did you guys get, that would require so much of your time?"

"It's at an antique bookshop," Lucy admitted, realizing that didn't exactly sound like such a time-consuming job. By the look on Alice's face, she was thinking the same thing. "It's huge, though," Lucy rushed to say as they stepped into the classroom. "And the owner does a lot of international dealings in antique books, so there's constant inventory and shipping and receiving."

"And training for *that* is intense?"

"Well, yeah." Lucy shrugged off her backpack and slid into her seat, giving Alice a serious look. "When you're handling books that are hundreds of years old, you gotta know what you're doing. Plus, you don't want to screw up an order that costs thousands of dollars."

Alice nearly choked as she took her seat. "*Thousands?*"

Nodding solemnly, Lucy confirmed, "Collectors really love their first editions."

Pulchrum entered then, the bell sounding in his wake. Lucy watched him as he smiled and greeted everyone as if nothing were different. Though she supposed nothing really was. He had always been an agent of the Gehealdan, hadn't he? She wondered how many other jobs he'd held as monitors elsewhere, and if he always served as a monitor. Czar had mentioned having new orders for him, which would imply that Pulchrum had other jobs besides keeping an eye on non-human teenagers.

While Pulchrum seemed relaxed enough during the class period, Lucy felt exhausted from how tense she'd been the entire time. Her stomach felt heavy and rotten as she worried that the class which had once been her favorite would now be something she'd dread. At least she'd only have until the end of the semester to endure it.

# Chapter 14
## Youthful Gathering

The Friday night before Halloween, Czar sent the trainees out on a recon mission. They had been given a file with of a fugitive strigoi who had been sighted in the area. The group wasn't to engage, just to locate and carefully stalk him to where he was sleeping. Then, after reporting back to Czar, they would be cleared to execute him the following night. Multiple names and photos were included in the file, since the strigoi evidently used several aliases. All that they knew was that he tended to be like the rest of his kind in that he was prone to do his hunting at parties. For some reason, strigoi were always drawn to parties. Perhaps because it was easier for a stranger to slip in and lure a random human off into the night.

Being Halloween weekend, there was quite an abundance of parties to choose from, and all of them were packed. Despite this, the trainees had visited three different parties without even so much as a scent of strigoi. They decided to try one more before simply calling it a night. Luck being the quirky mistress she is, they happened upon Kyle at the fourth party. Kyle called out to them from across a crowded living room, pressing his way through sweaty bodies in order to greet them with grins and hugs.

"Hey, guys! Been a while since I saw you at one of these!"

They smiled and agreed, no one wanting to mention how sick to death they were of parties by that point.

Kyle's gaze landed questioningly on Günter, who was an unfamiliar face, and he held out a hand in greeting, shouting his name over the cacophony of noise. Taking his hand, Günter yelled his own name back, then followed it up with a nod towards Eva and a simple "her brother."

207

Lucy had mixed feelings about finding Kyle there. She was happy to see him, of course, especially since she remembered that a dance was long overdue. However, she wasn't there to play. Kyle would prove to be too much of a distraction, she knew, and it would probably be best to part ways and try to avoid him for the rest of the night. The only problem with that was how could she avoid him without hurting his feelings and making him feel snubbed?

Bah, she was probably giving herself too much credit. Honestly, why would he care if she wanted to hang out with him? Most likely he already had some girl lined up to hang on his arm and share his dances and taste his scent on her tongue as he cradled her head in the crook of his neck.

"I'm getting some soda!" Lucy gave everyone a quick smile and wave before fleeing into the crowd. She realized that she should have asked if she could get some for anyone else, but hopefully they'd overlook her lapse of manners. Something heavy and distinctly dread-shaped hit the bottom of her stomach, as she only made it halfway to the beverage table before Kyle caught up with her and grabbed her arm.

"Luce, you mad?" he asked, pressing close enough so he could speak near her ear and not shout himself hoarse. "I do something wrong?"

Shit. "No." She let herself look at him, at the sincere pout that was so much more effective and heart wrenching than the puppy look.

"You sure?"

"Of course. Why would you think—"

"It's just that lately—" Whoever was in charge of the music had just put "Closer" on by Nine Inch Nails, resulting in several loud whoops resounding through the partiers. "Can we go outside?" he asked. Not wanting to, Lucy nodded and let him lead the way with their hands clasped together.

He'd never held her hand like that before, and even though it made her feel silly and juvenile to care, she couldn't help thinking about it. The party passed by her as nothing but a blur of color, sweat, and sound, her focus centered entirely on their clasped hands. His skin was naturally tan, even if he avoided the sun as much as possible, and it contrasted beautifully with Lucy's fair tone. Rather like a band of woven yellow and white gold. Kyle had warm hands. A little sweaty, perhaps, but soft. Artist hands.

A woman in a leathery Catwoman costume laughed hysterically and jerked back, jarring Lucy as she and Kyle passed. It worked to snap her out of her fixation with his hand, and she looked up at the room as if just discovering where she was. With the strong pull of a magnet, her gaze was drawn to a single pair of black eyes amongst the throng. Ren stared into her, glanced briefly to Kyle, and then it was if he couldn't see her at all. Thin lips stretching across crooked teeth, he carried on his conversation with an elegant goth princess with long, sleek, raven hair.

It felt like Kyle was tugging harder at her hand, and Lucy nearly tripped as she tried to keep up. They finally managed to make it out of the French doors leading to the back patio, which was surprisingly vacant. She absently pulled the doors closed with her free hand, unable to control the fleeting glance inside, nor the way the glance was drawn to a beige-clad figure in a sea of dark fabric.

"Luce." Kyle gave a little tug at her hand, pulling her a few steps closer to where he stood beside the railing. Flood lights mounted to the side of the house spotlighted them on the raised, stage-like porch, throwing their elongated shadows onto the dark lawn below. He was smiling at her, but the floodlights were highlighting the wrinkles of worry on his forehead and around his warm brown eyes. "Talk to me. Please."

She snorted a laugh with a levity she couldn't feel. "There's nothing wrong. Nothing to talk about." She reached out and tried to physically smooth his worry away with the wrinkles on his brow. Her hand didn't even shake, although she certainly felt a trill of energy along her nerves at the contact. Killing vampires obviously did wonders for her self confidence.

"But you and I never hang out anymore. You're always busy on the weekends. Even during the week, you always come up with some excuse."

"They aren't excuses." Looking into his eyes, she tried to gauge his feelings. "I really have just been busy."

"But not too busy to hang out with others. Seems you're always with Eva and Jim. I'm not the only one that's feeling abandoned, you know." She'd forgotten that he still held her hand, until he let it go. Suddenly her hand felt cold without the warm embrace of his. He leaned back against the railing as if he were bored, but his shoulders and movements were slightly stiff. "What's the deal?"

"Deal?" Lucy let out a short laugh again, because she didn't know how to respond. Avoiding his face and whatever clouded emotions were to be found there, she looked out at the backyard. Her eyes trailed the lamplight until it faded into obscurity, black trees rustling sleepily somewhere beyond. "I'm sorry you or any of the others feel abandoned. Like I explained to Alice the other day, we've all been working. Not to mention all the tests and projects I've had to focus on lately. And college applications, which require essays, and scholarship essays that I also had to—"

"Okay, okay, I get it. You've been legitimately busy, and you're not just trying to avoid me."

Even though she probably shouldn't have, she let her eyes slip away from their study of the backyard in order to take in his expressions. "Why would I want to avoid you?"

He shrugged, but she could tell he had some kind of notion. *"Maybe you found someone else,"* was the line never said, though it danced dangerously on the tip of his tongue and waved at her from behind his eyes. "Maybe I did something that pissed you off," he actually said, because it was safer.

Shaking her head, Lucy smiled and packed it with assurance and affection. "No, I told you, I'm not mad."

His shoulders relaxed a little, and his smile spread wide and pleased. "Good. Then I expect a dance with you sometime tonight, Lucy Goosey."

The resulting laugh that bubbled out of her in breathless chuckles was actually real, which made a warmth spread through her. She took another step closer, intending to reach out and draw him to her for a dance—the music still quite clear from where it boomed inside the house. Reading her intent, he stopped leaning on the railing, and an anticipatory grin lit his face far better than the flood lights ever could.

"There you are, you asshole!" The words were delivered with a laugh, sounding affectionate and teasing. A girl with black and blue streaked hair stood in the now opened doorway, the sounds of the party pouring out around her and onto the deck. She tilted her head, which made her wild pigtails perform a dance that was equal parts childlike and seductive. It went well with her outfit, which was a skimpy, punk bastardization of a Catholic schoolgirl's uniform.

Kyle stepped past Lucy and towards the newcomer, eyes only on the other girl. "Sorry, Chelsea. Some friends showed up, so I wanted to hang with them a little."

The girl—Chelsea—raised her pierced eyebrows and looked between Kyle and Lucy, her eyes clearly saying a skeptical *"some friends?"* Catching and misreading the look, Kyle hurriedly went about introducing them.

211

"This is Lucy, a friend from school. Luce, this is Chelsea, my girlfriend."

Girlfriend? Since when did he…? Hoping to hell that the smile on her face looked passable, Lucy said, "You didn't tell anyone about having a new girlfriend."

"New?" Chelsea wrapped her arms around his waist in a playfully endearing gesture, though Lucy clearly saw it for the ownership claim that it was. "We've been together nearly a month."

"I told everyone," Kyle went on to explain, his eyes apologetic even as he returned Chelsea's embrace. "Krysti knows. So does Alice. Hell, even Jim knows, I think, and he's been just as scarce as you. This is what happens when you stop being social, Luce—you fall out of the loop."

"I guess." Again she laughed, trying to keep everything light and friendly, as if this news didn't matter.

Chelsea made an impatient mew and pouted her dark blue lips. "C'mon, Kyle…I want to dance with you!" She ran her matching nails in a tantalizing trail down his front that had Lucy throwing up a little in her mouth. "You promised."

He took her wandering hand before it could get too low, and pressed it to his lips. "Such a spoiled little kitty. Let's go." As they turned to reenter the house, he looked at Lucy and smiled carelessly. "Catch up with me later, okay?"

She nodded, and they left, leaving the doors wide open. Turning away from it all, Lucy folded her arms along the top of the railing and again gazed out at the darkness. She'd been right about Kyle serving to distract her. There was no way she'd be able to casually stroll through this party in search of their target, without her gaze inevitably returning to Kyle and his girlfriend d'jour.

The sudden muffling of the party sounds let her know someone had closed the doors, but she was still somewhat startled when a young man moved to stand beside her. "Dangerous to be all alone these days, you know? Word is the Grin Reaper's in town." He held out a red plastic cup. "Coke? Well, vanilla Coke, but still."

Before accepting a drink from the stranger, she gave his appearance a quick sweep, as if she could determine his character and intentions that way. He seemed honest and unassuming enough, with big, chocolate eyes and a nervous-yet-encouraging smile. His brown hair appeared to have highlights added, and was mostly straight except for the tiny start of a curl at the tips. As he shifted, his long bangs occasionally brushed his eyelashes. The dark-washed skinny jeans he wore looked to be made for him, or perhaps they were simply one of an infinite number of things that he'd be able to pull off well. Hugging him just as much as the jeans was his shirt, which was tie-dyed with burgundies, blacks, and reds. Worn vintage lettering was splashed almost carelessly across his chest, saying LUCKY NUMBER 13.

"Hasn't really stopped people from going to parties, though, has it?" she asked, referring to his warning about the Grin Reaper. "Thanks." She took the cup and gave it a surreptitious sniff before taking his cue to clink it together with his own. The sound was more of a soft, plastic tap than a clink, but they both smiled and took long sips.

"Is that where he usually gets his victims? All I know is that he's a serial killer." The guy took another sip, even as he frowned at the thought of such a vicious predator.

"It is. From what I've read. Though I guess there's been no evidence of him actually in the area, yet." Her voice trailed off and she looked down at her cup. Lucy could taste something unfamiliar lingering in the aftertaste, and shot him an alarmed and suspicious look.

"There's rum in it, too," he said, not fazed by her look, and taking another hit from his cup. "I'd prefer Jack, myself, but

213

unfortunately someone took it upon himself to spike all the liters with whatever alcohol he damn well pleased."

Remembering what she'd heard about the potential dangers of unwanted chemicals secretly added to drinks at parties, Lucy regarded the dark liquid with trepidation.

"It was the host who did it. Didn't have enough booze for everyone, so he just spiked all the soda bottles. Spreads it out more that way. Don't worry, I don't even think he put that much in." He then shifted his drink to his left hand and extended his right. "I'm Venny, by the way."

"Lucy." She shook his hand briefly, then went back to contemplating her drink.

"You want to switch? You saw me drink from mine, so you can feel safe knowing I haven't slipped a roofie in or anything." As if to further assure her, he took another, very conspicuous sip.

Still unsure, she looked back at the doors and considered just returning to her companions. While she scanned the crowd for Eva, Jim, or Günter, instead she spotted Kyle and Chelsea grinding. Tan hands trespassed up pale thighs to disappear beneath a pleated plaid skirt. Turning away, Lucy took another long drink from her spiked Coke.

It wasn't so bad, really. She'd never had rum before, so would have expected it to have the same disgusting bite of things like whiskey or tequila. Maybe there really was just only a very little bit, so the soda was able to neutralize most of its unpleasantness.

"Man trouble, eh?" Venny leaned a little against the railing, and Lucy could feel his eyes studying her. "He your ex?"

Snorting into her cup, Lucy took another sip and tried to find the stars. "Have to be dating before we can break up." There weren't any. Perhaps they were obscured by clouds. No moon to be found, either.

Venny hummed in understanding while he moved to take another sip, so the vibration rattled along the red plastic. "So, instead he's in there with someone else, while you're left out here on your own."

"Rub it in, why don't you." She was getting more used to the rum aftertaste with every sip.

"Sorry." After looking contemplatively at his cup for a moment, Venny sighed and turned to prop his back against the railing. "I know you didn't ask for my opinion or anything, but," he started. Suppressing a groan, Lucy closed her eyes, took a sip, and awaited whatever cliché sentiment that was about to drip insincerely from his lips. "I think it's for the best that you and he aren't together." He turned his head to her, and with a very serious expression, continued, "I don't think you'd want his herpes."

Not expecting that at all, Lucy choked on her Coke, and had to spit her mouthful back into her cup. His serious expression cracked, and he laughed. It was a rich, warm sound that vibrated through her more than the beat of the overly-loud music. No one would be able to hear that laugh and not join, so she gave in to the inevitable.

*

Venny turned out to be exactly what she needed in order to get her mind off Kyle and the shock that was Chelsea. He was funny and charming, and she just felt comfortable in his presence. Any flirting he attempted was subtle and light and free of any pressure or expectations. He genuinely seemed interested in making a friend, not just looking to score.

At one point, they ran out of soda, so Lucy offered to get them refills. As she wove through the partiers, she kept her focus only on the drink table. When she arrived, she was pleased that she had no idea where Kyle was, and somewhat less pleased that she also couldn't locate the vanilla coke.

"Only have regular!" shouted the heavily-tattooed young man running the drink table, a spiked ball gleaming just below his bottom lip. "But it's got vanilla rum in it."

"Yeah! That!" Lucy shouted back, holding out her cups.

"You liked that shit? Take it! Mark finally arrived with the real stuff!" Instead of filling her cups, he just set the half-empty liter in front of her.

Lucy looked from it to the cups to the tattooed man, who had moved on to pour things into a shaker with ice. With a "why not?" shrug, she put one cup inside another in order to free a hand and grab the bottle. When she turned to go, she came up short to find Ren standing beside her. He was holding out a plastic martini glass as the tattooed man filled it with the contents of the shaker.

"Here you are, Mr. Bond; shaken, not stirred." The tattooed guy gave an amused nod, then turned to get someone else's order.

Ren took a sip from the clear drink, paused, then bobbed his head to the side in a hybrid shrug-nod. He was taking another sip as he turned to face Lucy, smiling at her over the rim and waving with his pinky. For some reason, she didn't walk away, and even seemed to forget where she was supposed to go. She stood unmoving as he finished his sip and leaned in with glistening wet lips to speak near her ear. Warm breath danced with her hair, tickling her skin and leaving behind the faint piney scent of gin. "You truly have no taste in men."

He didn't pull away, so she retreated, instead, leaning back enough to clearly see his face. A ghost-like image of herself stared back at her from his black eyes. Despite their close proximity, the low light prevented her from being able to discern where his pupils ended and the

216

irises began, giving the illusion that his eyes were circles of solid darkness suspended in voids of white.

"You know Venny?" she asked, mentally wondering why she didn't just walk away.

Those dark eyes turned towards the French doors, and Ren was quiet for a moment while he took a long sip of his martini. Appearing to be in deep thought, he licked the liquor from his lips, idly letting his tongue wander inward to trail briefly along the tips of his upper teeth. Lucy wondered what the martini tasted like. She watched his eyes look away from the doors, scanning the crowd and making a few snappy pauses, before turning to land on her again.

"I've heard of him," he finally said to answer her question.

"And? What have you heard?"

Ren shook his head, and went back to staring towards the doors. "Only cares about himself. Hurts everyone else."

Lucy pulled a skeptical face. That certainly didn't sound like the Venny she'd been getting to know. Embolden by the liquid courage she'd recently imbibed, Lucy smirked teasingly and said, "It just sounds like you're jealous, to me."

A smile came to Ren's mouth. Really, his top teeth weren't *that* crooked; it was more this bottom teeth that seemed crammed together. "You got me. So now that you know the truth, how about you ditch that creep and spend time with me, tonight?" His smile was gentle, but with a subtle curve to it that caused a peculiar fluttering sensation in Lucy's stomach. She had never seen such a smile on him directed her way before, more used to his sharp-edged smirks and cocky grins. He moved closer again and lifted his free hand to her face, gently brushing aside her long bangs and tucking the longest bits behind her ear. There his fingers curved, caressing the outer shell and lobe, sliding against her cartilage loop and causing her to shiver from the pleasing tingle that traveled along her nerves from that spot.

Brushing his thumb softly over her cheek and lips, he spoke to her in that rumbling purr she'd heard him use on the blond girl at the other party. "We could dance, go somewhere to talk, go grab a bite to eat, or perhaps…do something far more enjoyable."

It was difficult to do so, but Lucy broke eye contact and reestablished a safe distance. "You don't even know my name!"

That amused him, and his smile quirked up at one side, allowing a smirk to peek through. "Well then, tell me what it is I'll be moaning later."

"God." Lucy wasn't sure if she should laugh or choke at the gall he was displaying.

Black eyes widened and then gleamed with mirth. "Really now? Well, that'll make things easier. Usually people cry that out, anyway."

Rolling her eyes in disgust, Lucy finally broke fully away and headed towards the French doors. Over her shoulder she shouted back to Ren, "Not that you'll ever have need to moan it, but my name's Lucy!"

\*

"You have incredible eyes." Venny's cool fingers brushed aside Lucy's bangs to get a better view.

She laughed and turned her face away, letting her soft black hair serve as a veil while she moved to refill her cup. The bottle was far lighter than she expected, and she lifted it towards the light to find it was nearly empty. Still avoiding Venny's gaze, she shook her head and poured the rest into her cup. "That's such a cheesy line."

Venny stretched his legs out, the both of them sitting on the patio with their backs propped against the wooden railing. "No, I'm being serious," he insisted. "I've rarely ever seen such a shade. Reminds me of ice over a pool of pure, crystal blue water."

"Oh my *God*, just stop. The sappy clichés will kill me!"

They laughed, their shoulders sliding towards each other with a gravitational pull. Lucy found it hard to stop giggling, and she felt pleasantly fuzzy. Venny's laughter simmered down to warm chuckles that rumbled through her from the contact at their shoulders. Vanilla breath washed across her cheek, and Venny nuzzled playfully just above her ear.

A tiny voice inside her mind was telling her she should lean away—that she didn't know this guy, and shouldn't be letting him get that close. This voice was drowned out by the rest of her mind rationalizing that she liked him, and that the contact felt good, and really there was no reason to reject such pleasant sensations. Didn't she deserve a bit of happiness after everything she'd had to endure the past two months? It would be silly, this loud part of her brain said, to reject the attention of a cute guy who was sweet and actually seemed to *like* her.

"Lucy."

She had to blink a few times before the image in front of her came into focus. Kyle stood there, the French doors opened only enough to let him pass. His hair looked disheveled, but not in the intentional way he sometimes styled it. He looked concerned, though she couldn't imagine why. Squinting, she tried to assess every detail. The area around his mouth looked bruised, his eyeliner was smudged, and there was a red spot on his neck. A thousand possibilities ran through her mind—he'd gotten into a fight, he'd been pulled into a violent mosh pit, his girlfriend was abusive…

"Did you get into a fight with a vampire?" she asked, eyes constantly trailing back to the spot on his neck. If he'd found a vampire, maybe it was the one they were looking for. Then the others would be so happy! Their night wouldn't have been wasted, after all.

Her question caused his look to go from concern to confusion. Venny laughed beside her, the sound bright and sharp with delight. Kyle stopped staring at Lucy, and switched his attention to him. It was strange, Lucy thought, to see Kyle so serious and focused. The only other times she'd ever seen him like that were when he was drawing. Though he rarely ever stared at his drawings as if he wanted to punch them in the face.

"Been drinking, Luce?" he asked, even as his gaze remained pinned to Venny.

"Only a little bit, but it's mostly Coke." Tapping the bottle to indicate its label, she accidentally knocked it over. "Oops!" Giggles erupted from her again, Venny joining in as he wrapped an arm around her shoulders and pulled her tighter to his side. She felt him nuzzle at her hair again, and she turned her head into the crook of his neck. He smelled like musky cologne and fabric softener, with a subtle under note that made her think of dusty rooms no one had entered in ages. Maybe he worked at an antique store, she wondered.

"Let's play spin the bottle," Venny suggested, mouth brushing her hair and temple as he talked.

Lucy laughed and let herself relax into him. "There's only us."

"All the better."

Her thoughts were such a loud, garbled mess that she was too preoccupied with making sense of them to notice the thudding footsteps across the wooden deck. Kyle's sudden proximity startled her as he squatted in front of her folded legs. "Lucy, can you come with me for a minute?" he asked, hesitantly reaching towards her without actually touching.

From that close, she could better tell that the bruising around his mouth was smeared blue lipstick, and the redness on his neck was a hickey. Relief washed through her and she reached up to wipe at the bluish smudges. "You weren't attacked." Anger immediately smothered the relief, and she pressed at his cheek to make him go away.

Kyle had a look in his eyes as if she'd just plunged a stake into his chest instead of weakly turn his head with her fingers. Running from that look, she returned her face to the crook of Venny's neck. The arm around her shoulders squeezed tighter, and she felt safe and comfortable.

"Where's your girlfriend?" Again Lucy felt Venny's lips caress her hairline as he spoke, his voice vibrating through her.

"She went home." Kyle's voice was cold, and Lucy pressed closer to Venny to try escape the chill.

"Why didn't you follow her example?" The atmosphere was dropping in temperature by the second, and Venny's body wasn't providing sufficient shelter.

"I wanted to spend time with Lucy." Those words had her peeking out from Venny's neck. When Kyle saw her eyes, he made sure to snare them with his own, like he always could. For extra assurance, he added one of his most endearing smiles. "I'm still waiting for our dance."

Kyle reached out to offer her his hand, and Venny gripped her shoulder tightly. Body moving of its own accord, Lucy pulled free of Venny and took Kyle's hand. The reward was a brilliant smile as Kyle helped her to her feet. As an added bonus, he slid an arm around her waist as he led her to the door.

Venny called out to her, and she tried to stop to respond, but Kyle kept them in motion. "Come back soon," Venny was saying. "Don't leave me here waiting."

Then the doors were shutting him out along with the fresh night air. She choked when the humidity and stench of the party hit her. The music shook her brain, causing her ears to tingle oddly and her temples to throb in an awkward counter-rhythm. Leaning heavily against Kyle, Lucy fought back a swirling sense of vertigo and its accompanying nausea.

"Can't dance right now," she said into his ear, hoping it was loud enough to hear.

"I know." He wasn't yelling, but she heard him just fine. When his cheek brushed against hers, she realized how close they were, and her heart sped up. "Let's get you some water."

Ren was in the kitchen when they arrived, and he silently passed Kyle a red cup. To Lucy's surprise, Kyle accepted the offering with a grudging nod of thanks. "Here," he whispered to Lucy, pressing the plastic rim to her lips. "Drink up."

She closed her eyes and let him help her drink, even though she was certain she could do it on her own. The cup was filled with cold water, and she swallowed as much as she could before it felt like she was drowning. Kyle pulled the cup away when she gagged, and she felt his hand run soothing circles on her back. Words were murmured in her ear, and she knew they were intended to comfort, but she couldn't make sense of them. When he moved the cup close again, she batted it away with a protesting whine.

"Have to pee," she announced, trying to push past him in order to leave.

Kyle's hand on her shoulder kept her where she was, and propped her back against the counter. "I'll get Eva. You wait here, okay?" She liked it when he looked into her eyes like that, so she smiled and nodded, willing to agree to anything so long as he never turned his eyes away. Unfortunately, her agreement resulted in his swift departure, and she was left staring longingly at empty air.

Ren was still there, though she'd completely forgotten about him until he tried to disguise a snicker by clearing his throat. She glared askance at him, wondering why he felt the need to linger. "You're not my friend." There was a half-second delay until her brain registered that it was her own voice that she'd just heard.

Smirking—he was *always* smirking, as if his face had just gotten stuck that way—with wry amusement, Ren leaned back against the same counter. They were two cabinets and a sink apart, but it still didn't feel far enough for Lucy. "Have we already moved on to something more?"

Lucy glanced at the doorway, then returned her attention to the human embodiment of annoyance. "You're very full of yourself, you know?"

His only response was easy laughter, and it made a sensation of something sweet and needle sharp pass through Lucy. A smile forced itself onto Lucy's face without her consent, and something like a chuckle might have escaped her throat. Before her sluggish brain could formulate a response, Kyle was rushing back in with Eva.

*

The party was still loud, but it seemed to be dwindling as they made their way out to the car. Other party-goers were filing into cars, or standing in small groups as good-byes were exchanged and plans were made. Eva and Lucy were waiting by Günter's SUV while Günter had stayed inside to track down Jim. Kyle, for some reason, had tagged along.

Lucy leaned back against the cool, midnight blue metal of the SUV, and turned her attention to the starless sky. She was reminded of that first party she'd attended with Kyle, and how she'd propped herself

223

up against a car while waiting to flee for home. She really did hate parties.

A bump to her shoulder alerted her to Kyle's presence as he moved to join in her leaning. The contact turned to pressure as he slid into her. "I'm sorry." Softly spoken words that were little more than tendrils of warm air ghosted across her neck.

Turning her head towards him, she saw such a strange combination of emotions battling for dominance on his face, that it made her turn away again before she became dizzy. There was no reason she could see for him to be sorry, so she smiled in an attempt to calm the storm in his eyes. It only worked to veil it. Even tipsy—certainly she was not drunk, no—Lucy could tell he was slipping a mask on to hide everything else from her.

"Let's go." At first, Lucy hadn't recognized the voice, so she was startled when the SUV beeped to indicate it was unlocked. Günter was moving around to the driver's side, his posture tense and curling inward like a bow bending as the string was drawn back. It scared Lucy to see him like that, so used to him being an island of calm no matter the situation.

"I don't know why you're being so pissy." Jim was there, trailing petulantly in Günter's wake. He tried to project a casualness that was belied by his tense posture. His words serving as some kind of provocation, they reeled Günter back around the vehicle so that he could better face Jim. While everyone else in the area continued talking, the small world comprised solely of Lucy and her friends had been plunged into a chilled silence.

When it was obvious that Günter wasn't going to say anything, but merely glare at Jim with rage and disbelief, Jim killed the silence with a poisonous sneer. "What?" He stepped closer to Günter, tilting his head and looking more challenging than Lucy thought a human artist ever could be when facing off against a super-human athlete trained in various forms of combat. "Do we have a problem?"

Just when it looked as though Günter was finally going to say something, his attention flicked to Lucy and Kyle, then darted around at all of the unfamiliar faces in the area. Jim's eyes hadn't moved from their hard study of Günter's, and he took yet another step closer. "I was under the impression you weren't the kind to take issue over that," Jim nearly snarled. "Who'd have thought a brother of Eva's could be so closed-minded."

Günter pitched his voice so low that it would be difficult for anyone besides Jim to hear, so Lucy could barely make out his "Of course I don't— *That isn't the problem!*"

Eva walked bravely up to the unstable pair and asked her brother something in Japanese. When Günter switched his attention to her and offered a response in the same language, Jim released an angered cry. "Now, that's just not fair!"

Eva's eyes, sharpened to daggers and thirsting for blood, switched to Jim, causing him to involuntarily step back. "We need to go now," she said, and her voice was darker than that moonless night. "Get in the car."

There was no more arguing after that. Everyone climbed aboard and Kyle waved at Lucy through the tinted glass. She watched him as they pulled away, and thought she saw Ren approaching him right before her view was cut off by the trees and a sharp curve. Forehead on the glass, she watched the dark scenery whirl by, and closed her eyes against each sudden, harsh light of civilization they passed. No one spoke, and the tension was unnerving.

She wished she'd stayed on the porch with Venny.

DL Wainright

# Chapter 15
Sacrifices

Lucy awoke feeling as though she were falling, but she was already on the floor. Her head hurt and her mouth felt like it was coated in spray-on insulation. She must have made some sort of tell-tale sound, because Jim's voice came to her from somewhere, informing her that there was a bottle of Advil and a glass of water on the coffee table. Some bleary-eyed glancing around helped her locate the table at her side, and also sent spikes of agony through her skull with each shift of her eyes.

Propped up on the low table, she took the medicine and downed some of the water. After taking a few slow breaths, the room stopped spinning enough for her to see that she was in Günter's apartment.

That was odd. Usually they only stayed there on kill nights. Was it Sunday already? Then where had her Saturday gone? The last thing she clearly remembered was laughing with a cute guy at a party.

Oh right, the party. She forced memories out of her foggy mind, and tried to ignore the accompanying pain that it triggered. Realizing what kind of spectacle she'd made was just as painful, and she groaned as she buried her face in arms folded over her knees.

"You okay?" Jim's voice came from behind her, and she carefully turned around. He was sitting against some pillows on one end of the couch, his legs stretching out along the soft leather seat cushions.

"Not really. Thanks for letting me have the couch, by the way."

"What?" he scoffed, scooting up into a straighter position. "It was *my* turn, and you insisted. Repeatedly."

"I did?"

"Yeah. Until finally you just crawled into your sleeping bag and announced it was 'sleepy time,' and I was to shut up."

227

Groaning again, Lucy shifted so she was leaning back against the couch, her head resting near Jim's thigh. "Note to self: avoid rum and Coke in the future. Or, actually, just avoid booze in general, maybe."

He placed a soothing hand on her forehead and fiddled with her bangs. "Maybe you should just avoid creepy college guys."

"He wasn't creepy."

"From what I hear, he was trying to date rape you."

"He totally was not! It's not *his* fault I don't know my limit. He was just trying to keep me company so I wouldn't have to dwell on Kyle and his skanky new girlfriend. My fault I got drunk."

"If you say so." Her bangs were brushed into her eyes, and he chuckled when she made sounds of protest. The hair was swiped aside, but then his hand left her forehead. "So, was this not-creepy guy at least cute?"

"I think so, yes." She smiled at the memory of him, of his doe eyes and friendly grin. "Not usually my type, but still quite cute."

"Get his number?"

Lucy frowned, realizing that she hadn't, and would probably never see him again. "No."

"Sucks. And, not to rub it in your face or anything, but *I* met a living *god*, and was lucky enough to have exchanged digits."

"Who says 'digits'? Anyway, tell me about this guy."

"Can do better than that." Shifting around, Jim fetched his phone from the end table and tapped softly away at its touch screen before holding it in front of Lucy's face.

The lighting in the image wasn't the best, but it seemed like the man had dark blond hair that was short yet with enough length to show that it was naturally curly. Jim comparing the man to a god seemed apt, since his facial features looked as though they'd been molded from a

228

Hellenistic statue of Apollo. Looking at the glowing image before her, Lucy supposed he was attractive enough. In that factory-produced-in-order-to-sell-designer-clothing sort of way. She preferred men who were more unique, not considered "traditionally" handsome by most standards. Even so, she smiled and offered the obligatory "*Very* nice" that Jim was awaiting.

"Isn't he, though? And he's agreed to be my model. How lucky can ya get, right?"

"If things go well, perhaps *really* lucky." She punctuated her innuendo with an exaggerated eyebrow wag.

Retaliation came as a flick to the side of her head and a reprimanding "Cheeky girl."

A door could be heard opening, the clicking of the knob louder than the well-oiled hinges. Günter emerged from his bedroom, padding silently to the open kitchen and immediately going about rummaging in cabinets.

Jim glanced at him, then slid down a little and continued their conversation in whispers. Part of Lucy's fragmented memories recalled a fight, and she supposed it still had yet to be settled. "His name is Dorian, and he's in a band. Lead singer. The band's called The Ancient Mariners, and evidently they've been rather successful at obtaining gigs as of late."

Lucy wondered if she had that goofy, dreamy expression whenever she looked at Kyle. She hoped not. In her opinion, Jim looked a little silly as he mooned over the image on the phone, fingers reverently caressing the plastic as though it were a sacred object of the god Dorian.

"Somehow, though," he continued, eyes drinking in the digital image, "he's still going to find the time to model for me."

Günter approached, a mug in each hand, and Jim tapped the

phone's screen off, dropping it to his lap with a defiant-yet-wary expression. A mug was extended to Jim, accompanied by a soft smile. "It's the way you like it," Günter said, and Jim accepted it with a nod and hesitant smile in return. For an awkward few seconds, Günter did nothing but stare at Jim, obviously at a loss. Groping for distraction, or at least a way to banish the tension, Günter turned his eyes to Lucy and asked if she'd like anything.

"Naw. I've got the water, thanks."

The tension hadn't budged. Back stiff and straight, Günter sat at the opposite end of the couch from Jim. His thigh barely brushed Jim's socked feet. "So," came from his lips, but then he was drinking from his own mug and looking anywhere but at Jim. Lucy wondered what exactly had happened to cause this, considering the two had seemed to be getting close in the past month.

Finally Günter rested his mug on his thigh and looked squarely at Jim. "Does this mean you don't need me to model for you anymore?"

Jim slurped his coffee as he considered his response. "It's for the best to use more than one model, considering I'm doing multiple pieces. Wouldn't want them to all look alike, right?" His eyes fell to his drink. "But, if it's okay, I think I'll have Dorian be the model for Apollo. I think he suits the image better."

Günter's posture had started to melt as Jim talked, but the last line struck him like lightning and he tensed up again. "But, I thought you wanted me for Apollo because Eva was Artemis. Family resemblance and all that."

"Well." There must have been something quite fascinating in the coffee mug, considering Jim's transfixed gaze. "The Artemis piece was just practice, and isn't going to be part of the show, so that's irrelevant. But, I thought you'd be more suitable for Eros." Breaking away from the coffee, Jim looked up into Günter's stunned face. His next words tumbled out in a clumsy rush, and Lucy didn't see him blink even once. "That is, if you'd be comfortable posing with your wings out."

"I-I...um...yeah, sure, of course. I mean, if it wouldn't be too weird for you." Lucy had never heard Günter stutter before. Then again, she'd never seen him so obviously off kilter, considering he usually strove to be so composed.

A smile broke out on Jim's face, and he gently kicked Günter's thigh. "Idiot. How many times I gotta tell you it's incredible, before you believe me?"

Günter smiled too, looking happy and relieved. He regarded his own mug almost shyly, then rose to his feet. "I'll start making breakfast. Any preferences?"

And, just like that, it seemed they had reconciled. Jim asked for scrambled eggs, the smile still plastered across his face and peeking out from behind his mug as he drank his coffee. Lucy watched Jim while Jim watched Günter, and realized the expression in his eyes was infinitely more affectionate than when he'd been staring at his phone.

"Hey," she said, startling Jim as he seemed to suddenly remember her presence. "What exactly had you guys been fighting about?"

"What? When?" He glanced towards Günter in the kitchen area, then tried to hide behind his mug.

"Last night."

"Ah. Well. That was. You see." There was more glancing, until something managed to ensnare his fluttering attention. Lucy followed his now locked gaze to find Günter slamming down a frying pan and hanging his head.

"A misunderstanding," Günter said lowly.

"About what?" Lucy asked, glancing at Jim and seeing her

231

confusion mirrored back.

Lucy's voice sent Günter moving again, returning to the couch and looking somberly from Lucy to Jim. A laugh escaped his throat on a ragged exhalation, and he finger combed his long black hair out of his face. His gaze flicked between Lucy and Jim again, until finally settling on Lucy. She watched him take a breath, obviously trying to rebuild his composure. "I feel, considering everything we're going through together, that you have a right to know," he started to explain. "Both of you."

"To know what?" murmured Jim, who watched Günter in cautious anticipation.

Günter's eyes strayed to Jim for just a second before returning to Lucy. "Jim misunderstood my reactions to seeing him and Dorian together last night. He thinks it's because I don't approve of the person he likes' gender, but that would be very hypocritical of me. Considering my own orientation."

"You're gay?" The words were out of Lucy's mouth before she could think, and she literally bit her tongue in a belated effort to stop them.

Günter seemed to grow more uncomfortable, shifting his weight and unable to meet her eyes for a moment. "Yes," he said, forcing himself to face her, his expression reminding her of the night she'd learned he wasn't human. When he saw only confusion and no condemnation on her face, his tension leaked away and he turned to head back to the kitchen.

"Since when?" she asked, still unable to believe what she was hearing. Hell, it had almost been easier for her to believe he was a shape-shifting hybrid.

"Seriously," Jim whispered in shocked agreement.

Günter was laughing, and part of her was relieved to hear the sound coming out amused and easy. "Since as far back as I can remember."

All those years of doodling his name with little hearts, and she'd never stood a chance. True, she'd eventually moved on from that crush, but it still felt like such a waste. "How come you never told me?"

"Never told anyone except my parents and Eva." He took the carton of eggs from the fridge and went about cracking some into a bowl. "Well, and my very small list of ex-boyfriends. And Mick."

"Wait." Hangover forgotten, Lucy pulled herself to her feet and hobbled over to sit on a stool at the breakfast bar that separated the kitchen from the living room. "*My* Mick? Why tell Mick and not me?"

Whisking the eggs, Günter made a distracted "ah" sound. Lucy heard Jim snicker from the couch, and her dizzy mind reeled a little more. "For the same reason my exes knew," Günter eventually admitted, glancing at her from behind the fall of his long hair as he worked.

With a little groan, she rested her head on the cool surface of the bar. "Figures. My first ever crush, and my brother was the only one who ever really stood a chance." She didn't care about how Jim was laughing hysterically from the couch, or how endearing the sight of a blushing Günter was. She barely even heard him ask about her having had a crush on him, and she just weakly waved her hand in a dismissive manner. "Long time ago," she grunted, distracted by thoughts of the bizarre world that was her life. Mick had come out about being bi when he was thirteen, and she knew that he and Günter had become friends in high school, but she'd never even suspected. After all, she didn't even know Günter pitched for that team! It seemed rather rude that Mick had never told her that she might as well give up all hope. Cruel bastard had probably gotten a kick out of watching her moon in vain.

Closing her eyes, she tried to settle her whirling thoughts, the sounds of cooking working as meditation music. Her thoughts, however, refused to be ignored. Giving up, she opened her eyes and vocalized another query. "So how come Mick never said anything? I mean, he even knew about my crush."

"Probably didn't say anything because he knew I didn't want to 'come out.' Besides, we weren't really, like, *together* or anything. Just friends."

"Really, *really* close friends," speculated Jim, still snickering.

"Is that what you and Jim are? *Close* friends? Is that why you were upset about Dorian?"

Günter paused mid-whisk and looked up, his eyes flicking to Jim in alarm. "That's—"

"Considering he came out to the *both* of us just now, I'd say that's a very firm 'no.'" All laughter was gone from Jim's voice, and his interruption plunged the apartment into a cold, crushing silence.

Günter's expression closed off, his shoulders bunching like they had the previous evening. His knuckles around the whisk handle were as white as his kitchen tile. "I was taking issue with the *species* of Dorian, not his gender and not because I was jealous or anything."

"Which you could have *said*," Jim scoffed, bitterness tainting his tone, "instead of just snapping and glaring and dragging me away."

Günter's jaw was so tense that he barely moved it when he spoke, and Lucy thought she heard a growl. "You're right; *obviously* I should've just started talking about supernaturals *right there* in the middle of a *busy party*."

"It's not even like I was at some sort of risk of being abducted. I was just talking with a potential model in a professional manner."

"His hand was on your thigh!"

"Friendly contact, nothing else."

"Do you even know what he *is*?."

234

That got Jim to his feet, leaving his coffee safely on the end table. "I hardly see why it should matter. He was a perfect gentleman to me, so no matter what type of supernatural he may be, I'd hardly think he's a risk. Besides, I wouldn't expect *you*, of all people, to be discriminatory towards other supernaturals."

"No, that isn't—I meant—"

"Shut up." The words were spoken, but with the projection of an experienced stage actor. Everyone turned to look at Eva, who stood at the mouth of the short hallway which led to the bedroom and bathroom. Her pajamas were an assemblage of yoga pants and a loose T-shirt, not unlike her usual attire. DEFY GRAVITY was emblazoned on her black shirt in curly, green foil font. "It's too damn early for arguments, so just shut up. Besides, you're both just being idiots."

Lucy was grateful for Eva's intervention. While she was curious about exactly what kind of non this Dorian guy was, Lucy's head was pounding too hard to really care. Mostly she just wanted the guys to shut up, go away, or both.

Eva shuffled tiredly to the couch, but Jim stood between her and cushy comfort. "Go help Günter make breakfast," she ordered, glaring coolly from beneath messy bangs. He opened his mouth to protest, but she preemptively silenced him. "No. Go help my brother make breakfast before I make a mess of his living room."

Jim studied her face for a tense moment, then smiled and scoffed with attempted flippancy as he stepped around her towards the kitchen. "Good point. We probably don't want to witness *your* attempts at cooking."

"Yes, that's right," said Eva with a flat voice. "I certainly wasn't implying that I'd tear your limbs off and shove them down your throat." She settled on the couch with a small sigh that morphed into a yawn, and looked so comfortable that Lucy moved to join her.

Crawling onto the couch beside Eva, Lucy snuggled close and rested her head on her friend's shoulder. They pulled over the blanket Jim had used and wrapped it around them.

"Aw," cooed Eva, moving an arm around Lucy and drawing her closer. "Did the mean boys make your hangover headache worse?" Lucy whimpered in affirmative reply, and Eva stroked her hair soothingly. "Don't worry; I'll beat them up if they do it again." Jim and Günter chuckled from the kitchen, and Lucy thought she heard Jim mutter something about how he'd like to see Eva try.

Eva grabbed the remote and began channel surfing. After the twentieth channel, Lucy started to let her eyelids droop. She was warm and comfy; things were quiet, and the delicious scents of bacon and eggs were permeating the air. Just as she was starting to drift into a dream having something to do with Darth Vader making tea, she was startled awake as Eva jerked into an upright sitting position. When she opened her eyes and saw the look on Eva's face, Lucy knew something was wrong.

The volume on the TV was suddenly increased, so Lucy turned her attention to the large, glowing flat screen on the opposing wall. A live news report greeted her. In the foreground stood a brunette female field reporter, a familiar house behind her, its yard crawling with cops and people in black suits. "GRIN REAPER STRIKES AGAIN" was splashed across the bottom of the screen, next to the station's logo.

"Isn't that where we were last night?" asked Lucy, but Eva was too busy staring intently at the screen to reply.

"…at least eight confirmed dead, but the search still continues. Specialists will be making sketches of the victims based on what they can reconstruct from the remains. We ask that you please stay tuned to this station, as we will be receiving the sketches and all other information as it is released. Please help authorities by calling the appropriate numbers and reporting any information you have concerning the victims' identities, or potential suspects." Numbers appeared under the Grin Reaper headline, but Lucy didn't look away from the image of the house.

"Christ," she heard Jim gasp, all sounds of food preparation having come to an abrupt halt.

Eva looked to her brother, her eyes a battle between rage and misery. "We missed him. The target must have been there, but we missed him."

Günter shook his head, still watching the report. "Couldn't have. We combed the entire place, and never caught the scent. It must have arrived after we left."

"Or we weren't as thorough as we thought."

"No," interjected Lucy, watching the blurred images of officers moving from window to window. "The Grin Reaper wasn't our target. The guy we were looking for isn't the one who did this."

Everyone let that sink in, and it only served to make matters worse. They had just been there to locate and track down a random Treaty breaker, and had unknowingly escaped something far more dangerous. Only a month of being part of Gehealdan, and already they had grown cocky and over-sure. In actuality, they were small time newbies, splashing around clumsily in the kiddy pool because they weren't ready for the real thing.

Jim began furiously texting Dorian while Günter finished preparing breakfast and Eva called Czar. Lucy went for her phone, needing to make certain that Kyle was not among the victims.

She paced as the electronic ringing stretched on and on without interruption. When finally it terminated, a stranger's voice came over the line, striking Lucy dumb with panic. "Hello! You've reached Kyle's phone, but he is unable to talk at the moment. Can I take a message?

237

Hello? Um…is there anyone there?"

Snapping out of her stupor, Lucy resumed her pacing. "Who are you?" She was unable to keep the bite of impatience out of her voice.

"Conner. Who are *you*?"

"Lucy. Let me talk to Kyle."

"Well, sorry, but Kyle's currently passed out on a beanbag."

"Then wake. Him. Up."

Conner grumbled something away from the phone, and then there were rustling sounds. A garbled, distant voice came over the line, commanding someone to get up, and an equally distorted voice made some sort of incoherent reply. Eventually Kyle's voice came to her, clear but tired and confused.

"Luce?"

Breathing came much easier after hearing him, and a smile of relief touched upon her lips. "God, Kyle, you've no idea how good it is to hear your voice."

"Huh? Luce, is something wrong?"

Any traces of the smile ran away, and she looked at the TV. The scene hadn't changed, the reporter trying to wrangle an FBI agent into answering some questions. "Turn on the news. Like, right now."

"Why?"

"Just do it. Any local news channel should be fine."

She listened silently as he yelled for someone to turn on the news. There were voices raised in the background, and laughter, but it all died down once the news was playing. Kyle cursed, his voice rough from sleep and sudden fear. "Isn't that…"

"Yeah. It's why I called. Wanted to make sure you'd gotten out before…before the…uh…"

"Yeah. I—Yeah, I left not long after you guys. That Ren guy brought me along to his friend Nick's place. Bunch of us just hung out

238

here until we all finally passed out."

"So Ren's with you?"

There was a pause, and she wondered if Kyle had been distracted by the news. Right before she could repeat the question, he finally gave an answer, though his tone seemed rather preoccupied. "Yeah. Um, I mean no. He was. But he left close to four. Said he had an early day today and so was heading home for a nap."

He was safe, though, for which Lucy felt glad. She didn't know him that well, and he could be a little frustrating, but perhaps he was growing on her. Knowing that he and Kyle were safe and sound lifted the lead coat of dread that had been weighing down her shoulders. If only she had some way of contacting Venny, too.

"Lucy, thanks for calling and checking up on me. I'm going to call Chelsea, now. I mean, I know she left before I did, but I just want to be sure she didn't wander back at some point…and yeah."

"Of course!" The cheery, understanding tone to her voice rang false, but she was too strung-out to do any better. "I'll talk to you later, maybe. Okay, bye!" She clicked her phone off before he could respond, and stared at the slim device as though it were an alien artifact.

"How is *that* handling it!" Eva snapped, still talking to Czar. "Oh. I—yes, sir. Yes. Very well, sir." Eva clicked off the phone with a sigh. "The only information Czar felt inclined to give me was that the Grin Reaper is indeed a strigoi. His MO lines up with other accounts of strigoi throughout history, especially whenever Romania and Turkey fought. Evidently it was common practice amongst soldiers during wars between Turks and Romanians to cut off the lips of the corpses. Weakened morale. No one's really sure if the soldiers did it first or the strigoi, but one definitely was inspired by the other." She looked around the room at everyone, who were all frozen in place and hanging off her every word. "In any case, we're ordered not to concern ourselves with

239

the Grin Reaper. Says they're handling it. Also, he said that our target has already been confirmed as executed, so at least we don't have to worry too much about *that* particular failure."

"'It was common once,'" murmured Lucy, recalling the nightmare where she literally stumbled amongst the Reaper's victims. Everyone turned to look at her, and she wrapped her arms around herself. She tried to figure out how to explain, but every line that passed through her consideration just sounded crazy, and her fingers clutched desperately at her shirt. "Who feels like going to Cleveland today? I think it's time I have that talk with Branka about my dreams."

***

It was impossible to read Branka's face. The striga's eyes were directed at the coffee table, while she undoubtedly saw something else. Lucy had told her all that she could recall of the dream with the Grin Reaper, and she and the others were awaiting Branka's interpretation. Those mysterious ocean eyes finally rose, focusing on Lucy.

"He said 'the magician's hand'? You're certain?"

"Yes."

"And he's not the one you're looking for…" Branka's eyes lost their focus again, and Lucy exchanged glances with her friends.

"Does that mean something in particular?" Günter asked, leaning forward a little.

Branka looked tired, which made her seem older than the last time they'd seen her. Wrinkles were creeping in along her forehead and around her eyes. "The old man hasn't told you." It wasn't a question.

"Told us what?" Eva shifted into a position which mirrored her brother.

Branka's eyes roamed over their young, worried faces, seeming to only just then realize how pathetically ignorant they were. "There is a need to keep things secret." A sardonic smile slid across her face like a slowly rolling wave. "Sometimes that comes at a great cost."

Some of what she said must have registered with some previous knowledge imparted upon the siblings, because they were both nodding. "Father told us about the dangers of humans learning the truth." Günter's amber eyes were dark and serious, his jaw squaring in its tense clench. "That's the primary role of the Gehealdan, to maintain that secrecy."

The witch nodded, then stood up and moved to the window. She seemed to be searching the surrounding trees. "Yes. And that secrecy," there she hesitated, considering her words carefully. "It can be difficult. Sometimes a supernatural will do something foolish that jeopardizes all of us."

"Like being discovered killing and eating someone." Lucy felt her friends' attention shift to center on her, but she didn't care. Her entire focus was on Branka, and Lucy's expression remained eerily blank except for the ghost of vindictive fury haunting her eyes.

"Among other things, yes." If Branka noticed the echoes of old rage in Lucy's expression, she didn't let it faze her. In fact, she seemed entirely preoccupied with watching the skies and trees, glancing at times to the cats that roamed her yard. "And when that happens, the Gehealdan tends to send some form of distraction."

"Distraction." Lucy could hear the hollow tone of her own voice, and some strangely detached part of her shuddered at it.

Branka glanced at Lucy, studied her face for a fleeting second, and then resumed her worried monitoring of the outside. "A scapegoat. Someone on which the murders or disappearances can be blamed. He's often considered later to be a serial killer. In other words, the humans are presented with a perfectly human explanation. Then no one suspects

241

that there was ever the possibility of it being anything else."

"So the Grin Reaper is a distraction?" Lucy asked, thoughts threatening to be derailed by curiosity over Branka's concern for whatever she did or did not see outside.

A deep breath of air filled Branka's lungs, her eyes falling closed with the inhalation. As she exhaled, her beautifully disturbing eyes opened slowly. Lucy wondered what she saw with those eyes, somehow knowing that Branka was watching things that were taking place well beyond her house and yard. "We should not talk of this. You aren't to know."

"Wait, are you saying the Grin Reaper is an agent of the Gehealdan?" asked Lucy, rising from her seat. In her peripheral, she saw the others jolt and sit forward as if about to also rise. Branka's eyes came into focus again, and she turned away from the window to fully face Lucy.

"There's no other choice," she was saying, giving one more nervous glance to the window. "Our secrecy is important. For everyone."

"But all that death?" Once again her world seemed to be shifting beneath her feet. "All that *killing*?"

Branka looked away, back out the window. "He's a distraction, child," she said, as if to quiet Lucy's fears, but something in her voice belied her words. "There are many kinds of sacrifices that must be made for the greater good."

A coldness caressed along Lucy's back before enfolding her in its phantom arms. "Other kinds of sacrifices?"

Without looking at her friends, she knew they were all tensely watching Branka now. Branka met none of their eyes, turning her head away from the window and studying an abstract painting of owls on her wall as if it wasn't old and familiar.

"We are done here, I think. You should go."

No. Lucy refused to just leave it at that. "Tell us what you mean. What other sacrifices? You can't just say things like that and not *explain*."

Branka smiled with an irony that made the chill engulfing Lucy drop a few more degrees. "Can't I?" She looked away from the painting and met Lucy's eyes. Even though nothing about Branka's physical appearance had changed, Lucy was suddenly struck by how very different the striga was from a human. It was as if she could see the power that lurked just behind those mysterious eyes, as well as the reflection of times and ages that Lucy never saw nor would ever live to see.

All words died in Lucy's throat, not even surviving long enough for her to taste them on her tongue. No one spoke, and a clock in the hall ticked, the metallic sound strangely ominous. Each click of the gears marked another second of ignorance, time lost that could have been better spent saving someone from being *sacrificed*. An irrational urge came over Lucy to smash the clock and buy more time.

The smile on Branka's face twisted as if she'd swallowed sewage, and she moved away from the window. "You want to know more, talk to Hayes," she said. "See if he tells you any more than I have."

The group didn't move. Günter cleared his throat to loosen its earlier tension, and also to tactfully obtain Branka's attention. "If he's behind what's going on with the Grin Reaper, I'd doubt he'd tell us." Although Günter spoke with politeness, head slightly inclined, Branka frowned at them with impatience.

"It doesn't matter. You signed on to be a Gehealdan. You all did. His ways are now your ways." Again she glanced warily at the window. "And all we supernaturals are grateful for your efforts to keep us safe in

243

our secrecy."

"Really?" Jim suddenly asked, which was the first thing aside from salutations that he'd uttered since arriving. "Seems you don't exactly approve of all the Gehealdan's methods."

Everyone was watching Branka, waiting for her response to that. "You are mistaken," she assured, speaking clearly in a strong voice. Even as she spoke, she moved to a side table and fetched a pad of sticky-notes and a pen. "I and my kind owe much to the efforts of the Gehealdan. We would be in chaos without them to enforce order." Finished with the quick note she'd made, Branka set the pen and remainder of the pad back, then folded the note into a very tiny square. "You shouldn't concern yourself about things such as the Magician's Hand," she went on to assure, stepping up to Lucy and taking both her hands in Branka's own. The tiny note pricked against Lucy's palm, and Lucy made sure to cup it carefully as Branka's hands slipped away.

They waited until they were on the road to open the note. In small, cramped scrawl, it read: *Be cautious of Ravens. Trust only the snake that is a dragon wearing the skin of a wolf.*

# Chapter 16
## The Snake

Lucy sat in the War Room, absently rubbing at fingers that were sore from the firing range, and stared blankly at the book in front of her. It was the Yaxley one, which she was hoping would provide some insight into Branka's enigmatic note. Chapter thirteen was opened, but Lucy had barely read the first paragraph before her mind had wandered.

She wasn't sure if she should be there, be a Gehealdan. Not if it meant condoning things like the Grin Reaper. Then there were the other sacrifices hinted at by Branka. The very idea of it all made Lucy feel sick. While Phil had been supervising her training that day on the range, there had been a second-quick moment where she'd been tempted to turn the gun on him, to wipe out the monsters that could kill innocent people so easily and call it "good" and "necessary." It was the same burning feeling deep down that she'd felt about the vampire that had started all of this.

"Thought you were supposed to have finished that book by now." Pulchrum was sitting beside her, though Lucy hadn't even noticed him enter the room. He tilted his head to the side in order to better examine her face. Shaggy brown hair slid along his skin, curling across his cheek like the delicate fingers of a lover. It was hard to believe he was something ferocious beneath those soft eyes and gentle smile.

Looking down at the pages in front of her, Lucy tried to figure out why this book was the only one she hadn't already consumed cover to cover. It was the most important one, she felt. For some reason, though, it was like something nudged her attention away anytime she attempted to read much of it. Only the strigoi chapter had been easy to read, like a cleared patch in fogged glass. "I'm still working on it," she said with a shrug. They were the only ones in the room, and Lucy contemplated different ways of getting out of his presence without provoking him.

"That's an interesting chapter," he commented softly. "The vârcolac. It's native to my region of the world, actually. Thought to be hunted to extinction by those who worried they were too dangerous."

That worked to sufficiently derail Lucy's thoughts of slipping away, and she found her eyes able to start focusing on the words in the book. "They cause eclipses."

Pulchrum hummed in agreement. "But that's only part of what they are. There are two types." At that, he reached over and flipped forward a page to where there was a two-page spread of illustrations.

On the pages were creatures that looked like a cross between a dragon and a dog, mangy fur revealing scales. They had long, emaciated bodies that curled over themselves or twisted and stretched as they moved. One of the strangest things about them, though, was the mouths. There were so many of them, scattered across the creatures' bodies. Some were opened as if crying out, others gnashed their sharp teeth, while others remained placidly closed.

"No matter what, though, that's their true form. Some think they may be descended from the strix, like the striga and strigoi. But most theorize the vârcolac is something different entirely, and a remnant of the age of dragons. Likely some sort of mutt or bastardization, not a pure dragon."

Dragon. Branka's note. Lucy pulled the book closer and stared avidly down at the illustrations. "Tell me more about them. What are the two types?"

Pulchrum flipped back to the previous page, so that two bold headlines were visible: "Soma" and "Pneuma." "The Soma is the most common," he explained. "They consume flesh. The Pneuma are the most rare, and consume the darkness one gathers on their spirit or soul or consciousness, whatever you wish to call it. A soma can become a pneuma, and a pneuma can become a soma. For the former to happen, an existing pneuma must devour all of the darkness within a soma. Then, in order for the new pneuma to continue being a pneuma, he mustn't ever consume the flesh of animal or man again, nor shed the blood of another in violence or anger. If a pneuma vârcolac should eat flesh or bring harm to another, then they can no longer feed upon the darkness, and return to consuming the flesh."

Lucy scanned over the words, fascinated. "The darkness is better than the flesh?" she asked, seeing a line that suggested as much.

"Considerably," Pulchrum answered with a nod. "It's more satisfying, which helps stave off their insatiable hunger a little longer. See, vârcolaci are always hungry. Every moment when they aren't eating, they feel as though they are starving. It's hell, and can drive them mad. It's said to be easier for pneumas to maintain control, though." He flipped forward another two pages until there was another illustration on a page across from more text. "But, there's a way for both kinds to find temporary relief from the hunger, and it can even draw the most bestial back from madness."

It was an image of a woman with what appeared to be a string sprouting from her heart and floating up into the sky where a man gripped the other end tightly while also clinging to a bitten, bloody moon. "The folktales say that when a woman spins thread at midnight, a vârcolac uses that thread as a tether while he climbs into the sky to consume the sun or moon. If you cut the thread, it sets the vârcolac adrift." He smiled a little and chuckled, his eyes twinkling in the fluorescent light. "They're partly right. The reality is that a vârcolac finds a tether to humanity by way of a human lover. If there ever was proof of soul mates, the vârcolac is it."

At Lucy's questioning glance, Pulchrum sat back in his chair

247

and seemed to settle in preparation for a story. "Unlike with the tales the humans tell, the supernaturals have a better understanding of what a vârcolac is and does. Even so, it's still mostly theories. The vârcolac is one of the most mysterious creatures, likely due to its rarity even before the fervent hunting to eradicate their kind." He looked to the door for a moment and scratched his scruffy chin. When he looked back at Lucy, he seemed incomprehensibly sad.

"The theories say that when a vârcolac is born, his soul is born elsewhere within the body of a human. His soulessness is what causes him to always feel so empty, and drives him to consume in a desperate attempt at filling the gaping hole within. When the vârcolac comes across the human with his soul, the two cannot help but fall in love, because they are simply two halves of a whole. Once their love is consummated, a connection is formed. Affectionately dubbed 'the thread,' by their kind and others. That connection works to ground the vârcolac to his humanity, because it's as if the two lovers are sharing that one soul. As long as the connection exists, the vârcolac is sane and satiated. But, as soon as the human dies…"

Lucy frowned and looked back at the illustration of the man and woman. "The thread is broken, and he's adrift," she filled in almost sadly.

Pulchrum nodded and ran the fingers of his right hand through his hair as he bit his lip. "The vârcolac can potentially find his lover again, when the soul is born anew in another human. Even so, the chance is slim, and there's no telling how long it will take for the soul to be born again and grow to a marrying age."

"At least they don't only have one chance and that's it," said Lucy. "So, I'm assuming that means the vârcolac has a lengthy lifespan?"

"Very lengthy. I don't know if anyone's ever determined their limit, if they even have one. Another reason people think they might be descended from dragons. Dragons were considered the most ancient of beings until their extinction, surpassed only by creatures that existed at the start of all things, which some consider deities. There were a few dragons at the very start, though, I'm told."

"Are there any snakes that are dragons?" she asked, realizing that the question sounded odd.

"Snakes?" he echoed, looking thrown. "What, like the Eastern dragons, that were long and serpentine?"

Frustrated, Lucy turned back to her book and started flipping in search of chapter twenty in hopes it would help. "I don't know. I just. Someone said something to me recently about a snake that was a dragon."

"Oh?" Suddenly Pulchrum sounded distracted. When Lucy looked back up at him, he was again watching the door. "I'm not sure what they could have meant." For a moment, his eyes didn't look entirely human. It wasn't like with Günter and Eva, because they remained their usual greenish-hazel, but something about them made Lucy shudder. "Have you been shown the database, yet?" he asked as a strange non sequitur.

"No," Lucy said slowly. "I don't even know what database you're talking about."

Pulchrum clenched his jaw, but then his expression was soft and warm when he looked back at Lucy. "Come with me," he prompted as he rose from his chair. "Don't forget your book."

*

He led her down the long hall and into one of the rooms that Czar hadn't permitted entrance. Pulchrum's fingers had clicked at the

249

keypad with the ease of frequent use. The door itself had a draugr on it, looking like an angry zombie garbed in Viking armor and wielding a bloody war axe.

Within the room was what appeared to be an innocuous office space, much like Czar's office for the bookshop itself. There was a wooden desk with a single computer, a comfy-looking black swivel chair wheeled up to it. "Used to be we had to keep everyone's records as physical folders. Took a much larger space to hold it all," said Pulchrum, making sure they were both inside before closing the heavy door. "This is much more efficient, and allows for global updates to happen in real-time."

Pulchrum took the seat, motioning for Lucy to come and stand beside him. There was literally nothing else in the room, just wood panel walls, the same carpet from the store, a bare fluorescent light. She watched Pulchrum log in, and he seemed to be doing it in a slow, deliberate fashion as if to let her see what his username and password were. He glanced at her, making eye contact for a second, then nodded to the screen as he exited out and logged in once again. Lucy watched each key he typed, storing the information in her mind.

Once he was again fully logged in, Pulchrum motioned with the cursor to different portal titles. "This is the database for all registered supernaturals. You can narrow results to country, region, state, and jurisdiction. Czar's jurisdiction is the northern part of Georgia, up into South Carolina, and the bottom parts of Tennessee and North Carolina. There are chapters stationed throughout those areas that report directly to him, all headed up by a Commander. Anyone can access this database, once they are fully inducted into the Gehealdan and given an account on the portal so they can log in."

When Pulchrum seemed satisfied that Lucy understood, he pointed at a different link. "This is special. It requires high level clearance, usually only reserved to Commanders, High Commanders, and Agents." At that he smirked a bit, then clicked on the link. It required him to log in again, which he did just as slowly as before so Lucy could confirm what she'd memorized. "This is the database but with full information included in their listings. It includes those with black marks for executions as well as notes on all of the supernatural creatures who do not age, and thus require relocation after an allotted amount of time." With a few clicks of the keys, he was able to search for and subsequently pull up Hartmut Kuntz. "Jomei Tenno has her own entry, despite not being officially part of the Treaties, because all supernaturals must follow the codes so long as they reside in Gehealdan-enforced territories."

"I didn't know that," Lucy murmured, looking over Pulchrum's shoulder in fascination. "This says he only has a couple years left here, and then he has to...*die?*" She looked at him in shocked dismay. *"Seriously?"*

"Not literally. The man known as Hartmut Kuntz would be considered dead, while the werewolf himself would simply relocate under a different name and his timer resets. Tenno would likely go with him. In which case, the Gehealdan would gladly provide her a new identity with new paperwork. Just as they do for many other supernaturals."

"But what if Dr. Tenno were human?"

Pulchrum met her eyes again, and the sadness she'd glimpsed earlier returned. "The human lover of a supernatural is never to know the truth. If they should find out, they are made to forget. They're rarely given the option to join the Gehealdan and remember, unless they can provide a useful skill to the cause."

"So," Lucy felt choked as she tried to put voice to the sickening realization she was coming to. "You're telling me that the n-ah-

251

*supernatural* fakes their death, and their human lover is left to mourn them for no reason? You're saying the Gehealdan intentionally tears lovers—"

"And entire families."

"—and *entire families* apart? For what? To ensure complete secrecy?"

"It's deemed necessary," Pulchrum explained softly. "But there *is* a catch. Or, well, a stipulation, if you will. Concerning the children of such unions."

Lucy eyed him warily, not sure she wanted to hear it, fearing it would somehow make it all worse. "What?" she asked, bracing herself as if tearing off a bandage.

Pulchrum turned his attention back to the screen and seemed to be searching for someone in particular. "If their children prove to be supernaturals themselves, they must be registered and the truth must be explained to them. Then, if possible, they are reunited with the estranged parent so that they can learn about their abilities. Similarly, if a child is to somehow end up as a member of the Gehealdan, they are entitled to know the truth of their heritage, and the existence of the parent that was presumed dead."

"Okay, so what does that—" Lucy's words stabbed liked barbs in her throat, and her eyes burned when she registered the image on the screen. "How?" she tried to ask even though she couldn't find enough air to breathe let alone speak. All too soon the image on the screen became blurred by her tears, and she wiped them away furiously in an attempt to see him clearly again. The name beneath the photo wasn't the one she knew, but there was no mistaking those features. She saw their echoes everyday in the mirror, saw them replicated almost exactly in Mick. "Váli," was the primary name listed. She was sure she'd find the name she knew if she could read the notes through her tears.

Pulchrum was out of the chair and pulling her into a comforting hug as Lucy continued to stare at the screen and cry. "Go straight home," he whispered to her as he rocked her gently. "Tell no one what I've shown you. Not Czar or the others, not your friends, not your mother or your brothers. Czar wants to keep this truth from you, despite the rules, and we must be careful." He pulled back a little, and directed her attention up to him with a soft hand beneath her chin. "Take your book, and be sure to read all you can."

"I know that name," she realized, trembling. "He-he's the one that made Kuntz's kind." Something smelled like burnt plastic and the light overhead flickered for a moment.

"Read your book," Pulchrum repeated patiently. "Take a moment to calm down, dry your eyes, then go home and read your book."

"But, Dad is—"

"Don't tell anyone, Lucy. It's important that you act as if you believe him dead."

"Where is he?"

Pulchrum shook his head. "I can't tell you that."

"Is it in the computer?" She jerked back and out of his arms, turning to the computer with manic determination.

Before she could touch the keyboard, however, Pulchrum was pulling her back and turning her to face him once more. "You need to go home. Later, when you're calm, you can access the database and learn more. But right now you need to *go home*."

"But—"

He put a finger to her lips. "I've given you all the pieces you need," he whispered, green eyes flashing towards the door and back. "What happens next is up to you. Just know that I will be at your side, whatever you choose."

When she looked at him in desperate confusion, he lifted his hand to show her his wrist. For a moment, a tattoo of a writhing serpent appeared. It wrapped entirely around his wrist so that it bit its own tail. In a blink, it was gone, and his skin was clear and unmarked. "Read your book," he repeated. Pulchrum looked again towards the door. "Go now. The hall is clear."

As she slipped out the door, book clutched tightly against her chest, Pulchrum called softly, "See you in school tomorrow."

# Chapter 17
## For All We Know

A shadow-man stood in the center of the street, facing her where she watched from the window in the front door. Lucy wasn't sure how she knew he was watching her, when there was no discernible face; she simply knew he was. She entertained the possibility of moving away, so that he couldn't see her, but she really didn't know what good it would do by that point.

"We don't have a dog," her father said as he stepped up beside her.

"I know."

She didn't turn to look at him, because she knew that if she did, he wouldn't be there. That gave her an idea, and she wondered if the opposite were true for the shadow-man. Would it cease to exist once she looked away from it?

"At night they would dance," he went on to say, his rich voice enveloping her like a blanket fresh from the dryer. "They'd come as balls of light, and gather at crossroads or churchyards. There was a song, too, but I've forgotten the words. I just remember the dance. It was beautiful."

"That man out there isn't a ball of light."

"No." He shifted, and she watched the movement from the corner of her eye, wanting very much to turn and look at him. Something prevented her from looking away from the shadow-man, however. "He still meets them at crossroads and churchyards, though. Amongst other places."

"I've been to many churchyards, and I've never seen him or any lights."

"You don't want to."

255

His voice was different, and that was enough to startle her attention over to him.

Mr. Pulchrum smiled gently at her before reaching out to tug on the bottom of her sweater. "You're coming undone." Looking down, she saw that her sweater was unraveling, and he was pulling on a string. "I'll keep hold of this end," he explained, twiddling the bit between his fingers, "so that you won't get lost."

She was glad for that. The place was huge and unfamiliar. It had the air of a corporate office for a massive company. Or perhaps a government building. She couldn't be sure. Whatever it was, it was comprised of smooth surfaces and marble and glass. There were corridors that wound about her from all sides, as though she were in a random room tucked within a maze.

"Don't worry," he assured her, even as he urged her to start walking. "I won't let anything happen to you."

With those words as her shield, she pressed on into the labyrinthine halls. She found no doorways, but the architecture varied. Eventually she found herself in a dark place that looked like a honeycomb of rooms, open archways connecting them. Torches crackled to life whenever she took a step further into the rooms, following along with her like Pulchrum's protection. In the room she somehow knew was the very center, she found a man.

Or, at least she thought it was a man.

At first she'd confused it for a life-sized doll made of colored yarns, but then it moved, shifting away from the light she brought with her into the room. There were no eyes nor a mouth or nose. Just different colored strings, crisscrossing over each other to wrap around every inch of his body. The tails of some of the strands hung from him, slithering along the dirty stone floor and fraying at the tips.

"He doesn't want it," Pulchrum said into her ear, from all the

256

way back in that first room. There was a tug on her shirt, and she was leaning back against Pulchrum's chest, his arms coming around her to keep her close. "Have mercy," he said, "and leave him to his shadows."

Everything after that was confusing, even in the fractured rationality of dreams.

Sometimes they were in that large, mysterious building, and sometimes they were outside. Sometimes it wasn't 'they,' but merely her, walking along without anyone by her side despite the voices of conversation never stopping. Any questions she had, he'd answer, in a way that never made sense.

"Why can't I go that way?"

"It leads to the gardens."

"Why can't I go into the gardens?"

"Because of the dancing bird."

At one point she saw herself—not a reflection, but a completely separate her—down a corridor. At first she didn't recognize the creature with wild black hair and crazed eyes, which barely glanced up at her as it fed hungrily on the carcasses before it. Lucy thought she recognized the victims, one with hair like hers and broken glasses hanging half off his face, the other's brown hair matted with blood and his grey eyes staring sadly at her without seeing anything anymore. She didn't want to recognize them, just as she didn't want to acknowledge that she was the one chewing messily at their flesh.

So, she ran.

She ran past other things she didn't want to ever see. Creatures writhing up from shadowy crevices to reach for her with the desperate despair of a jilted lover. Statues of long-forgotten gods crying and crumbling and screaming in pain. Mirrors which reflected that feral creature from the corridor and a world of flames and death instead of Lucy and empty marble hallways.

257

"Soon," a voice whispered with the volume of someone shouting directly into her ear.

*

When her eyes opened, she wanted to scream, but her throat was closed and her jaw couldn't move. Suddenly the light was flicked on, washing away the darkness from her room. Something made a startled sound, and a familiar weight left Lucy's chest.

"You didn't burn the incense," Donnie said from where he stood just within the door.

Lucy sat up with a start, clutching the blankets as a weak barrier against the mara, even though the creature seemed to have already fled. She stared wild-eyed at her brother. "What?" she asked through panting breaths.

The way he was staring at her was something she'd seen him do before, but not for many years, not since their father died. Or, well, not since they *thought* their father had died. Donnie had been a strange child, starting from the moment he could form words. At times he'd make complete sentences that were not only far too advanced for a toddler, but were about unsettling things. He'd speak of the "Time Before," recalling memories of a life that was foreign from his own. Usually he would tell their father such things, speaking to the man as if he weren't his father but instead an old friend. Lucy remembered their father always seemed shaken after such instances, and avoided the subject whenever Diana tried to discuss it.

After their father's "death," however, Donnie hadn't ever spoken about the Time Before again.

"It helps if you leave the light on," Donnie said. "If you aren't going to burn the incense, you should at least leave the light on."

"You know about the incense? What it does?"

Donnie blinked at her, a small crease between his brows. His brown hair was a mess and the bags under his eyes spoke of interrupted sleep. "He told me, after the first night you burned it. What's wrong, did you run out?"

Lucy felt a chill and looked around the room. "Who told you?"

As if in answer, Donnie's eyes flicked to a shadowed corner of her room. "Doesn't matter," he replied almost sullenly. "You won't believe me."

"I will," she rushed to say, throwing the covers away and scooting towards the foot of her bed so she could be closer to him. "Who are you talking about?"

"I don't know his name. He doesn't really talk, just shows things with the shadows."

"Like a shadow puppet show?" Lucy asked, trying to pitch her voice as encouraging instead of alarmed.

Donnie looked skeptical and even glanced over his shoulder towards the hall. "In a way, but not as things projected on the wall. The others help him sometimes."

It took all of Lucy's control to withhold the violent shudder that wanted to rip through her. "Others?"

"They try to come out, too, like he has, but they can't fully. So, it's like part of them are here, and it makes them seem off, you know? Like partially-formed things. There's more of them when it's dark, which is why I always keep the light on in my room." He looked towards the corner again, and Lucy followed his gaze but couldn't see anything out of the ordinary. "I mean, none of them have hurt me or anything, but they make me feel uneasy. I think, if it were to ever get dark enough, they might be able to come out all the way, and it would be bad."

259

"Does," Lucy paused and licked her chapped lips. "Does he move around the house? Turn off lights? Go outside?"

Again Donnie seemed confused. "No, he can only be near me, as far as I can tell. He's always where I am, even if the only shadow in the room is tiny, he'll probably be peeking out from it, waiting to move with me somewhere darker."

What the *hell*. Lucy was overcome with the impulse to pull her brother to her and protect him. But how? Was she going to hack at the shadows with her axe? "How long has he been with you?"

"All my life, as far as I know." He shrugged as if it were nothing.

"Even...Even in the Time Before?"

That made Donnie's eyes widen, and he looked like he might run away. Instead, he took a deep breath and shook his head. "I don't think so. He seems familiar, though, so it's possible."

"Does he know who the one that turns off the lights is?" she asked, trying to paint over the desperation in her voice with calm inquiry.

Donnie just shook his head, eyes sad. "Go back to sleep, Lucy. And either burn your incense or keep your light on."

He closed the door behind himself on the way out.

Lucy was left sitting there trembling. It was as if all of the training and education for the past month or so with the Gehealdan hadn't even happened. All of the bravery and confidence she'd been starting to feel was bleeding out of her the more she realized just how little she knew and how useless she really was. Trying not to cry, she crawled back under the covers and wrapped them tightly around herself.

\*\*\*

School was hell the next day. While Lucy was no stranger to running on little sleep, this was different. It wasn't even like back when this all started, after the attack she'd witnessed, or when Günter had revealed the truth about him and his family. While last night she'd been reduced to a trembling mess, by morning her cracks had sealed over with anger and it left her rigid and cold.

Before classes started, Eva and Jim had kept casting her worried, confused looks, but she'd remained silent and stiff. Mr. Pulchrum was starting them on *Canterbury Tales*, and Lucy didn't pay attention to a single thing. He noticed that she'd not taken any notes, and frowned for a moment before plunging back into the lesson with his usual enthusiasm.

She envied him that ability, to be able to push everything aside and plaster on a smile. Then again, he was probably used to faking it. That tattoo she'd seen only for a second had seemed to be a dangerous sort of secret, a brand marking him as something other than Gehealdan. A spy, perhaps? And Branka was one too, maybe. Or at least knew about them. Which meant that not everyone approved of the Gehealdan and their methods. Lucy could understand that. There was no way she'd be able to continue blindly supporting an organization that murdered people as smokescreen and broke apart families with cruel lies. Not that she could back out, now. If she did, they'd just take her memory. Maybe there was something else she could do? Join Pulchrum's secret club or something.

But then what about Eva, Günter, and Jim? Was she just going to leave them? Let them keep working for such a deplorable organization? Pulchrum said she wasn't supposed to tell them, but how could she not? Besides, if Günter and Eva were registered, then the same restrictions would be applied to them that was applied to their father. How could they be okay with that? With knowing that if they'd

261

ever take human lovers, they'd one day have to break their hearts?

By lunchtime, Lucy felt like a pot of sauce left on the stove too long and reduced to a thick, burnt sludge. God, she was angry, but so damn tired and frustrated at the same time. It was hard trying to figure out what she could do, when she didn't even know what all of the paths were.

"Hey, Luce," Kyle greeted with his usual grin as he slid into the seat across from her at their table. "I was wondering if you're free this Friday? Chelsea and I split, and I could use some cheering up. There's this party over in Braselton, and you still owe me a dance."

Lucy thought about the last time he'd said that, about Chelsea and apologetic looks and wandering hands. "I'm busy," she grumbled at the contents of her lunchbox.

Everyone at the table fell silent and stared at her. She could feel them watching, heard Alice's sharp intake of breath beside her. "Oh," said Kyle. "Another time, then."

"No," Lucy said, shutting that assumption down as firmly as possible. "I hate parties."

"Well," Kyle started, his voice uncharacteristically hesitant. "I can understand how what happened at the last one would make you afraid to go to any more."

"It's not that." She snapped the lid back onto the container housing her sandwich and pushed it aside, appetite gone. Lifting her head, she looked him in the eyes to make sure there'd be no misunderstanding. "I hate parties. I don't ever want to go to another party. I certainly have no interest in going to a party just to watch you hook up with random chicks while you abandon me among a bunch of strangers."

"The hell, Luce?" Kyle was gaping at her, looking more hurt than angry.

"I don't have time to deal with your special brand of bullshit today, Kyle." Shoving all her food back into her lunchbox, she got up and walked out. Before she even made it to the door, she could hear some of her friends scrambling out of their seats and rushing to follow her.

"What was that all about?" Alice asked, voice gone high in shock and alarm.

"I say it's about damn time," Eva offered with an approving smirk.

"Ohmygod, Lucy!" Krysti practically yelled.

Jim didn't say anything. She could have kissed him for that.

Lucy huffed and stopped her strides in order to lean against a locker and press her forehead to the cool metal. "I've got too much shit to deal with right now," she ground out, even though she honestly didn't want to talk at all. "Kyle Raposo is so far down the list of my concerns, he's practically tied with who will win the Super Bowl."

"You hate football," Krysti felt inclined to point out.

Eva nudged the blonde with her shoulder and whispered, "That's the point."

"What's wrong?" Alice asked, placing a comforting hand on Lucy's shoulder and looking so unbearably concerned. Lucy wished she could tell her. Christ, but that would be such a relief, she thought, if she could just tell Alice everything, like she used to do before all of the vampires and Gehealdan crap formed a wedge of lies between them.

"Too much," Lucy offered up as a feeble reply. "I can't really get into it all right now. Maybe later?" She turned her head on the locker to smile weakly at Alice, hoping it was enough to placate her for the time being.

Alice seemed to hesitate before she nodded, rubbing Lucy's shoulder. "I'll hold you to that," she warned with sharp eyes despite the soothing touch. It made Lucy feel worse, because she knew she'd have to come up with more lies.

"She's probably just angsting over turning eighteen and still being single," Eva supplied, lies flowing far more naturally from her mouth than Lucy's. "Kyle, in his typical asshole way, invited her to another lame party without even realizing that's her birthday."

Lucy snorted and turned around to lean her shoulders back against the locker so she could see her friends. "That's it exactly," she joked with a roll of her eyes.

"That's right! It's your birthday Friday! We should do something fun," Krysti enthused. "Something you like."

God, all Lucy wanted to do was take a hot bath and forget the world for a while.

Forget.

She *could* forget. Previously, she'd balked at the very thought, but now she was questioning that reaction. Looking at Krysti and Alice, at how unburdened and light they seemed beside the weighted expressions on Jim and Eva's faces, Lucy wondered if ignorance really was bliss. There were countless people in the world who were oblivious to the truth, who would never look at a shadow and wonder if something was watching them back. Nothing horrible happened to them, did it?

*Tell that to the ones the Grin Reaper slaughtered,* she inwardly scoffed at herself. No, there was no salvation in forgetting.

"Maybe we could all gather at my place and just watch a movie or something?" Lucy suggested, desperately longing for a night of normalcy. She tried to not think about the thing that turned off the lights in her house, or the shadows that followed her brother wherever he went. Her house had been normal to her before, surely it could feel normal for her again.

\*

Lucy was almost feeling herself again by the time she reported to Pulchrum's room for assistant duty. He didn't mention anything that he'd revealed to her the previous day, just handed her some freshmen quizzes to grade and then buried himself in a stack of essays. It made her skin itch, until she finally convinced herself it was better this way.

As the period drew to a close, though, Pulchrum set aside the essays and stared straight at her. Outside, the late afternoon sun must have hidden behind a cloud, because it became as dark as night. There seemed to be a strange silence that accompanied the darkness, and Lucy glanced nervously at the windows.

"Ef el ay em ay en dee," Pulchrum said slowly, his eyes once again looking anything but human.

"What?" Lucy asked weakly. What new revelation was he about to dump on her now, she asked herself bitterly.

"Flămând," he said. "Remember it. All Agents have a universal key code that'll work for them at any Gehealdan location. That one's mine."

Oh. Oh god, he'd just handed her a virtual skeleton key to be able to enter any area within any Gehealdan base. She repeated the word and each of its letters in her mind over and over until she was certain they were ingrained.

"Use it sparingly and wisely," he warned. "Don't give anyone cause to check the logs."

"Why?" she asked. "Why are you telling me all of this? Everything yesterday, and now this. Why?"

He rubbed at his wrist. "Did you read the book?" he asked instead of answering her.

"Most of it," Lucy confirmed, annoyed by his dodging. "Chapter twenty is evidently about my father, and how he made the Nordic werewolves."

"Did you read about the Jörmungandr?"

"The serpent that circles the world, hidden beneath the sea. Its brother is Fenris and its sister is Hel. But Czar said Fenris is an organization, not a real wolf."

Pulchrum nodded. "Same with Jörmungandr. See, Fenris is comprised of three factions, Hati, Sköll, and Jörmungandr."

Lucy sat straighter in her chair. "Czar said my father heads up Sköll."

At that, Pulchrum smirked and even let out a little chuckle. "He heads up far more than just Sköll. He runs Fenris, second only to the Chairman."

While Lucy tried to process that, something clicked into place. "Your tattoo. The snake. It's Jörmungandr."

He flashed a second-brief smile. "That's right. The Jörmungandr is sort of the CIA of Fenris."

"You *are* a spy!" Lucy rose from her chair so fast that the stack of quizzes slid off the desk and fluttered fitfully to the floor.

Inclining his head, Pulchrum remained unruffled by her outburst. "I work for your father," he explained. "And I can get you out of the Gehealdan, memories intact."

It sounded too good to be true, and the force of it sent her back into her seat. "How?"

"We'll have to relocate you, get you out of the reach of not only Hayes but all other segments of the Gehealdan."

"What about my family?" she asked, unable to bear the thought of leaving them behind.

"That's something your father's been working on since before he was forced to leave you. We'll be doing everything in our power to get your mother and brothers relocated, as well."

Her family would be reunited, whole and complete after so long being torn and scattered. Yet, her smile froze partway to being formed, and she bit her lip. "And my friends? Eva, Jim, Günter?"

For the first time in that conversation, Pulchrum seemed hesitant. "If you feel they can be trusted, and if they express a genuine interest in joining our side," he allowed. "You must be cautious, though. If they don't share your views of the Gehealdan, then they may report you to Hayes."

"They wouldn't," she insisted, offended on their behalf for the very suggestion.

"I've seen it happen. And worse."

Lucy chewed on that for a while. The windows were still unnaturally dark, the area eerily quiet. "How long until you can get me out?" she asked, dreading the thought of having to play pretend with the other members of the Gehealdan, but willing to do so if it meant her escape would be soon.

"We're not fully prepared," Pulchrum explained. "Hopefully, we'll be able to act by the end of the month," he was quick to assure. "Sooner, if we can manage it."

Lucy laughed and rubbed at her face, wondering why this was her life. "So that means I have to pretend like everything's normal until then."

"It's just for a little while."

"And then I'll be out."

"And then you'll be out."

*Flămând*, Lucy reminded herself, resolving to check out the Gehealdan database thoroughly before making her escape. And it truly felt like an escape. The people she'd once considered allies had, in a dizzying moment of clarity, become enemies.

"Just tell me what I need to do and when."

Pulchrum smiled at her, then his eyes returned to normal, and the sunlight shown burnt gold through the blinds. "Thanks for your help with all this, Lucy. Have a great day."

Following his lead, she smiled and gathered up the fallen quizzes before tugging on her backpack. "Anytime, Mr. Pulchrum. See you later."

# Chapter 18
## Of Age

That Friday, Lucy had mixed emotions as she awoke to her mother and Donnie bursting into her room singing "Happy Birthday" and bearing gifts. It was a little difficult to celebrate when she was preoccupied with thoughts of fleeing like a fugitive. At least her family would be with her. The sooner she could get them away from everything the better. Especially now that she knew of the shadows following Donnie as well as the being that seemed to stalk their house. Despite her roiling mix of panic and uncertainty, she smiled at her family and opened presents. Lucy even managed to hide her worried glances at the shadows from Donnie.

Mick called from MIT before she headed off to school, just to wish her a happy one and chat briefly. His own birthday had only been a few days before, and she apologized for having forgotten to extend the same courtesy. When she explained how she hadn't even realized what date it was until Monday, he laughed in understanding. "Senior year can be a bit hectic at times," he said with nostalgia in his voice. "Just don't let yourself burn-out from too much stress, okay?"

She replied with affectionate assurances, inwardly resigning herself to far more stress to come. He said he'd try to get her to relax when he came home for winter break, so at least she had a little something to look forward to. What he didn't know was that they should be together sooner than that, if all went well. And with their father again, as well.

It was a thought that helped to ease at least some of her tension.

\*

As expected, most people at school paid no attention to the fact it was her birthday. Then again, she honestly doubted many even knew. This assumption was turned on its head at lunch, however, as her friends all surprised her with variously-shaped parcels wrapped in a variety of glossy colors.

Alice had been first, eagerly pressing into Lucy's hands a flat present wrapped in black and neon pink paper. It was a Voltaire CD that Lucy hadn't managed to find yet, and she hugged her friend in thanks.

"You should really come to Dragon*con with me next year, Lucy," Krysti said with a grin as she plopped an iridescent gift bag down beside Lucy's lunch. "He always comes, and you could see him perform live!"

Lucy gave a half smile of longing, even as she pulled the bag closer to inspect. "That con's so expensive, though. There's no way Mom would give me that much just to go spend a couple hours there." Besides, she'd probably no longer be in the state soon. It might be a long time before she'd have the chance to return to the area.

"Well, then you could spend the entire day with me!" Krysti's enthusiasm was too adorable for Lucy to crush it by pointing out how very unappealing she found a day filled with sci-fi panels to be.

"I'll think about it. Not even sure if I'll still be in the area next year, you know. Depends on which college I can get a scholarship for." Not a lie. Not entirely. Looking away from Krysti's contemplative pout, Lucy rummaged through the sparkly tissue inside the bag. She pulled out a book that was such a dark red it seemed almost black. The front of it had the words *Chains of the Damned: Bestiary* in raised gunmetal lettering. "A book for your RPG?" She raised an eyebrow at her geeky friend, wondering just how much Krysti had designs in corrupting Lucy to her ways.

"Well, yes, but just because I thought you'd find it interesting,"

270

Krysti explained, trying to fight back another pout. "It's got stuff on creatures from all over."

Well, that *did* sound interesting, actually. Cracking the book open, Lucy scanned the index, and was delightedly surprised to find it had strigoi, striga, and vârcolac listed. She also recognized a few of the other terms from their research. This book could be quite useful, she realized with a wide smile. "Thanks, Krys. This looks really cool." Her friend immediately brightened at the words, which made Lucy all the more pleased.

With nothing more than a quick "Here," Eva traded Lucy an envelope for the book. Lucy stared at her in bemusement for a moment, and Krysti let out an excited squee as she started asking Eva if she'd finally gotten interested in joining. Krysti was leaning across Kyle's lap to better talk to Eva, and he was glaring down at her in feigned annoyance as she separated him from his food.

Shaking her head with a little laugh, Lucy looked down at the envelope and pulled out the card. It was a simple piece of white card stock with "Happy Birthday" scrawled out by hand in black ink. Lucy tried to hide her disappointment, even as she flipped it over to find the other side blank.

"That's not the present," Eva explained, looking up from whatever page she'd been reading. "The real present is at the shop, and I'll give it to you later. Just couldn't give it to you at school, because then I'd also be giving the merry gift of expulsion." When everyone gave her a strange look, Eva smirked. "It's got quite an edge to it, let's just say." Eva paused for a moment, then her smirk somehow hitched even higher on that one side. "Actually, it's two things with edges, to be exact."

"That's when you'll be getting my presents, too," added Jim with a wink. "You'll understand when you see."

While all the others stared at them in blank confusion, Lucy grinned, eyes alight at the thought of what they could have possibly gotten her.

Kyle interrupted her thoughts as he set a small box in front of her lunch bag. "Happy birthday, Luce." Both his voice and smile were hesitant, no doubt due to the way Lucy had snapped at him earlier in the week. Neither of them had really talked much since then, even though they continued to eat across from each other at lunch every day.

"You didn't have to," she protested, looking at the box without making any motion to accept it.

"I know," he said softly, nudging it a little further across the table. "No one ever *has* to buy anyone a present." His smile dared to widen a little in an attempt to coax one from her. She gave a weak smile in return and slowly reached out to take the gift.

Alice leaned in a bit too close as Lucy unwrapped it, and her gasp was far more audible than Lucy's own. He had given her a set of earrings, both comprised of flat, silver suns dangling from a fine chain. A flat circle representing the full moon—complete with detailed etchings of craters—was set in the center of each sun, which rotated independently. Some sort of thin, translucent red lacquer coated the moons. The left earring had an additional chain, which connected to a tiny red loop—treated in the same lacquer—for her cartilage piercing.

"Try them on," Kyle insisted. His eyes still reflected how unsure he was of his gift's reception, but he tried to look upbeat.

Carefully removing her current black rose studs and black cartilage loop, Lucy swapped them for the new set. Kyle's smile softened, and he reached across to shift some of her hair away in order to get a clear view of the earrings. "Knew they'd look perfect on you."

Lucy was aware of the hush that had fallen at her table. In her peripheral she noticed Jim's gaping mouth and Eva's arching eyebrows and Krysti biting her lip to contain squeals of glee. Alice was grinning right beside her, and Lucy tried for a similar smile even though she knew it lacked the same wattage.

"So, I know you don't like parties," Kyle said slowly, then bit his lip for a moment, eyes darting down to the table with uncharacteristic shyness. "But, I was wondering if you'd like to hang out tonight? Just the two of us."

She blinked.

"As a date?" she asked, trying to sound interested, because she knew that's what everyone expected of her. This was the guy she'd wanted for so long, wasn't he? Yet as she looked across the table at him, she could only think about all of the times he had jerked her around. Eva was right, he was a fisher. The party of the Halloween Massacre had been the final straw, she realized.

He nodded, looking hopeful, and it made Lucy feel bad that she couldn't find it within her to care. Forcing her smile wider, she accepted his offer.

\*\*\*

When she entered Pulchrum's room for her period as his assistant, he called her to his desk with an unfamiliar tone to his voice. Instantly she assumed the worst, that something was wrong with the plan. Maybe he wouldn't be able to get her out as soon as they'd thought, or maybe the whole thing would be scrapped and she'd just be stuck.

Standing tensely in front of Pulchrum's desk, Lucy tried to steel herself for what was to come. The very last thing she expected was to see Pulchrum pull a box-shaped package in powder blue wrapping from a drawer.

"It's your birthday, right?" he asked, a smile lighting up his face. At her stunned nod, he held out the gift and let his smile tilt into a sly grin.

Her fingers didn't even tremble as she tore the paper. That surprised her, since she could feel her heart working double time to pump all kinds of hormones into her system that were guaranteed to wreak havoc on her composure. God, she was so glad that puberty was nearly over.

When she finally had it fully unwrapped and got a good look at what it was, she wished there were a chair for her to sit in. Since there was none, she settled for anchoring herself with one hand gripping the desk. Pulchrum had given her a very old, very *beautiful* leather-bound collection of the entirety of Emily Dickinson's poetry.

"This is…she's my favorite. How did you…?"

His smile was brighter than the golden sunlight streaking across his desk. "I've never seen anyone as enthusiastic about poetry as you were during her segment last year. Plus I've noticed that you use her meter and rhyme pattern most for your own works. So I figured this was a pretty safe bet for a present." He tilted his head to the side like a puppy. "Do you like it?"

Pale blue eyes—the same color as the wrapping paper—traced the curve of his hair on his cheek, then looked down at the dark brown leather. "I do. It's too much, though. Must have cost a lot. I can't…I shouldn't accept it."

She tried to hand it over to him, but he placed his warm hands on hers where they gripped the book. That's where her eyes focused while he gently pushed the gift back towards her. "Please. It's nothing, really. I've had it lying around for years, just collecting dust." Even after the motion stopped, he was slow to move his hands away. The brush of his fingertips along her knuckles made her arms tingle, and she had to

274

suppress a shiver.

Lucy set the book down in front of her and ran her fingers along the elegant scrollwork in the leather. "Thank you. For everything."

"You really don't need to thank me."

There were calla lilies in the corners, curling out of the border of woven vines. Like tendrils of hair across a cheek. Her fingers lingered on their curving stems.

***

"You seem a bit spacey."

"Hm?" Lucy looked up from the Dickinson book on her lap. Jim had turned around in the front passenger seat, and was studying her with amusement and mild concern.

"You've been zoned-out this whole time. You okay?"

Fighting back a blush, Lucy nodded and set the book aside on the back seat. "Yeah, fine. Just thinking."

For a moment, Jim continued to study her, his eyes going from the book to her pink cheeks. "It's a nice gift," he said eventually, his tone expertly neutral.

"She's my favorite poet." Lucy rubbed her fingertips along the top again.

The most recent dream flashed through her mind, with images of Pulchrum promising guidance and protection, as well as the scene where he had pulled her back against his chest and wrapped his arms around her.

Closing her eyes, she tried to focus on that instance. It had felt so real. So perfect. So right.

God, what was wrong with her? It wasn't the time to be fantasizing and daydreaming! Shit was getting heavy. She was conspiring with a spy against the organization that she worked for, and possibly had to go on lying to said organization for another month. Honestly, part of her feared what kind of person she'd become if she continued to work for the Gehealdan.

*Her own eyes staring up at her from a blood-splattered face. Fire. Screams.*

Shuddering, Lucy retrieved the book and clutched it to her chest. Her other dreams had held clues, truths wrapped in nightmarish images. Maybe the last one was a warning. Warning of *what*, though, that was the question. Of what was meant to be, or of what could potentially be? Was there a way to prevent herself from becoming that feral creature? Was there a way to stop the fires and the pain and chaos? There had to be, right? Or else what was the point of being warned?

\*

She was still rather quiet and in thought after they arrived at the shop and she was ushered back to the War Room. Günter was already there and waiting, and he greeted them with a smile as he pushed two messily-wrapped gifts further out onto the table.

"These are combined gifts from the three of us," Eva explained as Lucy approached the packages.

Setting aside thoughts of nightmares and warnings, Lucy tore into the skull-and-crossbones-adorned paper. They were a machete and an axe, which she already possessed, but these were obviously of higher quality. The machete was longer, widening suddenly towards the tip with a bit of an outward curve. With that added weight at the end, it made it a much better weapon for chopping, she realized as she tested it out with a few swift motions. It almost seemed to propel itself, minimizing the amount of effort she needed to put forth. The axe possessed a curved blade that was almost as elegant as it was deadly.

Opposite the blade, the head was broad and spiked like a meat tenderizer. She knew it would be perfect for shattering the particularly difficult bones, thus making it easier to chop the bodies into pieces. There was a strange pang in her chest at the knowledge that these would only be useful for another few weeks. Somehow she doubted she'd be an executioner once she became part of Fenris.

"Günter and I selected the weapons," Eva continued, after allowing Lucy time to open and examine them. "Jim created sheaths."

Yes, she had noticed the sheaths were particularly stunning. Jim had stained the leather in dark browns and rusty reds, incorporating knotwork and stylized wolves with wings. "Since it's like we four have our own little clan," Günter said with a gentle smile. "Something apart from the tengu or the wolf clans of mine and Eva's families. The four of us have created our own unit, it seems."

Lucy returned the smile, and she could feel the prick of unshed tears. Setting the weapons down, she took turns giving each friend a hug. "There are no other warriors I'd rather have at my back," she choked out. Somehow soon she'd have to speak with them about what she'd learned, and about leaving with her to Fenris. But not there, not where Czar or the others could hear.

Her gushing words of thanks were interrupted by Czar's sudden arrival. His face was grim, his mouth a flat, lipless line. All of Lucy's good spirits fled her, and she swallowed around a sudden lump in her throat. Czar settled his focus on Lucy and gave a nod of his head for her to approach him. She stepped from the table to obey, and he held out a sheet of paper for her to take. "This here's a list of books I want ya ta read. We're goin' ta start ya learnin' runes and old Norse. You'll likely need it fer later."

Lucy looked up at him in horror. Norse. Did he know, somehow, that she'd learned the truth?

"I realize it's yer birthday, an' you likely don't wanna spend it studyin'. Still. I want ya ta go fetch tha first couple an' meet back with me ta go over yer lesson plan. Don't worry, I'll let ya out early tonight so ya can go celebrate or what not." He patted her shoulder and offered a half smile, then moved past her to take a seat at the table.

"Just wasn't ever very good with languages," she offered up as quick explanation for her flash of fear.

"Won't be doin' it alone," said Czar. "Languages were always a specialty of mine. Hurry on now."

*

"What the hell are *you* doing here?"

Black eyes looked away from their examination of faded titles, rolling to focus on Lucy where she stood beside outdated foreign almanacs. Ren stared at her for a moment, then turned back to his search. Long, narrow fingers moved with the speed and grace of a figure skater as they followed his eyes' path along the spines.

"I'm shopping," he said, voice bored and practically dismissive.

"Are you stalking me or something?" Lucy glanced at the shelves nearest her. She should just grab the books Czar sent her for, but Ren's pale form was proving to be rather distracting.

He sighed as he carefully pulled a book partially out with one finger. After a brief study of the cover, he slid it back into place. "I believe I should be the one to ask that, since I'm almost always at the location first." He let Lucy see his smirk, knowing it would infuriate her even more. "So, what are *you* doing here? Do you work here? I've never seen you here before."

She made herself look away, focusing on the task of finding a book. "Sometimes. Right now, I'm supposed to get tutored on something."

"Interesting job feature. Are you to be tutored on stocking shelves? Because I believe that's just called 'training,' not 'tutoring.'"

Ah, there it was. Lucy pulled the book out, surprised that it wasn't as thick as she had feared it would be. "No, actually. I'm going to be taught about runes."

"Runes?" Ren turned to face her fully, and Lucy felt that now she couldn't just walk away. "Are you into fantasy games or something?"

With a sigh of her own, Lucy tucked her hair behind her right ear. Her fingers brushed her earring, and the flick of Ren's eyes towards the jewelry did not go unnoticed. "No, that's more my friend Krysti's arena." Thinking fast, she came up with a plausible excuse for her own interest. "This is for a project related to Norse writings."

"Isn't that a bit advanced for high school?" Even while he tried to focus on her face, Ren's attention kept returning to her exposed earring. Lucy found it to be mildly disconcerting.

"What? What is it?" she asked, hand coming up to touch at the dangling sun. "Is it bent or something?"

"Huh? Oh. No, it's just interesting, that's all. Both eclipses in one." Since he'd been caught, he went ahead and openly stared.

"Eclipses?" Sliding the hook from her lobe, Lucy held the earring in front of her to re-examine.

Ren stepped closer, making a confirming hum as he poked the red moon disk with his finger. In the dim light, the moon looked like it was coated in old blood, then it seemed to vanish when he rotated it perpendicular to the sun. "When it's a solar eclipse, it looks like there's a black hole in the center of the sun. Not like the phenomena, but as if someone just hollowed out the insides. All that's left is a ring of wispy light, too faint to illuminate the world." He tapped the moon again, so

279

that its craggy face was towards Lucy. "With lunar eclipses, the moon appears to bleed, until it's covered in its own blood."

She watched the charm sway where it dangled from her fingers, and wondered if Kyle knew what it meant. The fingers of her left hand skidded across the rough fabric skin of the book as she gripped it tighter. What a coincidence.

*"There's no such thing as coincidence,"* her father once told her. *"There's only inescapable destiny, which is sometimes generous enough to leave clues."*

"You didn't know what it was?" Ren asked with a mocking laugh to his voice. Lucy blinked and focused on Ren beyond the earring. He somehow pulled off an expression of condescending amusement. "Why did you buy them if you didn't even know what they were?"

"I didn't," she said almost petulantly as she slipped it back into her lobe. "It was a birthday present that I just got today."

"Oh, it's your birthday?"

"Yes," she confirmed hesitantly, confused by his sudden exuberance.

"And me without a gift! That just won't do. You're an adult now, right? That must be honored in some way. Let me see." He started rummaging in the brown canvas messenger bag he wore on one shoulder. Judging by his tone, Lucy couldn't be certain if he was being serious or if this was one of his jokes.

When he pulled out a spherical rock and presented it with a triumphant "Tada!" Lucy no longer questioned it. It obviously had to be a joke.

"A rock." Her voice was as flat as her stare, but she accepted the stone just the same.

"Not just any rock. It's a Schrödinger geode!"

"Did you pick this up in the parking lot?"

Ren tsked and looked disappointed in her lack of enthusiasm. "I got it quite a while ago, while I was out west."

"Uh-huh. So, you have a habit of carrying rocks around with you?" She turned it over in her hands, fingers learning its bumps and dents.

"It's not a rock; it's a Schrödinger geode," he repeated.

"And just what is that supposed to mean?"

He grinned as if having waited for such a question. "Well," he said, drawing out the word until it was practically unrecognizable, "if you split it open, there could be any number of things you might find. Perhaps it contains perfectly clear crystal, or milky quartz. Maybe it houses amethyst or fool's gold. Or, it could just be solid rock. As long as you *don't* open it, it's all of these things. It's only once you *do* open it that a specific option becomes the recognized reality."

"Were you dropped on your head often as a kid?"

He blinked at her, enthusiastic grin draining and twisting into one of his sardonic smirks. "Oh, far worse than that, but I don't see the relevance."

"I think it made you mentally unhinged."

Grin suddenly stretching wide in dark amusement, Ren chuckled. "No, I'm sure that's a result of many other factors."

"Yes. Well. I'm sure it is." Lucy took a step back, edging along the shelves towards the mouth of the aisle. "I should get back to Czar before he sends a search party. Thanks again for the…er…magical rock thing."

Ren's eyes were laughing at her, and his disturbing grin seemed to be slowly pulling impossibly wider. "Keep it with you. Might help keep the demons at bay."

Eva would be proud of Lucy's acting, since she managed not to let any of the guilty panic show on her face. Instead, she appeared curious and confused, pausing only for clarification, and not fear of being found out. "Demons?"

"Eclipse demons. You're wearing their symbols, so you should be careful. They aren't the sort you want to attract." His laughing eyes drifted smoothly into a lascivious leer.

Keeping the tension out of her posture, Lucy tilted her head quizzically. "You mean like vârcolaci?" Could he be...? Was Ren a supernatural? In that moment, Lucy realized with a sharp, growing panic that she'd only ever seen him during the night—even this meeting was taking place after sunset. And he'd been at that party on Halloween...

His dark eyes stared into hers, and his grin looked like it could cut diamond. "So full of surprises."

As she opened her mouth to retort, another voice smoothly intercepted hers. "Ren! Always a pleasure." She spun around to see Phil strolling up, his attention totally focused on Ren as he smiled with warmth and familiarity. "Unfortunately, we've nothing new in our French section."

Lucy scrunched her face up in confusion and looked from one to the other before settling on Phil. "French?"

Phil gave her a questioning look, as if wondering why she even had to ask. "Of course. Ren is French. He often comes by to snatch up any good French collections we manage to obtain."

"No, he's not." She looked back to Ren, who was barely withholding more laughter.

"Oui. Je suis." His accent was perfectly flawless, and even those few words flowed from his mouth with a natural grace. "My full name is René Sartre, and I'm originally from France," he explained. "I developed an American accent because I've been here for a while.

That's all."

"That's some damn good assimilation," she remarked, grudgingly impressed. Phil had been away from Greece for about ten years, and yet he had not fully lost his accent. Jim sounded just as British as he had when he'd first moved there four years ago. Even Dr. Kuntz and Dr. Tenno, who had been away from their homelands for over twenty years, still bore their original accents. Ren sounded like he was born and bred in America. Lucy's suspicions rose as she wondered just how long he meant by "a while," in order for his accent to have faded so much.

"In any case," he continued, dismissively turning away from Lucy to focus on Phil. "How about in one of the other languages?"

Phil had to consider his response for a moment, most likely trying to mentally review their recent inventory additions. "Might have a few. You'll have to ask Czar. You know how he sometimes likes to hoard things. Could be that we've gotten in something you'd like, but he just hasn't decided if he wants to put it out on the shelves."

Feeling quite put-out with how the two men seemed to be ignoring her, Lucy turned back to her task and pulled a couple more of her assigned titles. Phil must have been keeping an eye on her actions, even while he continued to talk about books with Ren, because he motioned wordlessly for her to follow him once she'd finished. Ren tagged along, the conversation never faltering as it shifted from books to what Lucy thought sounded a bit like gossip. Lucy eyed Ren as they walked, as if hoping to find a chink in his human appearance that would give her a clue as to what he really was. There was no way he was human, she was growing more sure of that by the moment as she scrutinized every past interaction with him.

Evidently everyone had moved from the War Room to the café area, as that was where Phil was leading them. Lucy and her friends tended to prefer the smaller, more intimate tables and the cushier chairs. Plus it didn't hurt having quick access to drinks that would help fuel them in their ceaseless researching.

Once they were back with the others, Czar welcomed Ren heartily and took him off to the side to converse with him in quick, fluid French. It left Lucy stunned for a moment, as she listened to the old man roll the language from his tongue as if he'd been born to speak it. Dazed, she wandered over to the table where her friends sat.

Eva greeted her by sliding a familiar book across the table to her. "I think we should take Krysti up on the offer to sit in on one of her RPG sessions," she said.

Confusion growing, Lucy set her stack of books aside and pulled the bestiary closer to look down at the pages that had been left open. She hadn't had a chance to really read it earlier, and now that she was getting a better look at it, something about the descriptions seemed familiar.

"Some of these are almost exactly like passages in that Yaxley book, verbatim," Eva continued, which helped explain any of the familiarity.

Brows coming together, Lucy re-read the passages a bit more closely, and realized that Eva was right. "Isn't that plagiarism, then?" she asked, eyes still glued to the page about strigoi.

"What are the odds that he has the same book?" countered Jim. "That thing was over a century old."

"Did I hear you guys right—did you say Yaxley?" Carmen was suddenly hovering between Jim and Günter. "I know Phil mentioned something about you guys having a Yaxley book, but I thought he was joking. You seriously have one? Can I see?"

Lucy blinked up at her, wondering if this haze of confusion would ever dissipate. "I thought Czar sent it to us to read."

"Sent it to you?"

"Through Agent Be—" Lucy glanced over at Ren. "Through Mr. Pulchrum."

Carmen's eyes widened. "He has a copy of Yaxley's manifesto?"

Everyone at the table was turned to give Carmen their undivided attention, now. Lucy even closed the book and folded her arms over the hard cover so as to have no distraction. "I assume this Yaxley bloke is of some importance?" Jim inquired, one brow regally arched.

Flicking him a mildly irritated glance, Carmen gave a curt nod. "Yaxley was an alias for a former Promethean." At this, she glanced over to Phil, who was participating in the French discussion with difficulty and determination. "They were a group primarily comprised of strigoi that used to protect humans, much like y'all's dad's clan." She flicked her fingers at Eva and Günter. "Also like them, the Prometheans swore off such protections after being hunted by the very humans they'd been trying to protect. They were a major influence on the Treaties. That book was written well after the Treaties were made, and it drew the angered attention of many factions."

Again Carmen glanced at Phil, and Lucy remembered him showing them his ring and talking about his adoptive father. An over-protective strigoi. "Most of the copies were destroyed," Carmen went on to explain. "The surviving copies are so rare that most believe them to be nonexistent. Czar's been trying to find one for years, with no luck." Fixing her eyes on Lucy, Carmen's voice grew quieter. "Interesting that an Agent would have one and never tell him."

Something cold rolled around in her gut, but Lucy met Carmen's eyes without hesitation. "Mr. Pulchrum likes to collect antique publications, so perhaps that's how he came about possessing a copy of it. I mean, he gave me an antique copy of Dickenson works today, so..."

"Is that right."

"Carmen! My darling!" Ren suddenly swooped around the table to scoop Carmen into his arms and give her a twirl. Her serious expression vanished in the span of a breath, and a smile was threatening to conquer her lips. After their twirl, Ren dipped her and came within a few inches of pressing his lips to hers, a grin splitting his face and his eyes gleaming. "Always a delight to see you," he purred, before slowly righting her.

Laughing softly, Carmen put a hand to his chest and pushed playfully. "You're incorrigible."

"No, my dear, I believe the term you meant to say was 'insatiable.'" His grin turned salacious and he winked.

"Not in front of the children, darling," she quipped back with a pointed glance to the table beside them.

"Children?" He turned and ran his eyes over the group of four. "I see no children. In fact," he drawled, his expression turning positively predatory, "I see nothing but beautiful people all around me. It's a veritable smorgasbord of delicious options."

Phil laughed as he strode up to join everyone. "Down, boy. Not sure your belt can hold any more notches."

"Look who's talking!" Ren's hand settled on Phil's shoulder with comfortable familiarity, friendly laughter punctuating his words. "Besides, I'm merely keeping up the part of the stereotypical Frenchman, here to seduce everyone."

Carmen sighed with feigned exasperation. "Yeah, well, they're a tad busy. Leave them be, and keep it tucked."

Lucy watched the three of them banter and laugh. She watched Ren's face light up and shift with each new emotion. Part of her wondered at how she could have suspected that he was anything other than just a normal guy. The rest of her, however, glanced at Phil's ring and tried to see if it was reacting. On the table beside her books, she had set the round rock. Twirling it idly, she filtered things in her mind like picking particularly colored puzzle pieces out of a pile. Everything would come together, she assured herself, once she'd collected all the right pieces.

"Kids," Czar barked, scattering her thoughts and pulling her mind away from Ren. With a nod towards the back, Czar ordered them to come along.

Lucy was honestly a little annoyed at having to return to the back rooms after only just getting situated there at the cafe. But orders were orders, so she gathered up her things and followed everyone through the shelves. When she glanced back over her shoulder at Ren, he was still chatting with Phil and Carmen, but his eyes flicked her way and that smirk of his returned. Face heating, she quickly turned back around and hurried along her way.

*

Mr. Pulchrum was waiting for them in the War Room, a file opened in front of him on the table with its papers spread out. As everyone gathered around, he and Czar had some kind of silent conversation involving eyebrows and thinned lips. Eventually Pulchrum looked to the newbies with a kind, apologetic smile, and reached out to tap his fingers against the file's contents. "We'd like you do to recon again tonight. Just for a little bit. Nothing major."

"It's yer birthday, though, Lucy, an' I know I said you'd have most of the night off," Czar began, his tone pointed, making Pulchrum wince.

"Um," she stammered, "it's fine. I mean, I had a date, but I can

287

just—"

"An' I know," Czar continued, the pointedness becoming a sharp tangle of brier, "that all y'all mightn't want ta be doin' another recon mission so soon after what happened at the last."

"They have to learn somehow," Pulchrum insisted, smile losing its gentleness as it grew brittle. He then turned guilty, sad eyes onto Lucy. "And I *am* sorry if this disrupts your birthday plans."

"No," she shook her head and gripped the round stone in her hand a bit tighter. "Like I said, it's fine."

"Y'all'll be released after this briefin'," gruffed Czar, arms folded across his chest and glare directed at the paper on the table. "Get yer date in, then go do recon."

"Oh, um, thanks." For some strange reason, Lucy felt a pang of regret, though. It was as if she'd rather be sitting in the cafe learning Norse than going on a date with the boy she'd crushed on for years. Which, honestly, that was ridiculous. Of course she'd rather go out with Kyle than study.

Pulchrum cleared his throat and, fingers still on the papers, pushed them forward a bit. "Here's the info on the Treaty breaker. We're having difficulty locating exactly where he's sleeping during the day and on Saturdays, which is why we were hoping you lot could spot him and—as stealthily as possible—follow him back to his resting place."

The friends moved to lean closer over the table and get a good look. "Another strigoi," murmured Eva, reaching out to pull a sheet closer.

Groaning, Lucy set her books and rock down to grab one of the papers herself. "Does this mean we have to go to another party?"

"Looks like," confirmed Jim, looking about as enthused as she was.

"There are a few potential parties he might be found at tonight,"

288

said Pulchrum, clasping his hands behind his back and watching them read the file. "Start with the top one listed, as it's the one we feel he's most likely to show up at, according to his typical habits."

"Anything else?" asked Günter, looking between Pulchrum and Czar. "Any other specific orders?"

"Just don't engage," was the command from Czar. "If ya do manage to find 'im, keep yer distance while maintaining a visual. Do not, I repeat do *not* approach him in any way."

"Understood," the four of them offered up at once, nodding almost in perfect sync.

He stared back at them for a heavy pause, then shook his head and waved one broad hand. "Y'all can go."

Lucy quickly fumbled everything back into her arms as she mentally composed the text she was going to send Kyle about having to bump their date up. They'd still probably have to cut it a bit short, since she was going to have to do recon later. Maybe they should just postpone it all together? Though that bore the risk of having it canceled entirely, and she'd have missed her one chance with him.

She gave Pulchrum a parting nod and shy glance before ducking her head and hurrying out of the room. All the way back to the parking lot with the others, she tried to convince herself that she would be disappointed if she missed out on this date.

# Chapter 19
## Trivialities and Terrors

"I'm telling ya, Luce, you should have seen his face." Kyle leaned over his plate a little as he laughed, a fry dangling forgotten from his fingers. "It was purple, he was so angry!"

Nudging the remains of her pasta about with her fork, Lucy cast a surreptitious glance at her watch. A smile was stretched almost painfully across her face, and she hoped the laugh she shoved out of her throat didn't sound nearly as forced as it felt. "I'm surprised that you weren't grounded for life!"

She had no idea why Kyle thought she'd be impressed by the story of his father having found his Marlboro and Smirnoff stash. Perhaps it was a story he often told his dates, she figured. When you spend your weekends hacking up bodies in a grave, however, cliché little attempts at teen rebellion just don't seem to matter. Speaking of which, Lucy was due back at her house soon in order to be picked up for that evening's recon.

Lucy and Kyle had forgone the movie and simply went to dinner, since Lucy had explained that she had other plans for the evening as well, and they had already gotten off to a late start due to her work at the bookshop. Kyle hadn't been happy to hear that their first date would be cut so short, but he'd relented when he'd gotten her to promise there'd be another to make up for it.

Now she was starting to wonder why it was she had ever wanted to date him. Maybe *she* was the fisher, she thought with a sense of self-disgust, watching his warm eyes twinkle with mirth and yet not feeling that familiar flutter in her stomach. Here she finally had the boy she'd been wanting for years, and all she could think about was getting rid of him so she could hunt down undead monsters. Maybe there was something wrong with her.

All attempts at discussing mutual interests such as literature—and she knew for a fact he'd read a lot of the same books as she had—had fallen flat. His eyes would just start to get a vacant look about them, and his smile would lose sincerity. Directing the conversation into his control simply resulted in a never-ending procession of stories about himself. It was painfully obvious that he was trying to impress her, but she couldn't understand why he'd feel the need to do so. Did he really not know that she'd had a crush on him for so long?

She found her mind wandering to thoughts of her father. There were memories she'd always held dear, snapshots of scenes to keep him alive in her mind. But, he was alive outside of her mind, as well. Would he be the same as she remembered? Or would he be different, now that she and the others would know the truth about him? There was also the possibility that her memories were inaccurate, skewed by love and eaten at by time. No matter what, though, she couldn't wait to see him again. It was a second chance she'd never thought she'd have with him.

"Hey, earth to Lucy." Kyle waved his hand in front of her face, and she sat up with a jerk.

"Sorry! I spaced out for a second there." She smiled contritely at him and set her fork down on her plate with a clink.

He studied her for a moment, and his smile from earlier faded away. "There you go being distant again, Luce."

Glancing aside, she shifted on the booth bench. "I don't know what you mean."

Kyle swirled a fry around in his ketchup as an excuse to not meet her eyes anymore. "Nothing, don't worry about it."

Part of her ached inside as she took in his disappointed expression. As she reached out to take his free hand, she shifted her foot to nudge their boots together. "Things have just been a bit hectic for me lately," she said, running her thumb over his knuckles.

He looked up at her through jagged bangs—he hadn't spiked his hair up with his usual gel—and smiled. Turning his hand over, he grabbed hers in return. "You know I'm always here if you need me, Luce."

*There* was that old familiar flutter. "Thanks."

\*

The rest of their short time together had passed pleasantly after that, though Lucy still found herself eagerly awaiting the time for her to go home and meet up with the others. When they found themselves lingering on her front stoop, Lucy felt a confusing mix of emotions. Part of her wanted to continue spending time with him, while part of her wanted to rush off to change and get ready. Just as she started to say good-bye, she felt his fingers combing back through her hair to cradle her head and pull her closer.

Ever since she was fifteen, she'd dreamed about kissing him. There were times when they'd share an art class, and her pitiful attempts at painting would go neglected while she watched his lips move as he talked to someone. She always imagined it would be like something from the movies, where she'd feel a thrum of rightness in the act, and the rest of the world would melt away into an inconsequential blur.

He tasted like the mints he'd crunched on after dinner, with just a lingering hint of the pickles from his burger beneath it all. His lips were surprisingly soft, and his tongue was almost shy about engaging her own. The kiss itself was disappointingly mediocre, but she liked the feel of one hand in her hair and the other pressing at the small of her back. When she pressed more aggressively into the kiss, it seemed to be the indicator he needed to stop holding back. The little moan he made as he tightened his embrace made her breath stutter against his lips.

Then, suddenly he was kissing her with a fierceness that had her clinging to him as the world finally—*finally*—started to become a diluted smear of drenched watercolors.

As they pulled away, he nibbled gently at her lower lip, sending pleasant tingles through her body. "You sure you have to be somewhere tonight?" he asked, lips brushing against hers with each word.

For one insane moment, Lucy was tempted to tell him everything and see if he'd like to join them. She hated that none of her other friends knew, that it was a secret she had to keep from all of them. Kyle could become part of the team, and he'd be someone she could confide in about all of her doubts and fears. But she knew that wasn't possible, and it was selfish of her to get them involved when tensions seemed to be simmering between some of the supernaturals and the Gehealdans.

"Yeah. I have to." Her fingers stopped gripping at his shoulder and moved up to twiddle with his hair, thankful that he'd forgone the gel. "But we could go out again soon, if you'd like." The dark strands looked almost to have blondish highlights thanks to the yellowish glare of the porch light. It might be nice to have another normal teenage experience before running away like a thief in the night to join a secret faction of supernatural beings.

His grin had her lips drawing back in response. "Oh, I'd like. God, Luce, you've no idea how long I've wanted you."

A startled laugh puffed past her lips, and she couldn't help but give him another quick kiss. "Ditto," she whispered, pressing her cheek against his. Kyle wrapped both arms around her waist and held her tight. *I'll miss this*, she told herself with a sudden sadness. *I'll miss him.*

Günter's SUV pulled into the driveway, its headlights casting their merged silhouette against the side of the house, and Lucy felt her heart sink a little. She tried to pull out of Kyle's arms, but he just squeezed tighter and gave her another deliciously rough kiss. "Next time," he said after they finished, and he could look her in the eye, "I'm going to require you spend a bit more time with me. No running off to be with someone else."

She would have laughed if it weren't for the seriousness she could see in his expression. "It's not like I'm running off to be with another guy or anything."

He opened his mouth, the sound of an aborted word escaping, but then clenched his jaw closed and broke eye contact.

"I'm not, you know," she assured, ruffling his hair and pressing her body flush up against his. "The only guys that will be near me are Jim and Eva's older brother. Jim you *know* isn't an issue, and Günter's like family to me."

Despite his responding nod, he didn't appear entirely convinced, but he loosened his grip all the same. The sounds of car doors opening and closing reached them, and Lucy stepped out of Kyle's arms. "I have to go get changed." There was an unsaid apology in her voice, and she grabbed his hand to give it a little squeeze.

"Yeah, okay. Hey," he squeezed her hand back to ensure her attention, "call me later, yeah?"

"Sure." Unable to resist, she leaned in for a quick parting kiss, then stepped out of his reach. "Bye."

"Bye, Luce. And happy birthday."

He gave her a slanted smile before turning away, and tossed a wave at the others as they approached. All too soon he was in his rusty old Camaro, and Lucy was left with nothing else to do but go inside and prepare for recon.

\*\*\*

She realized her folly all too late as she watched Kyle push towards her through the crowd, his face shadowed in anger. Eva's curse could be heard above the pulsing music, and Lucy wasn't sure if it had been uttered in frustration or sympathy. Günter and Jim had already fanned out to work the room, and she had the irrational desire to have them there beside her as back-up.

"The hell, Luce?" he spat in greeting, invading her personal space for reasons other than the necessity to be heard. "You cut our date short so you could go out partying? What was that about how you *hate* parties, and how Jim and Günter were going to be the only—"

"It's not like that!" she yelled back, the increased volume a reflection only of the atmosphere and not her emotions. To be honest, she didn't feel terribly upset, neither worried nor angry. Her mind was too busy maintaining the act of loyal Gehealdan while simultaneously trying to figure out how to convince her friends to join Fenris. Kyle's sudden appearance was little more than an unwanted distraction. Her words were sincere, however. It wasn't really what he thought it was. The very idea hadn't even occurred to her. This wasn't an outing of pleasure, but merely a job. A job nearly as unpleasant to her as hacking up bodies and feeding them to blue-and-yellow flames. No matter how many parties she had attended, they had never grown on her. Honestly, she'd much rather be doing just about anything else than attend another party.

"Oh yeah?" he shot back, arms crossing over his chest. He was wearing the same red long-sleeved shirt with black shadow monsters that he'd worn earlier on their date. It was a pretty fascinating shirt, she thought absently, studying the twisting, elongated forms. Some of them reminded her of the things on the doors in the back hall, and she also wondered if the things Donnie saw looked like that. "What is it, then?" Ah, that's right, he was angry at her and yelling, and she should be doing or saying something to patch up the situation, if she ever wanted him to kiss her again as he had earlier.

Before she could formulate a response, Eva was stepping in to intervene. "Don't blame her; she only came because I made her."

Kyle switched his attention to Eva, his eyelids fluttering for a moment as if he were having trouble passing from one thread of focus to another. "What do you mean? Why?"

Eva glanced away, looking every bit like someone who was embarrassed and entirely too vulnerable. It was quite entrancing to watch, considering Eva was not someone who would ever truly be that way. "There's a guy I like," she eventually confessed, as if the words had been forced from her against her will. "I wanted Lucy to come with me as moral support when I see him here. I'm not sure how he feels about me, and…well…I thought it would help me come across as more casual if I had friends with me. Less like I'm stalking or something, you know."

Amazingly enough, Kyle seemed to be buying it. Or, perhaps not so amazingly. The only really amazing thing about the entire affair was Eva's acting. Lucy nearly believed her, even though she knew better. Eva never had a crush on anyone, seeming incapable of it. When she'd asked Eva about it once years ago, they'd had a long conversation about how Eva was pretty sure she was asexual but still trying to figure out the romantic side of things. She was fairly certain she wasn't aromantic, but relationships in general just didn't really appeal to her.

Evidently Kyle didn't know Eva well enough to realize the impossibility of the situation, because he was melting and smiling in empathetic understanding. "Why didn't you say so? Eva, you know I'd totally be willing to help out, too!"

Again Eva seemed unable to meet his eyes. She wasn't overly fidgety or obvious. Her nervousness was subtle, with just enough of her usual stubbornness woven in to lend credibility. "It's not something I really wanted to talk about. I'm sort of new to all of this crap."

He laughed warmly and patted her on the shoulder before drawing her into a half hug. "Oh man, I totally get ya! Those first crushes can be tough! So, who's the lucky guy? Is he here yet?"

Lucy felt a trickle of panic breach her unnatural calm. There was surely no way Eva had had enough time to fully develop this lie. She'd be caught out, thus outing the both of them. There was really no need to worry, though, as evidenced by the totally not-panicked way Eva glanced around before settling on someone's face in the crowd and twitching her lips in a shy, secret smile.

"He's here."

Kyle and Lucy followed her line of sight, and something cold rushed through Lucy's veins when she saw the dark-haired man in the rumpled white shirt and pressed khakis. For an instant, she could have sworn that she felt the earth's rotation, and it made her swallow back a wave of nausea.

"The guy next to Ren?" she heard Kyle ask, knowing already what the answer would surely be.

"Not quite," Eva laughed with her perfectly imitated nervousness.

Kyle's arm gave her another quick hug, and he joined in her laughter, his eyes dancing with relief and delight. He glanced at Lucy, and his smile grew wider. Lucy hoped that none of her unease had shown, and that her smile seemed passable.

Her voice encouraged Eva to go over and talk to him, though she couldn't recall even commanding her lips. It was as if something else took over for an instant, loosening the tension of her shoulders and drawing out a happy giggle. Another girl was standing in her boots, wearing her clothes, and talking to her friends. It intrigued her more than frightened her, and she wondered if there was a way to capture this other being and make it do her bidding.

Then Eva was walking away, disappearing in the crowd and reappearing at Ren's arm, and Lucy stopped being so distracted by the stranger in her skin. Oddly enough, she was more confused by the sensations she felt watching those two together than she was by her own behavior. If she didn't know any better, she'd almost think she was jealous, which would be ridiculous. Lucy didn't even really like Ren. Much. Maybe as a friend, if anything. He wasn't even that cute. Sure, at first she had thought he was attractive, but that was before she'd really gotten a good look at him, or discovered his personality.

An arm wrapped around her waist and Kyle nuzzled playfully at her temple, his voice warm at her ear. "They'd make a good couple."

They would, she agreed, both vocally and mentally, even while something in her twisted and stabbed and gnashed at her stomach. She suddenly wanted to be anywhere but there at that party, witnessing this charade. Not even Kyle's arms around her or thoughts of seeing her father again soon worked to settle her. It felt as if there was a single, thin point jabbing at her chest.

What was *wrong* with her? She didn't even *like* him!

It was when her eyes started to sting that she panicked, turning away from Kyle and trying to untangle his arms from around her in an effort to escape. "I have to find Jim and Günter," she said in explanation, pressing into the crowd. Kyle was hot on her heels, saying he'd come help her look, but she just tried to up her pace.

This wasn't happening. She wasn't going to cry over some guy she barely knew and certainly had no interest in, especially when her long-time crush was all over her. The only solution she could think of was to get out of there and clear her head. If she got everyone to leave early, she wouldn't have to watch Eva's little performance. Which was another thing—why was she so upset, when she *knew* it was an act?

Glancing back, Lucy watched Ren lean close to say something into Eva's ear, her face aglow with amusement. It...it *was* just an act, right?

"No way! Lucy?" A familiar voice drew her attention away from the pair, and she was suddenly looking into Venny's big doe eyes. "I haven't seen you in so long!" He had a grinning brunette girl on his arm, and was wearing a shirt of The Joker from *Dark Knight*.

Relief crashed into her, sufficiently distracting her from her current dilemma. "Venny!" Throwing her arms around him, she nearly dislodged the brunette, who merely laughed and took no offense. "Oh my *God*, I was so worried for you!"

He chuckled and pulled back, resting one cool hand on her shoulder and giving it a little squeeze. "What for?"

Lucy blinked, frowning in confusion. "Because of the Reaper. That party we were at..."

"Ah." Nodding in realization, he gave her shoulder another soft squish. "Luckily, I left not long after you did. You've no idea how relieved I was to know you'd already gotten out. When I heard about what happened..." He trailed off and frowned, dropping his hand. His companion pouted sympathetically and tightened her hug.

"Luce, there you are, I thought I lost—oh."

Crap, she'd nearly forgotten about Kyle. The two boys eyed each other, Kyle with evident loathing, and Venny with dark amusement.

It was Venny who first broke the awkward silence. "Congratulations are in order, I see?" he asked Lucy, even as his eyes barely glanced away from Kyle's death glare. "Which reminds me! I'd like you to meet Angela."

The girl on his arm gave a giggle and a little wave, with a

sweetly-voiced "Pleased to meet you!"

Her presence and what it implied seemed to calm Kyle somewhat, though he shifted closer to Lucy out of both protectiveness and possessiveness. In a way, Lucy thought it was sort of sweet, if unnecessary.

Not giving a strigoi's scrote about the two boy's beef, Lucy kept on as if never having been interrupted. "Venny, maybe you can help me? I'm looking for a couple friends I seem to have misplaced. One's pretty tall, black with short dreads. Is wearing a scarf headband thing that's...er...reddish-orange? Has a sort of peasant hippie shirt on. Beige, a touch sheer. The other one's close to the same height, looks kinda Japanese, shoulder-length black hair. He's just wearing a black T-shirt, no logo."

Venny nodded along with the descriptions to show he was listening, then straightened his back so he could stand at his full height. He wasn't nearly as tall as Jim or Günter, but he was certainly a good bit taller than Lucy and a touch taller than Kyle. She hoped he would have better luck seeing over the heads of the crowd and spotting her wayward friends.

"Yeah, looks like the hippie's over there." Raising his free arm, Venny gave a large, exaggerated sweeping motion towards the far corner of the living room. "Talkin' with some curly-haired guy. As for the other one..." He looked around a bit, then frowned. "Heading over that way. Looks pissed as hell."

"Shit!" Nearly stumbling over her boots, Lucy spun and flung herself into the crowd towards the direction Venny had indicated. She barely registered the twin cries of her name, and the hurried footfalls of the small group rushing to catch-up.

Günter had already reached Jim before she managed to finally get there, and he was in the process of growling out a tirade in German.

Lucy skidded to a halt, and noticed that the crowd had seemed to draw away from the boys as if Günter's anger was serving as some type of repellent.

"Stop speaking in goddamn bloody German!" Jim finally snapped, pulling his arm free from where Günter had evidently taken hold.

Pain flashed across Günter's face, but not a reflection of the physical kind. No, it was something far deeper and more potent. His cheeks flexed as he clenched his jaw, and his chest rose and fell with deep, controlled motions. "Please," he said, the tight, injured voice somehow carrying over the noise of the party. "I told you that he's—"

"What? And do you really think *you* have room to talk?" Jim sneered and stepped away, moving closer to the curly-haired man. It was only then that Lucy managed to match the face to a name, remembering the photo of Dorian. "You need to stop over-reacting." The words were hissed through Jim's teeth, and his fingers were curling into tight fists.

Lucy watched, feeling helpless and alarmed. There wasn't anything she could think to say or do to diffuse the situation, and she hated it.

Then Venny was suddenly brushing past her, paying no attention to the arguing boys and strolling up to Dorian with a puzzled expression. "I know you from somewhere, right?" he was saying, and Lucy's attention was sufficiently pulled from her friends.

Dorian, who had been looking somewhat bored, suddenly started when Venny addressed him. He looked Venny over with a thoughtful frown. "Perhaps you saw me perform? I'm in a band called The—"

"Of course! That must be it! I remember now! Very captivating performance. Really seemed to snare the audience and hold them enraptured. Quite impressive." Venny was grinning as he started to pat himself down. "I just gotta get your autograph. I mean, if it's okay with you? Angela!" Looking over his shoulder, Venny gave his girlfriend a sweet smile. "Can you please go fetch me a pen and paper?"

Before Angela could do as asked, Dorian was raising his hand for her to stay. "No, I—no, sorry. I actually have to be going. I just remembered that I promised someone I'd meet up with them. Now. So, I have to go. Nice meeting you, er...?"

"Venny. Venny Fikus."

"Right. Well then, Venny." Tearing his eyes away from Venny, Dorian looked over to Jim, who had ceased arguing with Günter during the brief exchange. "Jim. I'll see you later, then. Call me when you need me to come model. Ah...Günter. A pleasure, as always."

Günter glared silently in response.

"So soon?" asked Jim, placing a hand on Dorian's shoulder in supplication.

"Such a pity," agreed Venny, his smile melting into a less-than-sincere pout.

Just as Dorian was pressing himself into the crowd, Eva was emerging into their spacious little corner. "What the hell is going on?"

"Where's Ren?" Lucy asked, attention flicking out to the crowded room to see if she could find his smudge of white in the sweaty, dark Monet. Beside her, Kyle moved closer and slid an arm around her hips.

Eva gave her a questioning look. "Had to leave early. Something about work in the morning." Then she was dismissing anything that didn't have to do with her brother and Jim. "You guys mind telling me what just happened? People are talking about how some crazy foreign guy started attacking someone."

"I didn't attack anyone!" objected Jim, placing his hand to his

302

chest in outrage.

"I'm pretty sure they were talking about Günter," Lucy supplied. "He was ranting in German, after all."

"I didn't attack anyone, either!"

"Tell that to my upper arm, you crazy, paranoid—"

"ENOUGH."

Jim and Günter—as well as most of the people in the nearby vicinity—fell silent at the tone and volume of Eva's voice.

Only Venny was brave enough to not let it shake him. He sauntered over to Eva and flashed one of his charming smiles. It had no effect, of course, but he didn't seem to let that deter him. "It seems there was just some misunderstanding, and perhaps continues to be. Boys will be boys, after all. I don't think they really need a lecture right now, though. Just some time alone to work out the issue."

Even if his smile had not worked, his words did, and Eva's shoulders lost some of their tension. "Fine. Yes. You're right." Then Eva seemed to realize something, and she actually looked at Venny directly. "Who the hell are you, anyway?"

"A friend of Lucy's. Name's Venny." When he extended his hand, Eva glared and pushed past him to approach Lucy and Kyle.

"That the guy?" she asked Kyle at Lucy's side. Kyle nodded, even as Lucy started to open her mouth to protest. Eva ignored her and turned to shoot an even more potent glare at the man in question.

"I can take a hint," Venny said with feigned insult, the corners of his lips tugging up in amusement as he retracted his hand. "It's okay; Angela and I need to get going, anyway. Don't we, Ange?" Collecting Angela, Venny gave Lucy a little wave and made his grand exit.

"That wasn't nice," Lucy berated as she watched the pair leave.

"Yeah, well, I don't tend to like men who try to date-rape my friends."

"He didn't!"

"He did." Kyle's voice was cold and hard, and he was also watching where Venny had departed.

Angry, Lucy pulled out of Kyle's embrace. "It was my own stupid mistake that I got drunk. It isn't fair for you guys to blame it on Venny. He wouldn't have done anything to me."

Kyle studied her face for a moment, before shaking his head, his expression a crumpled, twisted thing. "God, Lucy, you are so damn naïve."

She thought that was rich, coming from someone who was ignorant to the terrors she had witnessed. To the things she had done. What the hell did he know about danger and risks?

"Where's Günter?" Eva's question drew Lucy away from the path of disgust her mind had been about to wander. She looked around, just realizing that Günter had indeed vanished.

Jim had his arms crossed over his chest and was refusing to meet anyone's eyes as he shrugged. "He left." There was something odd about Jim's expression that picked at Lucy for a moment. Her friend looked almost confused, as if he didn't understand how things had gotten to that point. His brows were crushed together, and he kept worrying his lower lip, something she'd seen him do often when he was puzzling over a particularly difficult piece of artwork.

"Well then I suppose we should go find him, shouldn't we?" Eva's question left no room for refusal, and Jim gave a resigned nod.

"I have to go to the bathroom," Lucy said, not really in the mood to traipse through the party in search of the angry hybrid. She also wanted to get away from Kyle, and maybe Eva. Without giving anyone a chance to respond, she was gone.

\*

She didn't go to the bathroom, but made her way swiftly outside to take in deep gulps of fresh fall air. Dry leaves and stray gravel crunched beneath her boots as she wound her way along the dark road, moving farther and farther from the music and the laughter. At some point, she'd head back and see if the others were ready to go or if they'd located the target, but for the moment she just needed to clear her head.

"Hey," a deep voice murmured from the darkness beside her, making her heart slam against her ribs like a crash test dummy without a seat belt. Günter stepped out from beneath some trees, the shadows of the night accentuating the sad, haunted look in his eyes. "What are you doing out here?"

"Needed some air. You?"

"Same." Glancing back towards the party, Günter moved to walk in step with Lucy, and they continued down the road. "Eva still ranting?"

"Dunno. Might be. She and Jim are searching for you, now."

"I imagine." He was frowning and watching the pavement, and Lucy shifted her walking so she could give him a friendly shoulder bump.

"You can talk to me about it, if you'd like," she offered. "I promise not to rant or lecture."

His mouth pulled into a line, small dimples appearing in his cheeks, and Lucy thought he wasn't going to say a word.

"It's difficult," he eventually murmured into the night. "Being what I am."

"I don't think Jim really meant anything by what he said," she offered weakly.

Günter gave a little remorseful smirk which reminded Lucy very strongly of Eva. "Maybe. It's possible. Dorian's a child of Lamia,

305

which probably influences the way Jim reacts concerning him."

"Lamia? Shit, isn't she, like, an ancient succubus thing?"

A mirthless laugh huffed out of Günter. "Thus my concern. I keep trying to warn him. I had thought he'd understood. He even promised me that he'd avoid Dorian." He tilted his head back and stared sightlessly up at the stars. "Guess promises can't hold up against whatever kind of lure the guy has."

"Is that allowed?" she asked, confused. "Isn't that interfering with humans too much, for him to put them under some kind of sway?"

Darting her a sideways glance, he made a thoughtful sound. "Actually, it could be. I'll talk with Czar about it when we debrief tomorrow."

Anxiety slithered across her insides and made her wrap her arms around herself as if to ward it off. Czar. She needed to talk to her friends about Czar and about the Gehealdan, about the truth behind her father's "death," and how Czar wanted to keep it hidden from her despite the rules. She needed to convince them to come with her. "Günter, there's," she started, quiet and hesitant, eyes flicking nervously around at the trees and houses, "there's something I want to talk about."

Before she could say another word, however, she was interrupted by a muffled scream.

They shared a glance, then sped up their pace towards the house ahead. "Any weapons?" he asked, eyes turning gold.

"Knife, but that's it."

"Same." Except it wasn't the same, since *she* couldn't shape-shift into a powerful supernatural creature.

No lights were on inside, but the front door was unlocked. Günter wrapped his hand in his shirt before opening it, taking care not to leave any fingerprints. As soon as they crossed the threshold, he froze and placed a hand on her shoulder. "Blood," he whispered. "Fresh blood. Lots of it. The scent is strong."

Inhaling, Lucy thought she could smell it, too. That familiar metallic scent which permeated the air every night after a kill. Growing stronger with every chop of her axe or slice of her machete.

"Get your knife," he ordered as he reached back to draw his from where it was tucked in his pants.

Nodding, she bent down and drew hers from the hidden sheath within her boot.

Quietly they made their way through the dark house, Lucy following Günter's lead. At last they reached what looked to be a living room area, with a breakfast nook off to one side. The back door was opened wide, letting in the cool night air. In the corner it looked like shadows and moonlight were engaged in a twitchy, erratic dance. The music for the dance was comprised of wet chewing sounds and the rustling of feathered wings. For a moment, she thought it was crows or some other carrion bird. Moonlight caught one's face, however, and she realized they were something else, something strange and terrifying and not actually a bird at all. It had needle-sharp teeth and a face that wasn't sure if it wanted to be an owl or a human.

When Lucy glanced at Günter to see if he had a clue as to what was going on and what the things were, she noticed that his attention was focused away from the corner. She followed his gaze to a shadowed area near one of the windows, and felt her throat close up at what she found.

A man-like figure was sitting on its haunches, holding a long-haired head in one hand while he casually cut away at the face with the sharp claws of the other. She knew instantly that she was seeing a strigoi, since it bore somewhat of a resemblance to Isaiah Cartwright—who still had the dubious honor of being the oldest strigoi her little team had yet to kill. Looking at him, Lucy wondered if the strigoi had been a considerable inspiration for some of the images people created of the Devil. Isaiah Cartwright may have had the hooves and tail, as well as the ruddy appearance, but he had still looked at least partially human. The thing before her now barely held any resemblance to a human being.

His entire body was reddish in hue, from what she could tell despite the dark, blood-soaked clothing he wore. She supposed his limbs were somewhat human in how they were jointed, but his hands looked like fleshy bird talons and he had an extra, small thumb-like digit up near his wrist much like a dog or cat.

"Was that entirely necessary?" an accented voice asked from the opened door, before a man's silhouette stepped into view. The accent reminded her of the same not-quite-Russian sound that Branka's possessed.

"She knows him," replied the strigoi, not even glancing up from his task. "If I let her go, she'd tell him I was asking about him." His voice remained calm as he reasoned this, his sharp claws continuing their work. Blood painted his hands and wrists black in the moonlight, streaks snaking down his arms and dripping off his sharp elbows.

"And you don't think he'll grow suspicious if he hears of her death in the news?" asked the silhouette.

"Perhaps," agreed the strigoi with something almost a purr. "But everyone knows the Grin Reaper strikes seemingly at random, just so long as they're young and like to party." He seemed amused by his own words, and when he smiled Lucy could see that his mouth was crammed with abnormally long, sharp teeth.

His face reminded her of an owl. Or, really, like a couple kinds of owls. His eyes had the alien-like shape of a barn owl, yet the large irises were yellow. The way his pointed ears stuck out from the sides of his bald head, they looked like the pointed tufts of a horned owl. At first she didn't think he had a nose, but then he shifted a bit and the dim light hinted at thin slits making a V like an arrow pointing down towards his mouth.

"He's your age if not older," sighed the silhouette. "It's folly to think he won't recognize your style and know the truth."

"Belobog, why do you persist in nagging me so?" the strigoi groaned teasingly with a roll of his owl-like eyes. "Is it because I gave your dinner to the Old Ones? You know it's rude to deny them a meal."

Lucy and Günter tensed at the name Belobog. *Pulchrum*. All at once Lucy understood. *He wanted us here,* she thought. *He pushed Czar into sending us out on another recon, knowing that we'd run into the Grin Reaper here. He wanted the others to see what it means that the Reaper is an Agent of Gehealdan. Wanted them to learn the truth without me risking myself by telling them. Branka may have* told *us, but now they can* see.

"Agent Czernobog," tsked Pulchrum from the doorway, still employing that somewhat-familiar Eastern European accent. "You've already angered the Old Man with the stunt you pulled on Halloween."

"There were *witnesses*," hissed the Reaper, Agent Czernobog. "Can't keep a secret if others have seen it."

"The death count has risen too high. You risk us all by drawing such attention."

At that, Czernobog chuckled as he stood up on his hoofed feet and brought the head over towards the window. Lucy expected his legs to bend like a goat's, but they looked so very human aside from the hooves. He picked a pole up from the floor, only to plunge it effortlessly into the foundation. A hollow, metallic sound rang through the open room for a long moment, making Lucy's brain feel off-kilter from the vibrations. Even her teeth seemed to hum with the sound, and she opened and jiggled her jaw in a futile attempt at banishing the feeling. In the corner, the feeding things screeched in mild alarm, the squelching sounds of chewing giving way for a brief moment to the clamor of fluttering wings.

Humming a jaunty tune to himself, Czernobog went on to sink the head onto the pole with squishes and crunches. Once it was securely on, he proceeded to tilt it one way or another, stepping back on occasion to examine the arrangement. "It will end soon," he said distractedly, examining the current tilt of the head with a critical eye. "One of Yaxley's little followers has agreed to take the fall in return for a Second Life."

One of the things in the corner trilled a strange coo, then there was a loud, wet tearing sound. The feeding seemed to increase.

"You've found him, then?"

Czernobog clucked his tongue and moved away from the impaled head, closer to the door and Pulchrum. "I don't know why you'd doubt me."

"Didn't say that. I was simply confirming."

"Oh? For yourself? Or for our guests?" His head turned towards them, twisting a perfect one-eighty on his neck. Then slowly his blood-splattered body followed, until he fully faced him. Czernobog grinned at them, his teeth looking so sharp and glistening in the faint moonlight. Bits of flesh were wedged between some of those teeth, the sight making Lucy's dinner try to rush up her throat.

"They've a right to know," said Pulchrum, reaching into the house and placing a warning hand on Czernobog's shoulder. "They are members of Gehealdan, same as we. They keep the secrets and uphold the Treaties."

"I know who they are," said Czernobog. He tilted his head, rotating it like an owl would. A shudder ran down Lucy's spine. "But why are they here?"

310

"Recon, looking for a certain Treaty Breaker, like they were on Halloween."

"Come closer, children," Czernobog summoned, motioning with his bloody talons. "Come now, I won't hurt you. We're on the same team, you and I."

Günter made sure to place himself in front of Lucy, but neither of them moved further into the room. "We didn't mean to intrude, sir," Günter offered with such stunningly calm politeness. Lucy could feel his tension, could practically taste his fear. Yet he did his best not to show it to the Agents inside the gruesomely decorated room. "We heard a yell and came to investigate. But it seems you have everything in hand, so we'll just go back to our duties."

Though Czernobog's chuckle was low, it possessed the same effect as nails screeching down the entire length of a chalkboard. Both Lucy and Günter shuddered at the sound and involuntarily recoiled. "What's the matter?" he asked, tone mocking and cruel. "I've never seen executioners quite so squeamish at the sight of blood."

"Leave them be," insisted Pulchrum, tightening his grip on Czernobog's shoulder. "They're still green."

Czernobog snorted and motioned with his sticky-wet claw. "Go. Run back to your Very Important Task. Leave the adults to handle things here."

Lucy and Günter didn't have to be told twice.

# Chapter 20
## Warning

"You sure you want to do this?" Eva gave Lucy a questioning glance. "We can leave if you want. Nothing forcing us to go in there."

Rolling her eyes, Lucy grabbed her friend by the arm and pulled her the rest of the way up the front steps of the quaint house of wood and stone. It stood beside a similar style home in an unfinished subdivision. To its other side was a vacant lot, still waiting for the developers to have the funds to turn it into a home. From the darkened windows of most of the houses in the small development, Lucy was willing to bet that not many of the finished houses had been purchased yet. It seemed this particular house was the only one in that corner of the neighborhood with any sign of life.

She rang the bell while Eva glared at the decorative glass set into the door. A silhouette fell upon the glass before the door was eased open, dark eyes heavily lined in kohl blinking at them. "We're Krysti's friends," Lucy said in greeting.

The girl at the door nodded, moving aside to let them pass. She was dressed in a corseted black gown with a hooded robe made from sheer black fabric sporting a spider web pattern. "I'm Arachne," she said. "Vanora told us you'd be coming tonight."

"Vanora?" both Eva and Lucy asked in unison.

Arachne snickered. "That's right, I forgot; you guys are new to this."

They were led to a large living room lined with couches and comfy chairs, pillows piled in random places on a plush rug. All these cushy surfaces were occupied with young men and women dressed in various assortments of costumes or even just normal clothes. A few books and papers were scattered about, some of the occupants looking over them with single-minded interest. A stereo in the corner was softly playing something that reminded Lucy of Donnie's music, only maybe a little more electronic and jazzy.

A high-pitched squeal overpowered all of the music and the friendly conversation as Krysti jumped from her seat on a sofa to dash over to her friends. She was dressed in something tattered and gauzy that could perhaps be considered a dress in a very loose interpretation of the word. "You guys came! This is so exciting! Oo, oo! Do you know what you want to be? I'm a bean-sidhe named Vanora!"

Rubbing at her ears, Eva let out a groan. "Yes, and your voice certainly brings about great woe." Krysti pouted at Eva's remark, and Lucy bit back a laugh.

"Be nice," Lucy admonished, Krysti nodding along.

"Hello there." A handsome man with short dark hair and strikingly light brown eyes strolled up and slung a casual arm around Krysti's shoulders. Lucy surreptitiously elbowed Eva to get her to stop glaring. "You must be the friends Krysti was telling me about. I'm Darin, the creator of *Chains of the Damned.*"

Lucy switched on a high-kilowatt smile and shifted subtly closer. "Krysti gave me the bestiary for my birthday, and I thought it was fascinating. Actually, I was wondering if I could talk with you a bit about some of it. See," here she ducked her head in a shy, insecure way and fiddled with her hair, glancing up at him through long dark lashes. "I've been doing some related research myself, and I'd really like to get some good recommendations for reference sources."

Darin grinned, obviously delighted to see such interest in the subject. "Of course. After the game, I'd love to talk with you."

It was Eva's turn to give a sneaky elbow jab, and she let Lucy see the distress in her eyes for a second before masking it with bored indifference. Biting her lip as yet another show of shy schoolgirl nerves,

Lucy made her eyes look large and entreating. "Oh, okay. I suppose we could wait. I was just really excited to talk with you about some of my own findings. Like, there's this one book I read by a man named Yaxley that's just fascinating."

Darin's smile tensed, and his eyes locked with Lucy's in sudden understanding. "You know what?" he asked with a laugh, giving Krysti's shoulder a friendly squeeze. "Krysti and Devon had been wanting to lead the group. Came up with a little side-story, right?" Krysti nodded happily at his question, eyes sparkling. "Well then, why don't you two go on and get that all set up. I'll have a little chat with your friends for a bit. We'll be right over there in the corner if you need me."

For a moment Lucy worried that Krysti would object to not having her friends participate, but it seemed her excitement over getting to lead the group out-shined anything else. She let out another little squeal, gave Darin a hug, then bounced off to who Lucy assumed was Devon.

Once she was gone, Darin took on a very serious air. His light eyes studied them both, and he exhaled a heavy sigh. "You two are very interesting and not what I expected," he said. "Come on."

The three of them made a private little circle of chairs in the corner farthest from all of the action. Krysti could be heard explaining the evening's turn of events, and there was much rustling and shuffling as everyone gathered to begin. Darin relaxed back into his armchair, eyes darting over to the crowd. "She doesn't know, does she?" he asked.

Eva's answer was a question of her own. "Know what?"

He turned his full attention to her. "That you're not human. Or, as the Gehealdans would say, a 'non.'" His lip curled a bit with derision at that word, as if it were a foul insult to him and his kind. Lucy realized that to them, it probably was, because it centered humans as the default.

Frowning, Eva turned her head to watch Krysti. She was moving her hands about in large, exaggerated motions as she addressed the group. There was a glow of happiness about Krysti, making her tattered outfit appear almost ethereal. "No." Eva's voice was chilled, her walls trying desperately to keep back any emotion. Lucy resisted the urge to take her hand.

Darin nodded, unsurprised. "Though honestly, I don't think she'd have a problem with it if you told her. She'd probably flip out in uncontrollable delight."

Eva snorted and switched her attention to a lamp, its brightness dulled compared to Krysti's exuberance.

"Are you Yaxley?" Lucy asked, feeling they should just get to the point.

He frowned, glancing again at the group. "I was once. Right now my name is Darin Monico."

"You were a Promethean."

"Yes. A long time ago." Tilting his head, he looked closely at Lucy. "But what about you?" he asked. "You aren't like your friend here. Yet..."

"I'm not important."

Squinting, he gave her a strange look. "That's not true. Everything's important. What nature are you?"

"What? Nothing. I mean, I'm human." She tried to continue meeting his eyes, but it was difficult.

"Are you certain?" That gaze was intense, penetrating, and Lucy wondered what he was seeing as he stared at her.

For a moment, she questioned her own certainty about her humanity. Eva even turned to give her a funny look when she didn't offer an immediate reply. Why would he question her humanity unless he found a reason to? It would make sense if she was something else, considering who and what her father was. Maybe it could explain the mara and the prophetic nightmares they were delivering. Maybe it could explain the darkness that followed Donnie, and the shadowman that seemed to haunt her house. It could explain so many things. Just because her mother was human didn't mean Lucy was.

Swallowing, Lucy found her words. "Far as I know, I'm human. My mother's human, my father was…is…something else, it's true." She glanced at Eva, but her friend thankfully wasn't letting anything show in her expression. After she and Günter had seen the Grin Reaper in person, they'd all left the party and holed themselves up at Jim's place. There, she'd told them everything, writing it down on paper, making them pass it between themselves before burning each piece.

Darin offered a slow nod, but his eyes didn't turn away, and Lucy was certain they hadn't even blinked. "Your coloring reminds me of someone, but I can't quite place who. Or what." With a soul-deep sigh, he finally broke eye contact and looked to Eva. "So, what may I do for you two, who know my old name and obviously came seeking an audience with me?"

Eva and Lucy exchanged a quick glance. "We're of the Gehealdan," explained Lucy, "from the local chapter."

"Gehealdans?"

"Yes."

He looked at them from the corner of his eye and then seemed to come to a decision. Leaning back into the chair, he watched them warily. "What business do you have with me?"

"Why did you never check in with High Commander Hayes?" asked Lucy, also leaning back in her seat.

Darin frowned and glanced away before answering. "It's not mandatory."

"For you it is," corrected Eva. "The Prometheans were prominent figures in the forging of the Treaties. All organizations signed to the Treaties are subject to their enforcement."

"But," he argued, "the Prometheans have since dissolved. I can't very well be considered a member of a group that doesn't exist."

"Even those outside of the Treaties are expected to at least check in with the local Gehealdan, as long as it's within Treaty-run territory." said Lucy, remembering what Pulchrum had shown her.

A small scoff escaped Darin as his lips pressed hard and thin in disapproval. "This nation shouldn't even be considered as one under Treaty law, and the Gehealdan should technically have no power here. Not a single one of the local folk of this land signed on, but still the Gehealdan came over with the colonizers and enforced their rules on this continent's denizens."

"You're hiding," said Lucy, cutting through his excuses and having little patience for an impromptu history lesson. "You didn't check in because you're trying to disappear."

He inclined his head. "Sometimes it's best to do so."

Lucy snorted and turned her head to cast a pointed look at the crowd of role-players. "Way to stay low profile."

His lips pulled taut in a mockery of a smile. "I have my reasons for the game." When the girls merely gave him skeptical looks, he again glanced away towards the group. "They have to know. It's important for them to learn."

Eva looked at him as if he'd just claimed to be an alien from Mars. "So you choose a role-playing game to teach them?"

His gaze returned to her, and he studied her silently, reading her eyes in the same skilled way Hartmut Kuntz could. "It was pop culture that taught them the lies. Why can't it be pop culture that teaches them the truth?"

317

"Counteract the conspiracy." Lucy nodded at the logic, even if she personally didn't think an indie role-playing game necessarily counted as popular culture.

"Baby steps," he said, as if he could read her mind. "Trust me on this."

"Fine." With a heavy sigh, Lucy stretched out in her seat and crossed her clunky boots. "Let's get back to the more important issue: namely, your wanting to remain 'invisible.'" When she locked eyes with him again, he was the first to look away. "Hiding from something?"

To the casual observer, Darin appeared to be monitoring the status of the game. Those sharp eyes were roaming over each face, assessing and analyzing every expression and laughed comment. Beneath his good looks, Lucy could see he was as brittle and weathered as metal left to rust for centuries. There was a bleakness in his eyes, a fatalistic acceptance in the line of his mouth. For a moment she could not ignore the stark differences between them in age and experience. She almost felt foolish for speaking with him in such self-assured tones.

"There's so much left to do," he whispered. "I can't let them end me, yet."

Eva and Lucy perked up their ears at this, both of them shifting forward in their seats. "What?" asked Eva in a whisper just as hushed and tense as his had been.

Those haunting eyes glanced negligently at Eva before boring into Lucy. "There is a giant wolf bound in impossibility," he said, and his voice somehow evoked the mental image of dark words shared across crackling fires. "It waits until the time is right. Then it will snap its massive jaws closed upon the Old Man, heralding in a New Age."

"Fenris," breathed Eva.

Without looking at her, eyes still focused with disturbing intensity on Lucy, Darin nodded. "I have to help them, in any way I

318

can. Have to aid the cause. Report me, execute me, whatever you need to do. Just, please, give me a little more time."

"We won't do that, won't hurt you," Lucy assured gently. "We're here to help."

"Don't lie to me, child," said Darin, unblinking. "I know what the Gehealdan does to those who leak the Truth."

Lucy squared her shoulders and affected a serious manner. "My father is Váli."

The corner of Darin's lips twitched, but his amusement was not light. "So you are wolves in sheep's clothing."

Lucy thought of the scene she and Günter had witnessed on her birthday, remembered the words Czernobog had said. "The Magician's Hand knows where you are," whispered Lucy. Eva glanced at her when she said this, then leaned forward to stare at her clasped hands. "He plans to kill you, and one of your players has made a deal to turn himself in as the Grin Reaper."

"You know they won't stop at me," Darin whispered sadly. "Any of the old factions or clans that used to protect the humans are under close watch. If any member dares revert to their old ways..."

When it looked as if Eva was about to bolt from her chair, Lucy stilled her with a hand on her knee.

"Why?" Lucy asked, because her friend was too upset to voice it.

Darin eyed Eva curiously, replying with a distracted tone. "For the sake of secrecy. For what they consider the Greater Good."

Someone laughed while another cried out in objection. Krysti's voice rose above it all and called for order. The three of them turned and watched as the humans pretended to be monsters, making up battles and mimicking discord.

\*\*\*

Her father's entry had no current address. After he was known as Walter Kincade, it was as if he'd vanished. The notes contained theories and updates from various Gehealdan members, but nothing was conclusive.

Lucy glanced at her phone to make sure she hadn't received a warning text. Out in the hall, Jim was serving as lookout while using the excuse of quizzing himself on the creatures depicted on the doors. So far so good. Günter and Eva were supposed to be distracting Czar and Phil with questions about different factions and the proper protocol for non-registered supernaturals breaking Treaty Law within territories held predominantly by Treaty-bound factions. Montenegro and Carmen were working in the shop, as usual, so hopefully they wouldn't need to wander into the back hall anytime soon. It was Friday, and the college kids would be showing up to the shop soon, so Lucy figured that would keep them busy.

It had been Sunday when they'd gone to visit Monico, and Lucy's first opportunity to sneak back into the room didn't come until the following Wednesday. Pulchrum had been dropping hints with her since Monday that Friday was her deadline, and once she'd finally gotten the chance to access the database again, she understood Pulchrum's urgency. The Gehealdan were planning on executing Yaxley, known currently as Darin Monico that Friday. Not only execute *him*, his file stated, but as many of the people he'd spread the truth to as possible. Which was ridiculous. Absolute utter bullshit. The man had created a *role-playing* game, for Christ's sake. It wasn't like he was training them as some secret army.

Technically, though, he'd been part of the Treaties, and thus vowed to never tell humans the truth about *any* of the supernatural

320

world. The book he'd written had been bad enough to earn him a black mark, but like Lucy's father, he'd managed to seemingly drop out of existence since the publication. According to the Gehealdan, his execution was long past due. The only reason they were also executing the role-players was because the Gehealdan wanted to set an example, it seemed.

Günter didn't plan to jump ship like Lucy, but he had agreed that this was an unwarranted execution, and *especially* agreed that the players of his game shouldn't be targets. Considering Krysti was on the list of those to be silenced, Eva was definitely in Lucy's corner. Nothing in the world was allowed to come close to harming Krysti so long as Eva was still living and breathing. Günter's hesitance was rooted in the horror stories told to them by their father of the time of hunts and trials, and he didn't have something like Eva did to overpower that fear.

"The secrecy is *important*," he'd objected, voice just as hushed as the rest of theirs, where they had huddled close in Jim's studio that Wednesday night. He and Lucy had witnessed the Grin Reaper only a few days ago, and yet still he hadn't been able to fully condemn the Gehealdan and their methods. Still, at least he was willing to help Lucy and Eva get out of the Gehealdan safely. He just wasn't going with them.

Jim was staying as well, but for different reasons than Günter. For Jim, asking him to leave and join Fenris would be asking him to give up his entire life. He'd have to abandon his family and art career, and all for a cause in which he had no investment. It was safer for him, he reasoned, to stay where he was. He'd do what he could from within the Gehealdan to help people, maybe see if there was a way to work towards some type of reform. So, like Günter, he'd aid in getting Lucy free. After that, it would be good-bye.

Lucy tried not to think about that, about how she was not only going to have to leave behind Jim and Günter but also all of her other friends. Hopefully it wouldn't be forever. God, she really hoped it wouldn't.

Pushing aside heart-piercing thoughts about Alice and Krysti, Lucy continued her digging into the database. She tried searching for Ren, but there was nothing. Absolutely nothing. Even a search for Jomei Tenno resulted in an entry about how she was a non-registered supernatural residing in Gehealdan-maintained territory. It was like René Sartre didn't even exist. At least, not according to the Gehealdan. So maybe she was wrong, and he was human after all.

Biting her lip, Lucy pulled up Agent Czernobog. There was no photo, and the only information in the file was "Magician's Hand" and "Handler: Agent Belobog."

But...she thought Pulchrum was a monitor.

Lucy checked her phone again, then clenched and unclenched her hands before typing in a search for Agent Belobog. There was a lot more information in Pulchrum's file, including his picture. It had him listed as a monitor, with a primary focus on the Kincade children. Lucy froze, fingers trembling where they hovered over the keyboard. She and her brothers were evidently marked as "high risk," due to their father, even if they had thus far not exhibited any supernatural traits. It made sense, she told herself, trying to shake off the unjustified feeling of betrayal. He was just doing his job. It also didn't invalidate any of their interactions. Of course not.

Her phone's screen lit up, and Lucy quickly exited out of the database. She texted Jim back, asking if it was clear, then waited anxiously by the door until he replied in the affirmative. Eva and Jim were waiting for her in the hall, Jim looking pinched and nervous while Eva smiled casually.

"Got a text from Krysti," Eva said by way of greeting, nodding with her head for them to head down the hall towards the main entrance. "She needs us to go help her out with some homework."

Lucy followed along, confused but willing to trust that her friend had some type of plan. "What subject?" she asked.

"Chemistry," was Eva's careless reply. It was enough to let Lucy know that this was a cover-up for something else. No way in hell would Krysti, who had the highest grade in Chemistry, need any of their help. Eva could only mean one thing—it was time. Despite going back to warn Monico of the planned execution, all week they'd been hearing from Krysti about how the game was preparing for a trial run of the LARP mechanics. The fool should have disbanded the game and left. Though Lucy wondered if that would even matter to the Gehealdan, or if the players would still be marked as targets for execution.

Once they were all out into the main shop area, Jim broke away from them. "Günter and I have some more training we're going to work on here." His smile was there and gone, like he was one of those old hologram cards someone was tilting back and forth. "I don't take Chemistry, anyway. I'd be no use."

Eva nodded and looked like she was going to say something, before she shook her head and offered a little wave. "See ya in school tomorrow, dork."

"Yeah," he returned as he stepped backwards away from them down an aisle. "See you."

Lucy didn't understand why her stomach was filling with dread and her chest felt like something was crushing it. "Bye, Jim."

He turned around and kept walking, waving over his shoulder.

They didn't see Günter on their way out, but Eva didn't hesitate as they crossed the threshold and out into the parking lot. Lucy did, though, glancing back one last time to see if she had missed Günter amongst all the shelves. But then she was walking again, following Eva to her car, where it was parked beside Günter's. Brushing her fingers against the side of Günter's SUV, Lucy sent a silent farewell to the boy who had been like a brother.

# Chapter 21
### Ready or Not

A scream tore through the night, sounding nothing like the staged screeches of horror films. It clawed its way roughly across the nerves of the spine and filled the stomach with a pestilence that poisoned the rest of the body into petrifaction. Lucy fought the urge to freeze, to hide, to flee.

She and Eva ran through the trees, but they were hardly doing so together. Hindered by the necessity of having a flashlight to see, Lucy stumbled and tripped her way through the darkness. Eva leapt and dashed with all the grace of the predator Lucy kept forgetting she was. The only times Lucy managed to catch up with her friend was when the hybrid girl had discovered blood or a body.

Lucy hated those times.

The first time, she'd nearly puked all over the mangled corpse of a boy missing the lower half of his body. Every twitch of his dying muscles was going to haunt Lucy's nightmares, she was certain. There was no way she'd ever rid her mind of the way his intestines glistened in the grass like a nest of muddy snakes. Or of the sound his throat made as some still-living instinct tried to breathe and bring oxygen to the blood of a failing heart.

None of the others they'd come across were much better. Eventually, Lucy stopped looking at the things Eva found. All that mattered, she told herself, was that none of them were Krysti. Which meant that Krysti was potentially still alive. Somewhere. Out in those trees. With the Reaper.

There was another scream.

This time, Eva's head jerked in its direction, her golden eyes trying to see past their limit. "This way!" she cried, changing direction

325

and increasing her speed.

Lucy cursed and bumbled after her. She nearly slipped at one point, and she didn't even want to look down to see what it had been that was so slick beneath the tread of her boot.

The closer they got to the screams, the more distinct the sounds became. There were two voices. One of them yelled out words between incoherent cries of panic. Eventually, sobs could be heard as a staccato bass drum to the wailing. "Help," Lucy heard. "Medic!" There were also questions. The questions that people always seem to ask in those sorts of situations. "Why, God, why?" Questions like that, with no real answers. Or, maybe it's just that the inquirer asks the wrong god.

Eva came to an abrupt halt, and Lucy shuffled to a stop behind her. The screams were now only a few feet ahead, and there were forms barely distinguishable in the moonlight. Krysti was beneath a tree, cradling a bleeding woman in her arms and rocking. Memory superimposed itself onto reality, and Lucy saw her brother Mick with Diana, trying desperately to comfort his shock-quiet mother while shedding his own tears of mourning. That momentary flash was disrupted by Eva invading the scene, and Lucy had to remind herself that there were things to do.

Eva tried to reach their friend through the thick layer of trauma that was blinding her from reason. When finally she recognized her rescuers, Krysti began rambling and sobbing uncontrollably. The woman was gently moved aside by Eva's steady hands, and Lucy noticed that her chest was still shallowly rising and falling. With hushes and murmurs, Eva tried to pull the blonde into her arms and calm her hysterics. Even though the trees surrounding them could be host to any number of dangers, Lucy could not look away from them, and could focus her hearing on no other sounds than Krysti's hiccuping words.

"Why didn't he-he-me-I was trying to get to Ja-Jackie and she-I don't know how-how-people-how do you just-how can you-PEOPLE DON'T EAT PEOPLE! Eva, he-it-he wasn't-that wasn't-and Devon was with him-and I call, but the medics—"

"Shshshhhh… We're here. We'll protect you. Were you hurt?"

"No. No, he just-just grinned. Grinned and winked. Said they-they'd be back for me. His laugh. Wasn't human."

"No. He's not human. He's a strigoi."

Krysti looked up at Eva then, her eyes seeming to gain some level of clarity. "Strigoi. What level?" The flicker of sanity in her eyes was a lie, the shock still preventing rational thought.

"Not a level. This isn't a game, Krysti. He's a real strigoi."

When Krysti shook her head, the motions were short and twitchy, and Lucy saw the dying boy in the trees when she blinked. "They aren't real. That's a creature from the game."

"Krysti, where did they go?"

"Don't leave me!" Bloody hands gripped at Eva's shirt, clinging like desperate, starving creatures latching to their only source of food.

"I won't. I'm going to stay right here and protect you. I swear to you. Do you know where Darin is, Krysti?"

One hand released the fabric and shakily pointed towards a small gap between two pine trees. Lucy and Eva exchanged looks, and Lucy felt her head nod as her fingers undid the strap keeping her machete sheathed. Facing the Reaper on her own was certainly not ideal, but Pulchrum should potentially be nearby to back her up if needed. Besides, she only planned to find Darin and double-back to Krysti and Eva. She would attempt to avoid direct contact with the Reaper at all costs. And in any case, she was still technically a member of Gehealdan. The Reaper was an Agent, and so theoretically wouldn't attack her. Well, hopefully.

Behind her, Krysti was screaming for her to stay, and Eva was wrestling to keep her voice calm and comforting. A footpath snaked through the brush, and Lucy followed with the sense that she was a lamb being led to slaughter. She cursed the way the dead leaves beneath her feet whispered with muffled crunches that resounded overly loud in the tension. Every crack of branches above or groan of a bending bough had her light flicking around in aimless searching.

Minutes passed, but the continued silence brought no comfort to her strained nerves. How far had she wandered? There wasn't even the hint of Krysti's sobs anymore, so she must have gotten decently far from the others. A glance up revealed a sliver of a moon through the skeletal arms of trees. She wished Günter had come, so he could watch her from above.

Someone cried out in pain, and Lucy sped up, moving towards what she estimated to be the source. She only managed a few steps before a dark mass was hurtling through the brush and stark saplings, only to come to an abruptly painful stop against the trunk of an ancient oak. Ducking back behind another tree, Lucy clicked off her flashlight and watched the mass shift and groan. Another figure stepped through the trees and stopped a few feet from the crumpled shadow of a person.

"Gone soft, it seems," said a voice so familiar that it seized Lucy's breath and shoved it back down her throat as jagged icicles. The Grin Reaper.

"You're being used," wheezed the man on the ground, his voice also startlingly familiar. Darin was still alive somehow, and Lucy wondered if he had tried to flee without even lifting a finger to help all of the humans, or if he'd gone to face Czernobog himself in an attempt to stop the slaughter. If it was the latter, he had failed completely.

"Interesting thing for a Promethean to say. At least I'm not betraying my own kind. How's that going for you, by the way? Has it proven to be at all worth it?" The Reaper hauled Darin up by his hair

328

and snarled in his face. "You and yours killed a lot of dear friends of mine, I'll have you know. Now you want to bring it all back, the hunts and trials and systematic murder of our people?"

Even in the scant light, Lucy could see Darin struggle, see his hands claw uselessly at the Reaper, and she was confused as to why there seemed to be such a difference in strength. In a desperate move, Darin shifted forms—bird, wolf, cat, then something so small Lucy couldn't see and the Reaper was grabbing at air and cursing. A few beats later, and Darin was tumbling to the ground seemingly out of nowhere. He tried to crawl a bit, wheezing and groaning, and Lucy realized why the power differential seemed so great: Darin had already been severely injured.

Darin was facing her by this point, and he lifted his head to look at her even as he collapsed in pain. Their eyes locked, mirroring each other in their unblinking fear, and she saw him mouth the word "run." Even as Czernobog descended upon him, sinking those razor teeth deep into the yielding flesh of his neck, Darin repeated the word.

It's what she should have done from the start, she knew. It was a lesson Czar had been beaten into them from the start, to run when faced with a supernatural foe too powerful to fight. God, it was so foolish of her to have gone on alone! She should have stayed with Eva, taken Krysti and gotten the hell out of there. In fact, that sounded like a fantastic idea.

Her muscles wouldn't move, however, no matter how much her mind screamed at them. Instead, she watched as Darin's face flickered between monster and human, bloody spit trying to glue his busted lips together. With a satisfied purr, the Reaper tore away half of Darin's neck with his jaws while simultaneously tearing through his back with his talon-like claws. A great part of Lucy felt the acid-tipped stab of guilt as she watched, but there was nothing she could think to do.

329

Trying not to stumble over her own feet or the forest itself, Lucy quickly backed away before turning to run as fast—and as quietly —as she could. Once she deemed herself far enough away, she clicked the flashlight back on and kept it trained on the ground directly in front of her. She was fairly certain that she was heading in the right direction, but every step brought her closer to doubt.

In her flight, she did not see Czernobog raise his head from his consumption of Darin's freshly-removed heart. She also failed to see those bloody lips drawing back in a grin as he stared after her retreating form.

*

"Lucy," a voice hissed from the shadows ahead of her, causing her feet to shuffle to a startled stop.

Her flashlight's beam fell on the face of a young man peeking out from behind a tree, and she squinted in an attempt to better see his features. "Kyle? But, what are you doing here?..."

Kyle smiled as if she'd told a mildly amusing joke, and stepped out onto the tiny path. "There you are! Lucy, I'd been looking everywhere for you."

For her? No, that wasn't right. Kyle wouldn't be at Krysti's LARP, and certainly wouldn't be expecting to find Lucy there, as well. She stepped back, something inside her urging her to move. Something was off.

"Lucy, you okay?"

Not Luce. Kyle would call her Luce. She took another step back, drawing her machete and bringing it up in front of her. "Who are you?"

The Kyle-that-wasn't-Kyle stopped, tilting his head curiously.

330

His eyes said clearly that he thought she was being silly, and his smile was angled perfectly to melt her heart. "It's me, Lucy. What? No good?" He laughed, and she blinked, the sound jarring her mind and making her feel as though waking from a dream. That wasn't a laugh. She'd misheard. Somewhere a dog had been baying while an owl screeched and a cat wailed. That's what she'd heard.

As her mind and thoughts settled like sediment in water, she realized her flashlight was shining at empty air. Someone had been there, hadn't he? No, no one had been there. No one was meant to be there. She had to press on and find someone. Something. Someone. There was someone she was searching for.

"It's dangerous." The flashlight beam spun as if of its own accord, and her eyes followed it around to the way she'd come. "Lucy, you shouldn't be out here alone!" Pulchrum was saying, rushing to her through the trees, pushing low branches aside in aggravated urgency. "Thank God I found you!"

"Pulchrum!"

"What are you doing running around by yourself?" he asked, brows crinkled adorably in concern. "Where're the others?" Pulchrum darted a cursory glance around at the nearby trees. "Are you hurt?" His steps had slowed, and he was approaching her with relief and caution, his eyes flicking to the machete in her hand.

"I'm fine. Eva's with Krysti, keeping her safe. I was just coming out to find Darin…" She lowered the weapon, but kept her grip firm. The words were fading away in her mind even as she spoke them, and she mentally tried to grasp at them in vain.

His face hardened for a moment, but then it was melting like butter in the hot summer sun. "You shouldn't have done that on your own. Why couldn't you have waited for me?"

"We couldn't wait. We had to find…to find…" Who had she set

out on her own to find, again? Or was she hunting something? Turning her head, she looked at where she had a vague notion of someone having once stood. There was something out there that she was after. Something important. Or was she supposed to be running away from it? Something dangerous lurking in the shadows and stalking her with its owl-like eyes.

"Lucy, look at me." So, she did. Pulchrum was little more than a foot from her, and she could clearly make out his face, despite the low light. He was smiling that shy smile of his, and his shaggy hair was caressing his cheek. "You look amazing like this, you know."

She was tempted to look down and see what he meant, but she couldn't look away from his beautiful eyes. They were so warm, so open. When he stepped closer, his hand moved to touch hers on the handle of the machete. "You don't need that," he said softly, his voice rumbling in such a delicious way. Her fingers slackened, and the machete fell to the carpet of leaves. "That's a good girl. So, so pretty. You have the most amazing eyes, Lucy."

"Not as nice as yours." Fingers touched her cheek, and she leaned into their touch, eyes closing to slits. She didn't want to close them entirely and lose sight of him. "I've always liked looking at your eyes."

His chuckle rolled over her like a gentle wave, and the fingers on her cheek slid back to comb through her hair. "Only my eyes?"

"All of you," she confessed, voice a whisper, heart beating violently against her ribs.

"Seems we have a lot in common, then." A shudder traveled along her spine as he whispered those words into her ear, and she couldn't help but lean forward to clutch at him for support. Lips brushed at her temple, and the hand at her back slid up under her shirt to press cold flesh against her burning skin. "Oh yes, this is much better." The amusement in his voice confused her, but when she tried to pull back to look at him, he kissed her.

She cursed the chilly weather and subsequent necessity to wear jeans and a sweater. A skirt and tank-top would provide much easier access for his soft, cool hands. Her combat boots made her feel clunky and awkward whenever she tried to lift a leg to wrap it around his hips. If she had kicked him, though, he didn't seem to mind, and his hand cradled her thigh in order to keep her leg in place. There was no question as to how much he was enjoying this, and she rocked against his hips with hungry whimpers.

"Yes," he whispered heatedly against her neck. "Yes." There was a question, for which those words had been answer, and Lucy's excitement became laced with tingling nervousness. She'd never done it before; what if she got it wrong…

Just as his hands had worked their way between them in order to get at her belt, he was suddenly torn from her arms. Lucy stumbled from the movement and force, staggering forward from the tree and looking around in a daze.

"Get away from her," Eva growled, with a secondary sound as undercurrent—something that vibrated like a rough coo. Lucy saw something silver flicker in the darkness—where had her flashlight gone?—and she realized Eva had her sword drawn.

"Hello, child." Pulchrum's full attention had been turned to Eva, and his grin was wide with teeth that gleamed sharply in the night. "Calm down; I wasn't doing anything with her that she didn't want."

"She doesn't want it with *you*." But she did! She tried to reach out for Pulchrum to bring him back. "Lucy!" Eva cried, and Lucy's hand fell. "Open your eyes!" For a moment, Lucy managed to look away from Pulchrum, and she saw Eva standing there looking wild and fierce. Her face wasn't entirely human, but something caught between a wolf and bird. There was a beak, and yet still Eva had fanged teeth that she bared by parting her mouth in a cry of warning. Eva was unlike anything Lucy had ever seen. Beautiful in her horror.

Pulchrum looked at Lucy, his face full of sorrow. "Help me, Lucy," he pleaded. "Don't let her kill me."

With a nod, Lucy ducked and retrieved her machete, brandishing it in front of her threateningly. "Let him go, Eva."

"She won't listen, Lucy," Pulchrum was saying, his eyes pleading, and oh, God, she wanted to help him so much. "Stop her."

She would have. In that moment, she wanted to do nothing more than sink her machete into Eva's flesh and slice until she could never hurt Pulchrum ever again. Just as Lucy tensed to move, however, Eva released a loud, shrill screech.

Again Lucy felt as though waking from a dream. No, really it was more like snapping out of one of those strange half-asleep trances she'd slip into when watching the TV after a tiring day. That hazy state of not-quite-consciousness where the details of the real world bleed and mix with shadows of dreams.

Slowly, the shadows died, leaving only the real world for her to view. Eva was holding her sword at the ready, bright gold eyes focused intently on Pulchrum. No, not Pulchrum. Even in the darkness, Lucy could tell it was someone else. How hadn't she noticed before, when he was right in front of her? When they were *kissing*. Lucy swayed on her feet, feeling ill.

In a flash, the not-Pulchrum was lunging at Eva and she was slicing a gaping wound in his shoulder. He fell back with an animalistic scream before turning and fleeing into the trees.

"Lucy," Eva cried again. "I want you to turn left and run until you find the burn disk. Get it ready."

"I can't see—"

334

"There's a lantern beside the disk. It should still be lit." Without waiting for a response, Eva dashed off in pursuit of her quarry. There was no sign of Krysti, and Lucy could only hope Eva had hidden her somewhere safe before coming out in search of Lucy.

Lucy steeled her nerves and then went the way Eva had instructed her. It was as she nearly stumbled over a fallen log that she started quietly cursing herself for having forgotten to retrieve her flashlight. No helping it. All she could do was press forward and hope she was keeping in a straight line.

There! Up ahead! A small glow flickered between the low brush, and she knew it had to be the lantern. At least, she *hoped* it was the lantern. When she finally cleared the last bit of bramble and found herself in the tiny clearing with the burn disk, she nearly fell to her knees in relief.

She had only taken a few steps when she felt a hand land on her shoulder and Pulchrum's voice called out her name in a hush. Without even hesitating, she spun around and swung the machete. It sliced through the Reaper's hand as he tried to pull away, sending the four fingers of his right hand flying into the darkness. He hissed, but then started to laugh as he seemed to realize that the blade hadn't been coated in garlic.

"You're just a one trick pony, aren't you?" Lucy scoffed. While Czernobog was distracted with laughing at his injured hand, Lucy pulled the spray bottle of garlic extract—one of several field items that had been mandatory in the Gehealdan—from its holder on her belt. "I mean, you could at least take some other form. Maybe look like Eva or Krysti."

"Sorry, old habit to take the form of what people desire most." He smirked at her with Pulchrum's mouth.

Indignant fury rose up in her, giving her the sudden burst of speed to catch him off guard and spray the garlic juice in his face. Growling in rage and pain, the Reaper stumbled back and rubbed futilely at his eyes. The image of Pulchrum faded, revealing the true monster beneath.

His temporary blindness provided the perfect opportunity to run, like she'd been instructed. Instead, she quickly pulled her hunting knife free and unscrewed its handle compartment to get the cloves of garlic Czar required them to always keep in fresh supply. Taking a deep, steadying breath, she rushed him, shoving the handful of garlic down his throat whenever he opened his mouth for one of his pained gasps. To her shock, it looked as if he tried to fight back on the instinct to bite down, and he kept his mouth open as much as possible. Even so, her flesh caught on his numerous teeth as she withdrew, slicing her arm from just above the wrist and taking chunks from her hand.

Letting out a pained cry of her own, she stumbled back and cradled her bleeding hand. She was glad to have had the forethought to use her non-dominant hand. At least she'd still be able to function somewhat normally while her wounds healed.

As soon as her hand was free of his mouth, Czernobog fell to all fours, gagging and trying desperately to rid himself of the garlic lodged in his throat. "Stupid…ungrateful…" He choked out the words and tried to crawl towards her.

Lucy sniffled, unable to control the tears of pain, and turned away from him to work on getting the fire started. Thankfully, it seemed Eva had already poured the natural charcoal. All she had to do was pour the grain alcohol and light it. She did just that, then cried out for Eva as loud as she could.

"Keeper…of…the flame…" The Reaper seemed to try to laugh through his gagging, and he fell onto his belly, no longer able to crawl. "Fitting. Perfect."

"Shut up."

"Eyes…like the hottest…flame."

"I said shut up, you son of a *bitch*!" Abandoning the fire, Lucy walked back over to him and kicked him soundly in the ribs a few times with her steel-toed combat boots.

He laughed between grunts of pain, the sounds muffled by his face being pressed into the dirt. Finally the kicking rolled him over, and he grinned up at her, dirt caked into the black blood oozing from his lips. Lucy tried not to shudder at the look in his avian-like eyes.

"How's…your hand?"

"Don't you ever *shut up*?"

Czernobog laughed again, the sound a sickening gurgle as more blood—this time some of it a bright red—bubbled up from his mouth. "You're…being…quite…stupid."

"And you're being quite annoying." Frustrated, she tilted her head back and yelled out for Eva again.

"They'll kill…you. Or…wipe memories. Stupid."

"They won't be able to find me. And if they do, I'll have plenty of people on my side. People like my *father*."

"Clever…clever girl. He'll…be so…proud."

She was about to yell at him again, but the sound stopped short in her throat as her mind finally registered his words. "Who?"

The Reaper merely smiled up at her, yellow eyes narrowed in sadistic glee.

*No,* she reprimanded herself, *don't rise to his bait.* All he was doing now was trying to buy himself a little time, or get one last laugh at her expense.

Letting out an annoyed "Tch," she returned to the fire. The alcohol was burning blue, and had already caught the coals on fire, which added wisps of white and gold and orange. She watched the flames dance, using their fluid ballet as a way to settle her anger.

Her meditation didn't last long, however, as the Reaper started calling her name and making motions like he was trying to roll over so he could crawl.

"Stay there."

He ignored her, reaching out his good hand to claw at the ground and drag his body sideways. Lucy screamed for Eva again, and tried to remember where she'd dropped her machete this time.

The arrow didn't make a sound until it pierced flesh and bone and rooted itself into the earth with a dull *tunk*. For a moment, the Reaper simply stared at his outstretched hand and the long shaft protruding from it. Then, his disturbing eyes switched skyward and he grinned.

"The wolf of ill omen," said the Reaper, making no move to pull his hand free.

Eva landed almost soundlessly, bow gripped tightly in her hand. "What's he babbling about?" As soon as her wings were tucked back into her skin, she was pulling her shirt back on and smoothing it down.

"He's just trying to screw with us." Lucy felt almost dizzy with relief when she saw Eva. Then a twitching pain reminded her of what had happened to her left hand, and she realized she was dizzy for an entirely different reason. She didn't recall seeing Eva move, but suddenly she was there at her side, steadying her and pulling Lucy's hand to examine it.

"How did you manage this?" she asked with concern, carefully pressing at torn flesh to get an idea of the full extent of damage.

Lucy cringed and looked away from the wound like she did whenever the doctor was about to give her a shot. "Shoving garlic down his throat."

"Seriously?" Eva's tone sounded both worried and impressed.

338

"Let's get this cleaned out and dressed." Releasing her hand, Eva darted around the site to fetch what she needed. "Shit," she said at last, pausing to cast a lost expression around at the few items near the fire disk. "The first aid kit's in the car."

An idea came to Eva, and she was suddenly in motion again. "Not a problem! We'll just do this!" The speed at which Eva returned to her side made Lucy's head spin, and she blinked slowly as she tried to focus on Eva. Gently taking her arm above where the wounds started, Eva lifted the limb and began cleaning the wounds out with the grain alcohol.

It stung worse than anything Lucy had ever felt, hurting more than when the wounds had been made. Tears pricked at her eyes, and she tried to blink them back, hissing uselessly between her teeth. Eva was patient with her, holding her arm still despite Lucy's reflexive jerking. Once that was done, Eva tore the bottom of her shirt to make bandages. Beside them, the fire roared high and hot, and seemed to burst brighter with Lucy's every wince.

"The hell—" Pulchrum's voice had them both turning, Eva pausing as she was just about to tie the final knot of the makeshift dressings.

The Reaper chuckled darkly, watching without fear as Pulchrum advanced. "Welcome," he wheezed, and it was a wet, painful sound, "to the party."

"I thought you two were saving who you could and pulling out?" Pulchrum asked the girls, even as he continued to study the injured strigoi.

"He attacked us." Eva tied the bandage so tightly it made Lucy hiss.

Lucy nodded weakly, blinking slowly through her pain. "So I had to incapacitate him until you got here."

"What?" That snared Pulchrum's full attention, and he looked over at where Eva was finishing up with the dressings. "How?"

"I shoved garlic down his throat."

Pulchrum gaped at her, then shook his head. "Full of surprises."

At this, the Reaper laughed. "She's not...only...one!" Black and red blood continued to gurgle up from his mouth every time he attempted to talk, but he didn't seem to mind.

Returning his attention to the vampire, Pulchrum proceeded to walk around him. He cocked his head to the side and smiled pleasantly. "Were you *really* surprised?"

On the ground, Czernobog's form was trying to shift into something different, dark hair growing from his scalp and a nose forming where none had been. The garlic poisoning his system caused the transformation to almost instantly wilt away, until he looked like his true self once more. "Trai...tor."

Chuckling, Pulchrum turned away to pick something up off the ground. Ah, so *that's* where Lucy had dropped her machete. "I think that all depends on which side I've been on from the start. Don't you?"

That only seemed to bring on a new wave of amusement for the Reaper. "Snake."

"Hiss," Pulchrum replied mockingly as he dropped to his knees beside Czernobog. The Reaper tried to shape-shift again, parts of him shifting in and out of something that looked almost like a dog, but inevitably, the poisoning won out.

Without another word, Pulchrum plunged the machete into the Reaper's chest. Bones cracked and flesh made wet sucking sounds as he dragged it through Czernobog's ribs. All the while, the Reaper seemed to laugh through his unquestionable pain.

The screeching laughter grated at Lucy's frayed nerves, causing her head to pound and her vision to pulse. Or was that the fire, pulsing like a strobe light in the small clearing? As Pulchrum reached in to pull the heart out, Czernobog's eyes rolled to lock on Lucy. It was difficult to tell if it was simply him cringing, but he seemed to be winking and grinning at her, even as Pulchrum's arm slowly withdrew accompanied with a gushing spray of blood. Her vision blurred for an instant, warping and duplicating the Reaper's face like a ghost ripping itself away from its host. Blinking heavily, she banished the double-vision and regained her equilibrium. By the time the world was steady again, Pulchrum had fully-removed the heart and Czernobog was rigidly still.

"I'll get to dismembering him," Eva offered, taking the task from Lucy due to her injury.

Pulchrum merely nodded, his blood-streaked jaw clenched tightly as he moved to drop the organ over the flaming coals.

Head still spinning, Lucy sank to her knees and tried to apply pressure to the rapidly dampening cloth around her hand. The stench of burning vampire flesh made things worse, and she shifted to sit fully on the ground.

"We'll get you all out and safe once we're done here," Pulchrum said softly, his eyes watching the heart burn. "Your friend, too. She won't be safe otherwise."

"My family?"

Pulchrum nodded. "Others are taking care of that at this very moment. You'll all meet back up when you get to Headquarters. We have to finish up here quickly, then you and Eva need to go here." He handed her a folded slip of paper with an address scribbled on it, his attention still mostly on the burning heart. Lucy tucked it in her pocket quickly in an attempt to prevent getting too much blood on it. "I have to stay behind to do clean-up as part of my duties to the Gehealdan. Don't worry, you'll know the people you'll be meeting up with there."

She gave a shallow nod, and then turned her eyes towards

where Eva was chopping up the body. Partway through the procedure, Eva looked up and over at them. "What happened to his fingers?"

"Ah." Lucy lifted her right hand a little, then returned it to applying pressure onto the wounds of her left. "That was me. He touched me."

Eva grinned at that, and Lucy felt herself smile, some of the tension finally draining from her.

Wait a minute, where was— "Where's Krysti?"

"In the car with my gun," Eva said before swinging the machete down for another chop. "Don't worry, I'm keeping an ear on her. She's fine."

"Good." Lucy felt her muscles trembling, and she hoped it was just the cold.

Pulchrum turned away from the fire and knelt beside Lucy, taking her wounded hand gently in his to get a better look. "I can help with this," he offered softly. "It's kind of weird what I'll have to do, though."

"He'll have to lick the wounds," Eva said absently as she hacked away at Czernobog. "Won't completely counteract the enzyme in the vamp saliva, but it'll probably help a bit. Werewolf spit is useful." She chuckled as she worked.

Pulchrum lifted Lucy's hand higher and helped her remove the bandages in a manner that wouldn't stress the wounds. As each inch of flesh was revealed, Pulchrum swiped his broad, flat tongue along it. It stung, but not nearly as much as the grain alcohol had, so Lucy simply gritted her teeth and bore it. The whole time, Pulchrum kept his eyes averted, as if silently apologizing for any pain he was inflicting and the awkwardness of the situation.

When all of the blood had been lapped up, Pulchrum tore some of his own shirt to re-wrapped the wounds, and threw the bloody scraps into the fire. Face heating, Lucy forced herself to stare at her wrapped hand as she thanked him. Her breath was still coming harsh and labored, tugged down by pain and exhaustion.

Eva finished chopping and began tossing the body parts onto the fire. Satisfied that Lucy was taken care of, Pulchrum moved to aid Eva. Lucy closed her eyes and listened to the crackling fire, the rustling forest, the wet thunks as piece by piece Czernobog was added to the coals. Taking a deep breath, she smelled the garlic and the blood and the cooking flesh and the oncoming winter. It was over. She wouldn't have to be an executioner anymore. After tonight, she would be free.

Both Eva and Pulchrum inhaled sharply, and Lucy hesitated to open her eyes. "What?" Lucy asked, almost afraid to hear the answer. Part of her wanted to look and see what they saw, but the rest of her was conjuring frightening images of the Grin Reaper reassembling himself and crawling out of the flames.

Everything seemed strangely quiet all of a sudden, the only sounds in their little clearing were her gasping breaths and the crackling fire. Slowly, she opened her eyes to look at the fire and confront whatever it was that had shocked the others into silence.

At first she didn't notice anything strange or different, but then when she did, she didn't fully believe what was happening. Rising up on unsteady feet, she stumbled closer to the burn disk. Her breathing grew deeper and more ragged with each shuffling step, each second of realization setting in like cold rot.

The flames breathed with her, rising with each exhalation, shrinking with each inhalation. A stuttering gasp made them splutter and flicker, and she could deny what she saw no longer. She choked on a scream, and the flames reacted to that as well, threatening to blink out in an instant.

"What—" she managed to force out of her tight throat.

Pulchrum caught her as her body went suddenly limp, smearing black blood across her arms. "What?" she breathed into his shoulder.

It was too much. On top of everything else, it was just too much for her in that moment. She knew it shouldn't be a surprise, considering who and what her father was, but she was tired and hurting and scared and now this was just *too much*.

As her vision went dark, so too did the clearing.

# Epilogue

"Donnie, please set the table."

"In a minute," he called back distractedly, too focused on the TV and the special live report. Supposedly the Grin Reaper had been found, his home containing evidence such as plastic containers filled with human remains. Authorities were already optimistic that the DNA samples would come back as positive matches to previous victims. His name was Devon Michalson, evidently, and he was shown briefly from a distance as police escorted him out of his home. Even blurry and from a distance, his clothing looked to be covered in blood. The reporter explained that he had been interrupted during another killing spree that evening, apprehended when he had to go home to retrieve more containers for his abundant kills.

Diana popped her head around the archway separating the living room from the kitchen. "Now, buster. Dinner's almost ready. Set a place for Lucy, too, in case she gets home early."

Donnie sighed and stood from where he'd been sprawled across the carpet. "You know she won't," he grumbled back, dragging his feet as he headed into the kitchen.

"Well, you never know," chirped Diana, fussing over the wok where veggies and meat were sizzling. Her hair was pulled back in a messy ponytail, and her faded daisy-print apron was splattered with brown sauces. "She said she wasn't camping tonight, so she should be home at some point."

Just as Donnie was setting down the third plate, the doorbell rang. "I'll get it," he offered, eager to get out of setting the table. Before Diana could object, he was out of the kitchen and nearly to the door.

He opened the door to find a young man with a faded green dress shirt and pale khakis. The yellowish porch light glinted almost green off his shaggy black hair, and made his skin look sickly and sallow. "Hi there," the man greeted with a smile, which curved curiously when his black eyes flicked over Donnie's shoulder before focusing on him.

Donnie glanced behind himself, but there was no one there. No one, that was, except for the shadow that was always there. That made Donnie regard the stranger differently, suspecting there was something more to him. "Who are you?" Donnie asked, squinting up at the man.

"Could you fetch your mother, please?" the man asked instead of answering Donnie's question. "I need to speak with both of you about something very important."

Eyes still on the stranger, Donnie leaned back into the house a bit and yelled over his shoulder for his mom. She arrived quickly, wiping her hands with a dishcloth. When she spotted the man at the door, Diana moved to take Donnie's place with him safely behind her. "Can I help you?" she asked, smiling politely.

The stranger produced a business card seemingly from nowhere and passed it to Diana. "I'm Dr. René Sartre," he said, finally introducing himself. "I'm a psychologist who was hired to assist in a revelation that may prove to be very jarring."

Diana's eyebrows squished down over her eyes in confusion. "What are you talking about?" Then a sudden realization seemed to hit her, and she stood straight and stiff. "Has something happened to Lucy or Mick?"

Dr. Sartre shook his head and spoke with a reassuring voice. "Your daughter and eldest son are fine, don't worry. They'll be meeting up with you later, somewhere safe."

"Safe?" Diana reeled back, dropping her dishcloth and reaching behind her to grab at Donnie's shoulder. "What do you mean?"

"My client feels it would be best for you to relocate tonight, right this instant, in order to prevent your family from being split up even more than it already has. The same organization which took him from you could potentially take Lucy, as well."

"What?" Diana's voice broke a little and her hand tightened on Donnie's shoulder.

"Why don't I let my client explain?" asked Dr. Sartre, as he motioned towards the darkness behind him.

Another man stepped forward, as if melting out of the very shadows. It wasn't like the shadow that followed Donnie, which wasn't *really* a shadow. Instead, it was like an actual shadow had detached itself from the darkness, only to melt away to reveal a solid person.

The new man had a beard that forked into three points and long hair, but that couldn't disguise who he was. Even if there hadn't been photos of him all over the house, Donnie would recognize those eyes and the cut of his facial features. Walter Kincade was always clean-shaven with messy, short hair in all of the photos and in Donnie's vague memories. How he looked now, though, sent a jolt of deeper recognition through Donnie. He knew then that he wasn't looking at Walter Kincade, but Váli, from the Time Before.

"Walt?" Diana asked, voice hesitant and trembling. Then she was rushing at him and practically collapsing against him. Her fists took turns pounding at him and gripping at his black shirt, as if she couldn't decide to be angry or glad to see him there after so many years. "How?" she sobbed, sliding those contradictory hands up to run through his hair as she studied his eyes. "*Why?*"

"I'll explain on the way," Váli promised, wrapping his arms around his wife and looking happy enough to cry. "But we have to leave now, otherwise we won't be able to be together. They'll come and take your memory of this, of me. You'll still think I'm dead."

Diana was shaking, looking between Váli and Dr. Sartre. "I

347

don't understand."

"As he said," Dr. Sartre explained gently, "we don't really have a great deal of time to get into it right this second. I'll do my best to help explain things as we're en route to a safer location. Please, if there's anything vitally important, go get it now. Otherwise, we should probably just leave."

"Clothes and necessities will be provided for you there," Váli quickly assured. "Anything else, we can have agents come and retrieve later."

Nodding like a bobblehead, Diana clung to Váli and let him lead her down the walk towards a black SUV sitting idle at the curb. Donnie reached out and touched Dr. Sartre's sleeve before moving to follow, grabbing the man's attention. "You see him, don't you?" Donnie asked quietly.

Again Dr. Sartre's gaze flicked to where the shadow lurked, and his perpetual smile tilted into a smirk. "Let's just say you're lucky I was the one hired for this job."

"You know what he is." It wasn't a question.

Dr. Sartre's eyes were dark, darker even than the shadow they were discussing. "I'm probably one of the few people alive who does." He tilted his head and seemed to study Donnie. "You're very calm about all of this, seeing your father back from the dead and being told to run off in the night."

Donnie shrugged one shoulder then moved past Dr. Sartre and towards the SUV. "I knew he wasn't really dead."

It was strange, Donnie observed, as Dr. Sartre stepped up to walk alongside him. The shadow and his lesser-formed brethren seemed to move further away, despite the darkness of the night surrounding them. A glance up at Dr. Sartre found the man smiling and humming. He winked down at Donnie before opening the back passenger-side door to the SUV and motioning for the kid to load up.

Usually Donnie couldn't stand being in a confined space in the dark, but somehow Dr. Sartre's presence kept the shadow things at bay. He was able to feel safe all night as they drove. While Váli and Dr. Sartre cautiously explained the truth to a nearly hysteric Diana, Donnie remained quiet and calm. Lucy and Mick were safe, and that was enough for him. All the other stuff? Donnie wasn't surprised. It wasn't much more than what he'd seen in memories of the Time Before, and he only felt long-awaited validation.

"And what are *you*?" Diana asked Dr. Sartre, her hand squeezing Váli's so tightly a lesser man would probably complain. Or, well, a human would.

Donnie turned away from his bored observation of the void-black world whizzing past the window, curious to hear Dr. Sartre's reply.

Sartre was still smiling his soothing smile, and he let the words drip carelessly from his lips. "I'm a vegetarian."

DL Wainright

The story continues in book two of
The Hollow Sun series:

# Fractured Masks

# Acknowledgments

There are so many people to thank, that it's hard to know where to start. Of course I thank my parents for encouraging my tendency to come up with weird little stories, and for allowing me to grow up on horror movies and other assorted spooky things. I thank Tommy for believing in me, and for the endless hours of discussions to hammer out details of this book. He's also to thank for some of Ren's lines, most notably the "Schrodinger's geode." I want to thank my friends who read through various incarnations of this book and helpfully provided input to make sure it all made sense. These angels include: Ollie, Matt, Ashleigh, Chantel, and Carrie. Last but certainly not least, I want to thank all of my family and friends who helped me with figuring out the title, cover, and other tricky concepts for this publication. I couldn't have done this without your help.

# DL Wainright

is married with two cats, and loves folklore, horror stories, and long walks on the beach at night.

You can find a multitude of ways to contact DL by going to thehollowsun.com.